Trace whisked her back into the crowd of swaying couples.

Hand against her spine, he brought her as close as the full skirt of her wedding gown would allow. Poppy let her body sway to the beat of the music, relaxing now that the big picture moments were finished. Their first dance, the toasts, the cake-cutting and endless picture-taking.

All of which had prompted an extended trip down memory lane. "Remember our very first dance?"

"The senior prom? You quarreled with your date a few days before..."

"So he ended up taking someone else."

"And I stepped in, as your friend."

She'd come very close to falling head over heels in love with Trace that night. But knowing how he felt about romance in general, she had come to her senses in time to preserve their growing friendship. To the point they hadn't even shared a good-night kiss when he'd finally dropped her at her front door, at dawn.

"And you're still doing it."

The Texan's Christmas Bounty

CATHY GILLEN THACKER
&
NEW YORK TIMES BESTSELLING AUTHOR
TINA LEONARD

**Previously published as *Lone Star Twins*
and *The SEAL's Holiday Babies***

PLEASE RECYCLE · THIS PRODUCT IS RECYCLABLE

Recycling programs for this product may not exist in your area.

ISBN-13: 978-1-335-47146-8

The Texan's Christmas Bounty
Copyright © 2020 by Harlequin Books S.A.

Lone Star Twins
First published in 2015. This edition published in 2020.
Copyright © 2015 by Cathy Gillen Thacker

The SEAL's Holiday Babies
First published in 2014. This edition published in 2020.
Copyright © 2014 by Tina Leonard

All rights reserved. No part of this book may be used or reproduced in any manner whatsoever without written permission except in the case of brief quotations embodied in critical articles and reviews.

This is a work of fiction. Names, characters, places and incidents are either the product of the author's imagination or are used fictitiously. Any resemblance to actual persons, living or dead, businesses, companies, events or locales is entirely coincidental.

This edition published by arrangement with Harlequin Books S.A.

For questions and comments about the quality of this book, please contact us at CustomerService@Harlequin.com.

Harlequin Enterprises ULC
22 Adelaide St. West, 40th Floor
Toronto, Ontario M5H 4E3, Canada
www.Harlequin.com

Printed in U.S.A.

CONTENTS

Cathy Gillen Thacker is a married mother of three. She and her husband reside in North Carolina. Her stories have made numerous appearances on bestseller lists, but her best reward is knowing one of her books made someone's day a little brighter. A popular Harlequin author, she loves telling passionate stories with happy endings and thinks nothing beats a good romance and a hot cup of tea! Visit her at cathygillenthacker.com for information on her books, recipes and a list of her favorite things.

Books by Cathy Gillen Thacker

Harlequin Special Edition

Lockharts Lost & Found

His Plan for the Quadruplets

Texas Legends: The McCabes

The Texas Cowboy's Quadruplets
His Baby Bargain
Their Inherited Triplets

Harlequin Western Romance

Texas Legends: The McCabes

The Texas Cowboy's Triplets
The Texas Cowboy's Baby Rescue

Visit the Author Profile page at Harlequin.com for more titles.

Lone Star Twins

CATHY GILLEN THACKER

Chapter 1

"Christmas has come early this year," Poppy McCabe announced from her impeccably decorated living room in Laramie, Texas.

Lieutenant Trace Caulder stared at the screen on his laptop. He'd never seen his best friend look happier.

The only bummer was that they were separated by thousands of miles, as was usually the case. Determined to enjoy every second of their video-slash-web chat—despite the fact he was currently stationed on an air base in the Middle East—he kicked back in the desk chair and drawled in the native Texas accent that mirrored hers, "Really, darlin'? And how is that?" Given that even Thanksgiving was still several days away.

"You remember when you were home on leave two months ago?"

Hard to forget that weekend in Fort Worth. For two

people who'd never been in love and likely never would be, they sure had amazing chemistry.

Oblivious to how much he wanted to hold her lithe, warm body in his arms and make sweet love to her all over again, Poppy persisted on her verbal trip down memory lane. "When we went to the Stork Agency and met Anne Marie?"

That had been the only serious part of the entire rendezvous, but important nonetheless. "Sure, I remember," Trace said, pausing to take in the sexy fall of her thick, silky mahogany hair. A sweep of bang framed her oval face; the rest tumbled over her slender shoulders. Lower still, the five-foot-seven interior decorator had shapely calves, delicate feet, a taut tummy and trim waist, and full, luscious breasts that were meant to be worshipped. Very little of which he could actually see, given that the image on the screen only showed her from the ribs up…

But then, given how much time he'd spent paying homage to her lovely form, and vice versa, he didn't really need to see her body to remember it. Fondly. He could tell by the way she often gazed at him that Poppy felt the same.

"Anne Marie was a nice kid." And at seventeen years old, Trace recollected, way too young to be pregnant. That was why she was giving up her children for adoption.

"Well, she's picked us to raise her twins!" Poppy exclaimed with a joyous twist of her velvety-soft lips.

"Seriously?"

"Yes! Can you believe it?" She paused to catch her breath. "There's only one itty-bitty problem…"

Trace saw the hesitation in Poppy's dark brown eyes. Waited for her to continue.

She inhaled sharply. "She wants us to be married."

Whoa now. That had never been on the table.

Trace swung his feet off the desk and sat forward in his chair. "But she knows we're just friends—" and occasional lovers and constant confidantes "—who happen to want to be parents together." He thought the two of them had made that abundantly clear.

Poppy folded her arms in front of her, the action plumping up the delectable curve of her breasts beneath her ivory turtleneck. Soberly she nodded, adding, "She still gets that neither of us want to get hitched."

No woman prized her independence more than the outspoken Poppy. For a lot of very different reasons, he felt the same. "But?" he prodded.

Wrinkling her nose, she reluctantly explained. "Anne Marie's decided she would feel better if we were actually married at the time of the adoption. And, as it happens, the Stork Agency apparently has a requirement of their own—that any time more than two children are adopted simultaneously, there be two *married* adults with a long-standing relationship doing the adopting."

"The agency officials didn't say anything about this when we were there, meeting Anne Marie and the other girls."

"Apparently they didn't expect Anne Marie to choose us…but they wanted to give her a basis for comparison. As it turns out there was another couple that was also in the running, which Anne Marie's mother met and prefers, and they *are* married. But in the end, Anne Marie decided she wants us. On the condition," Poppy reiterated with a beleaguered sigh, "that we get hitched and the kids have the same last name."

"I have no problem with you becoming a Caulder," Trace said. "In a nontraditional sense, of course."

"Or you could become a McCabe." Removing a coated elastic band from her wrist, she swept her hair up into a messy ponytail on the back of her head and secured it there.

Aware when she wore her hair that way it reminded him of her college cheerleading days, he volleyed back. "Or, better yet, you could just drop the Elizabeth—" her middle name "—and change yours to Poppy McCabe Caulder. Like a lot of married women do, for practical reasons, to cut down on the confusion."

Silence fell.

Finally, realizing this was one battle she wouldn't win with him, Poppy conceded, "Fine. If you *insist*."

"I would." Thanks to two parents who couldn't stop marrying—and then divorcing—he'd been saddled with a lot of different "family names." He had no intention of ever inflicting the same on any offspring. Whatever it started out with was what it would stay.

He studied the ambivalence in her dark brown eyes. "You're sure you want to get married, though?"

Trying not to think that if things had gone the other way, he and the woman opposite him might very well *be* married now, Trace watched her rise to pace around the room, then return, her taut-fitting jeans doing very nice things for her waist and hips.

A river of desire swept through him.

He wished they were close enough to touch.

Kiss.

He wished he could inhale the tantalizing apple blossom fragrance of her soap and shampoo.

Meanwhile she looked perfectly content with the way things were; the two of them thousands of miles apart.

"It's a big step," he cautioned her. "Even if it is only on paper."

She twisted off the top of a water bottle. "I'm sure I want to adopt those twins with you." She paused to take a long, thirsty drink then shrugged. "And since this is the only way…"

Travis knew how frustrated and upset she was, deep down. And with good reason. He and Poppy had abandoned contraception ten years ago, when she'd told him she wanted to start a family, on her own. As her best friend, because he still felt responsible for a very sad time in her life, he had readily agreed to help her achieve her goal of having a child on her own.

After six years, and many a passionate rendezvous, she still hadn't been able to conceive. She hadn't wanted to see a fertility doctor, because she didn't want to risk having multiples. So she had signed up to adopt. Again with his full emotional support. For the first two years, strictly on her own, as a single woman. When that hadn't panned out, he had signed on to be the dad in the proposed arrangement. Except that they hadn't been selected by any of the mothers wanting the type of open arrangement they did.

Hadn't even come close. Until now.

But there was a catch.

The babies were twins.

And, of course, when he'd agreed to all this a couple of years ago, he had never considered the fact that he and Poppy would have to get married.

That, for a lot of reasons, neither of them wanted.

Yet with both of them thirty-five and her biological clock ticking, passing on the marriage requirement and waiting for another baby to come along—a single-birthed child this time—did not seem wise.

It would be foolish to not do whatever was deemed necessary to make this happen. Even if getting hitched wasn't something they would choose under any other circumstance. "What's the timetable?" Trace asked finally, aware that nothing about their long-standing relationship was exactly conventional.

"According to the agency, we'll need at least three weeks to get all the legalities in order, *after* we're married. That is, if we want the babies to come home from the hospital with me."

"And naturally we do." After waiting so long, Poppy would be heartbroken if she had to miss out on a single second of motherhood.

She took another long, thirsty drink. "The twins are due on December twenty-fourth."

That gives us less than a month, all told. Trace frowned. "Only one problem with that. I'm still deployed and not due for leave again until next spring."

Suddenly looking plucky as ever, Poppy beamed with her trademark Can Do attitude. She might not have been a twin or triplet, like her five younger sisters, but she knew how to go after what she wanted, no matter the obstacles in her way. "Fortunately, I have a solution." She pushed on. "A marriage by proxy."

Trace had heard the term bandied about by his fellow airmen and women, mostly as a joke. Realizing he was thirsty, too, he got up to get a bottle of water from his room's mini-fridge. He returned to the desk, his dog tags jingling against his chest. "You can really do that?"

"In exactly four states in the USA. California, Texas,

Montana and Colorado. Luckily—" her grin widened "—we are both permanent residents of the Lone Star State."

"So how does that work?" he asked curiously, wishing he'd had time to clean up since coming off duty before they'd connected.

Poppy sobered. "I can't speak to the process in the other three states. But under Texas law, a member of the military who is deployed out of the country can request to be married by proxy. Generally, there need to be extenuating circumstances—like the birth of a child or some other reason for urgency—and the ceremony will have to take place here in Texas. We'll just get someone to stand in for you at the courthouse."

Physically take my place? Next to Poppy? His jaw tightening, Trace tried not to consider how much that rankled, or why it might. "You're kidding," he said gruffly and then paused as he studied her slightly crestfallen expression. "You're *not* kidding?"

"This is the only way we're going to be able to adopt Anne Marie's babies," Poppy reminded him. "And you know how long I've been on the waiting list."

Forever, she had often lamented.

A fresh wave of guilt stung Trace. He was part of the reason Poppy had had such trouble getting the family she'd always wanted. Although no one but he and Poppy knew about the specifics, at least in her hometown of Laramie. Mostly because she hadn't wanted anyone else to know about the tragedy and he'd had no choice but to abide by her wishes.

"Anne Marie is also the only one who's ever been amenable that we want to raise these children more as friends than anything else. The fact you're constantly deployed in the military, like her late father, actually gives you a heroic edge in her view. Just as the fact that I was big sister and eventual babysitter to both the twins and the triplets gives me a unique perspective on what a child in that situation might feel or need."

That was certainly true. Poppy had been through a lot even before they'd hooked up. Mostly because, as the oldest sibling and the only single-birthed child in the Jackson and Lacey McCabe brood, she had often been overlooked in a way that the other girls had not.

Not that she had ever complained about it.

Rather, she'd joked it had given her a freedom and autonomy her other siblings could only envy.

Poppy inhaled deeply. "I mean, what are our chances of *ever* finding someone else who thinks our situation is ideal for the children she's relinquishing?" There was a long pause. "We just have to comply with the agency's requirement and demonstrate our lifelong commitment by getting married."

Well, put that way…he supposed it didn't seem too much to ask.

"You're right," Trace said finally. "This is our chance."

Poppy took another deep breath, the action lifting the soft swell of her breasts, and then slowly released it. Steadfastly, she searched his face. "So you're okay with a marriage by proxy?" she asked.

Trace pushed any lingering reservations he felt aside. This was Poppy they were talking about. A woman who knew her own mind and had more than proved over the years she wouldn't go all fickle on him, no matter what happened.

He nodded. "It's not as if a piece of paper or a marriage pretty much in name only is going to change anything between us."

Poppy smiled, her eyes crinkling at the corners in the way that always made him want to take her in his arms and hold her close. "Right," she said.

Wishing he was close enough to hug her, Trace continued. "And if it sets Anne Marie's mind at ease, so much the better."

Visibly relaxing, Poppy laid a hand over her heart. "So you'll do it? You'll request a marriage by proxy?"

Trace knew he owed Poppy this much—and more. Hoping this would finally balance the scales between them and allow the last of her lingering grief to slide away, he nodded. "Yes, darlin'," he promised. "I'll talk to my commanding officer right away."

"About time the two of you decided to tie the knot," Jackson McCabe said when Poppy stopped by the hospital to inform her parents of their plans.

Her dad had just come out of surgery and her mom was winding up a long day on the pediatrics floor.

"I agree." Lacey beamed, looking as lovely as ever in her blue scrubs and white doctor's coat.

As always, feeling a little in awe of her super-successful, still-wildly-in-love parents, Poppy followed them into her father's private office. She held up a hand. "You both understand that Trace is still going to continue on with his life's work in the military and I'm still going to be running my design business here. *Right?*" That was actually a blessing in disguise. There would be no risk of getting too romantically entangled, since they both wouldn't be under the same roof most of the time.

"You may change your mind about that when the babies actually get here," her mom predicted.

Her dad nodded. "Little ones have a way of changing even the best-laid plans."

"Well, not ours," Poppy said stubbornly.

If there was one thing she loved—and Trace was adamantly against—it was living in the rural Texas town where she'd grown up and he'd moved to briefly as a teen. Luckily, the two of them had attended the same college, where they'd gotten even closer, and had almost everything else in common.

"We're just doing this because it's required of us if we want to adopt the twins from the Stork Agency."

"It's still cause for celebration!" Lacey picked up the phone with a wink. "And that means family!"

Half an hour later Poppy was ensconced at her parents' Victorian home in downtown Laramie. Her folks were busy opening champagne and setting out food, picked up from a local restaurant. Trace was once again connected via Skype, as were her San Antonio-based twin sisters and their families. The triplets had arrived with their families, too. And, as always, everyone had an opinion about what would be best for the oldest of the Jackson and Lacey McCabe brood.

"You can't get married at the courthouse," her mom said.

Poppy caught Trace's handsome countenance on the monitor. His expression might be carefully casual, but she could tell by the look in his hazel eyes he was as opposed to all the calamity as she was. What, she wondered with a pang, had she gotten them into? Why hadn't they just eloped via proxy?

But it was too late now.

The news was out.

"All five of us want to be your bridesmaids. It's tradition," the ultra-romantic Callie declared via Skype.

Poppy wished she could lean up against Trace's muscular six-foot-four frame and take the comfort only he could give. Since that wasn't an option, she did her best to throw a monkey wrench into the plans. "What about groomsmen, though?" She looked at Trace, expecting him to bail her out.

Instead he shrugged. "I've got fellow airmen stationed at the military base nearby I can call on to escort them down the aisle."

Poppy moved closer to the computer camera and gave him a look she hoped only he could see. To her frustration, Trace remained as ruggedly composed as ever. His brawny arms were folded in front of him, his broad shoulders relaxed.

And his chest. How well she knew the sculpted abs and lean waist beneath his snug T-shirt. Not to mention...

Oblivious to the direction of his daughter's privately lustful thoughts, Jackson asked, "What about the best man?"

"I'll arrange for that, as well as the groom, sir," Trace promised with his usual calm command. "It will all be military. If that matters in terms of color scheme or anything."

Poppy rubbed her forehead, already exhausted just thinking about this. "It's too much trouble," she declared, doing her best to take charge of her very overbearing family. She turned away from Trace and made eye contact with everyone else there in person and on the additional laptop screens. "Especially given the fact that Thanksgiving is just a few days away and for the adoption to proceed as planned, Trace and I need to get married in the next week." Couldn't anyone see a big McCabe shindig was *impossible*?

Again, she looked to Trace for help.

Instead he said, "I'm fine with whatever Poppy wants."

"Well, what Poppy wants—what she deserves—is a wedding every bit as wonderful and meaningful as we all had!" Callie insisted. "I mean, it's not as if this is ever going to happen again for either of you, is it?"

Poppy and Trace exchanged glances and simultaneously shook their heads. *Not in this lifetime… This one marriage that wasn't* really *a marriage was it.* At least they were both on the same page about that.

"Well, then, there you go," Callie's twin, Maggie, an event planner, said. "Poppy's wedding to Trace needs to be every bit as special for her, as all of ours were for us. Luckily, I can pull a ceremony and reception together for you and Trace, even on very short notice."

Poppy had been afraid of that. When her five sisters put their minds to something, there was nothing they could not achieve. Especially in the romance milieu.

"I'll handle the wedding announcement and invitations," veteran publicist Callie volunteered.

Lily smiled and squeezed her husband's hand. "Gannon and I will take care of everything on the legal end that needs to be done here through our firm."

Rose leaned against her rancher hubby, Clint. "I'll donate all the food for the reception from my wholesale business."

Physician Violet looked at her doctor-husband, Gavin. "We'll hire the caterers to cook and serve it."

"We'll provide everything else," her mother said. "Down to the flowers, venue and dress!"

"And anything else you might want or need," her dad finished quietly.

Aware she actually felt a little dizzy, Poppy had to sit. She rubbed at an imaginary spot on the knee of her jeans, wondering how her life had gotten so far out of her control so fast. Especially when she had worked so hard not to let events overtake her, not ever again.

Inhaling slowly, she lifted her chin. "I know you all want to give me a beautiful wedding, and I truly appreciate it, but don't you think that's all a little over the top since the *groom in question* won't actually be here? Except to watch via Skype—"

Trace, who never made a promise he couldn't keep, cut in. "I may not actually even be able to do that."

Her father frowned, knowing, as did the rest of them, that military orders could change on a moment's notice.

Lacey moved to stand beside her husband. Her arm curved over Jackson's bicep as she studied Trace's image on the screen. "What about your family?"

This time Trace did grimace, Poppy noted, glad to see she wasn't the only one who felt events had spiraled completely out of control.

He squinted. "I haven't told them yet but I imagine my parents will both want to come." He paused, reluctantly adding, "My mom and dad will likely want to be seated well apart from each other, though."

Poppy groaned inwardly. It didn't matter what the situation, Trace's parents never got along. Never had. Probably never would.

Jackson seemed to read her mind and again deftly nixed his daughter's effort to call off this calamity before it happened. "It's important you both have family there, so whatever we need to do to ensure your folks are comfortable, Trace, will be done."

"After all," Poppy's mother added, "the two of you are making a lifelong commitment, not just to each other but to the twins you're planning to adopt. So it's important you do this right. Or as right as can be, under the circumstances."

More excited chatter followed.

Not sure whether she was going to suffocate or to scream in frustration, Poppy picked up her laptop and headed upstairs. "I need a moment alone with Trace before he signs off." She ducked into the bedroom she'd had as a teen and shut the door behind her. "Still there?"

"Oh, yeah." This time he didn't bother to hide his exasperation.

"We should call this ridiculous wedding off now," Poppy declared, "before it goes any further. And just find a way to elope by proxy instead!"

Looking ruggedly fit in his desert fatigues, Trace folded his arms across his brawny chest. "You really think that will work—with your family?"

He had a point. "You're right. It's probably best to know what they're planning rather than be surprised at the courthouse."

Trace gave the look that usually preceded him taking her into his arms and holding her until all her troubles eased. "Exactly."

She rubbed her temple. "Besides, given how complicated this marriage by proxy is, it's probably best we have all the help we can muster." She studied the taut planes of his handsome face. "Have you talked to your commanding officer?"

"The paperwork from our end is under way."

Another silence fell; this one only slightly less tense. He studied her, too, his expression gentling. "You going to be okay?" he asked in that tender-tough tone she loved.

Poppy thought about the family she had always wanted, the twins just waiting to be born and about to come home to her. "I don't have any choice," she told Trace. "I have to be."

So she would be. It was as simple—and complicated—as that.

Chapter 2

"I can't tell." Violet peered at her older sister closely, four days later, as the two of them stood in Poppy's old bedroom at her parents' home. "Are you about to cry—or burst into the 'Hallelujah Chorus'?"

Poppy grinned at the reference to her favorite Christmas music compilation playing in the background. "How about a little of both?" she quipped as she stepped into the wedding gown her sister held out. The truth was she was *incredibly* happy about fulfilling her long-held dream of having babies of her own in just a few short weeks. But not so thrilled about being pushed into a marriage neither she nor Trace wanted. What if it ruined what they had? Changed their relationship in a way neither expected?

"Everything has happened so fast," she admitted as the heart-pumping finale of the "Messiah" ended and the more bluesy sounds of "I'll Be Home for Christmas" began. "It all feels a little surreal."

Violet secured the hook at the top of the bodice and then moved around for the full effect. "Well, you look absolutely gorgeous, sis."

A little sad Trace wasn't here to see her in the gown, Poppy moved to the mirror to check out her reflection. "I just wish we'd arranged for the ceremony to be at the courthouse instead of the community chapel." The downtown venue had been the site of many a McCabe wedding. And, unlike hers, the marriages embarked upon in the century-old building, had been hopelessly romantic, incredibly satisfying and long lasting!

Violet studied her sister with a physician's caring intuition. "Are you also wishing Trace was going to be here—in person—instead of just watching someone else stand in for him?"

Yes, and no, Poppy thought, pausing to pin on her tiara and veil. Having him here beside her would make it feel as if they were entering into a traditional union instead of the modern arrangement they had agreed upon. So she was glad, in that sense, her best friend in all the world was thousands of miles away.

But not having Trace here depressed her on a soul-deep level, as well, since she always missed him when they weren't together.

The twins burst into the room, both looking elegant and beautiful in their silver satin bridesmaid dresses. "When did you say Trace's buddies were supposed to arrive?" Maggie asked.

"I'm not sure," Poppy admitted, trying not to flush.

"I haven't actually been able to contact him for a couple of days."

Callie did a double-take. Romantic as ever, she pressed a hand to her heart. "He hasn't called you?" Or video-chatted or answered her emails. Poppy slipped on her satin pumps, once again feeling like the odd woman out, since not only was she the only non-multiple among the six McCabe daughters, but the only one not gloriously in love with her man, too.

"He might be out on assignment." Otherwise, there was no explanation.

As expected, all five of her sisters exchanged worried glances. Luckily, just then, Jackson McCabe appeared in the door. "I just had a text. The military contingent from the air force is about ten minutes out. So we better get a move on if we want to get to the chapel before they do."

"Thanks, Dad."

Her sisters chatted excitedly as they all made their way downstairs.

Poppy, with her voluminous skirt, entered the limo, along with her mother and father. Her sisters and their spouses and children followed in a caravan of pickups and SUVs.

Thanksgiving had been two days before.

Yet the downtown streets were already decorated for Christmas. Wreaths with red-velvet ribbons had been strung on every lamppost in town. Twinkling lights and decorations adorned many of the front yards as well as the businesses that lined the major avenues.

Once again, it seemed to Poppy, time was passing far too quickly.

The limo idled in front of the century-old chapel. Her

mom got out and went in with her sisters and their families, and a steady stream of guests.

Finally even that dwindled. "Nervous?" Jackson asked gruffly.

Awaiting her grand entrance, Poppy nodded at her dad. *More so than I ever have been in my life.* Though she was damned if she knew why.

After all, Trace wasn't even going to be here.

It was just her…and whomever he had chosen to stand in for him. And maybe, if she was lucky, her groom was back from wherever he had been and would be watching the ceremony via Skype.

So there was absolutely nothing to be anxious about.

A few more minutes passed. Finally her dad's phone chimed. He grinned as he looked at the text message. "Trace's military buddies have arrived. They just went in through the rear of the chapel."

Another few minutes. Another text. Jackson opened the door and got out. "Showtime!"

Her jitters increasing, Poppy inhaled a bolstering breath. Accepting her father's hand, she gathered her skirts in her other palm and stepped out.

Her hand tucked securely into the crook of her dad's elbow, they stood at the top of the steps, out of view, and awaited their cue as the rest of the bridal party entered to the strains of Pachelbel's Canon.

Finally, it was time. Poppy and her father glided through the vestibule and into the chapel.

There, in front of the altar, stood seven tall, strapping men in uniform. Most handsome of all was the sandy-haired air force pilot next to Reverend Bleeker.

Poppy blinked. And blinked again.

Trace?

* * *

She was surprised, all right, Trace thought, staring back at her. Although no one was more surprised than he was to find himself in Laramie, Texas, for his own wedding, no less.

But now that he was finally here, he had to say he was damn glad he'd taken advantage of the opportunity given him and had headed back to the good old US of A.

Because watching Poppy come through the chapel doors on her father's arm was enough to stall his heart.

She looked like a princess in the white satin gown. The high neck and long sleeves, closely fitted bodice and poufy skirt covered every sweet, supple inch of her. Her silky, dark hair was caught up in elaborate curls pinned to the back of her head. If he found fault with anything, it was that the veil covered her face and he couldn't see the expression in her eyes.

Until she reached the altar and the reverend asked, "Who giveth this bride away?"

"I do," Jackson McCabe said in a deep, gravelly voice. He turned, lifted Poppy's veil and bent to give her a reassuring smile and to kiss her cheek, and then he handed her off to Trace.

As they faced each other, Trace could see the conflicting emotions in Poppy's gorgeous sable-brown eyes.

Confusion. Delight. Anxiety.

Aware he was suddenly feeling all that and more, he followed the minister's directive and took both of Poppy's hands in his.

The ceremony was a blur. He repeated what he was supposed to say. Poppy did the same. Until finally the reverend said, "I now pronounce you and husband and wife. Trace, you may kiss your bride."

Poppy gave him the look.

The one that warned him not to overdo it.

So of course he did.

Poppy didn't know whose gasp was louder—hers or
their guests—when Trace took her in his arms, bent her
back from the waist and planted one on her.

A roar of delight went up, followed by cheers, wild
clapping and a yee-haw or two.

And still he kept kissing her; the touch of his warm,
sure lips as magical as ever. A thrill swept through
Poppy, followed swiftly by a surge of pure happiness.
Unable to help herself, she wreathed both her arms
around his neck and kissed him back with the same
abandon.

It took the discreet cough of the minister to break
it up.

The heat of her embarrassment flooding her face,
Poppy opened her eyes.

Grinning triumphantly, Trace slowly shifted her upright.

More cheers followed, drowned out by the beginning
of the recessional.

In the aisle, the airmen in dress blues stood with their
ceremonial swords drawn into a canopy. Gallantly tucking her hand into the crook of his elbow, and still beaming proudly, Trace escorted her beneath the canopy.

"I can't believe you're here," Poppy murmured as
they stepped to the front of the receiving line in the
chapel vestibule.

Eyes darkening possessively, Trace gave her waist
an affectionate squeeze. "Surprised ya, huh?" he whispered back.

And then some, Poppy thought, still tingling from his recklessly impulsive kiss.

"You look so beautiful," he said, his eyes twinkling with delight.

Poppy grinned, aware he wasn't the only one who'd had his breath taken away. "Right back at you, Lieutenant," she murmured happily.

Then all was taken up by the formalities of greeting their guests. And it wasn't until the two of them had dashed down the church steps, through a shower of bird seed and well-wishes, and were sharing the limo to the reception that Poppy finally had the chance to talk with him privately. "I gather this is why I haven't heard from you in two days?"

Trace ran a hand beneath his closely shaved jaw. "I was on standby on several of the flights, so I wasn't entirely sure I was going to make it in time for the ceremony."

"But you did make it." And he'd obviously found time to shower, too, she noted, the joy she had felt upon seeing him in the flesh still staggering in its intensity.

"It appears the only thing most folks love more than an impromptu wedding that needs all the help it can muster to be pulled off, is one between an active-duty airman and his bride."

Poppy knew that was true. There was something about star-crossed lovers that appealed to just about everyone. Star-crossed lovers in the military, even more. Still…

She studied the just-cut perfection of his short, sandy-blond hair. "Why *did* you come?" Especially when he had never so much as hinted that it was a possibility.

A shadow crossed his face and he hesitated, as if not

sure how to respond. Finally he said, "You seemed so overwhelmed when we last Skyped. I thought you might have trouble handling all this on your own."

Disappointment jabbed her in the stomach, putting to rest any of the wildly romantic notions she'd had when she had walked into the church and seen him standing next to the minister.

Poppy gathered her thoughts slowly. "So you came to *rescue* me?" And not because he had suddenly discovered he was madly in love with her, as she knew everyone else who had witnessed their nuptials was probably thinking. But because he was her good *friend*. And friends helped each other out.

He nodded. "Turns out it was a lot easier to get permission to use some of the leave I'd accumulated than to push a proxy marriage request through military channels in the swift time frame you needed."

Poppy stared at him in confusion. "But you did manage it! Liz Cartwright-Anderson showed me the paperwork this morning."

"Yeah, but I didn't know if it would come through or not when I left a couple of days ago. At that point, the request was still in limbo. So to make sure the pending adoption went smoothly, I called in every marker I could."

"And came back to Texas."

He shrugged, as if it were no big deal. When she knew darn well it was a very big deal. "I haven't spent the holidays Stateside in years."

Mainly, she thought sympathetically, because he hated being caught up in the midst of his own quarreling family.

"Well, here's hoping that this yuletide will be memorable," Poppy said softly.

"I have a feeling it will be." He took her hand in his and examined the wedding band. He didn't have one, because she hadn't expected him to actually be there. Thus they had forgone that part of the ceremony.

Winking at her, he drawled, "At any rate, we're married now."

Clearly, from the joking way he'd said it, it didn't mean much, if anything at all. That was good. Wasn't it?

Poppy swallowed around the sudden constriction of her throat. Honestly, the pending adoption plus all this chaos had her brimming with unchecked emotions.

Bypassing what she normally would have done at this point in one of their private reunions—climb onto his lap and really show him how glad she was to see him—Poppy stayed right where she was. Maintaining her ladylike demeanor, she met his eyes and asked casually, "So how much time do you have?"

Oblivious to how fast and hard her heart was beating, he flexed his shoulders beneath the formal blue uniform coat. "Total? Thirty days. Of which I've already used two."

Trying not to dwell on how much she really would like to forget about the reception and kiss him again, Poppy quickly did the math. "So...twenty-eight." Compared to what short time they usually got—this visit was going to last forever! And yet compared to what she really wanted—Trace stationed somewhere close enough they could see each other all the time—not nearly enough.

His hazel eyes twinkled down at her. "Of course, I'll need a couple of days of that for travel time when I head back to the Middle East. But I'll be here for Christmas. And the birth of the twins," he promised as the limo reached the hotel where the reception was to be held.

It had all worked out perfectly, Poppy thought. So, then, why wasn't she happier?

Chapter 3

"I'm so sorry your father didn't show up tonight," Bitsy, Trace's mother, told him two hours later as he and Poppy came off the dance floor. "I mean, I knew he'd ditch the ceremony," the gregarious San Antonio society florist declared unhappily. "That's just the kind of heartless man Calvin is. But I thought for certain he would make the reception."

Not sure what to say, Poppy did her best not to react to the bitterness in her new mother-in-law's voice.

Trace hugged his diminutive, platinum-haired mother. "It's okay, Mom. It was short notice. I'll catch up with Dad before I leave the States."

Bitsy gave Poppy another warm hug. "Well, just so you know, dear, I'm so glad the two of you have finally come to your senses and made it official."

Trace scowled. "Mom…"

Bitsy straightened the hem of her beaded jacket. "Oh, hush. The two of you have essentially been married—albeit long distance—for years now. Even though you won't admit it, everyone knows you're head-over-heels in love. Isn't that why you finally decided to adopt a child together?"

Uh, not exactly, Poppy thought.

"What I don't understand is why you're not trying for a baby the old-fashioned way."

Actually, they had been, although that was a secret, Poppy thought.

"Unless you're worried the distance imposed on you by Trace's stint in the military will make conception all but impossible," Bitsy finished practically.

"Mom, I am not discussing this with you," Trace said firmly.

Make that me, either, Poppy thought.

Bitsy peered up at him. "But you do admit you want a baby with Poppy—badly?"

And I want one with him. Badly, as it were, Poppy noted. But just because they each wanted a family, and were willing to have one together, did not mean they were "essentially married," never mind head-over-heels in love.

Exhaling roughly, Trace rubbed at the muscles in the back of his neck, reminding Poppy that the only thing he hated more than having his life choices dissed or second-guessed, was to have someone assign emotions to him that he did not feel.

"Ah, it's not just one. It's twins, Mom," he said.

"Oh." Bitsy paused in the act of adjusting a diamond earring, as if not sure what to make of that. "Well, that's wonderful," she said finally. Spying her latest beau, Donald Olson—a commercial Realtor from San Angelo, who was now first in line at the open bar—she waved and started to glide off. "Just make sure the little darlings call me Bitsy, not anything grandmother-ish." She smiled over her shoulder.

"Will do," Poppy promised.

Trace bent to whisper in her ear. "Maybe if we head back to the dance floor, we won't have to endure so many blasted questions and theories and…"

"Advice?" Poppy quipped as she slipped her hand into his. "Don't forget, we've been getting plenty of that, too. Like 'don't let the sun go down on your anger.' Or 'make-up sex is the best.'"

Which was ironic, since she and Trace never, ever quarreled.

Trace whisked her into the crowd of swaying couples. Hand against her spine, he brought her as close as the full skirt of her wedding gown would allow. "My favorite is, 'never miss a chance to hold her in your arms.'"

Poppy let her body sway to the beat of the music, relaxing now that the big 'romantic' moments were finished. Their first dance, the toasts, the cake-cutting and endless picture-taking.

All of which had prompted an extended trip down memory lane. "Remember our very first dance?" Poppy tipped her head up to his as one of their favorite songs, the hopelessly romantic ballad "Wherever You Will Go" began.

His eyes crinkled at the corners, before making a wickedly provocative tour down her body. "The senior prom? You quarreled with your date a few days before…"

Reveling in the cozy feel of his hand clasping hers,

and the even more possessive look in his eyes, Poppy let out a quavering breath. "So he ended up taking someone else."

Trace nodded, recollecting fondly, "And I stepped in, as your friend."

She'd come very close to falling head-over-heels in love with him that night. But knowing how he felt about romance in general, and infatuation specifically, had come to her senses in time to preserve their growing friendship and keep things light and easy. To the point they hadn't even shared a goodnight kiss, when he'd finally dropped her at her front door at dawn.

"And you're still doing it."

The slow song ended. A faster up-tempo one began.

Trace offered a mock salute, brought her hand up over her head and twirled her around to the lively beat. "My pleasure, ma'am."

"That's Captain Ma'am to you," she teased as he tugged her back into his arms then spun her out again, dipping her backward.

"Outrank me, huh?" His low voice radiated the kind of easy joy she always felt when they were together.

Doing her best to rein in her reckless heart, she admitted, "In some things..." Although at this moment she couldn't think what. Not when she was matching her steps to his in the energetic beat and wearing a wedding ring he'd slid onto her finger. Had he ever looked more devastatingly handsome, more inclined to just have fun?

Even though the rational side of her knew this was all a formality, undertaken for the best of reasons—the babies they were soon to adopt—she couldn't help but be swept up in the moment as the song ended and another much slower, sultrier one began.

Clueless to the hopelessly conflicted nature of her thoughts, Trace pulled her in tight against him.

Their bodies swaying as if they were made for each other, he drawled, "Well, then, Captain Ma'am—" with the pad of his thumb, he traced the curve of her lower lip and looked deeply into her eyes "—I guess I'll just have to do what you say…"

Trace had been kidding when he said he'd follow her orders. But hours later, when she first laid down the law, he realized by her hands-off expression that she hadn't been.

He stared at her in disbelief. She'd been getting more distant as the night wore on. He'd attributed it to fatigue and the stress of allowing people to see only what they wanted to see.

"You want me to sleep in the guest room?" he repeated, sure he must have misunderstood what she meant. "On our *wedding* night?"

She headed through the upstairs hall of her cozy bungalow, the voluminous skirt of her white gown hiding the delectable shape of her hips and swishing lightly as she moved. Steadfastly avoiding his gaze and keeping her back to him all the while, she stood on tiptoe to reach the top shelf of the linen closet at the end of the short hall, trying but failing repeatedly to reach the stack of clean linens and pillows. "You have to understand." She frowned, rocking back on her heels, her soft lips sliding out into a sexy pout. "I didn't know you were coming home for the ceremony."

What did that have to do with anything? When had it ever? One of the things he liked best about her was that she was so easygoing and—usually—up for just about anything.

Not tonight.

He frowned. His presence was supposed to be a happy surprise, not cause for complaint. "I don't get it."

She lifted a desultory hand and waved it in the direction of the master suite. "My bedroom's a mess."

He cast a look over his shoulder. That much was true. Not only did the elegant retreat look as if a tornado had gone through it, spilling everything from lacey undergarments to high heels in its wake, but there was a good deal of Christmas stuff, too. Gift catalogs. Lists. Even what appeared to be the makings for homemade holiday cards and ornaments.

Not about to be sidetracked, when he had missed her so damn much, he caught her around the waist. Anxious to make up for lost time now that they were finally alone, he trailed a string of kisses down her silky-soft neck. Lingered at the sensitive place behind her ear. Felt her quiver in response. Satisfaction roared through him.

"So we'll throw a few pillows on the floor," he teased, reaching for the zipper of her dress.

Stiffening, she wedged her elbows between them. "No." She wiggled free. "Trace…"

Not about to push her into anything, he dropped his arms and stepped back. Looked down into her face. "What's wrong?"

Her dark brown eyes took on a troubled sheen. She brushed past him into the mess that was her bedroom. "When we agreed to get married, we said this wouldn't change anything."

He followed lazily, making sure to give her the space she wanted. Lounging against the bureau, he surveyed the soft blush flooding her cheeks. The turmoil twisting her sweet lips. "You not wanting to make love with me is definitely a change."

Hand on the bed, Poppy bent to remove her high heels. "Don't you see?" She let her skirt fall back into place, but not before he'd gotten a tantalizing glimpse of her long legs.

Trace felt his body harden in response.

Poppy shook her head. "After everything we've just been through the past six hours—"

"Seven," he corrected. That was way too long. Usually, after months apart, they were in bed within minutes of reconnecting, which was why they usually met up at a hotel first.

Poppy frowned. "Okay, seven hours," she corrected with an exasperated scowl. "If we were to make love now after all of that…"

He saw where she was going. "The vows?"

She nodded in what abruptly seemed like regret. "And the toasts and the cake-cutting and the first dance." She went around the room, snatching up discarded clothing and stuffed it into the hamper so the lacy unmentionables were out of view. Whirling to face him, she swallowed. "Can't you see it would be too confusing?"

For her maybe. Not for him.

With effort, he ignored the ache in his groin. "It doesn't have to be," he said. As far as he was concerned, vows or not, absolutely nothing between them had changed. They were still free to do whatever and to be whomever they wanted.

She folded her arms beneath the inviting lushness of her breasts. "Right now, everything feels pretty traditional. And you've never wanted that. And…" She hesitated slightly before continuing even more stalwartly. "Neither have I."

Once again their gazes collided.

As was their custom, neither wanted to be the first to look away.

He jerked off his bow tie and loosened the first couple of buttons on his shirt. "So what are you telling me?" he rasped. Feeling pretty damn stifled, he let his uniform jacket go by the wayside, too. "That now that it's properly sanctioned, we'll never hook up again?"

She blushed at the ridiculousness of that notion.

"Of course we will," she said softly, her desire for him momentarily shining through. She paused to wet her lips; her defenses sliding stubbornly back into place. "Just not tonight. Not when we're both so tired. And confused."

Trace was confused, all right. He'd pulled every string it was possible to pull, and come an awfully long way, to get turned down cold. On their wedding night, no less!

Sweeping past him, she went back to trying to get the stack of linens off the top shelf. Stumbling slightly, she managed to grab hold of the bottom corner and pull them toward her.

He caught her in his arms as she caught the linens in hers.

Inhaled the sweet fragrance of her hair and skin.

Felt another tidal wave of desire ripple through him.

Damn if he didn't want her all over again.

That was, assuming he had ever stopped.

Which, of course, he hadn't.

"Thanks." Arms full, she wiggled free, pivoted and rustled toward the only other bedroom on the top floor of her bungalow.

Currently a home office, it also housed a sofa bed for guests.

When he visited her in Laramie and bunked at her place, it was always opened up and the covers dutifully rumpled every morning. But only for show. In case someone in her family happened to drop by, unannounced.

Although he doubted anyone really believed they were, or had ever been, just good friends.

No, his place was in her very comfy queen-size bed. Like her, sans clothes.

But, apparently, not tonight.

Poppy knew she was disappointing Trace. But, really, she reckoned as she entered the guest room to make up the bed while he went downstairs to get his suitcase, she was doing them both a favor, giving them each a little breathing room.

The last thing she had ever wanted was for him to feel as trapped as his dad apparently had, whenever he was married, or to ever do anything that would spoil their relationship.

Come morning, he'd be thanking her for it.

Meantime, where was he?

Getting a bag couldn't possibly take that long.

Nor could she hear any sounds of him moving around.

Perplexed, she called out. "Trace?"

No answer.

Grabbing the skirts of her wedding gown, she rustled down the stairs.

Trace was sprawled in the oversize club chair she'd brought into the house just for him. His long legs were stretched over the matching ottoman and his chest moved with deep, even breaths. It looked as if he had sat down, just for a second, and fallen fast asleep.

He was more handsome than ever, in repose.

Tenderness swept over her and she knew she couldn't wake him. Instead she eased off his shoes and took a throw from the back of the sofa and spread it over him.

As expected, he didn't stir.

She stood there another long moment, just drinking in the sight of him, realizing all over again just how much she missed him when he was away.

In need of a little comfort herself, she slipped into the kitchen and extracted the nearly empty peppermint ice cream container from the freezer. Taking that and a spoon, she headed back up the stairs, suddenly feeling near tears again.

What was with her these days? Poppy wondered as she moved into her bedroom and sat to finish what was left of the ice cream. Was it the prospect of adopting the twins that had her so emotionally overwrought? The knowledge that while she was getting *part* of what she wanted, she was still eons away from getting it all? Or just the fatigue?

Poppy had no answer as she let the minty, holiday flavor melt on her tongue and soothe her yet again. Finally she put the empty container aside. Then, taking a moment just to chill, she laid back against the pillows.

The next thing she knew sunlight was streaming in through the windows. It was just after nine in the morning. And—was that her doorbell ringing?

Poppy sat up with a start.

Thinking it must be some sort of emergency, she rushed down the stairs. Too late, Trace had already awakened and moved to open the door. Mitzy Martin stood on the other side of the threshold, work bag over her shoulder.

If Poppy's childhood friend was surprised to see them still in their wedding finery, she managed not to show it. "Hey, sorry to intrude. But I really need to talk to both of you."

Gallantly, Trace ushered the social worker inside.

The vivacious Mitzy pulled out a sheaf of papers attached to a clipboard and pen. "The Stork Agency wants an amended home study done ASAP."

Hence, Poppy thought, the surprise visit. One of several she'd endured during the past few years. "Why?"

"You've already interviewed us both extensively," Trace pointed out.

Mitzy looked around, bypassing the chair with the throw still on it, and took a seat on the sofa. "You weren't married then. Or planning to marry."

Feeling a little self-conscious to be caught, still in her wedding gown, her hair askew, Poppy snuck a furtive glance Trace's way. He looked as bedraggled as she did. His once-pristine military uniform was wrinkled, and from the look of his bloodshot eyes, it appeared he'd had a pretty rough night.

Clearing her throat, Poppy shook off the rest of the cobwebs. "But they asked us to do this!"

"Exactly my worry." Mitzy sobered. "Is that the only reason you tied the knot last night?"

Poppy locked eyes with Trace, not sure how to answer that.

"Yes," he said, blunt as ever.

"So if the Stork Agency hadn't required it?" Mitzy took a clipboard full of papers, and pen from her bag.

Trace shrugged and took a seat in the same chair

where he'd spent the night. "I wouldn't be here today. I'd be back in the Middle East."

Mitzy wrote on a preprinted form. "Is it your intention to be in this marriage for the long haul? Or just until the adoption is final?"

"Until the kids are grown," Trace said firmly. He glanced at Poppy. "Or longer."

Mitzy turned to Poppy. "And you?"

"When Trace and I decided to adopt children together, we agreed we would behave as a family from this point forward."

"So there was no end date?" Mitzy challenged.

Aware her knees were suddenly a little shaky, Poppy perched on the wide arm of Trace's chair. "No. Being a parent is a lifelong commitment."

Mitzy looked at Trace. "Do you agree?"

He nodded. "For better or worse. Just like marriage."

"Are you expecting the worst?"

Trace returned, "Are you?"

Ignoring his insolence, the social worker rose. "Are you going to live here?"

Poppy and Trace nodded in unison.

Mitzy continued to study them. "Mind if I take a quick look around the premises?"

"You've already done that," Poppy protested. When the upstairs wasn't such a total mess!

Gaze narrowed, Mitzy paused. "Is there a reason you don't want me to look around?"

Yes, Poppy thought, knowing if the social worker went up there, she would quickly realize that neither bed had been slept in. "No," she said out loud.

Her manner all business, Mitzy made her way through the dining area and into the kitchen, which, unlike the upstairs, was neat as a pin. From there, she peeked into the powder room then took the stairs. Poppy and Trace were right behind her.

She paused in front of Poppy's bedroom, which was still a mess, the covers rumpled from where she'd slept.

"Where will the babies sleep?" Mitzy asked, still making notes.

"In here." Poppy pointed to the office-cum-guest room.

Wordlessly the social worker took in the perfectly made-up sofa bed, Poppy's desk and computer.

"Obviously, everything's happened so fast, we haven't had a chance to set up a nursery," Poppy said in a rush. "But I'll get it done in the next couple of days."

"Call me when you do. I'd like to add it to the report," Mitzy told her. "Where are the two of you planning to sleep?"

Trace quirked his brow at Poppy as if he'd like to hear the answer to that, too.

Flushing, she pointed to her bedroom. "Exactly where you'd expect. In my—er, *our* room." There wouldn't be a whole lot of choice once the nursery was set up.

Mitzy turned back to Trace, her expression as poker-faced as his. "Does that square with your plans, too?"

"Unless she relegates me to the sofa," he replied in a joking tone.

Poppy recognized an attempt to lighten the mood when she heard one.

Unfortunately, Mitzy chose to ignore it. "Is that likely to happen?"

"Well…" Trace exhaled slowly, his expression turning even more maddeningly inscrutable. "We are married, after all."

"And?" Mitzy persisted.

Trace lifted his broad shoulders in an affable shrug. "Sometimes spouses disagree, and when that happens, one of them generally ends up on the sofa. Unless they are really ticked off and go to a hotel."

Another joke.

That did not go over well.

"And you would know that because…?" the social worker prompted.

Abruptly, Trace lost all patience. "Come on, Mitzy. Everyone in Laramie County knows my mother's been married eight times, my dad three. So I've seen my fair share of discord. And, for the record, I was kidding around about the sofa."

"Except the sofa bed upstairs was made up," Mitzy pointed out with a Cheshire smile.

"And no one slept in it," Poppy noted. But wisely did not elaborate.

Mitzy looked pointedly at Poppy's rumpled wedding gown and Trace's uniform.

In an effort to smooth over any rough edges, Poppy shrugged lightly. "It was a long day and an even longer night. We were both exhausted by the end. Suffice it to say…" She paused, took a breath and turned to look Trace in the eye, giving him a wordless apology for her unprecedented cowardice. "Nothing went according to plan."

He smiled. *Apology accepted.* Then he reached over and clasped her hand. Tightly.

A taut silence fell.

Mitzy frowned. "I'm just trying to get a feel for how real this union is going to be."

Trace countered in a smooth voice, "As opposed to?"

"A sham marriage." Mitzy walked down the stairs. "Which, I don't have to tell either of you, would be a very bad thing to have to report on."

How could things have gone so far south so fast? Poppy asked herself glumly as she and Trace followed. It hadn't even been fifteen hours! Feeling as if it was her turn to defend them, she said hotly, "It's *not* a sham. It might not be traditional by someone else's standards, but it's definitely going to be real enough according to ours."

Mitzy took a seat in the big comfy chair, leaving the two of them to sit side-by-side on the sofa. "I gather since the original plan was marriage by proxy—until Trace showed up in person, anyway—that this was almost a mere formality."

Before it turned oh, so real, Poppy thought.

"And now it's not," Trace said snidely.

Aware she was getting under his skin, Mitzy made another note. "So how long had you been thinking about getting married before you made the decision?" she asked.

Trace continued the battle like the true warrior he was. "Five minutes maybe."

"I don't mean when you actually proposed," Mitzy said.

Figuring the truth, and nothing but the truth, was the way go to, at least as much as possible, anyway, Poppy put in, just as cavalierly, "Actually, it was my idea."

Mitzy did a double-take. "You proposed to Trace?"

Proposal meant romantic. Hers hadn't been. Poppy made a seesaw motion with her right hand. "Mmm. More like… I…presented the option."

Trace draped his arm around her shoulders and shifted closer. "And I accepted."

"Because of the agency requirement regarding the adoption of more than one child at one time," Mitzy ascertained.

Poppy and Trace both nodded. She, reluctantly. He, as if to say, what's the big deal here?

Was he more like his oft-married and divorced mother in this respect than she knew? Poppy wondered uncomfortably.

Mitzy turned the page on the preprinted questionnaire she was working through. "Do you have a prenup?"

"No," Trace said.

"We trust each other," Poppy agreed.

Mitzy looked up. "What about an actual marriage contract, verbal or written?"

"No," they said firmly in unison.

Mitzy tapped her pen on the page. "Surely you have some sense of exactly how this is all going to work."

Somehow, Trace managed not to sigh—even though Poppy could feel his exasperation mounting. "I'm in the military," he stated bluntly. "I'll be here whenever I can, as much as I can. The rest of the time Poppy will handle everything on the home front, like most military wives."

Military wife. Poppy kind of liked the sound of that. All possessive and gruff-tender.

Mitzy's expression softened ever so slightly, too. "Will you come home to see them every time you get leave?"

"I always do," Trace said.

And Poppy knew that was true. Whenever he had time off, the two of them managed to steal time together. Even when it meant they rendezvoused in a third central location.

"So in that sense—" Mitzy smiled, still writing "—nothing will change."

Trace and Poppy nodded again.

"So is this it?" Trace asked, looking impatient. And still jet-lagged.

Another long, thoughtful pause.

"Actually," Mitzy said, riffling through the content on her clipboard, "I have several more pages—"

Pages! Poppy thought.

"—of questions to ask for the amended home study. But I can see it's a bad time, the two of you being on your honeymoon and all. So what do you say we get together at another time, when you have the nursery done, and finish up then?"

"What else could you possibly need to know?" Poppy asked, only half joking, getting to her feet.

Mitzy slid everything in her work bag. "Well, for one thing, we need to revisit your individual family histories."

"We did that before," Poppy pointed out.

"Individually. Not together. Now that you are married we have to make sure there has been full disclosure between the two of you and that there are no underlying issues there, either."

"Sounds like a test," Trace grumbled.

That Cheshire smile again. "It is, in a way," Mitzy said. "So, if there's anything you haven't told each other—and should—now is probably the time."

Trace was about to say there was nothing he and Poppy hadn't told each other when he caught the fleeting glimpse of unhappiness in his new wife's eyes and realized maybe there was. What it could be, though, he had no idea.

He waited until they had showed the social worker out before voicing his concern. He cupped Poppy by the shoulders and looked down at her. "What's wrong?" he asked gently.

Poppy extricated herself deftly, swirled, lifted the skirt of her wedding dress in both hands and headed up the stairs. "Didn't you see the way she was looking at us?" She was fuming.

He caught sight of the layers of petticoat beneath the satin skirt. And couldn't help wondering what was beneath that.

Casually, he caught up with her in the short hall that ran the length of the second floor of the bungalow. "Like a social worker doing her job?"

Poppy stormed into the bedroom, still in her stocking feet. Reaching behind her for the zipper, she pouted. "She thinks our marriage is a sham."

Trace stepped in to gallantly unhook the fastening at the nape of her gown. Once that was free, the zipper came down easily. "Why?" he countered huskily. "Because she obviously figured out you and I didn't consummate our marriage last night?"

She shivered when his fingertips grazed her bare skin. "Please don't say it that way."

Hands on her shoulders, he turned her to face him. "Since when have we parsed words or dealt with something other than the truth?"

Poppy raked her teeth across the delectable plumpness of her lower lip. "Never."

"So what's the problem, then?"

She stared at the open collar of his shirt. "The fact

we didn't make love makes us—our whole union—look suspect."

"Well, then," Trace drawled, taking her in his arms and doing what he should have done the night before, *would* have done if she hadn't been so skittish and he hadn't been so damned jet-lagged. "There is only one way to fix that."

Chapter 4

Poppy knew she and Trace would eventually make love as a married couple. She had just convinced herself it wouldn't be until she felt *emotionally* ready.

She splayed her hands across the hardness of his chest and ducked her head to the side. "You can't kiss me."

He chuckled, stroking one hand down her back, molding the other around the nape of her neck. "Actually, darlin'…" He left a trail of light kisses across the top of her head, down her temple, along the curve of her cheekbone, to the ultrasensitive place just behind her ear. "I think I'm supposed to…"

"Not yet." Not until her sentiments were in order, her heart secure.

"Then how about I help you out of this dress," he said.

She moaned as his tongue swept the shell of her ear. "Trace, I—"

"Unless you're really going to wear your wedding dress all day."

Gently, he eased the unzipped gown from her shoulders.

Poppy caught it, one hand to her chest.

His brow lifted. "Something you don't want me to see?"

Actually yes. "My sisters…"

He waited.

"Well, they got me this, um…"

As always, he knew where she was going almost before she did. "Lingerie?"

"As a joke."

His husky laughter filled the room. Devilry sparkled in his hazel eyes. "Then I really have to see it."

Letting her go, he removed his jacket and the tie still loose around his neck and unbuttoned a few more buttons on his shirt. That came off, too. Leaving only a white cotton military-issue T-shirt and uniform dress pants.

With a sweep of his arm, he cleared a place on the side of the bed where she'd been sleeping and sat, propped against the headboard, both hands clasped behind his head.

Her heart pounding, she stammered, "Y-you really expect me to give you a show?"

"Well…since you've outlawed the romantic approach I was intending…having a little fun seems like the way to proceed. Unless—" he dared her with a wolfish smile "—the Poppy I know no longer exists?"

Poppy planted both hands on her hips, forgetting for a moment she'd been holding up the front of her dress. The bodice tumbled down, revealing the ridiculously sheer and tight-fitting, low-cut bustier that laced up the front.

His grin widened even more as she decided, against her better judgment, to just leave it where it fell, draped low across her waist. "You know, married or not, I am just the same."

"Ah…" He undid his belt then his zipper. "Then prove it."

Her gaze followed his hand.

The bulge she saw pressing against his fly made her mouth water.

"Unless," he said, going back to simply watching her, his eyes dark and seductive. "You don't want to give me something to fantasize about when I am far, far away?"

Trace had meant the remark as a jest. Incentive to forget the tumultuous pressure of the past five days and return to their usual horsing around. But the reminder of an eventual departure had set the time clock that always surrounded their reunions running.

"All right, Lieutenant," she said.

Sashaying forward, she turned, giving him a 360-degree view of the dress peeled down to the waist. Facing him, she continued her striptease.

Not wanting it to be over too soon, Trace goaded. "No music?"

Poppy stopped. Rolled her eyes. Sauntered over to the CD player on her bureau and pushed Play without even looking. The strains of the "Hallelujah Chorus" burst forth, prompting them both to burst into gales of laughter.

"Good choice," Trace said, getting immediately to his feet.

"What are you doing?" Poppy asked.

"Isn't it customary to stand for the finale of Handel's Messiah?"

She knew full well, as did he, that it was.

But it wasn't the rousing sounds of the traditional oratorio that had his heart pumping. Or hers, either, he guessed. Today it was all them…

But not wanting her to know—just yet anyway—how wickedly excited he was, lest he ruin the mounting anticipation for her, too, he waited for her to make the next move.

Her sable brown eyes lit with a lively, impetuous light. Inhaling deeply, eyes locked with his, she stepped out of her dress and then the petticoat. Then slowly, erotically, moved toward him in nothing but the bustier, garter belt and thigh-high stockings, and the tiniest bikini panties he had ever seen.

When she was just out of reach, she stopped.

It was all he could do not to groan in frustration, as she began taking the pins from her hair, until it, too, spilled over her shoulders in a tumble of dark, silky-brown curls.

Unable to hold back, he breathed, "You are so damn beautiful."

The adrenaline rush of Handel playing in the background, Poppy sashayed closer still. "Mmm-hmm." She tilted her face up to his mischievously. "Your turn." Her eyes drifted over him appreciatively. "Lieutenant…"

Aware he was already way too aroused to hold back for long, he warned, "Poppy…"

She stepped away and tilted her head tauntingly. "Unless you don't dare?"

Oh, he dared, all right.

Still appreciating the view, he tugged his T-shirt over his head. Spun around, just as she had.

Her soft laughter filled the room.

Hands spread on either side of him, miming a model showing off the garments, he let her look her fill, then hooked his thumbs into the waistband of his pants and pushed them down.

Instead of the white military-issue briefs he knew she was expecting, he was wearing a pair of black silk boxers with red hearts all over them.

Chuckling merrily, she let her gaze drift lower, to the outline of his male anatomy pushing against the silk.

No hiding his desire now.

"Nice," she said softly as the first song ended and "Have Yourself a Merry Little Christmas" began.

Unable to wait a second longer, sensing she wasn't either, Trace prowled toward her. "Not as nice as you," he said, running his thumbs over the crests of her breasts pushing against the sheer fabric.

Her arms came up to wrap around his neck.

Rising on tiptoe, she moved all the way into his arms. Then, pressing her body flush against his, she threaded her hands through his hair, all the tenderness he had ever wanted to see shimmering in her misty brown eyes. "Now, you see? This is why you always end up seducing me." She kissed him soulfully.

"Really?" Cupping her face in both hands, he returned her kiss with every ounce of pent-up passion that he had. Feeling her shudder, he took her by the hand and led her over to stand next to the bed. Satisfaction roared through him. "Because all this time, I thought it was *you* seducing me."

She watched as he unlaced the front of her bustier

and the luscious mounds of her breasts fell free. "You know it's mutual."

Relishing the sight of her partially dressed as much as completely undressed, he turned his attention to the convenient little bows on either side of her bikini panties. A tug of each and those, too, slid right off.

Her eyes darkened. "You're going to ravish me, aren't you?"

Still kissing her, determined to give her all the pleasure she deserved, he backed her playfully to the wall. His palms and fingertips made a leisurely tour of her body. "Oh, yeah…"

With a soft sigh of acquiescence, she lifted her arms to his shoulders. Trembled when he found the sensitive place between her thighs. Desire shot through him. He loved the way she responded to him, the way she insisted, even now, on giving back, by sifting her palms over her shoulders, down his spine, to cup and mold his buttocks.

He moved his mouth to her breasts, nibbling and suckling, making sure there was nothing he missed. Her nipples pebbled all the more, her eyes widened in excitement, and the satin of her skin grew as hot as the fire burning inside him.

Damn. But he loved her like this. All soft and womanly. Rocking against him, so reckless and open to everything…

He rose and took her mouth again, determined not to let it go by too fast, yet able to tell from the quickening meter of her breath she needed more, too, just as he did. Wedging his knee between her legs, he spread them wide and brought his leg up, so she could ride his thigh. She moaned and melted into his body, rubbing, seeking, finding, her tongue tangling with his, until he was as lost in their embrace as she was. Her breath caught even more as he stroked her, finding her center, the wet, velvety heat.

"Trace?" She kissed him again.

He kissed her back, still stroking and touching, making her his. Quivering, her hands found the waistband of his boxers, slid inside to cup him. She whispered, "I don't think I can wait…"

Another thing he loved about her.

She was okay with living in the moment. And then finding another. And another…

Grinning, he peeled off his boxers. She climbed his body and still resting against the wall, wrapped her legs around his waist. One clever move on her part, and he was inside. Overcome with the feel of her slick, wet heat, he pushed even deeper. "This isn't how it's supposed to go, darlin'."

He moaned as she clamped even tighter around him, bringing him home…

"Exactly what I thought when you first undressed me. And yet…" She pressed her mouth to his, kissing him softly, erotically, finding the same easy timeless rhythm of penetration and withdrawal. She sighed wantonly. "Here we are…"

"Together again," he rasped, letting her call all the shots the first time they made love during a reunion, the way he always did. *Being each other's soft place to fall…*

Two additional bouts of hot lovemaking and a short nap later, Poppy and Trace finally showered and headed to her kitchen for a long-delayed first meal of the day

"So what's on the agenda for today?" Trace asked.

Glad things were finally returning to normal between them—meaning not too serious or intense—Poppy took out the coffee. "Well, I was going to make a new wreath for the front door. Then, I have to run over to the office-supply and craft stores to buy supplies for the Holiday Cards for Soldiers project at the elementary school later this week."

He lounged against the counter, crossing his arms over his chest "That's right. You help out with that every year, don't you?"

Wondering if she would ever get tired of admiring his taut, hard body—never mind the things it could do for her!—she shrugged. "The whole school does. It's a way to show our military how much we appreciate all they do for us."

"Want help with it?"

"Actually, I bet they'd like you to speak to a class or two, too. Tell them about your job."

His mouth quirked. "I think I could do that."

"Great!" Poppy grinned as their eyes met. "I'll let the teachers know. Then…" Sobering, she took a deep breath, not sure how he would feel about it, never mind the timing, since he hadn't even been back a full day. "I had planned to go to Fort Worth to visit with Anne Marie this evening. I wanted to let her know that we were married and to thank her for having so much faith in us."

He moved so she could get into the cupboard behind him. "Want company?"

Did she ever.

Poppy's thigh brushed his as she reached for the filters. "I'm sure she'd be thrilled to see you." She stumbled slightly and Trace put a hand beneath her elbow to steady her.

"The only thing is... I was planning to spend the night in a hotel there, rather than drive the two and a half hours back tonight." She felt oddly clumsy. Almost a little dizzy.

Must be the accumulated fatigue.

He slid her a look. "Do you have a hotel reservation?"

Poppy put the paper filter in the basket. "Yes."

He watched her grind the beans. "Am I going to need my own room or can I bunk with you?" he asked as the aroma of fresh-ground coffee filled her kitchen.

In the past they had done it both ways, although they usually ended up spending most of their time together, anyway. Aware of his eyes upon her, Poppy added water and hit Brew. "I suppose we could share," she said dryly, "in the interest of economy and all."

And the fact that given a choice, I'd like nothing more than to spend another night making wild, passionate love with you and then sleep snuggled up together.

He nodded. "What time did you want to leave?"

Poppy got out the orange juice. "I said I would be there around seven, so...maybe three-thirty."

"Sounds good."

A feeling of peace descended between them. And something else a lot deeper and harder to identify.

"So...back to the wreath," he continued affably as she busied herself pouring them each a glass of juice. "Do you want any help making that?"

Say what? "I thought the only thing you ever did for your mom's florist business was deliver orders!" As the mood between them began to lighten, she pushed on. "That she wouldn't let you near the creative side because you were all thumbs."

"True enough." He grinned at her playful needling then winked. "*Maybe* on purpose…"

"Ah. The old male trick of trying to get out of something through demonstrated incompetence?"

He rubbed the flat of his hand across his stubbled jaw. "Not that you would ever do the same thing."

Poppy called on her inner Texas belle. Flattening a hand across her throat, she drawled, "Why, whatever are you talking about?"

His brow raised at her thick Southern accent. Still laughing, he said, "I seem to remember a flat tire or two…"

"Okay." She flushed as his eyes surveyed her lazily, head to toe. "So I *might* have feigned feminine incompetence when we were in college, to avoid getting my clothes smudged with tire yuck." A perfectly understandable ploy, in her view.

He put his glass aside and moved toward her. "And I might have enjoyed coming to your rescue."

"That's right." Poppy gazed down at their suddenly linked hands. "The first time we ever made love was after you rescued me and came back to my apartment to shower and get cleaned up."

He kissed her knuckles. "And we ended up in bed instead."

Tenderness flowed between them. "Amazing, how long ago that was." Poppy sighed contentedly.

"How long we've been together."

And she knew it was all because they had never been foolish enough to put restraints on each other, and what they each wanted out of life. Or to do anything really crazy like, say, get married.

Only now they had.

Would that change anything?

And what would happen to their long-standing friendship slash love affair if it did?

Trace noticed the shift in her mood. He asked lightly as she moved away, "Was it something I said?"

A joke. Yet not a joke. Poppy turned the oven to preheat it. "No."

"Then what's bringing you down?"

Poppy wished she knew why her moods were so mercurial these days. It was like being on a roller coaster. Over the moon one minute, incredibly sad and weepy the next...

She brought out the bacon and began layering it in the bottom of a cast-iron skillet. "Is that another way of saying I've been frowning too much?"

"Looking near tears."

Poppy retrieved the package of ready-to-bake buttermilk biscuits from her freezer. "I know I've been emotional lately." What she couldn't say—maybe didn't really want to know—was why.

She got out the eggs.

Seeing the coffee was finished, Trace reached for two mugs. Poppy put up a staying hand. "Maybe later."

He settled against the counter, aromatic beverage in hand. "Is it because you're finally about to adopt twin babies?" He paused. "Or because of what happened years ago?"

Poppy should have known he would bring *that* up. He always did, whenever he was worried about her, in this sense.

And maybe, she thought ruefully, he had a right to be.

Glad she had him to talk with, Poppy released a weary

sigh. "I admit I feel a little jinxed when it comes to me ever having a family."

"Because of the baby we lost?"

God. How was it possible it could still hurt so much? After fourteen years?

Swallowing a lump in her throat, she concentrated on her task. "I know I was barely through the third month." She broke eggs into a bowl and tossed the shells into the sink. "But I really thought I would carry that baby to term. And I would have, had it not been an ectopic pregnancy."

"Instead, you lost the child and the tube and ovary."

That had left her with two-thirds of a working reproductive system. And roughly half the ability to even get pregnant.

"Even after all that, you know, when I had finally gotten past it and we decided to actively try to conceive, I had hoped it would happen. That we'd be successful." *Have the perfect baby that was half me and half you.*

"Only it never did."

"So, can you blame me for being a little worried something might happen?" She hitched in a breath. "Again?"

Trace took her in his arms. "First of all, I don't think it will. I think you're finally going to get everything you want. Even if it is via adoption instead of pregnancy."

You're…going to get what you want…

He wasn't talking about himself. Or them, Poppy thought sadly. Just her. But why should that even surprise her? she asked herself. Up until the past few years anyway, it had always been just her thing. Trace had merely been a willing participant and a good friend. A guy who was willing to be "The Dad" in the equation whenever he came home on leave. And how often was that? At most, once or twice a year?

He studied her expression, remorse tautening the ruggedly handsome features on his face, misunderstanding the reason behind her malaise. "But even if something does go wrong with this adoption——"

She pressed her finger to his lips. "Don't say that," she whispered.

He kissed the back of her hand gently. "I'll be right there with you, to make sure you get the family you deserve to have." This time it was his voice that sounded a little rusty. "It's the least I can do."

Guilt. Again.

Poppy's spine turned as rigid as her heart. "You're not responsible for what happened, Trace."

"Come on, Poppy." He stepped aside as she grabbed a whisk and the mixing bowl. "We both know if I hadn't gotten careless, you never would have become pregnant, never would have lost the baby, and a good portion of your fertility, to boot."

She whisked the eggs with a vengeance. "I could have had an ectopic pregnancy anytime. I could still have one in my remaining fallopian tube, if I ever did get pregnant, which we both know now is unlikely to ever happen."

He grasped her wrist and put the bowl aside. "The point is, darlin', I'm here for you. I always have been. And I always will be. The same way you're here for me."

Warning herself to calm down, she took a deep, enervating breath. "As friends."

"And lovers." He tucked her hair behind her ear. "And now, husband and wife."

Poppy mugged comically at the wry note of humor in

his low tone. "Can you believe it?" She held out her left hand, examining the plain gold wedding band. Then she looked at his hand, which did not contain a ring because she hadn't expected him to actually be at the ceremony. "Because I still can't!"

He shrugged affably, still looking as though he wanted to do nothing more than sweep her up into his arms, carry her up the stairs and make love to her again. "The notion's beginning to grow on me," he admitted gruffly. "Especially since it means we can now make love wherever, whenever, without suffering any raised brows. Or, in your case, parental concern."

Yes, Poppy thought, wincing slightly, there had been that.

Her parents were big on tradition. Marriage. Grandchildren. Forever love.

Trace paused as his cell phone began to buzz. "And speaking of parents…" He grimaced. "My dad is calling." With a sigh of resignation, he answered the phone, listened and then said, "Where are you?"

More talk, mostly on the other end.

Trace covered the phone. "Dad's got a gift for us. Mind if he comes over to drop it by? Or would you prefer I meet him somewhere downtown?"

Not an unexpected question, given the crusty, oft-highly-irascible nature of his rancher father.

"Tell him to come here," Poppy said, realizing it was past time to turn the bacon and get the biscuits in the oven. "And ask him if he'd like a late brunch."

Trace relayed her message. "Okay. See you in five minutes, then." Trace turned to his bride. "He's not going to stay. He just wants to come in for a minute."

Somehow she wasn't surprised. Calvin Caulder had never been—would never really be—a family man.

A fact that was confirmed when the six-foot-two cowboy walked in the door, hat in hand.

Everything about him said he was in a rush. "Sorry I wasn't at the ceremony," Calvin declared after greeting them both perfunctorily. "I didn't want to chance a run-in with Bitsy."

Trace accepted the apology with the sincerity in which it was given. "It's okay, Dad."

"Besides," Calvin continued, looking so much like an older, sun-weathered version of his big-hearted son that Poppy wanted to cry, "you know how I feel about weddings."

Trace recited, deadpan, "After three of your own, you don't care if you never go to another one as long as you live."

A nod and an acknowledging smile. "Three divorces will do that to you." The cowboy reached into his pocket and handed over an envelope. "I figured with twin babies set to arrive any day that cash might help the two of you more than anything. In any case, I know Poppy will put it to good use."

"Thank you, sir." She smiled, noting the check was made out to her alone. Which made sense, right? Since she was the one with the local bank account. "And, yes, you're right, I will."

She followed him to the door, wishing he'd done more than throw the money and run. "Are you sure you don't want to stay?" She knew it would mean a lot to Trace.

Calvin shook his head. "I'm on my way to Wichita Falls to see an Angus bull I've got my eye on. I want to get there before daylight ends."

Poppy did her best not to see the raw disappointment in his grown son's eyes. "Let me get you a cup of coffee for the road."

As soon as Poppy had disappeared into the kitchen, Calvin looked at Trace. "Walk me out?"

Figuring whatever his dad had to say was probably not something his new wife should hear, Trace nodded. He grabbed his jacket on the way and walked down the bungalow's front steps to his father's pickup, which sat in the drive next to the house.

"You sure you know what you're doing?" Calvin asked. "It's probably not too late to plead insanity, ask for an annulment or something."

Trace sighed. *Here we go.* "Dad, come on."

The older man didn't even have the good grace to look apologetic. "Look, I know you want a family, son. And I'm all for that. But adopting twin infants when the two of you haven't even lived together is not wise."

The hell of it was, the sensible part of Trace thought so, too. Or would have, if he and Poppy had actually been planning to live together full-time. Thanks to his commission with the military, they weren't. Life would go on, as usual. With the two of them seeing each other enough to stay connected but not enough to drive each other crazy.

"I want what Poppy wants."

Calvin rubbed his jaw ruefully. "That's what I thought when I rushed to the altar with all three of my wives."

Trace let out a breath. "I'm not like you, Dad."

"Sure about that?" Calvin settled the brim of his Resistol low on his brow. "This all sounds pretty impulsive to me. And impulsiveness is what has always gotten me in trouble."

No foolin', Trace thought just as Poppy rushed around the corner, her face a telltale pink. She had a travel mug in her hand. "Here you go!" she said cheerfully.

Calvin accepted the coffee. "Thank you, sugar. Well, good luck. Both of you." He climbed into the cab of his pickup and started the engine. With a final wave, he drove off.

Trace turned to Poppy.

Without surprise, he noted she was not looking him in the eye. Suspecting the worst, he snapped, "Just how much did you hear?"

And, just like that, their vow to always be one-hundred-percent straight with each other went by the wayside.

"Nothing really," she said.

Chapter 5

"Is this how we're going to start our married life?" Trace asked brusquely. "Lying to each other?"

Regret shimmered between them, as tangible as the cold December air. "I wasn't trying to eavesdrop."

"But my dad isn't exactly soft-spoken."

Finally she did look him in the eye. "I have to ask." She dropped her gaze then looked back at him slowly. "I know it hasn't even been a whole day yet, but...*do* you want out?"

His gut twisted. "No. Do you?"

Shivering, she wrapped her arms around her. "No."

Trace did his best to put aside the calamity his father had brought. "Then why are we standing out here when there is still brunch to be made?"

Poppy flashed him a bright smile that did not quite

reach her eyes. "Good question." She held out her hand. He caught it.

They walked back into the kitchen. Poppy poured him a fresh mug of coffee, herself another juice, then slid the biscuits into the oven to bake.

Just that swiftly, the companionable mood they'd shared had been broken.

He was disappointed, but not all that surprised. Poppy had always been elusive. Keeping her deepest thoughts and feelings to herself. Heck, she hadn't even told anyone in her family what had happened when they were in college. Or even that she was minus one ovary and one fallopian tube.

And he understood that.

She hadn't wanted her parents to know they'd been having a no-strings affair, and worse, been careless.

Understanding her need for privacy, that had suited him just fine.

But now, suddenly, he could feel her holding him at arm's length for reasons he didn't understand. And that did bother him, even as she went back into perfect hostess mode.

"So…*husband*. What kind of fruit do you want?"

He returned her genial smile, knowing she would give him everything she had—except a way past the barricades guarding her heart. "What do you have?"

She opened up the fridge to survey the shelves. "A fresh pineapple. Oranges. Some grapes and strawberries."

Enjoying the way she looked in faded jeans, boots and a bright red sweater, with her hair spilling loosely over her shoulders, Trace shrugged. "How about all of the above?"

"You got it."

Not shy about enlisting his help—in the kitchen, anyway—she handed him the pineapple, serving bowl, cutting board and knife. She went to the sink and began rinsing the strawberries. "Can I ask you a question?" she said finally.

He could tell by the tone of her voice that she didn't think it was one he would welcome.

"What was it like with you and your dad when you were growing up? I mean, I know you rarely saw him when your mom briefly moved to Laramie in your senior year in high school."

Ah. So this was what was bothering her. Their upcoming Q-and-A session on their families, with the social worker.

Trace cut the ends off the pineapple, then the sides. "I didn't see him that much before then, either."

"How come?" Poppy moved to the other side of the island and set her cutting board opposite his.

Trace frowned as he cut out the core. "When he was with my mom, he was always working his ranch. And she insisted we live in town, so she could be close to her florist shop—which at that time was located in San Angelo." He exhaled slowly and a muscle in his jaw flexed. "Then, when they divorced and he remarried, his next two wives weren't keen on having the scion of a previous romantic relationship around. So even when my dad and I did see each other, things were…tense. Plus, I had half a dozen stepbrothers and sisters with those relationships. So there wasn't ever a lot of one-on-one time with my dad, in any case."

Poppy accepted the bite of pineapple he pressed

against her lips, smiling as the sweetness hit her tongue. "And your mom remarried and had stepkids, too."

"Six times before I graduated college and began my military service. Twice since, although from what she hinted last night, husband number nine is on the horizon."

Poppy licked the pineapple juice from her lips, and he felt himself grow hard.

"What was her shortest marriage?"

Trace grimaced. "Two days."

"And her longest?" Finished with the strawberries, Poppy began de-stemming the grapes.

Trace shifted his weight to ease the building pressure against his fly. "The five years she spent married to my dad."

"How many stepsiblings did you have altogether?"

"At last count? Twenty-seven."

Poppy joined him at the sink to wash her hands. "In that sense you put even the McCabes with their big families to shame."

He nudged her with shoulder and hip. "We Caulders have to exceed at something," he told her playfully. "And since it's not marriage…"

Poppy handed him a dishtowel. "Maybe you and I—with our newfangled attitude about what marriage should and should *not* entail—will change the tide."

Trace sure hoped so. He would hate for him and Poppy to end up the way his parents had. Either giving up on relationships completely, like his dad, or continually searching for that elusive happily-ever-after, like his mom.

He braced his hands on the granite countertop on either side of her, before she could move away. "Does that bother you? The fact I didn't come from a family as well-grounded and loving as the McCabes?"

Her gaze turbulent, Poppy shook her head. "No. I just feel sad for you, that your childhood was so tumultuous."

"And worried about our twins? That some of my family angst will somehow transfer to them?"

She splayed her hands across his chest. "I know you'll be a great father. That they'll be very loved by both of us."

She always had believed in him. Just as he had always believed in her. He pulled her to him for a long, lingering kiss. She melted against him, soft and supplicant. When they finally came up for air, she had a glazed look in her eyes that thrilled him nearly as much as the way she surrendered to his kisses.

He tucked an errant strand of hair behind her ear. "By the way. I never had a chance to ask. Do we know the sex of the kids we're adopting?"

"A boy and a girl."

He took a moment to imagine him and Poppy with a son and a daughter. "Well, that couldn't have worked out better."

The flush of excitement in her cheeks said she thought so, too. "Should we be talking about what we're going to name them?" she asked.

The timer on the oven went off.

Reluctantly, Trace stepped back to let her pass. "You can decide that."

She cast him a surprised glance over her shoulder. "Seriously?"

He nodded. "Poppy, I want you to have everything you want, exactly the way you want it."

She paused then turned to take the tray of fluffy, golden-brown biscuits out of the oven.

Trace didn't need to see the slight slump to her shoulders to know that he had disappointed her. Why, he wasn't sure. Any more than he could comprehend why she had asked him to sleep in the guest room the evening before. When she had to know, deep inside, that they would only end up where they had this morning—making love in her bed.

Figuring this was proof enough he wasn't cut out for traditional marriage, any more than she was, he steered the conversation on to something they could deal with. Their road trip later that day.

Trace wanted to drive, so they took the SUV he had rented for the month, rather than her minivan. Poppy sat beside him in the passenger seat, reflecting on the events of the past week and trying not to fall asleep. That was not an easy task, given that Trace was unusually quiet, too. But that was to be expected, she told herself as she relaxed to the soothing Christmas music filling the interior of the car, since he had a lot to process, as well.

Finally they reached the north Texas branch of the Stork Agency Home for Expectant Mothers.

Located on five acres in a quiet suburb of Fort Worth, the four-story dormitory rivaled those at college campuses with its private rooms and cozy gathering areas, outfitted with televisions, sofas and chairs. A second building housed an infirmary, counseling center, classrooms and cafeteria. A large atrium bridged the two brick structures and served as a lounge for the young women and their guests.

"You didn't tell me you were bringing Trace!" Anne

Marie squealed when they walked in a few minutes before seven that evening.

As usual, the tall, golden-haired teenager had a textbook in front of her and a cell phone close at hand. Maybe it was the fact Anne Marie had grown up on military bases around the world, Poppy noted, or the recent loss of her dad combined with the predicament the teen found herself in, but she looked more mature than her seventeen years in some ways and tons younger in others.

Poppy clasped her outstretched hand warmly. "We wanted to surprise you."

Anne Marie put her textbook aside and beamed at them both. "So you *did* get married!"

"Last night," Trace affirmed.

Anne Marie checked out the gold band on Poppy's left hand. Then looked at Trace, frowning when she saw he did not have a wedding band.

He lifted a cautioning hand. "We're still working on that. Not to worry…it'll be there by tomorrow."

"That's good." Anne Marie tucked her phone into a compartment and zipped her backpack closed. "Because everybody needs to know you're married, too." She looked at Poppy earnestly. "Don't you agree?"

Not if it made him feel hemmed in, Poppy thought. Out loud she declared as candidly as possible, "I think it's always best not to have double standards when it comes to men and women."

"Amen to that!" Anne Marie high-fived Poppy in a celebration of female power. Using one hand behind her for leverage, she settled in a side chair. "Do you have any pictures of the wedding?"

Glad for the rapid-fire subject change, Poppy got out her phone. "A few."

Anne Marie scrolled through them avidly. "Wow. It was really pretty. You look like the perfect couple."

Trace and Poppy sat on a loveseat, kitty-corner from her. "Thanks."

When she'd finished, Anne Marie handed over the phone. "So did the local social worker come and visit you? My counselor here said they were going to send someone to amend the original home study."

"They did, and that process has already started."

Anne Marie looked as surprised as Trace and Poppy had felt that very morning. "It may take a week or two to complete, though," Poppy continued.

Anne Marie ran a hand over the end of the French braid that fell over one shoulder. "It's kind of a pain but it's also kind of good, too, you know, that they check out everything so well."

"It is," Trace and Poppy agreed in unison.

The teen looked at Trace. She shook her head fondly. "You look so much like my dad. Even when you're not in uniform..." She sighed wistfully, the grief she still felt showing on her face.

"How are you doing, sweetheart?" Trace asked Anne Marie gently, the military man in him coming through.

"I still miss him," Anne Marie admitted, picking up on the conversation she and Trace had had the previous time they'd met. She absently rubbed a hand just beneath her collarbone. "And get sad sometimes. But it makes me feel better that the twins are going to end up with a military dad, too. I know, if he were still alive, he would like that."

Anne Marie shifted in her chair, as if unable to get

comfortable. That was easy to understand, given her growing girth. The slender young woman had gained close to forty pounds, all of it carried in a basketball-shaped mound in front of her. "What about your mom?" Trace continued, recalling there had been trouble there, too.

Anne Marie winced. "We're still barely speaking, but she's not as mad at me as she was." She leveraged herself out of her chair and began to pace, as if trying to walk off her physical discomfort. "The counselors have helped us both understand that I made impulsive choices out of grief over my dad's death, and ended up pregnant. And my mom was so mad at me for making everything harder than it already was because she was grieving, too."

Trace and Poppy followed the teenager over to the Christmas tree in the corner of the lounge. "So you think everything is going to be okay with you and your mom?"

Fingering a snowflake ornament, Anne Marie nodded. "Yes. Once things get back to normal." She grimaced again. Her hand went to the center of her chest.

"Are you feeling all right?" Poppy asked.

Anne Marie sighed. "I get heartburn every time I eat now."

"Is there something you can take to alleviate the discomfort?"

Anne Marie grinned. "Geez, you sound like a mom. And the twins aren't even here yet! And, yes—" she comically mimed compliance "—I already did. It just hasn't completely taken effect yet. In the meantime, I have a favor to ask."

"Whatever you need," Trace said with customary gallantry.

Anne Marie beamed. "Do you think next time you come, you could maybe bring me pictures of the nursery? So I can show my mom. And help her understand that you and Trace are way better than my second-choice couple on the list."

"Is your mom still having second thoughts about us?" Poppy blurted before she could stop herself.

Anne Marie shrugged. "You know my mom. She's really old fashioned. She likes the fact that the other couple has been married for a long time. But she also knows it's my decision. And I know, once she hears you-all got married, and sees the pictures of where the babies are going to live, then she'll know everything really is going to be all right."

"I thought our selection as the babies' parents was a done deal, at least once we pass the amended home-study portion," Trace muttered when they left the campus and went to check into their hotel.

Trace and Poppy walked out of the lobby, key cards and map of the establishment in hand. "It is, as far as Anne Marie is concerned."

Trace climbed back behind the wheel. "You don't think her mom might influence her to change her mind?"

"Not about this, no. Anne Marie is as stubborn as I am. Once she makes up her mind about something…"

"It's decided."

"Pretty much. Yeah." Poppy watched him fit the key in the ignition. "Why? Are you getting nervous?"

"No." Trace draped his hand along the top of the bucket seats as he backed out of the space. "I know this is right—that I was meant to raise a family with you, and vice versa."

Except he wouldn't be there most of the time.

He braked as he came to a sign directing which way to go for which set of room numbers. "Everything okay with you?"

Poppy read the sign and pointed in the direction he should take. "Believe it or not, I'm getting heartburn."

"From the grilled chicken and veggies we ate en route?" he asked wryly.

"Don't laugh."

"I'm not." He drove around until he found a space closest to the door.

Poppy unfastened her seat belt. "I think I'm so worked up about the impending birth of the babies I'm getting sympathy pangs."

"Like some new dads."

She met him at the tailgate. "Last time I drove over to see her, which was a few weeks ago, she was having lower back pain, and by the time I got to my hotel, I had lower back pain."

He laughed at her dramatic recitation.

She playfully punched his arm. "You promised you wouldn't laugh!" Even though she had known he would.

He shook his head, sobering. "That just seems so unlike you."

"Yeah, well…" Poppy watched him lift the gate and take out their overnight bags and laptop cases. "I suddenly have a lot of sympathy for the birthing partners that just have to sit around and wait." She pressed her lips together ruefully. "I think it's probably harder than actually being pregnant yourself."

"I'm not so sure about that, in normal situations." Realizing what he'd just said, he brought himself up short. "But maybe…in yours…" His voice trailed off.

An uncomfortable silence fell.

The light in the parking lot casting a surreal light over them, he shut the tailgate then locked the SUV via the keypad. He caught her wrist before she could pivot away from him. "Is it hard for you, seeing other women carry a child?"

Poppy stood, handbag slung over her shoulders, her laptop bag held in front of her like a shield. "Not as much as it used to be, but, yeah." She forced herself to look him in the eye. There was enough compassion there to mend anything broken in her heart. "It hurts. I'm not going to sugarcoat that. But—" tears pricked behind her eyes and her voice took on that telltale catch "—I think that will pass when I become a new mom."

Wordlessly, he moved her hand holding on to the laptop bag to the side and enfolded her in his arms. She let her head rest against his warm, sturdy chest.

Yes, she thought as she reveled in their closeness and the comfort he brought, she could definitely find a way to get over their past loss, if he were with her. Like this.

Trace set their bags down inside the hotel room. Able to see from her expression and the way she kept rubbing her sternum, she was really uncomfortable, he said, "I'm guessing you don't have anything for heartburn."

She did not.

"How about I find a drugstore that's open?"

Her body sagged in relief. "Are you sure you wouldn't mind?"

He thought about all the times he hadn't been there to hold and comfort her when she was sick or stressed, or just blue. He was glad he was here now. "That's what husbands do, right?"

For that, she had no answer.

Tenderness rolling through him, he kissed her forehead. "I'll be right back."

Trace quickly learned that all the pharmacies in the area had closed. But there were several supermarkets that were open until midnight, and all of them had a medicine section. Not sure which type of antacid would work best, he picked up a selection, as well as a couple of additional things that might help, and headed back to the hotel.

Wondering what she'd packed in her overnight bag—he'd brought a change of clothes, a toiletries kit and nothing else—he used his keycard and walked in.

His fantasy that she would greet him in something as sexy as the second night of their honeymoon—such as it was—would warrant, quickly vanished.

Poppy was in work mode—something he was equally familiar with.

Clad in a pair of pink flannel pajamas, she had ballet slippers on her feet, a sketch pad across her lap and a lot of discarded papers around her.

Which meant…what? She'd brought clothes for any eventuality? Or just hadn't planned on having a wild and sexy time in the first place?

Hoping it was the first option, he moved close enough to smell the apple-blossom fragrance she favored. "Feeling better?"

"A little. In the way I always do when I wash my face and put my hair back, after a long day." She nodded at the grocery bag. "So, did you find anything?"

"Several kinds of antacids and indigestion meds." He handed her four small boxes. "Pellegrino. Crackers. Lemonade. And—" He whisked out a plastic green strand adorned with white berries and held it over her head. "Ta-da! Mistletoe!" He kissed the top of her head. "In case you get to feeling better later."

Poppy grinned at his clowning. She worked open the packet that declared instant relief. "You just can't help yourself, can you?"

"Around you, darlin'? Apparently not." Determined to make her as comfortable as possible, he reached for the ice bucket on the dresser, unfolded the plastic liner and set it inside. "I'll get us some ice. Need anything else?"

She worked the chewable tablets out of the foil-and-paper wrapper, paused, medicine in hand, and looked up at him gratefully. "I'm good. And thanks for being such a great—"

"Husband?"

She rolled her eyes in a way that reminded him they weren't really married, not in the traditional sense. "I was going to say friend."

That was what she had always tagged him. And it had never really bothered him.

Until now.

So what had changed? Why was he suddenly feeling so driven to protect and care for her? Was it the fact they were about to become a family—albeit a non-traditional one. And he was already slipping into the role of 'dad'? Or something more…?

By the time he had returned with the ice Poppy had gone back to drawing. She had turned the Sunday-night football game on TV. For him, obviously. Poppy wasn't into football. He wasn't, either, *this* evening. Maybe because it wasn't a particularly exciting match-up.

He poured her a glass of Pellegrino over ice and took it to her, along with a packet of crackers.

She looked up in irritation. "You really don't need to wait on me."

He set both down on the table beside her chair with a thud. "Probably not, but I want to anyway." He paused to survey her languidly, then added tautly, "Is that a problem?"

Poppy inhaled sharply and gave him an adorably contrite look. "No. I'm sorry. Forgive me?"

Trace could see she was stressed out, so his temper quickly cooled. "Of course." Settling in the chair next to hers, he inclined his head at her sketch. "Do you really need to do that tonight?"

"Yes, unfortunately." She pinched the bridge of her nose, as if trying not to cry. "If I'm going to do the nursery right away—"

"To help the process with Anne Marie along."

She pulled herself together, as always. "I've got to figure out what I'm going to need."

He'd always admired Poppy's ability to set a task and get it done well, and with remarkable efficiency. He picked up some of her discarded sketches. Saw different views of nurseries. All looked fine to him. And not that different. But, apparently, to her, they were. Maybe she just needed inspiration. The retail kind.

Once again, he threw himself on the sword for her. "Want to go shopping tomorrow?" he asked casually.

Poppy's eyes lit with excitement. "Yes, but not where you'd think."

Chapter 6

"You want to purchase the wedding ring first or go look for baby stuff?" Trace asked late the next morning, after they had stopped by McCabe Interiors to leave his SUV and pick up the small moving truck she used for her business.

Poppy waved at a fellow business owner who was putting up a yuletide display in her store windows, then continued driving toward the storage complex at the edge of town. "You don't need me to do that. Do you?"

Trace caught the flex of her shapely thighs as she moved her foot from accelerator to brake. His body ached with the need to make love to her again.

"Don't you want the bands to match?" Hers was gold with some sort of decorative ridge around the edges.

"I got it at the jewelry store on Main Street." She paused in front of the security gates and held an electronic fob against the reader. The light turned from red to green. The automatic metal gates opened and she drove through. "They can look it up for you."

"Which means you don't want to go."

"I don't think I have time. At least, not right now."

That was clear. She'd been up half the night working on her sketches while he'd watched football on the hotel room TV. Then she'd fallen asleep shortly after taking a second dose of antacid. This morning, she'd been in a rush to get back. So they'd grabbed breakfast at the buffet off the hotel lobby and headed out. On the drive back from Fort Worth she'd made a series of business calls on her cell phone. Most of them related to the nursery she was setting up.

"I mean, that's okay, isn't it?" She grinned at him as they emerged from the truck. "You can handle it?"

That wasn't really the point.

He'd figured, as long as he was going to be here, they'd spend as much time as they could together. She clearly did not feel the same.

Reminding himself that Poppy was a woman who needed a lot of personal space, he walked with her into the long building. A brightly lit cement-floored aisle ran the length of the building. On either side were aluminum garage doors. She opened three of them, one right after the other. He stared at the amassed contents inside. "Do you have a secret life as a hoarder?"

She tossed him a look. "Ha, ha. This is all stuff for my business."

And there was plenty of it. Sofas, dressers, lamps, chairs. Steamer trunks, decorative wall signs, paintings, even chandeliers. The second unit had rolled rugs, patio furniture, sconces, desks, china cabinets and bookcases. And the third…well, that was all nursery stuff.

Lots and lots of nursery stuff. And holiday stuff galore, too. She had at least a dozen cribs in there. Youth beds. A variety of glider rockers. Plus more wall art. "This is what you meant by going shopping."

"Yes. I'll actually have to buy the inventory I choose from my business, although I can give myself an employee discount."

As long as they were talking the mechanics of things… "We should split the cost."

Twin spots of color highlighting her cheeks, she spun away. "That's okay."

Money. It could be harder to talk about than sex. He followed her past a row of change tables. "I'm serious. If I am going to be the dad to these twins, then I am going to be financially responsible, too."

Temporarily foregoing the baby stuff, Poppy stacked the Christmas things she needed to decorate her bungalow on a wheeled cart and pushed it toward the exit.

Trace took over for her and loaded it into her truck. "Obviously, you don't agree."

She accompanied him back into the building, spine stiff. "It's my house, which makes any change in the decor my responsibility. Financial and otherwise."

He helped her move two dissembled cribs out into the aisleway. "Except that the changes are for the kids we are *both* adopting."

Leather cowgirl boots clicking across the cement floor, Poppy marched back into the storage unit. Trace didn't know what he admired more. Her purposeful sexy strides or the way her lower half looked encased in those skintight jeans.

Poppy shifted several boxes away from a glider rocker the same hue as the cribs. "The thing is, I can afford to raise these kids on my own. I planned on doing that all along. So—" She grabbed the matching ottoman while he carried the chair out and set it next to the cribs.

He stopped. "You don't need my money? Is that it?"

Poppy had no immediate answer for him.

"You accepted the check from my dad."

"Because it was a gift. His heart was in the right place. It would have hurt his feelings if we hadn't accepted it."

"I have feelings."

"You know what I mean, Trace. And I'm putting the money he gave us in a college fund for them. But I won't even do that until after the adoption is final. So, technically, although I have a check from him, I haven't actually accepted any money from him, either."

"Boy, you're prickly."

"And you're pushy!"

They stared at each other in indignation.

Was this their first fight?

The harbinger of many to come? Trace wondered uncomfortably.

He'd promised himself he would never have a marriage like those of his parents. Yet, here they were, not even two days in, rubbing each other the wrong way… over nothing.

Poppy looked just as nonplussed.

Luckily her phone rang before they could say anything else to each other. With an irritated sigh, she glanced at the Caller ID. "I have to get this." Lifting the phone to her ear, she walked a short distance away. "Hi, Will. Yeah, sure. He's here." Her fingers grazed his as she pushed her cell phone into his hand. "My cousin wants to talk to you."

Still savoring her gentle touch, wishing he could haul her right back into his arms, and make sweet wild love to her until all this tension between them faded, Trace turned his attention to the task at hand, and said instead, "Hey, Will. What's up?"

Will explained.

Trace went into action mode. "Sure. I'll be at the Laramie airfield at seven." Promise made, he ended the call.

"What's going on?" Poppy asked, delicate brow furrowed.

Not surprised she'd picked up on the fact a situation was brewing, Trace closed the distance between them and handed Poppy her phone. "They need an experienced medevac pilot for an air ambulance flight to Nashville tonight. The gal that was going to fly it is down with the stomach flu. I figured you wouldn't mind." *That maybe you might even appreciate the personal space...*

"Of course I don't. And you don't have to ask me, remember?" She pivoted to look at him. "We're still independent operators."

Funny that he'd thought differently.

He wasn't normally the romantic type.

Anything but, in fact.

Jerked back to reality, Trace looked at the furniture yet to be loaded and the additional Christmas decorations she'd set aside while he was on the phone. "I don't want to leave you in the lurch. I know you were planning to get most of this done today."

She nodded with a little grimace. "And I will. So

long as you can help me load it on the truck and move it back to my house."

An easy task, compared to his efforts to understand what had been going on with her since the moment they'd said their I Do's. "No problem."

She flashed him a smile that was both determined and aloof. "Then let's get started."

"So how's married Life?" Rose teased when she, Lily and Violet arrived at Poppy's house that evening.

Hard to say, Poppy mused. Ever since they'd said their I-'Sort-Of'-Do's, she and Trace had been completely out of synch. Wildly in lust one minute, unusually at odds the next. She waved an airy hand. "Oh, you know. Busy," she fibbed.

Her sisters exchanged looks.

Clearly, Poppy noted, they were disappointed she wasn't more forthcoming with tales of utter bliss in this season of joy...

Rose set down a wicker picnic basket full of organic fruits and local yuletide goodies from her wholesale business. She took off her coat and scarf.

"Sad for you, to be away from your handsome hubby so soon after the ceremony, though."

It was, Poppy thought. Because even though she and Trace hadn't actually figured out how to be married while not really married, yet, she did love being with him. And she missed him desperately when he was away. Too much, really...considering their circumstances.

"Is he coming back tonight?" Lily unveiled a luscious-looking Brie in puff pastry.

Poppy got out the plates and silverware and passed them around. "Tomorrow morning. If the weather holds."

"Well, that's not too long then," Violet soothed. Both doctors, she and her husband were used to spending many hours apart. It seemed to only bring them closer, Poppy noted enviously. Especially now they had adopted an adorable infant, Ava, who after a rocky start, was now thriving. "Since you decided not to paint, at least for now," Violet continued, "we should have the nursery done before he gets back."

Poppy nodded. Thanks to her sisters' help, they would.

"So what's the matter?" Lily asked compassionately. "Why are you so glum?"

While they ate, Poppy talked about how weird and unsettling the past two days had been. How everything was absolutely fantastic one moment and then awkward or not so great the next. "And worst of all," she concluded, "we nearly had our first fight this morning at the storage unit."

"Over what?" Violet asked.

"Trace wants to pay for half of the nursery!"

"And that's a problem because…?" Rose, the ace negotiator in the family, asked.

Poppy blew out a breath. "First, I don't want to tell him how much everything costs, despite the employee discount I'm going to give myself."

Lily frowned. "He's never struck me as cheap."

Poppy's dinner sat like lead in her stomach. "He's not the kind of guy who's going to want to pay three hundred dollars for a framed painting, either." The thought of disagreeing with him on anything left her feeling ill.

Struggling to contain her feelings, Poppy sat back. "I mean, you know Trace. Since he's been in the military, he's always stationed around field hospitals. He practically lives out of a duffel bag."

"Maybe that's because he's never had a real home of his own to go to or to leave his stuff in." Rose carried her plate to the sink. "He might feel a lot differently if he did."

Poppy and her other sisters got up, too. "Or he might not." She sighed. "The point is I don't want to fight about this stuff with him. And this is the kind of stuff married people argue about. I know. Because I'm in the interior design business and I hear about it all the time. Although sometimes the situation is reversed and the wife is the one who doesn't want to spend the money."

Lily wrapped her arm around Poppy's shoulders. "So tell him how you feel. Because you're in interior design and these are your first kids, you want everything to be really special. Surely he'll get that."

"He did come all the way back here to marry you," Violet reminded her, hugging her, too.

Poppy scoffed. "Only because he thought the paperwork wasn't going to come through in time for the marriage by proxy."

"The point is—" Rose stepped in to gently offer her support "—he *was* here. And he loves you."

"Like a best friend," Poppy insisted.

The triplets exchanged looks. Now she wasn't the only one who was worried, Poppy noted.

"I think your situation is more romantic than you know," Violet said firmly as the three of them headed upstairs to clear the office-slash-guest-room of other furniture.

Poppy stared at the sofa bed where she'd wanted Trace to sleep that first night here. "I know you all want to think that I've found the love of my life, and he me, just the way you all have with your spouses…" She shook her head slowly. "But what Trace and I have isn't like that."

Violet—who'd lost her first love to cancer before finding happiness with Gavin Monroe, advised sagely, "Well, whatever it is, enjoy it, Poppy, because before you know it Trace'll be back on the other side of the world again."

Poppy took her sister's advice to heart, so when Trace finally arrived home the next evening, after multiple weather delays, she gave him the kind of warm, wonderful greeting he deserved. He returned her hug and kiss just as wholeheartedly. "Get the nursery done?"

She nodded.

He held out his hand. "Let's see it."

Up the stairs they went. Trace stood in the doorway long enough to make her heart pound. Then he walked in, grinning approvingly at everything, it seemed. The pastel chenille rug spread out across the wood floor. The glider rocker and ottoman. He even seemed to like the striped window treatment and the twin off-white cribs with the blue and pink bedding.

"Nice." He paused in front of the framed Beatrice Potter print on the wall; took in the wide bureau with the padded change-table top. "Really nice. I can see you in here with the kids." Taking her hand in his, he hooked his arm around her shoulders and tugged her close to his side. "Anne Marie is wild about it, too."

Poppy gazed up at him, her heart hammering in her chest. Was this how all wives felt when their warrior husbands returned home after a day away? "She texted you, too?" she asked, practically bubbling with joy.

"Yep. She said it's better than she ever could have envisioned. She especially likes the fact they're going to share a room." An impish smile tugged at the corners of his mouth. "The question is…are *we* going to be sharing a room tonight?"

"I don't know. It depends on how you behave," she teased.

"I can be good." He promised, mischief in his eyes. Wrapping an arm around her waist, he brought her close. Dropping his head lower, he shifted his lips over hers.

Tingles swept through her.

Lower still, she felt the stirrings of his desire, too.

"Or bad," he caressed the shell of her ear with the tip of his tongue, "if you prefer…"

Her shivers of awareness turned into a cascade. The truth was, she liked him any way. Every way…

He lifted his head, stared deep into her eyes.

After a moment, she said quietly, "We're really doing this. Aren't we?"

His gaze turned warm, possessive. He rubbed a hand up and down her spine. "We are…"

And it felt so good, Poppy thought. So right. To finally be getting the family she had wanted with him for so long.

And speaking of the babies they were about to adopt… "Anne Marie also asked me about the names."

Trace wrapped an arm about her waist. Together, they headed back down the stairs. Bypassing the boxes of Christmas decorations yet to be put up, he stripped off his coat and shoes and knelt to build a fire. "Have you decided anything?"

Poppy watched him angle the wood just so, the taut

muscles of his shoulders and arms bunching and flexing as he worked.

Lower still, his thighs were really hot, too. "I really think this is something we should do together."

"Okay." He wadded up a little newspaper and stuffed it in the middle. "Hiram for a boy and Henrietta for a girl."

"Trace…"

"Persephone for a girl and Pegasus for a boy?"

She handed him a match. "I know you're not serious."

"Well, they are going to be Texans." He lit the paper and watched it flame. "So the boy could be Tex and the girl could be Tessa…"

She stepped back and propped her hands on her hips. "Is alliteration really necessary?"

He squinted. "You prefer we name them all flower names, like your folks did you and your sisters? Except I'm not sure how that would work with a boy." He set the screen in front of the fire and stood. "Is there a flower name that would be appropriate for a boy?"

Poppy rolled her eyes. She loved it when he teased her this way; a fact he very well knew. "I was thinking more along the line of Trace Jr. for the boy. And a pretty, old-fashioned name, like Emma, for our little girl."

He tucked a strand of hair behind her ear. "You're serious?"

She hadn't realized how serious—until now.

Taking her by the hand, he walked her over to the sofa. Settled beside her. "I hadn't really thought about naming our son after me. But is it fair to you if our son carries my name and our daughter's moniker is the only one that's the same category as yours?"

Leave it to Trace to consider the situation from all angles. Poppy covered his left hand with her right and tried not to worry about the absence of a wedding ring. "We could put McCabe as her middle name. Emma or Ella McCabe Caulder. And Trace McCabe Caulder for him."

"No preference for the girl's name?"

"I like them both equally. I expect I'll know for sure when I meet the babies for the first time. In any case, I'd like their names to carry an equal connection to both of us."

His lids dropped sexily. "Me, too."

Poppy grinned and leaned over to kiss his cheek, her worry over the future fading as fast as it had appeared. "I think we just made our first joint decision as parents-to-be," she announced happily.

"The first," Trace agreed, kissing her sweetly, "of many to come."

Chapter 7

"Busy day ahead?" Trace asked the next morning after breakfast.

Poppy rushed around, getting ready for work. Thanks to the fact that they'd made love twice last night —once before they went to sleep and another time just before dawn—she was running late this morning.

Not that she was complaining.

Her body was humming with that well-loved satisfaction only Trace could bestow on her. She smiled, loving the way he looked, lounging on the rumpled covers of her bed, clad in a pair of low-slung navy pajama bottoms and a body-hugging gray T-shirt. "I'm decorating Beau and Paige Chamberlain's ranch for the holiday. They'll be home from Europe tomorrow and they're throwing their annual open house the day after that."

"This is something you do every year, isn't it?"

"Yes." Poppy put on a pair of gold Christmas tree earrings that Trace had given her as a joke five years prior. Although they were actually quite nice. Poppy spritzed on perfume and spun away from the mirror. "And the decorating theme changes every year, too."

"And this year it's…?"

"A New England Christmas."

His eyes twinkled. "In Laramie, Texas."

Poppy ignored the shimmer of sexual attraction between them. If she acted on it, she'd never get to work. "It's going to be lovely."

"Want some help?"

Wistfully, she let her eyes rove over his solidly built frame and powerful shoulders. "Actually, I have a full crew."

He rose, went into the bathroom and came out, toothbrush in hand. "I could still help."

Her master suite was small and cozy. Too cozy she sometimes thought. Ruing the fact that bath and bedroom opened directly onto each other, she said, "I appreciate the offer."

He went back to the sink, which was located just inside the door, rinsed, spit and then lounged in the open portal. "But?"

He closed the distance between them in two steps. She could feel his body heat and breathed in the enticing fragrance of mint and man. "It will go faster if you're not around distracting me."

He rubbed his jaw in a thoughtful manner. His gaze took her in head to toe. "If I promise not to hit on you… like any newlywed might hit on his wife…"

She laughed at the exaggerated innocence in his low

tone. "You're determined to milk this for all it's worth, aren't you?" she asked, her heart kicking against her ribs.

"You can't deny you're enjoying our honeymoon, too." He caught her in his arms and kissed her softly and slowly, leaving her longing for more.

Although she knew she could be late and leave most of the work to her staff, she also knew if they got back into bed again, they'd never get out. Not today, anyway.

Forcing herself to be the responsible business owner in this equation, Poppy splayed her hands across his hard chest. "Surely you can find something to do. I know you're at loose ends. Maybe another short flight for Will's charter air service?"

He dropped his hold on her and stepped back. "Already checked."

Apparently to no avail.

Poppy went to her closet and pulled out a navy fleece vest to go with her plaid shirt and jeans. "Well, then, Rose's husband, Clint, usually has a lot going on with his horses and his cattle. Particularly in the winter. You could always offer to lend a hand, since you used to do all that for your dad, growing up."

Poppy followed him into the bathroom. She loitered nearby, watching him spread menthol-smelling lather over his chiseled cheeks and jaw.

He lifted his chin as he ran the blade beneath his jaw. "I know you mean well, Poppy, but I don't need you to solve my problems for me."

Hmm. Poppy worked her feet into her engineer-style work boots. Propping them on the edge of the tub, her stretched out thigh perpendicular to his, she laced them up efficiently. Straightening to her full height, she prodded in the most civil voice she could manage, "Was I nagging?"

Still shaving, he slanted her a glance. Suddenly, looking equally peeved. "More like managing—in the way that a lot of wives do."

Surprised at how swiftly they were slipping into traditional roles in their non-traditional arrangement, Poppy flushed.

Next thing you knew she'd be writing him a Honey Do list. Calling him to see what time he'd be home for dinner.

Swearing, Trace shook his head, then looked her in the eye. "I don't mean to whine like a kid at the start of summer vacation with too much time on my hands."

Was that why he'd been initiating so much sex? He was *bored*? Poppy wondered, even more mortified.

Oblivious to her worries, Trace continued. "I've got cabin fever. I'm just not used to being at loose ends."

Poppy straightened. Found the belt for her jeans hanging on the hook, next to her robe. Ducking her head, she threaded it through the loops. Asked what she couldn't bear to while looking at his face. "You trying to tell me you want to go back to your unit? Spend the holiday with them?"

He bent over the sink and washed the residual shaving cream from his face. "Can't. Even if I wanted to," he said, his face buried in the towel, "my commanding officer is insisting I take the full thirty-day leave this time."

Wow. It just keeps getting better.

Trace took in her expression. "Not that I'd do that," he amended hastily. "I want to be here when the twins come home from the hospital. Help you celebrate their first days."

Uncertainty coiled in her gut. "Right," Poppy agreed with a smile. Afraid what else she would discover if she lingered, she grabbed her bag and swept down the stairs. "Well, I've got to go. And I'll be late getting home!" she called over her shoulder. "Most likely, sometime after eight."

Trace didn't need a marriage expert to know he had failed Poppy, in that same way his parents always failed their various spouses, without ever meaning to or ever really knowing why.

Otherwise she wouldn't have rushed out the door as though the hounds of hell were suddenly after her.

Was this marriage?

Or just his DNA?

Regardless, he could do better.

Figuring he might as well make himself useful, he showered and dressed. Did the breakfast dishes and got out the Christmas decorations she'd taken from storage two days before.

There were, he soon discovered, a lot of them. Everything from candlesticks and a variety of wreaths and garlands, to Christmas ornaments for the tree.

That they didn't yet have.

Suspecting picking out the evergreen might be something good for them to do together—and the kind of thing that Poppy might enjoy—he concentrated on stringing colored lights on the eaves of her bungalow. He then wrapped the remaining white lights around the stone columns fronting either side of the steps and used what was left to frame the front door.

Unfortunately the last strand of bulbs wasn't quite

long enough and there was a one-foot gap on one side of the door frame.

He bit back a curse. Evening it out would require undoing everything he had already put up. So, instead, he took a colorful yard ornament of Woodstock and several little bird friends, all carrying presents and wearing Santa hats, and propped it next to the door, hoping to disguise the shortfall.

Stepping back, he realized you could still see the problem with the lights. That meant there was only one solution. He'd have to stop at the hardware store to try to find a light strand long enough to completely frame the door.

In the meantime, only two and a half hours had passed.

So he headed for the jewelry store.

There, the owner's wife, a flamboyant redhead, was only too happy to assist him. She looked up Poppy's wedding band. "You know, I told her she should order you one at the time, but she wasn't sure you would want to wear one." Trace ignored the suspicion in Mrs. Brantley's eyes.

"I intend to wear one. So if I could just buy it—"

She cut him off with a shake of her well-coiffed head. "We don't have it in your size. We're going to have to special order it."

"How long will it take?"

She walked over to her computer. "Hard to say, this time of year. Could be one week, could be six…"

"Then maybe I should buy one that doesn't match."

An officious smile. "I really would not recommend that. Poppy wouldn't be happy and in the long run, neither would you."

Trace handed over his credit card for the deposit. "Okay, then special order it."

"Wise decision." Mrs. Brantley walked back to the display case. "So, have you thought about what you're getting Poppy for a push present?"

Trace blinked. "A…what?"

"A push present. The gift all new dads give all new moms for pushing the baby out." She lifted out a tray of diamond tennis bracelets for him to peruse.

Aware he'd never seen Poppy wear a bracelet, period, Trace lifted a staying hand. "We're adopting."

She nodded. "Which, as I understand it, is even more work. But in the end, you have a baby, and a new mom, and new moms like push presents."

Did they?

Trace hadn't heard any of his guy friends talk about it.

But then, he avoided any conversation centering on marriage. Wives. And efforts—often futile, from what he could see—to make them happy.

Aware Mrs. Brantley was waiting for him to pick something out, he said lamely, "Poppy's not a jewelry kind of gal." Unless it was something jokey. Like the Christmas tree earrings or Easter bunny necklace he had gotten her.

Poppy liked anything that was funny or fun.

Mrs. Brantley looked down her nose at him. "All women want to be recognized at this special time."

"Is it true?" Trace asked Poppy's brother-in-law, Clint McCulloch, when he stopped by the ranch to help put out feed for the horses and cattle. "All women expect a 'push present' when they become a mom?"

Clint retrieved a bale out of the back of the truck and handed it to Trace. "That's a tricky question."

Trace cut the twine holding it together and spread it across the ground. "Help me out, man."

Clint got in behind the wheel. "Always err on the side of generosity. So if other new moms get push presents, get your wife one, too."

Trace rode shotgun. "Poppy always says that stuff like that doesn't matter." She considered it superficial.

Clint drove a little farther along the pasture. "Rose doesn't buy it. She thinks Poppy just says that because, up to now, anyway, she's been so fixated on whatever it is that she has with you, to ever be in a position to receive it from someone else. I mean, she's never dated anyone since the two of you started hanging out together. And from what I understand, it's been the same with you."

"No time." No interest.

Every other woman pales in comparison.

"So it's a good thing you two put each out of your misery and got hitched. All this time Poppy felt she was missing out, not being married, not having a family. Now, thanks to you, she won't have to suffer that gap in her life anymore." Clint grinned over at him. "She'll get the babies she has always wanted. You'll have a wife and kids to come back to whenever you're on leave. *And* you'll both still have your freedom. Bottom line? Everyone will be happy."

But would they? Trace had sensed that Poppy wasn't as ecstatic as she should be.

His feelings were cemented when she came home that night, her expression anything but delighted as she walked through the front door.

"What's wrong?"

Poppy set down her work bag and keys, the aloof look back in her eyes. "Nothing. Dinner sure smells great."

"It will be."

She tilted her head. Her mouth smiled but the rest of her did not. "All that and modest, too."

Okay, something was up. He might not like fighting with her—if you could even call their mild disagreement the past couple of days that. But he definitely did not like their playing games with each other. He caught her elbow as she tried to breeze past. "Come back here and tell me why you had that look on your face just now."

Her defenses went higher. "What look?"

Not about to admit how impatient he'd been waiting for her to come home, or that he'd stood at the window, watching her get out of her minivan and cross the lawn, Trace pulled her outside onto the porch.

She gazed at the twinkling lights up and down the street. Then back at her bungalow.

It was true, thanks to the lack of his design skill, theirs weren't as elaborate as some others. But wasn't the spirit of the season still obvious? Apparently, given the slight rigid set of her shoulders, not.

"It's really nothing."

He stepped close enough to inhale her sweet and sultry scent. "It's something, Poppy. So just spit it out already."

Her attention turned briefly to the front door, obviously noting the replacement strand he had gotten was a good two feet too long, which had required it be doubled back on either side of the door frame. But, hey, hadn't he been able to move the Woodstock and his friends yard ornament out in front of the house, where it belonged?

Wanting to know just why she was so unimpressed, he came closer still. "I'm waiting."

She released a sigh that smelled like peppermint. "That's the inside wreath." She pointed to the door.

Inside, outside. "What the heck's the difference?" It was the new one she'd made the other day, and hadn't had the time or interest to put up. He had figured she would want to put it on the front door, where everyone walking by could see.

Her brow lifted. "The holly leaves and berries on it are made of silk. They are too delicate to stand up to inclement weather. And it always either rains or spits a little snow in December, so…"

So he was an idiot.

"But that's okay," she rushed to reassure him as if suddenly remembering her manners. "It doesn't matter."

He really didn't want her lying to him, even to spare his feelings. "Except to a class-A designer, it does."

"It's the thought that counts. And it means a lot to me that you went to all this trouble."

Except it clearly wasn't right. "I can fix it."

"No. Really…"

"I've done enough?" he goaded in a low, silky tone.

Maybe it was because she'd had such a long day, but abruptly she stopped trying to sugarcoat the situation and became the straight-spoken woman he adored. "Look, Lieutenant—"

An even better sign. She only called him "lieutenant" when she was getting worked up. And getting worked up always led to one thing.

She crossed her arms and fixed him with a withering stare. "You doing all this for me is kind of like me randomly deciding to fly a plane to help you out. My intentions might be good, but the results would be calamitous."

He laughed. "You're saying my decorating is a disaster?"

She pointed to the oddly wrapped lights around the front door. "Interesting."

He prodded her wordlessly.

"Uneven," she continued, stepping past him to enter the house.

"To the point you'd rather not look at it anymore?"

Reaching back, she grabbed his wrist, tugged him across the threshold and shut the front door behind him. "To the point I..." Whirling, she thrust herself against him, went up on tiptoe and cut off all further discussion with a hot and steamy kiss. Stopping only to wrestle her way out of her coat.

He watched her toss it on the coat rack, pivot and sashay to him once again. "Was that a thank-you?"

She leaped, so her legs were secured around his waist, her arms around his neck. "It was a 'please shut up and properly welcome me home.'"

Grinning broadly, he carried her into the living room where a fire was already blazing in the hearth. "Well, darlin', *that* I can do."

He sank onto the big chair she'd gotten just for him, taking her with him. Combing his fingers through her hair, he trailed kisses across her temple and cheek, lingering on the sensitive spot behind her ear. "I'd make love to you beneath the Christmas tree, but we don't have one yet."

Poppy groaned. Settling more intimately on his lap, she went back to kissing him. "Please stop talking decorations..."

Not hard to do when he felt her thighs straddling his. Awed by her beauty, he took his time unzipping her vest and unbuttoning her shirt, touching and kissing as he went. She trembled in response, her flesh swelling to fit his palms. Lifting her to her knees, he kissed and caressed her creamy breasts and rosy nipples. His fingers traced from base to tip, then laved the tight buds with his tongue, until her skin was so hot it burned.

"Oh, Trace," she whispered, kissing him again and again. "I want you so much."

"I want you, too."

His body shaking with the effort to rein in his own pressing needs, he took her onto the floor, in front of the fireplace. He let her go just long enough to remove the rest of her clothes and for him to strip down to his skin.

Her eyes widened at the sight of his arousal.

He parted her legs, then touched and rubbed and stroked. She caressed him in turn, moving her fingers lightly from base to tip, then back again. They lay on their sides, the V of her thighs cradling his hardness. They kissed and kissed as he throbbed against her surrendering softness. And when the tip of his manhood pressed against her delicate folds, she moved to accept him.

Then he was going deeper still, harder, slower. She whimpered low in her throat as his thumb found the most sensitive part of her. Rocking against him, until he was embedded as deep inside her as he could be.

"Trace," she whispered, climaxing.

He joined her, the pleasure fast and fierce.

And as they clung together afterward, still shuddering, he knew. This was more than friendship or a longtime affair, more than a legal arrangement born of necessity.

Much, much more, he thought as Poppy lay with her head on his chest, her pulse slowing, even as he stroked a hand through her hair. "Damn, you smell good." And she felt good, too.

She cuddled closer. "Like sweat and hot glue?"

"Woman and evergreen," Trace drawled, rolling her onto her back.

The second time they made love was more leisurely but no less passionate. Finally, they ended up in the kitchen, in their pajamas, eating the dinner he had picked up earlier. Steak tacos with all the fixings and the peppermint ice cream he knew Poppy loved.

She sighed contentedly, looking as happy and relaxed as he felt, as she helped herself to a little more ice cream. "I could so get used to this."

That made two of them. Trace grinned. "Tell me about your day."

She did, in great detail.

He listened, impressed by all that went into decorating the ranch house of the movie director and his film-critic wife. She had just finished her recitation when her cell phone chimed, alerting her that an email had come through. His buzzed at the same time.

Poppy read, yawned. "It's Mitzy, reminding us we need to be in her office tomorrow at nine sharp for the continuation of the interview."

Trace gathered up the dishes and carried them to the sink. He turned to ask her if she wanted any coffee, then grinned at what he saw. Poppy sitting with her head propped on her hand, fast asleep.

"Sweetheart." He touched her shoulder lightly.

She sighed and did not budge.

There was only one cure for this, he knew.

He lifted his sleeping wife in his arms, cradled her against his chest and carried her to bed. As he laid her down, a wave of tenderness swept through him.

If this was marriage, it was definitely okay by him.

Chapter 8

"Wardrobe crisis?" Trace asked at eight-thirty the following morning when he emerged from the bathroom after his shower. Clad in nothing but military-issue briefs, he was in the process of spreading shaving cream over his face.

And then some, Poppy thought glumly as she watched him return to the bathroom to shave with careful, even strokes.

Not about to tell him the real reason why—which was too many stress-provoked bowls of peppermint ice cream lately—she waited until he rinsed his face and razor, then continued rummaging through her closet for something suitable to wear.

"You really want to know the dilemma?" The one she could tell him anyway.

He slapped aftershave on his jaw as he returned, the fragrance of sandalwood and man filling the room.

"I want to know everything."

She finally picked out a long-sleeved jersey-sheath dress that fit, no matter what time of the month it was, and eased it off its hanger. "Well, I want to demonstrate by my attire how important this meeting with social services is to me."

She slipped off her robe, as enamored of the way he ironed a shirt, as he was of watching her get ready. "However, there's going to be an abundance of glitter, glue and marker at the elementary school card-making session you volunteered to help me with later, and although the art supplies will all be washable, I just don't think I should wear wool or cashmere since we're going there right after our interview with Mitzy." Aware of his eyes on her, she shimmied into the red dress and released a sigh. "You, on the other hand, have no such dilemma since you've been asked to wear your everyday uniform and talk to the kids about being a medevac pilot in the air force." And his daily uniform was machine washable.

He stepped into his desert khakis then sat on the edge of the bed to pull on his boots. "But otherwise you'd wear cashmere to our meeting with Mitzy?"

"Or my best wool skirt." Assuming she'd be able to get into it, which, to her frustration, she hadn't been able to do today.

As he moved closer, she turned so he could zip her dress. Reaching for a cotton cardigan, she slipped that on, too. To her relief, a quick glance in the mirror showed no evidence of the five pounds she'd gained since Halloween—and would definitely need to work off. Probably would work off without even trying once the twins were home and commanding every bit of energy she had.

He put his hands on her shoulders, said gently, "You're really that nervous about our second interview with Mitzy?"

She shrugged. "Aren't you?" So much was riding on this amended home and character study.

Wriggling free of his steadying grip—lest they be tempted to make love again—she rummaged through her jewelry box for her favorite Christmas angel pin and secured it to her sweater.

His turn to shrug. "All she's going to do is ask us some questions. All we have to do is answer."

"I hope you're right," she said as she found her coat and bag and they headed out the door.

Unfortunately Poppy's instincts that the morning could be tougher than Trace thought, proved correct.

Mitzy started out by handing them a long questionnaire based on each other's family histories that they had to fill out on their own. Then she moved into verbal questioning that was even more intense.

"You're both notoriously independent. Any idea where or when this started?"

Poppy knew success meant digging deep. Even if she would have preferred not to do so. "It probably comes from being the only single-birthed daughter, as well as the oldest of six siblings."

"A lot of responsibility there."

As well as often feeling like the odd woman out since she didn't have anyone exactly her age to pal around with.

Mitzy zeroed in. "Did you enjoy having twins and triplets for sisters?"

Poppy sucked in a breath. "I love them all dearly."

"But?" Mitzy coaxed.

Trace was studying her, too. With good reason, since she'd never really talked about this stuff.

Determined to be as candid as the situation required, Poppy admitted, "As a kid it could be a little rough. As firstborn, I was used to being in the spotlight, then the twins came along when I was three, and I..."

The social worker guessed. "Didn't get a lot of attention?"

"I did."

"Just not the way you were used to."

Poppy nodded.

"And when the triplets arrived two years later?" Mitzy persisted.

Forget it. Poppy inhaled sharply. "We all had to step up and be more autonomous and responsible. That is true in all big families."

Nodding, Mitzy turned. "Trace? How were things for you growing up?"

Realizing that the social worker was digging for deficiencies, he said in a clipped tone, "My parents were each married and divorced so many times, I had to learn how to handle myself, no matter what the situation."

"Do either of you think your inherent independence might undermine your ability to forge a truly workable marriage?" Mitzy asked.

"No!" Trace and Poppy said firmly.

Mitzy made a note in her file. "Regarding marriage... Poppy, why have you never even considered marriage to this point?"

Because the only person that even seemed remotely possible with was Trace, Poppy thought as the heat of embarrassment rose in her chest and spread into her neck and face. And he was not the marrying kind. At least, he hadn't been until circumstances warranted it.

Mitzy frowned. "Don't parse your answers, Poppy. Tell us."

Perspiration beading her brow, she waved a dismissive hand in the air in front of her. "Is this why they call it the hot seat?" she quipped to lighten the tension "Because I'm suddenly hot all over." She stood and took off her cardigan.

Trace gave her a weird look. As if she'd lost her mind.

"Aren't you both hot?" Poppy persisted, a sweat breaking out, all over.

"Actually, I think it's kind of cold in here," Mitzy said, pulling her blazer closer to her chest.

Stunned, Poppy turned to her husband.

As ready to come to her rescue as ever, he said, "I think it just feels warm in here because it's so cold outside today." His brows drawing together, he looked over at her. "Actually, now that you mention it, your face and neck are kind of red." He touched the back of his hand to her forehead. "Are you sure you're not getting sick?"

Poppy pulled away, the way she always did when someone did that to her.

"I feel fine," she returned irritably, wiping her suddenly damp forehead. "I'm just hot." She waved off the mutual concern of the two others in the room. Then babbled on offhandedly. "This has just been happening to me a lot lately. One minute I'm cold as can be, the other completely burning up…"

Mitzy nodded, her expression changing from concern to feminine understanding. Clearly, Poppy noted, her childhood friend had another idea why that might be.

Trace's expression reflected a light-bulb moment on his part, too. "And if either one of you makes a crack about early menopause..." Poppy warned.

Because that absolutely was not happening here!

Trace lifted both hands in abject surrender. "Hey! I would never be *that* dumb." He mugged at her comically. "I'm Bitsy's son, remember?" And his mom was forever ageless.

Poppy couldn't help it. She laughed.

"Okay, you two quit horsing around and answer the question. Poppy, you first," Mitzy demanded in a stern voice. "Why have you never considered marriage up 'til now?"

Having had ample time to compose herself, even though she was still sweltering from the inside out, Poppy finally said, "I never found the right man at the right time." Out of the corner of her eye, Poppy could see that Trace looked...was that *hurt*?

Mitzy noticed, too. "Trace?" she prodded.

He flexed his broad shoulders. "I'm not sure I believe in the traditional version of marriage, and that's all most women seem to want."

Nice and vague. And hurtful, too. What had he meant by "most women"? Had he thought about hooking up with or marrying anyone else? Even in the abstract?

Mitzy tapped her pen. "You didn't want family?"

"I have one. In the military."

"Do you think this one with Poppy and the twins will work?"

Trace nodded, exuding confidence. "Yes, because we're not going to be locked into the usual domestic situation where we both have to sacrifice everything we care about just to make the other person happy."

"But if a situation arises where Poppy or the children need you there—say if one of them gets ill—do you intend to be there?"

"Of course," Trace said immediately.

"Although that sort of depends on where you are stationed and whether or not you can get emergency leave, correct?" Mitzy pressed.

Trace nodded, a flash of something that might have been guilt—or worry—flashing in his eyes.

"Which means you'll likely miss most of the routine stuff. Like the first ear infection, or cold, or sleepless night due to any number of things."

Trace shrugged. Although Poppy could see the thought of leaving her to handle absolutely everything on her own with the kids was beginning to get to him. Her, too, really, although there truly was no need. She jumped in, "I have plenty of family in the area to assist me with all the challenges. And let's not forget that both my parents, as well as a sister and brother-in-law are all doctors."

Mitzy asked Poppy, "So you don't mind that the four of you are going to spend a lot of time apart?"

Of course she wished the situation were otherwise! Poppy thought in frustration. She hated knowing that Trace likely would not see—in person anyway—the twins first steps, or their first emerging tooth, or hear them utter their first word. But they did have Skype! And email. And Instagram, and all manner of social media tools to help them stay connected.

But of course, that wasn't what Mitzy was asking.

Poppy smiled, demonstrating she and her new husband were on the same page. "Trace and I both like our freedom. That doesn't mean we won't be good parents or good parenting partners, because we will."

Mitzy paused. "So there was never a point in which marriage seemed that it might be a possibility for you two, before now?"

The two of them exchanged looks. Poppy could tell they were both thinking the same thing. "No," they said at the same time.

"And yet," Mitzy continued, "when I spoke with your commanding officer, Trace, he told quite a different story."

Poppy tensed.

"What do you mean?" he asked with a frown.

"He said you never intended *not* to be here to marry Poppy in person." Mitzy gestured affably. "That the paperwork for the proxy was only put through as a failsafe measure, in case you got hung up somewhere along the way—due to inclement weather or a canceled flight—and didn't make it in time for the ceremony."

Poppy looked at Trace in astonishment. To her frustration, he was poker-faced.

The social worker leaned forward. "Your CO said that the minute you heard someone else was going to be standing in for you during the ceremony, you were adamant you be here."

Heart pounding, Poppy noted Trace did not deny it.

Mitzy turned to her. "Did you know this, Poppy?"

Her feelings in turmoil, she said, "No." The situation Mitzy described didn't sound like the man she knew. Or thought she knew. He had never been jealous. Territorial. Possessive.

"Which is why I'm surprised to see you're not wearing a wedding band, Trace," Mitzy continued.

At least this was something they could easily explain! "We haven't actually had time to get one, although we did talk about it," Poppy said at the same time Trace said, "We've got a band that matches Poppy's on order."

Another shocker. She blew out a breath. "We do?" She thought he had forgotten all about it, since he hadn't mentioned it again.

Not that it really mattered in any case.

Trace slid her a look. "I went Monday, while you were working at the Chamberlain Ranch. I guess I forgot to tell you."

"Well." Mitzy smirked, triumphant. "Seems like you two have a lot to talk about and catch up on."

No kidding, Poppy thought, still a little dazed by all that had been revealed.

Mitzy slid her notes into a thick manila folder and stood. "Look, I know you two are due over at the elementary school at eleven-thirty to work on the Cards for Soldiers project. So how about we finish this on Friday, if that works better?"

Poppy was silent as they left the social services building and made the short drive to the elementary school. He could hardly blame her. Frankly, he felt as if they had been put through the wringer, too. Although he supposed it was par for the course. Mitzy Martin had to make sure he and Poppy knew what they were doing. And they did.

"Sorry I forgot to mention the wedding band," he said gruffly as they gathered up the art supplies they were donating to the project. Shutting the tailgate of his rented SUV, he turned to face her.

"That's okay." She shifted a shopping bag to each hand. He did the same. She slanted him a look as they walked through the sea of cars in the school parking lot. "I'm more interested in what your commanding officer had to say." Her voice had a little catch in it. "Did you really plan to be here for our wedding all along?"

Trace inhaled a ragged breath, suddenly at a loss for words. He was surprised she didn't know by now. He would do anything for her. She meant that much to him.

Aware they had a little time and this was something that needed to be talked about in private, he slowed his steps accordingly. "Yeah. I mean, there were a lot of variables that could have thrown a monkey wrench into the plans. I was thousands of miles away. Transportation needed to be arranged, leave okayed, orders put through. I honestly wasn't sure I could pull it off in time and, given what happened during your sister Maggie's first wedding—"

Poppy grinned. "Her legendary bolt as she started to walk down the aisle?"

"I didn't want to be the groom that didn't show—or appeared to change his mind." And he especially hadn't wanted to disappoint Poppy.

She searched his face, her heart in her eyes. "So why go to so much trouble, then?"

"Put yourself in my situation, darlin'. Would you have wanted another woman standing in for you during our wedding ceremony, if we'd conducted a proxy wedding where I was stationed instead?"

She pursed her lips. He waited.

"No. I really wouldn't have wanted any other woman in my place," she finally admitted. "Even if you hadn't kissed 'the bride.'"

He grinned at the territorial look in her pretty brown eyes and then immediately sobered as a disturbing thought hit him. "Were you planning to kiss my stand-in?" he demanded.

She squared her slender shoulders, the movement making her breasts stand out. Delectably. "No. Of course not."

"Not even a peck on the cheek?"

"Not even a handshake," she affirmed in a way that left him feeling much, much better. "You, on the other hand—" her glance trailed over him seductively "—would have received a kiss blown your way via Skype."

Good to know she felt that way.

Poppy came to a dead halt as they neared the entrance to the school. She stepped back, so they were standing next to the lawn. He moved back, too.

"We never talked about being exclusive," she murmured, her eyes darkening in the way they always did when she felt ill-at-ease. "We just sort of were in that 'best friends turned lovers' way." She set her shopping bags down and shrugged. "But at the same time, I knew that if you ever did meet the love of your life," she said, her voice going abruptly hoarse, "I'd do the honorable thing and let you go, wishing you only the best."

He nodded, not sure what she was asking him, only knowing what he felt deep inside. "And up to now," he admitted, cupping her cheek in his hand, "I've always known that I would do the same for you." Even if he sure as hell would not have wanted to. "Because," he pushed on, his voice sounding a little rusty, too, "all I've ever wanted, Poppy, is for you to be happy."

"Only now we're married," she said.

Yes, they were.

And as long as they were…

"So maybe it's time we shut down that avenue for good," he declared.

* * *

Trace's matter-of-fact pronouncement was as practical as he was. So why, Poppy wondered, was she disappointed?

What had she expected? That he would use this moment to tell her his feelings had begun to change, just as hers had? That all of a sudden he found himself falling in love with her?

That wasn't him.

It wasn't her, either.

The notion that it might be…well, it was just a sentimental time of year. And an emotional one, too, now that she was finally about to get off the waiting list and adopt twins and have the family she had wanted since… forever.

"Poppy? You okay?" Trace's handsome face was etched with concern.

She nodded. "Yes. I just have a lot on my mind."

Very little of which I can share.

Fortunately she had no more time to think about it as she and Trace went in to help the fifth-grade classes with their Holiday Cards for Soldiers project.

The teachers made introductions and Poppy explained where the cards were going and why. Then Trace took the floor for questions while the kids worked.

"Tamara and Bobby are going to be so sorry they missed this," one of the little girls said.

Curious, Poppy asked, "Where are they?"

"Stomach flu," one of the teachers said. "It just started going around. Hopefully, that's the beginning and end of it."

Poppy hoped so, too. "I hope they feel better soon."

"Maybe we could make them Get Well Soon cards

when we finish," the head teacher suggested. "In the meantime, who has questions for Lieutenant Caulder?"

A sea of hands quickly shot up. Trace took the floor. Looking incredibly handsome and buff in his military fatigues, he pointed to a pudgy child in the front row.

"Do you like being a pilot?" the child asked.

He nodded. "Very much."

"Don't you get scared, being around sick people so much?" a bespectacled kid wondered.

"No. They need my help. And I'm glad to give it."

"Where are you stationed?" another girl asked shyly.

The teacher pulled the map of the world down over the chalkboard. Trace showed them.

For a moment all was silent.

It was an awfully long way away, Poppy thought wistfully.

A little girl raised her hand. "How long does it take to get there?"

"Usually around a day or a day and a half," Trace responded patiently. "It depends on the travel arrangements, but…a long time."

And he was always gone a long time, too, Poppy thought, her heart panging in her chest.

"What about at Christmas?" another boy asked.

"I'm usually there during the holidays, too," Trace admitted. He tossed an affectionate look Poppy's way. "Not this year, though."

She was happy about that, too.

"Isn't it hard being so far away from your family all the time?" a little girl asked. "Especially at Christmas?"

Yes, Poppy thought, for her it would be.

For Trace?

"The military is my family," he said gruffly.

"Except now," a teacher interjected quickly to amend, "you have a family here in Texas, too. Since the lieutenant and Ms. Poppy just got married last week."

A chorus of excited "Ohs" followed. Poppy blushed despite herself. Trace just looked…satisfied, in that distinctly male way.

"And rumor has it," another teacher said, "they're about to adopt twins!"

"Twins!" The kids' eyes lit up.

"Cool," declared one.

"That's a lot of babies," warned one student.

"A lot of dirty diapers, too," giggled another.

"So will you take Ms. Poppy and the babies with you when you go back to the Middle East?"

"No. It's too dangerous over there right now for that."

A contemplative silence fell as the kids went back to decorating the holiday cards for the servicemen and women.

Finally one of the kids frowned and piped up, "So does that mean you won't get to see your new babies at all, Lieutenant.?"

"I'll see them," Trace said in a low, determined tone.

Just not as much as either of them would like, Poppy thought sadly. And that was something their kids, like her, would just have to learn to deal with.

Chapter 9

"Problem?" Trace asked.

Their stint at the Holiday Cards for Soldiers session finished, goodbyes and thank-yous said, they walked out to the parking lot.

Poppy lifted her phone for him to see. "The usual. Several emails from clients who, having been unable to make up their minds for months now, suddenly have decided and want everything done yesterday."

Knowing how much he liked to drive when he was back in the States, she handed him the keys to her minivan.

He opened the passenger door. "What are you going to do?"

Smiling at his sudden show of gallantry, Poppy slid into her seat. "Write them back and tell them what the time frame is for delivery of services. And then see what they want to do. Move forward or find somebody else."

He shut her door then circled around and settled behind the wheel. "Are you going to be able to work once the babies come home?" He fit the key in the ignition.

Acutely aware how "familial" this conversation was, how much they had already started acting like husband and wife, Poppy shifted toward him. Her eyes briefly holding his, she admitted, "I'm not going to take on any new clients for a few months. I'll have my team of contractors and painters and stagers finish out the existing work. Then go from there."

Trace draped his arm behind her as he backed out of the space. "Are you going to be okay financially?"

Please tell me he's not going to try to call the shots now that he's slipping into the husband role.

"Yes, dear," she teased at his too protective tone.

Wanting him to continue to see her as his equal in every way, she told him, "I've been putting money aside for this for years. So I'd be able to take as much time off as I need when I finally became a mom." And not have to worry about anything but savoring the moment. Just as she was trying to do now with Trace.

Trace frowned. "Like I said before, if you need assistance…"

"No, really, it's okay. I've got it covered."

He nodded, believing in her, as he always did. "So where to?" he asked casually.

Poppy turned on the car radio. The nostalgic strains of "Silver Bells" filled the air. "Home. At least for me. I've got twelve dozen chocolate-crinkle cookies to make before tonight's cookie swap with the family over at my mom and dad's house."

He flashed her a wolfish grin. "Am I invited?"

"Of course." Which would make one of her favorite holiday events all the more special this year.

"Don't laugh."

Poppy couldn't help it. "You look ridiculous in that frilly apron." The print featuring reindeer and Santa's sleigh was okay. Sort of. But the ruffles along the straps and edges was not. Plus, something that was meant for a woman of average height and weight did not exactly fit a solidly muscled, six-foot-four man.

He turned this way and that, preening comically. "I think I look rather dashing."

"That's one word for it."

"Just not the correct one?" he teased back.

She grinned. Both of them had changed into jeans and flannel shirts the moment they'd walked in the door and then headed for the kitchen to get right down to business. Or so she'd thought.

Poppy shook her head at him remonstratively, then put baking chocolate over the double boiler to melt. She motioned him closer. He complied with a masculine ease that made her heart pound.

"Stir this." Hand over his, she demonstrated what she wanted him to do.

His palm heated beneath hers. He ducked his head, the side of his jaw brushing her temple. "Why not do it in the microwave?"

Poppy inhaled the heady sandalwood-and-soap scent of him. Would she ever be less physically aware of him?

"Because it is way too easy to burn it that way," she said, moving so he could manage the task himself. And she could stay focused.

He seemed skeptical.

She quirked a brow. "Have you ever smelled burned chocolate?"

His gaze tracked the careless way she'd piled her hair up high on her head, with a few wispy strands escaping, and she could tell that he was thinking about taking it right back down.

"No," he said, "can't say that I have."

Trying not to think about the hot, hungry look in his eyes, Poppy swung away. "Then be glad." She stood on tiptoe and took out the rest of the ingredients. "It's horrendous enough to turn you off chocolate forever."

Trace's glance moved lovingly over her hips to her waist and breasts. "Well, now," he said in that sexily gruff voice she loved, "that would be a shame."

Not, Poppy thought, if she still had him.

With him to keep her company, she wouldn't need chocolate to boost her spirits. Or peppermint ice cream, either. She'd have company and sweet, arousing kisses…

And lots and lots of…sex.

While he was stirring, Trace squinted at the fireplace.

Uh-oh, Poppy thought.

Noting it was all melted, Trace removed the pot and bowl atop it from the burner and set it aside to cool. Then, furrowing his brow even more, he strode toward the living room. "Have you been switching the wreaths around?" Poppy added sugar to the melted butter in the mixing bowl then turned the stand mixer to low speed. She tried not to flush. "Ah, maybe."

He spun toward her with a snort. "When?"

Oh, dear, oh, dear, oh, dear.

Poppy broke the required number of eggs into a glass dish, picked out a piece of shell and then slowly added them to the mixing bowl. She kept her gaze averted. "When I had a moment…"

He trod closer with panther-like grace. Stood just next to her. "When was that?" he taunted, chuckling softly. "When I was sleeping? You know, you didn't have to do that in secret. You could have done it in front of me, or even asked me to help. I wouldn't have minded."

But what if he had?

They would have quarreled.

And she really did *not* want to quarrel with Trace. Any more than she wanted to hurt his feelings. Or to have hers hurt, either.

Was this where living together—even temporarily—got them?

Poppy began measuring out the flour in yet another big bowl, added salt and baking powder and whisked them all together. "I appreciate what you tried to do."

His jaw tightened. "I just didn't do it right."

She saw she had really touched a nerve with him. "And this reminds you of…?"

Was that a barely audible sigh she heard?

"Many of my ex-stepparents."

Ouch. When had life gotten so messy and complicated? "I'm sorry." And she was.

His expression softened. "Don't be." He rubbed his thumb across her cheek. "On you, that perfectionist streak is kind of cute."

Just as on him…

She really needed to get back to cooking. "I think the chocolate is cool enough." Together, they worked to slowly add the chocolate to the mixing bowl. When it was fully incorporated, they added the dry ingredients to the wet.

He stood next to her, watching. "Nice."

This *was* nice, she thought wistfully. Making Christmas cookies together. "Now for the sticky part," she cautioned.

"Sounds…interesting." He flashed a wicked smile.

She flushed—as he meant her to.

"Pay attention, Lieutenant," she said sternly.

"Yes, ma'am." He gave her a salute.

Her pulse racing, she showed him how to take a teaspoonful in the center of his palm and roll it into a ball. And from there, dip it in confectioner's sugar and place it on the baking sheet.

He studied his handiwork. "That's it?"

"That's it one hundred and forty-three more times."

His lips quirked ruefully. "And how did you talk me into this?"

She wiped a smudge of confectioner's sugar from his jaw. "You volunteered."

"Which is what usually gets me into trouble," he growled.

They worked for several more minutes until they had a dozen cookies on a sheet, ready to put in the oven.

Poppy paused to wash her hands. "Trace?"

He joined her at the sink and washed his palms, too. "Hmm?"

She lounged against the counter, pivoting to face him. "Do you regret saying yes to me…about getting married?"

Hands braced on her hips, he brought her against him. "What do you think?"

Think or hope? Poppy swallowed around the sudden dryness in her throat. "That you're as excited about starting a family as I am."

He bent his head and kissed her, showing her just how much. Dimly, Poppy heard a buzzing sound. She was inclined to ignore it until she remembered it was the signal that the oven had preheated and was ready for the first batch. Reluctantly she broke off the clinch. They were both breathing raggedly as he pressed his forehead to hers. "The cookies…" she gasped.

"Will get baked," he vowed, kissing her again, hard and hungrily, until she could barely remember her own name. With a grin, he took her by the hand. "But right now we need some R and R…"

Their rest and recreation ended up taking an hour. That left them on a strict schedule for the rest of the marathon cookie-baking session.

Finally finished, they packaged the freshly baked confections then rushed upstairs to change for the party. And it was when they were just about ready to walk out the door that the call came through.

"Hey, Will," Trace said, answering his phone, "what's up?" He listened, his expression sobering. "Sure. I can help you out. No problem. See you in ten."

"Ten?" *Please tell me it's not—*

"Minutes." That was about the time it took to get to the Laramie airstrip from her place. Poppy's heart sank, even as she warned herself not to be so selfish. "Another flight?"

Trace nodded, already in rescue mode. "There's a heart that needs to be picked up ASAP and flown to Minneapolis for a transplant. The pilot who was going to do it just came down with the stomach flu. I told Will that I'd do it."

She felt a sudden twinge of guilt. These were problems much bigger than any she had. "Of course."

He frowned, his voice full of regret. "I'll miss the party at your mom and dad's."

Poppy clasped his shoulders and tilted her chin up to brush her lips against his. "I'll save you some cookies."

He reached for his keys and wallet, already focused on his mission. "I've got to go."

Nodding, she crossed her arms at her chest. "Be safe."

Just that swiftly, he came back and kissed her, harder and longer this time. He muttered something beneath his breath she couldn't quite catch and then was gone.

Poppy stood there watching until he was long out of sight. With a sigh, she loaded up the cookies herself and headed for her parents' home.

All five of her sisters and their families had already arrived. Christmas music was playing. Kids were everywhere. As were the sounds of laughter and teasing.

"Hey, Mom, Dad." Poppy set down the huge box of cookies and hugged them both.

"Trace parking the car?" Jackson asked.

"No." Doing her best to put on a brave front, she explained.

"Good for him," her dad said. In this instance, a surgeon first.

"But not so good for you?" her mom suggested in a disarmingly perceptive tone.

Poppy wasn't sure what to say except, "I understand." And she did. Helping others was important. Especially at this time of year. And this was a matter of life and death.

"Yet you wish he was here," her mom concluded.

Of course she did. The last thing she had ever wanted was to be the only single woman among a sea of married sisters. And even though now, technically, she was married, she wasn't married in the way every other woman in her immediate family was, with all her heart and soul.

And that did bug her.

More than she cared to admit.

Even to herself.

Poppy squared her shoulders. "Can we not talk about this tonight?" Or maybe ever?

Before her parents could respond, Rose's triplets spied her. "Aunt Poppy!" they shouted and ran up to give her great big hugs. Lily's two children followed. Then Maggie and Callie's kids. Even Violet's daughter, Ava, toddled up to her to say hi.

As soon as the commotion ebbed, Poppy made her way to the drink station that had been set up in the living room. Her stomach suddenly feeling a little too unsettled to handle champagne, she selected sparkling water instead.

"I heard about Trace," Violet said, coming over to give her a hug.

"Bummer," Lily agreed.

Rose smiled. "But he's out there doing good in the world. As always. You can't argue that."

No, Poppy couldn't.

That made her private disappointment that much harder to bear. As long as she was married now—on whatever level—she had wanted her first holiday with Trace to be different.

Special.

Instead it was shaping up to be the same old same old.

"How's the adoption process going?" Callie asked.

Poppy wanted to lie and say, "Good."

Suddenly she needed to vent. "Not really sure."

All her sisters were suddenly listening. "It was almost going better when Trace and I weren't married."

No one looked surprised by that revelation.

Poppy explained the amended home-study process thus far.

"Mitzy Martin is sure doing her due diligence," Violet said. "She came over to the hospital and grilled me and Gavin."

Rose nodded. "She's asked us all if your union is the real deal."

"And, of course," Callie said, "we all told her that you and Trace have been wildly in love with each other forever."

Except they hadn't, Poppy thought.

Infatuated, fond of, had fun with, could always talk to or use as a sounding board, sure. But none of those things constituted being head-over-heels in love.

Her mother joined the group. "Your father and I both told Mitzy we thought you were destined to be together all along."

Except, Poppy mused, that wasn't necessarily true, either. Because she knew that had it not been for the requirement they be married to adopt the twins, they would not be married now.

In fact, the subject would never have even come up. Ever.

"Oh, forget all that!" Callie said with an exasperated huff. "What I really want to know is what you're giving each other for Christmas. I hope it's not the usual jokey stuff."

She and Trace had had a competition in previous years. Who could deliver the corniest or silliest present? It was usually a tie.

Poppy's stomach churned. She took another sip of sparkling water. "The twins and the marriage are present enough."

"Sure about that?" Lily asked.

"If you haven't discussed it," Maggie advised seriously, "you should. Because the last thing you want to be is short-handed."

Yet something else she did not know about her new husband, Poppy thought pensively hours later as she headed home alone, a huge assortment of holiday cookies in tow. Did he or did he not want to exchange real Christmas gifts with her? And if he did, then what?

She was still thinking about how to manage this latest dilemma, without coming right out and asking him, as she put on her pajamas and got ready for bed.

Unfortunately no solution to the problem immediately came to mind. Sleep seemed similarly out of her reach. So, wanting to do something productive, she turned on her computer and answered the work emails she hadn't had time to respond to earlier in the day.

She'd just finished and gone upstairs with a book when her phone rang.

The name flashing across Caller ID made her smile.

Was he missing her, too? Had he known she was thinking about him? "Hey, stranger," she said, feeling a little like old times.

"So you are still awake." His voice was a sexy rumble.

She snuggled under the covers where she and Trace had recently made love. "I can't wind down from the party." From a lot of things...

"That fun, huh?"

Not without you. It was never as much fun. "Let's just say there was no shortage of McCabes," she said dryly.

He chuckled. "I'll bet the kids are excited that Santa Claus will be coming soon?"

As would theirs be next year. "And then some," Poppy confirmed affectionately. "I take it everything went okay on your flight?"

"Went great." Trace inhaled. "The transplant team already has the heart."

Poppy thought about what his efforts must mean to the family of the recipient. "That must make you feel good."

"I've got clearance to fly back tonight."

Even nicer. But…

"Sure you don't want to get some sleep and fly back tomorrow?" she asked, amused to hear herself sounding so protective now.

He made a dissenting sound. "I want to be home."

Home, she thought longingly.

"With you. As much as I can, while I can."

So it wasn't her imagination. They *were* getting closer.

"Miss me that much?" she teased.

"As a matter of fact…" She could hear the sexy promise in his voice. "I do."

Joy filled her heart and she felt tears spring to her eyes. "I miss you, too."

"So I'll see you before dawn?"

"I'll be waiting."

He paused again. She heard voices in the background. "Listen, the plane's ready. I've got to go."

"Travel safe," she said softly.

"Will do."

The call ended.

She sat there staring at the phone in her hand.

They weren't supposed to be married in the usual sense. Yet she felt that way. A fact that was only going to make their impending separation when he had to leave right after Christmas that much harder.

Trace parked his rented SUV on the street and tiptoed in, tired but anxious to see his wife.

Was this how the married guys all felt when they headed home after being deployed? Excited as hell, yet their hearts aching a little bit, too, realizing that the togetherness wouldn't last?

But he was here now. Even if it was nearly five in the morning.

Wary of waking her, he took off his coat and walked soundlessly upstairs. She'd left a light on and was asleep on her side, her features even more delicately beautiful in repose, a cloud of silky dark hair flowing across the pillow. He stood there a moment, admiring her, then stripped down to his T-shirt and briefs. Still marveling that she was his, he pulled back the covers and climbed into bed.

As he cuddled up to Poppy, she let out a soft little moan. "Hey, sweetheart," he whispered in her ear.

She moaned again. More insistently.

Was she…dreaming?

"Poppy?" he said quietly.

Her eyes fluttered open.

She pressed a hand to her mouth, struggled to sit up, and bolted from the bed.

Chapter 10

"Well, that was some welcome home," Poppy said miserably several minutes later when she finally lifted her head from the toilet bowl.

Trace hunkered beside her, cool, damp cloth in hand.

She pressed it against her mouth.

"Do you want to get up?"

Her stomach roiled at the thought. She took a shaky breath. "I hope you don't come down with this, too."

He touched her arm gently. "You think it's the stomach flu?"

"Probably. We were at the elementary school. And as Will and his sick pilot can attest, it is making the rounds."

Trace sat beside her on the floor. Once comfortable, he touched her forehead with the back of his hand.

This time, Poppy didn't mind. In fact, she was ridiculously glad to see him. "I don't think I have a fever."

He dropped his hand and pressed a light, reassuring kiss to the top of her head. "I don't, either."

Another moment passed.

Then another.

"Think you're going to be sick again?" he asked softly.

Poppy softly sighed. The nausea that had been plaguing her for the past hour or so seemed to have gone away. "I think that was it."

He gave her a hand up. She stood on shaky legs, paused to rinse her mouth in the sink and then brush her teeth.

Trace walked with her back to the bed. Once he'd helped her settle beneath the covers, he started to climb in, as well. "I don't think you should sleep with me tonight," Poppy said, aware it was inching toward dawn.

He smiled. Unafraid. "I've seen someone get sick before..."

"And you handled it like a pro," she praised him, just as kindly. "But I don't want to give you my germs." She patted the pillow beside her, motioning for him to get cozy, and swung her legs over the side of the bed. "So why don't you stay here and I'll go downstairs to the sofa."

He caught her wrist before she could go anywhere and tugged her back down to the mattress. "In sickness and in health, remember?"

Except that they hadn't really meant their vows. Not like that, anyway. Had they?

"I'm not going anywhere," he repeated sternly. "Not when you're sick."

"But I've already had nearly a full night's sleep."

He leaned closer and gave her a tender glance. "We were exposed to the same germs at the school, remember? So if I'm going to get it, I'm going to get it. Lay down. Close your eyes." He brought her into the curve of his body and spooned with her. Kissed her ear. "And go to sleep."

Poppy didn't think she would be able to do that, but figuring she could slip away once he was asleep, and spare him that way, she reluctantly closed her eyes. The next thing she knew sunlight was streaming in through the windows. It was late morning. And Trace was still asleep.

She eased from the bed and went downstairs.

And there, on the blinking phone, all kinds of messages awaited.

Trace heard Poppy get out of bed and slip out of the room. Aware she might need her privacy, he gave her a few minutes' grace. When he heard her moving around on the first floor, he got up, too, and ambled downstairs.

Poppy was sitting at the kitchen table, a glass of ginger ale and a plate of saltine crackers positioned next to her laptop computer. Her hair tumbled over her shoulders, the vivid color in her cheeks matching her pink-and-white-checked flannel pajamas.

Thinking the smell of coffee might make her nauseated, he helped himself to a glass of ginger ale, too. She looked alarmed. "Are you sick?"

He smiled at the protectiveness in her eyes. "No."

She scowled. "Then you don't have to drink that."

"Really?" He closed the distance between them and

made an exaggerated show of examining her visually. "And I thought misery loved company."

Poppy moaned and buried her face in her hands. "Trust me. You don't want what I had last night."

Wondering if maybe she did have fever, he once again pressed his hand to her forehead. She felt warm, but just ordinarily so.

Poppy glared at him. "You're aware the only other person who does that is my mother?"

Her sarcastic tone made him smile.

If she was this irascible, it had to mean she was on the mend. "It's a fairly reliable indicator when there are no thermometers to be had." He dropped his hand and pulled up a chair.

She rolled her eyes, grumbling, "Unless you're in the desert."

"Even then." He waited until she looked him in the eye. "Fever usually feels like the skin is burning up from the inside out."

Another eye roll. "'Cause it is."

But she seemed to be calming down.

"Seriously." Trace settled so his knees were touching hers beneath the table. "How are you feeling now, darlin'?"

Poppy swallowed. "Okay, actually." She paused before nodding at the plate of crackers and glass of ginger ale. "I just don't want to push it. So—" she inhaled a breath that lifted the soft swell of her breasts "—I thought I would start with this."

Having been there when she got sick, he didn't blame her. Figuring she might want to talk about something else, he nodded at her laptop. "Why were you frowning when I walked in?"

Poppy sighed. "A couple things from clients. One has decided a lamp she was completely in love with three months ago just doesn't go with her home. Another's decided she should have had the mother-in-law suite in her home redone, as well, and wants to know if I can completely overhaul the two rooms before her in-laws visit in four days."

He hadn't realized her job could be so exasperating. "And the answer is?"

"No. I understand the panic—when you have guests coming you suspect aren't going to be happy. But this couple is on the kind of budget that dictates they are going to have to live with whatever major changes they make for years to come."

"So there's nothing you can do."

"Not on that scale. I'm going to suggest they freshen up the suite with a new coat of paint, fresh bedspread and bath towels—that's something I can arrange on short notice. And it won't break the bank. But they are still going to have to decide exactly what they want, and that can be tough, too." Poppy typed something. Paused.

"You're frowning again."

Poppy turned her laptop so he could see the monitor. "We also had an email from Mitzy. She forgot to give us a list of what the twins are going to need."

Trace shrugged. "Okay."

Poppy pointed to what she wanted him to see.

"'Each infant will require ten diapers daily for the first month. Six to eight four-ounce feedings of formula…'" Trace read aloud in shock.

Quickly, he did the math.

"That's twenty diaper changes a day! And twelve to fourteen bottle feedings, too," he noted in amazement.

Poppy was the most capable and independent woman he knew, but could *anyone* handle that?

She scrawled a few numbers on the piece of paper beside her, noting serenely, "Or one hundred and forty diaper changes a week and fifty-six bottle feedings."

Trace helped himself to one of the crackers. "You don't look at all surprised."

"I come from a family of multiples. I knew from experience it was going to be a lot."

Not for the first time, Trace felt a current of guilt for leaving her so soon after the twins arrived. Yet what choice did he have? He was in the military. He went where they told him to go.

She picked up a cracker and took a very small bite. He watched her savor the salty snack. "How are you going to manage it?"

She tossed her head, the thick, silky strands swishing softly around her shoulders. "After you leave, my plan is for me and the babies to stay with my parents at their home, nights." Clasping her hands in her lap, she settled deeper into her chair. "During the days, I'll be here, and I'm going to bring in someone to help, probably for the first six months or year. Which won't be a problem," she said, warning him with a look not to offer her money again. "Although I wouldn't have needed to make such elaborate plans if I had adopted one child, as I originally thought I was going to do. I could easily handle one baby on my own."

Trace imagined that was true.

Poppy paused and raised one hand to point a little farther down on the email. Fresh color sweeping into her cheeks, she continued her tirade. "What bothers me is the fact that Mitzy not only felt the need to tell me this, as if I hadn't already calculated all this on my own. She's also requiring us to submit a written plan for how we are going to care for the twins once they come home and you leave. And that makes me think that she isn't so certain we'll make great parents, after all."

Trace not only understood Poppy's concern, he shared it. So when Poppy settled down to make the first of several calls to clients, to discuss their issues and possible solutions, he went out to take care of some "errands."

First stop—the social worker who had caused his wife such worry.

He caught her at her office on her lunch hour.

Mitzy looked up from her desk. "You know our final Q-and-A session for the amended home study is not for another three days. And that's really just a wrap-up-any-loose-ends-and-hear-the-decision kind of meeting."

Trace lounged in the open doorway. "I just dropped by to make sure that you got the care plan Poppy emailed you this morning."

Mitzy took the last bite of salad, then closed the lid on the container and slid it into her insulated lunch sack. "I did." She studied him with a poker face. "But that's not the reason you're here."

Trace wasn't accustomed to begging. But if that's what it took—to get Poppy what she deserved—then so be it. "Do you have a minute to talk?"

"I've got five before my next appointment." Mitzy motioned for him to take a seat.

Trace shut the door and settled in the chair she'd indicated. "Poppy has the feeling you may not be gung-ho about us adopting the twins."

Mitzy uncapped her thermos and poured herself some

lemonade. "I know she'd be a great mother. The problem is…the Stork Agency requires us to ensure a couple of things."

"Such as?"

"First, they require a good rapport between the birth mother and the adoptive parents, since they specialize in open adoptions that foster an ongoing relationship. You and Poppy have that, since you are clearly compatible with Anne Marie. And vice versa. Second, the agency has a policy that when more than one child is adopted at a time, there be two parents in a longstanding relationship who are also married, taking on the challenge. They also want to make sure that the marriage will last and that the couple is equally devoted to each other, as well as the idea of adoption."

"So the kids don't end up in broken homes," Trace concluded.

"Right."

"Makes sense. So am I right in assuming that I'm the problem in this scenario? Maybe because of my parents' history of multiple marriages and divorces?"

Mitzy leaned forward, hands clasped in front of her. "Actually, it's more you, Trace."

He hadn't felt this much on the hot seat since he'd been called into the CO's office to explain why he should be granted immediate leave so he could make it home in time for his proxy wedding.

Mitzy's glance turned even more serious. "So far, I'm not seeing much of a commitment from you toward these kids—or Poppy, for that matter."

Trace scowled. What the hell was she talking about? He was here in Laramie, wasn't he? Not to mention that he'd had to call in every favor he'd accrued over his long career just to get here.

"I'm in the military."

She raised a brow at his curt tone. "I know."

Trace cooled his temper with effort. "What do you want me to do? Quit?"

Mitzy tilted her head. "Would you?"

Half a dozen errands later Trace returned home to find Poppy in the driveway, cutting the twine securing a Scotch pine to the top of her minivan. Her color was good. She was in a dark green Polartec fleece jacket, white tee, jeans and boots. She smelled good, too—like the apple blossom soap and shampoo she used. He parked his SUV behind hers and got out, container of chicken soup in hand. "Feeling better, I take it?"

"Much." Poppy smiled. She walked around to the other side of the minivan, utility scissors in hand. "In fact, I don't recall when I've ever recovered from the stomach bug so quickly."

He set the takeout bag on the hood of his SUV and ambled over to her. "That's good to hear." He had hated seeing her sick.

She grabbed the trunk of the tree and pulled it toward her. He leaned in to assist. "You know, I would have helped you with this, if you'd told me you were going to do it." He felt a little hurt at having been left out, oddly enough.

Poppy shrugged, recalling, "You've never been that into Christmas."

With good reason, he thought. Given how tumultuous and angst-filled his holidays had been as a kid. His parents often either fighting over where he should be and when, or worse, trying to foist him off on one another so their own plans could continue without the hassle of trying to include a son from a previous relationship who—he readily admitted—had been a little surly and a lot uncooperative.

"I like it, as much as anyone." Now that he was a grown-up, he could appreciate the value of Christmas as much as anyone and liked a good meal, a holiday movie or a little carol singing. If only because it reminded him of his homeland.

Together, they carried the tree up the walk, with him taking most of the weight and Poppy guiding the cone-shaped treetop. "I'm just usually not here."

Poppy paused to unlock the door then wedge it open. "True."

He upended the tree and, angling it just so, carried it inside. "Although you have a point," he said as Poppy knelt to help him set the base in the metal stand. "The one year I was home for the holidays in Laramie—my senior year in high school—both my parents were in the midst of yet another set of divorces."

"Not fun."

"Not in the slightest." He stepped back to admire their handiwork. Finding it leaning slightly to the right, he hunkered down to re-center the pine in the middle of the stand. "Which is why, after that, I always stayed on campus and worked through the holidays."

Poppy checked the trajectory. Finding it satisfactory, she knelt to tighten the screws on the other side. "Well, now you have a reason to come home." She smiled warmly.

He stood. "I do." He extended his hand. She grasped it and he helped her to her feet.

Before she could move away, he whipped the mistletoe out of his pocket. One hand gliding down her spine, he swept her against him and indulged in a sweet and lengthy kiss. The ultrasexy kind he knew she liked.

"You are such a distraction," Poppy breathed.

Trace waggled his brows. "As are you." He bent his head and kissed her again until she pushed him away.

"But we have to get this done," she said sternly, pointing to the boxes of decorations. "I want it up in case Mitzy or anyone else involved in the amended home study decides to stop by unexpectedly again."

In that case...

Trace reluctantly put his desire to make love to her aside for another time.

"Speaking of which, Mitzy called while you were out. She mentioned you had been by her office."

He shrugged as if it were no big deal when it had turned out to be a *very* big deal. "I dropped by to see if there was anything else we could do to speed up the approval process."

"And is there?" Trace opened a box marked Tree Lights and pulled out several carefully wrapped strands. A quick check with the plug showed them to be in working order. "She wants to see more of a daily commitment from me."

Poppy's spine stiffened. "Well, that's impossible." She moved to help him unwind the miniature bulbs. "At least when you're deployed overseas."

Not exactly how he had planned this, but...

Trace moved around to the other side of the tree. "That was probably her point. If I'm going to do this, maybe I need to be all-in."

He anchored the lights near the top.

Poppy strode closer. Tipped her face up to his. "In what way?"

"By requesting a hardship transfer back to Texas."

Her mouth dropped open and she stared at him in shock. "Can you do that?"

Not sure if this was a good thing or a bad thing in her view, he shrugged. "Already have. I talked to my CO a little while ago. He said it's going to take at least six months. Maybe more."

"Oh." Poppy laid her hand over her heart. Slowly, joy spread across her lovely face. "But, still…if we were to tell Mitzy that, it would have a positive impact on the process!"

"But would it be enough," he said carefully, "for you?"

Poppy was not sure how to answer that. Buying herself time, she went back to stringing the lights.

"I would never tell you what to do with your life. Any more than I would want you to tell me what to do with mine," she told him.

Finished with the lights, they moved on to the ornaments.

Trace fit the star on the top, made sure it was secure and stepped back. "Is that why you didn't tell me you were pregnant back then, and probably wouldn't have if I hadn't been with you when you realized something was wrong?"

Aware he had never asked her this—or any other hard question—before, because they had been so determined to keep things light and easy between them, Poppy shrugged. "We had just graduated from college. I'd started a new job. You were just a few weeks away from heading off to flight school."

His face remained impassive. "So?"

Had she let him down?

Poppy bit her lip and tried again. "I know how gallant you are, at heart, Trace."

He narrowed his gaze. "And that's a bad thing?"

Poppy attached a pretty glass bulb to a branch. "It is when it leads you to do something that eventually ends up feeling like a lie." She took out another bulb and handed one to Trace, too. "Bottom line, I was afraid if I told you we had a baby on the way that you would do what our parents would have considered the right thing, and stick around and marry me."

He didn't deny it.

Poppy looked him in the eye. "I didn't want to trap you. And it would have felt like a trap if I'd told you, even if it was an unintentional one."

He remained silent, neither agreeing nor disagreeing.

Aware at times like this she really didn't understand the strong, silent guy beside her, Poppy attached several more glass bulbs in quick order. "Besides, I knew I was independent enough and savvy enough to have a baby on my own."

He came near enough she could feel his body heat. "No one's disputing that," he said huskily in her ear.

"Then?" Poppy turned to face him, her arm grazing his in the process.

He reached out his hands to steady her. Looked down at her. "I would have wanted to share in the responsibility."

The ache in Poppy's heart moved to her throat. "And you would have had a part in that baby's life—as much as you wanted," she explained softly. "*After* you had achieved your dream of becoming a military pilot. You wouldn't have had to marry me to do that, or forfeited your desire to serve and protect our country. And I knew you would realize that you could have both, once you actually entered flight school and started realizing your dream." She blinked back the tears pressing behind her eyes.

He rubbed the pad of his thumb across her lower lip. "So maybe I'm not the only noble one in this family?"

Poppy rose on tiptoe and kissed him with all the affection she had in her heart. "Let's just say I learned from the best."

They shared another kiss.

Trace hugged her tightly then stepped back.

"But that's not all I have to tell you," Poppy said.

His mouth quirked, as if he wasn't sure what could be more life-changing than what he'd just said.

Poppy went on excitedly. "Anne Marie wants us to be at the birth. To do that, we have to take at least one Lamaze class. So I've signed us up for the one here in Laramie, which meets at the hospital tomorrow night."

Trace favored her with a bemused smile. "Sounds… interesting," he said finally.

"I know." Poppy had had the same initial reaction. Trace and her? In a *Lamaze* class? Together? She hadn't been sure whether to laugh or to worry.

She squeezed his hand. "We're going to be like two fish out of water. But we can handle it."

To her relief, he seemed to think so, too.

"In the meantime, do we have any plans for tonight?" he asked in that low, gravelly tone she adored.

Poppy hesitated. "Not that I know of. Why?" She looked at him closely. "What do you have in mind?"

He flashed that sexy grin. "Our first ever date night."

Chapter 11

"You want us to have a date night?" Poppy stared at Trace in surprise. She'd never known him to be romantic. Sexy, kind, funny, smart and chivalrous? Yes, he was all that and so much more. But given to established courtship rituals? No. He steered as far away from those as possible. Yet here he was, asking her for their first actual "date."

His brow lifted. "Yes? No?"

"I don't know?" She was already feeling way too romantic and overly sentimental herself, so to do something like this would only add fuel to that fire.

Yet he was apparently dead serious.

A slow smile tilted the corners of his lips. "You want to be persuaded?"

"Maybe."

Tucking his thumbs into his belt loops, he rocked

forward on the toes of his boots. "All the married folks I know have them. So we should probably start the tradition, too."

Ah, yes. Tradition. That was exactly what the military was run on, too. No wonder he was suddenly so hot to take her out.

"I thought we weren't going to run our relationship like everyone else runs theirs," she countered, still trying to figure out if she could do this without getting her heart broken in the end.

He shrugged amiably and flashed her a sexy grin. "Some activities that come with marriage sound good." He stepped close enough to inundate her with the soap-and-man scent of him. "Besides, what else do we have to do?"

Make love, Poppy thought. Again and again and again. She straightened abruptly. "You're right. Maybe we should get out of the house for a while."

While she went upstairs to freshen up, he took out his laptop.

By the time she returned, still defiantly wearing the same old jeans, Polartec jacket, tee and shearling-lined boots, he was grinning from ear to ear. Her only obvious concession had been to take her hair down, run a comb through it and spritz on perfume. Although, he noted, she'd touched up her makeup.

Determined not to make more of this than there actually was, she sauntered close to him, able to see he'd shaved, though she wasn't sure how she'd missed him upstairs. The scent of sandalwood and mint clung to him. "Since this was your idea, big guy, where do you want to go?"

He donned a leather aviator jacket over his charcoal-gray sweater while she grabbed her scarf and the dark green all-weather outer shell to her fleece jacket.

"The town square," he said.

Poppy allowed him to help her on with her coat. She told herself the long-running spate of masculine gallantry didn't mean anything. "Is the community sing-a-long tonight?"

"Yep."

She spun around to face him. "Just when I thought you couldn't surprise me any more than you already have…"

He grinned at her triumphantly, taking her hand and leading her out the front door. A companionable silence fell between them as they walked through the beautifully decked-out neighborhoods. When they approached Main Street, the sounds of the high school band and choir could be heard, along with a spate of familiar yuletide melodies. Everyone was encouraged to join in.

When the concert broke up, Poppy and Trace turned to the food venders set up along the avenue. It seemed that every booster organization in the county was selling something.

"No need to play favorites," Trace decided after they stopped for mini brisket tacos.

"I agree." Poppy wound her way over to the cranberry-apple tarts.

Thirsty, they stopped for chilled bottles of water and hot mugs of peppermint tea.

Together, they wandered the streets contentedly, looking at the window displays on all the shops and saying hello to old friends. Admiring the festive wreaths and red velvet ribbons everywhere, as well as the twenty-five-foot Christmas tree in the center of the town square.

It was small-town life at its best.

And, Poppy noted, Trace seemed to think so, too.

He inclined his head at the booths still doing business. "Want anything else?" he asked her.

Poppy shook her head. She let her hand rest against her middle. "I'm stuffed."

"Me, too." He rubbed his thumb across the curve of her cheek.

Poppy cocked her head, sensing a building emotion in him. "Want to take the short way or the long way home?"

He took her hand in his. "Why don't we walk down a few extra streets? See what kind of decorations everyone's put up this year?"

Poppy savored the warmth of his touch. "You're really enjoying this, aren't you?" she observed.

His fingers tightened around hers. "What's not to love?"

She thought about what kind of change this signified. "I never thought you were suited for life in a small West Texas town," she admitted wistfully.

He pivoted toward her, the soft glow of the streetlamp making him look more ruggedly handsome than ever. "Never saw us married, either," he said huskily.

"And yet here we are," she noted as they began walking. They passed a particularly cute Santa and his elves display. "Doing okay. So far, anyway."

Trace wrapped an arm around her shoulders and tucked her into his side. "Are you going to be okay when I leave again?" he asked in a low tone that told her she could tell him anything and he would understand.

"I always am." She flushed, hoping he would ignore the slight catch in her breath.

He brought her in even closer. "This time you'll have two infants."

Poppy turned her glance to a display of angels as a torrent of need swept through her. "It's not as if you aren't coming back." She swallowed hard. "You are, right?" In the meantime, she had to be strong. Resilient. Keep to the agreement that had served them so well these many years...

Tightening his grip on her shoulders, Trace stopped and turned her to face him. His lips thinned. "There are only so many open pilot slots, Poppy." He paused to let his words sink in. "I've requested to be transferred back to the continental US as soon as possible, but there is no telling where I'll be, within the country, when that finally does happen sometime next year."

Poppy shrugged; abruptly aware she had an ache in her throat and an even bigger one in her heart. "So maybe the twins and I will move closer to you."

Trace frowned. "I would never ask you to do that. You have a business here."

Ignoring her disappointment, she continued, pretending it was no big deal. "With my background in interior design, I could work anywhere."

"But you wouldn't have the familial support network you do now," he retorted.

"I'd have you." The words were out before she could stop herself.

Guilt flashed in his eyes and his jaw tightened. "And I would be off on missions more than I was actually home."

A troubled silence fell. "So you don't want me and the twins to follow you around," Poppy declared, aware personal sacrifice had never been part of their deal. Just the opposite.

His eyes softened, as did his touch. They resumed walking. "I would never ask you to upend your life that way."

"Then what do you want from me?" she asked, her voice quavering as they moved up her porch steps.

He caught her in his arms, reading her heart as readily as her mind. His mouth lowered, lingered over hers. "This."

The feel of his lips on hers sent a jolt of electricity racing through her. Moaning, Poppy wrapped her arms around his neck, opened her mouth to the plundering pressure of his, and pressed her body to his. And once they made contact, there was no stopping with just one kiss. He stroked her tongue with his. She cajoled and teased with hers. Until they were both gasping for breath as if they had just finished a 5K run.

Aware they were still standing on the front porch, Trace pulled back. The air between them vibrated with escalating passion and fervent emotion. He dropped kisses at her temple, along her cheekbone, the delicate shell of her ear and the pulse in her throat. Lifting his head once again, he looked at her and promised huskily, "I'll come home to you and the kids, Poppy. All the time."

She knew he would. Knowing nothing had ever felt this right, Poppy kissed him again, sweetly, tenderly. "And I'll be waiting," she whispered.

His brow quirked roguishly. "If this is any indication of the homecoming I'm going to get..."

"Oh, it is." She took out her key, unlocked the door and turned the knob.

Pushing the door open with the flat of his palm, Trace accompanied her inside.

Poppy turned the tree lights on and closed the drapes while Trace put away their coats and lit the fire.

Their mood was quiet, contemplative and achingly sentimental as their first-ever date night came to a close.

He pulled her to him and bussed the top of her head, clearly planning to make love to her then and there. "Do I need mistletoe this time?" he rasped.

Poppy shook her head.

The truth was he hadn't ever needed it.

She was his, for the taking.

And he was hers.

Trace knew that Poppy still wasn't getting everything she wanted. A happily-ever-after like all her sisters had experienced. The ability to get pregnant by the man she loved and to deliver not just one, but several happy, healthy babies.

He wanted to bring her joy just the same. And there was one kind of satisfaction he was very good at bringing her.

He found her clothes, divested them one by one.

Let her remove his.

Before she could look at what she'd uncovered, he guided her onto the sofa and dropped to his knees.

Parting her thighs with his hands, he leaned in to kiss her. Slowly, evocatively, until she was sliding to the edge of the cushion. Her hands were in his hair and she was holding him close, the taut tips of her breasts rubbing against his chest, even as her inner thighs provocatively cradled his hips.

"Now," she breathed.

Lowering his head, he flicked the tip of her breast with his tongue, while lower still, his hand found her most feminine core.

A wordless cry escaped her.

His fingers paved the way, finding her rhythm in a way that left her shuddering. She rocked up against him. Hung on to him for dear life.

He shifted her, moving her onto her back, then stretched out over top of her, already hard as a rock. Her eyes were unwavering, letting him know that all that mattered was the here and now. The two of them. The chance to spend the holidays together at long last. And the life—and home—they were building.

He gripped her hips, leaving no doubt about who was in charge, and tilted her in a way that pleased him, pleased them both. With a soft, willing smile, she arched up into him, being creative with how she moved, inciting him to be creative, too. And still he kissed her, and she kissed him back, offering him refuge, until their hearts beat in tandem. What few boundaries still existed between them dissolved.

Reveling in the soft surrender of her body against his, trembling with the need to make her his for all time, Trace slid his hands beneath her, lifting her. He penetrated her slowly, then deeper still. Her hands ran down his back and she kissed him insistently, taking even more of him deep inside her. She opened herself to him and he claimed her with unchecked abandon.

When her release came—fast and hard and wild— his came, too. Hitting him with shocking force. Blasting him into oblivion.

Afterward they clung together, still shuddering, breathing hard. "So this is married sex," he murmured, dropping down to kiss one taut pink nipple then the other.

She quivered at his touch. Not completely with pleasure, he noted in concern. "Too much?"

"Never. But, yeah," she admitted shyly, "I'm a little, um, tender."

"Just here?" He cupped her breasts.

She flushed. "Actually, all over."

They had been unable to keep their hands off each other the past few weeks. "Honeymoon-itis," he sighed, knowing this meant they were going to have to give it a rest, at least for the remainder of the evening.

She laughed at the face he made and shifted so the length of her was draped over top of him. "There are worse things than simply cuddling," she chided.

He kissed her gently; acutely aware of the satisfaction he got from simply holding her in his arms. "But none better, either…" He winked.

She chuckled again and pulled a cashmere-soft throw over them.

No more willing to move than she was, Trace lay with her on the sofa, wrapped in each other's arms, looking at the lights on the tree.

Still loving the silken womanly feel of her, he caressed her bare shoulder with his left hand. Exhaled. Who would have thought contentment could be so easily had?

Without warning, Poppy caught the gleam of gold on his left hand. "Hey! You're got your wedding ring!"

"I was waiting for you to notice it." He held out his hand so she could get a good look at the band that proclaimed him a happily married man to one and all. "I picked it up this afternoon."

Delight radiated in her gaze. "How does it feel?"

She seemed to be asking about more than the band. He was serious when he answered, "Exactly right."

And, as it happened, so was the rest of their very first date night.

Although they had requested, in lieu of wedding gifts, donations be made to one of several organizations that helped military families, there were still many thank-you notes to be written. Trace and Poppy tackled it together the next morning after breakfast.

"I've been thinking," she said as they wrote. "We need to do something more to thank everyone who pitched in to help with our impromptu wedding."

Trace stuffed, sealed and stamped several envelopes. "What did you have in mind?"

She let her gaze rove over him. It was amazing how handsome he was, even with his hair delectably rumpled and a shadow of beard lining his jaw. She could really get used to having him around like this. Feeling so much a part of him, so…*married.*

Realizing he was awaiting a response, she said, "A party for all your military buddies. Here or closer to the base," she added practically, "if you'd prefer that."

Respect and admiration shone on his face. "I'd prefer to have them all here at the house, if that's okay with you."

She forced herself to remain matter-of-fact. "Sounds perfect. Next question is when?"

Like her, he appeared to think the sooner the better. "Saturday night?"

Nodding, she finished another note. "If you give me

a list of email addresses, I'll prepare an e-vite and send it out."

He waved off her suggestion. "We don't have to be that formal. I'll fire off an email to everyone, inviting them."

There was nothing like her husband on a mission. "What about RSVPs?"

"I'll ask them to let me know if they're coming or not." He paused, his gaze roving her upswept hair, as if he were thinking about taking it down and tangling his fingers through it.

"Anything else?" Poppy asked lightly, trying hard not to think how much she would have liked him to do just that.

"Yeah. Write me a To-Do list. Make it a long one. Since I'm the one with all the free time on my hands."

Grinning, Poppy got up to get a yellow legal pad. When she found it, she came back to the table. She wrinkled her nose at him playfully. "You may regret volunteering to do this."

"Doubt it," he teased right back, pulling her onto his lap. He settled her over the hardness of his thighs. "But if I do—" he cupped her face in his big hand and bestowed a hot, lingering kiss reminiscent of their lovemaking the night before "—you'll just have to find a way to make it up to me."

Poppy grinned against the seductive pressure of his lips. If that way included a lot more hot lovemaking, she knew it would be no trouble at all.

Chapter 12

"Got everything?" Poppy asked that evening when she arrived just in time to leave for the hospital.

Trace held up the cotton duffel bag containing the supplies the Lamaze instructor had said they would need to bring. Most of which had been borrowed from her sisters. All of whom had already successfully given birth.

Trace inclined his head at the kitchen. "Are you sure you don't want something to eat before we head out?"

Poppy's stomach vibrated with butterflies. "No. I can do that later," she said with a smile. *When I can relax.* Turning the attention back to him, she moved closer, inhaling the brisk soap and sandalwood clinging to his skin. "Did you get something to eat?"

"A sandwich a while ago."

His gaze drifted over her before returning ever so

slowly to her face. He took her hand in his and gave it a comforting squeeze. "So I'm good."

"Then let's go." She led the way out the front door and into his SUV.

"Why are you so nervous?" he asked as he drove the short distance to the hospital.

"I don't know," Poppy fibbed.

He lifted a reproving brow.

She ran a hand over her eyes and turned her gaze to the holiday wreaths on the lampposts as they passed. "It's just I've had a hard time being around pregnant women in general since I…"

He pulled in and parked in the hospital lot. "Lost our baby."

"Yeah." Poppy got out of the SUV. She met him at the rear, where the duffel was stowed. "I mean, I can do it on a one-by-one basis. Like, with my sisters. I just focus on the person and their happiness rather than their actual condition," she told him quietly. "But whenever I do have to go to the gynecologist and I end up in a roomful of pregnant women, or worse—at the hospital around a ton of women who have just given birth—it sort of brings it all back to me." She forced herself to go on despite the tightness in her throat and the ache in her heart. "And I know that sounds selfish and awful…"

"It sounds human." He consoled her gently, taking her in his arms.

Snuggling against him, Poppy sought solace in his warmth and strength. "I'm sure it will pass as soon as I do adopt. Because I'll be replacing the last of my lingering sorrow with joy."

Surreptitiously he removed a sprig from his pocket. "'Tis the season for that."

She pursed her lips at the plastic leaves and berries suddenly dangling above her head. "Mistletoe again. Really, Trace?"

"Hey." He used his free hand to cup her chin. "It comes in handy. Especially when you're standing there looking so lovely." He ran his thumb along the outline of her lips.

Desire caught fire inside her. "We're going to be late for class."

"Some things are more important."

His mouth slanted over hers before she could murmur another word. He kissed her as if she were the only woman on earth for him, and she kissed him back, just as passionately, savoring the hard warmth of his body.

The feel of Trace pressed against her sent sensations rippling through Poppy's core. Suddenly the sadness, the devastating loss she'd felt, all fell away. All they had in front of them was the brightness of their future, the realization of family and the perfectness of this moment.

It was as if all her Christmas wishes had suddenly come true.

Until they heard a discreet cough, that was.

Blushing, Poppy and Trace broke off their hot and heavy make-out session. And turned in unison to see her very happily married brother-in-law, Gavin Monroe, leaving the hospital. He chuckled, shaking his head. *"Newlyweds!"*

Poppy grinned.

Indeed.

Maybe she and Trace hadn't done things the traditional way, but they were happy together and that was all that counted.

* * *

Course instructor Meg Carrigan looked up as they entered the classroom. The longtime nursing supervisor, and family friend, pointed to the empty floor mat in the center of the room. "You're right there. Everyone, this is Trace and Poppy Caulder."

"Uh, McCabe," Poppy corrected, blushing slightly. "I haven't changed my last name yet." Although it was something that would need to be done. And soon.

"I'm with you, hon," a vivacious brunette with an artful streak of blue in her hair said. "I didn't change mine, either, when I got married. And good thing, too," she added, hand on her swollen belly, "since it didn't last." Her companion coach, which appeared to be her older sister, rolled her eyes.

Poppy didn't know what to say to that, so she merely nodded and smiled.

Another mom-to-be, a petite redhead, interjected, "I'm Louann. This is my husband, Jack." Her eyes went to Poppy's tummy. "I'm guessing you're newly pregnant?"

Trace put a hand on Poppy's shoulder. "Actually, we're adopting," he said.

The awkward silence in the room was palpable. Just as Poppy had expected.

"We're going to be part of the birth team in the delivery room." *If we ever get the final approval from social services and the agency,* Poppy thought anxiously. "So we have to take the class."

Meg grinned. "Well, one of you is going to have to be the pregnant one. The other, the coach. The question is which of you is going to actually coach the birth mom?"

Although they hadn't discussed that, Trace immediately pointed to Poppy.

She raised her hand. "I guess it's me."

"Then, Trace, you're going to have to be the one expecting."

Everyone laughed.

"Are you a good actor?"

He flashed a devil-may-care grin. "I think I can be."

Oh, dear heaven, Poppy thought. Give that man a stage. And a joke…and there was no telling what could happen.

Despite their conversation earlier, Trace had felt Poppy tense and had caught a fleeting glimpse of her past heartbreak in her eyes the moment they'd walked into the classroom. He knew her well enough to sense she could easily burst into tears at any second, if things got too serious.

He was determined not to let her humiliate herself that way. She'd been through enough already.

"All right. I want the coaches to sit behind the moms or beside the moms," Meg said, gesturing toward the comfy looking floor mats placed around the room. "Which means, Poppy, you'll be behind Trace," she directed.

Poppy nodded, her cheeks turning that telltale pink before the storm. So Trace did the only thing he could. He put his hand to his middle and groaned. Dramatically. "Oh, my word! It's coming!" he shouted.

Everyone broke into laughter.

Meg glared at him. "You're not in labor yet."

"Then what is this? Arghhhh!" Trace moaned.

More laughter.

"Okay. We can work with this," Meg said. "Poppy, massage his shoulders. Whisper comforting words in his ear. Get him to calm down."

Trace's "partner" leaned forward and began kneading his upper torso, her touch not exactly gentle. "Stop embarrassing us."

"Ohh-hhh-hhh." Trace groaned even louder.

Meg stepped in to demonstrate. "Like this." She massaged his shoulders firmly but gently then handed the task over to Poppy.

Poppy mimicked the instructor. As always, the feel of Poppy's hands was pure heaven. Trace began to relax, despite himself. But when he glanced over his shoulder, to see how his wife was doing, he could see she was still on the verge of tears.

That left him only one alternative.

Still hamming it up, he sighed in ecstasy. Turning his head toward her and pulling her face down to his, whispered in her ear, "Oh, sweetheart, I'm *so glad* you're here."

"I thought for sure you were going to get us kicked out of the class," Poppy scolded an hour later as they walked out of the hospital.

"Just trying to lighten the mood."

For which she was grateful. His antics had kept her from bursting into tears. Several times. "Oh, you did that, all right," she drawled, pretending to be more upset than she was. "I don't think anyone completely stopped laughing the entire class."

He wrapped an arm around her waist and tugged her closer to his side. "You look pretty when you smile, you know that? And even more gorgeous when you get the giggles."

She knew she'd been practically delirious with laughter, as had a number of other couples. "Stop now."

He moaned, as if having a contraction, and gave her a comically exaggerated come-hither look. "Coach me!"

She elbowed him in the ribs. "I mean it."

He amped it up even more by doing the rhythmic breathing exercise that brought air in slowly and then let the tension out—by groaning.

Afraid he was going to attract even more attention, Poppy trapped him in the shadow of his SUV and kissed him.

He stopped clowning around and kissed her back until her nipples were tingling, her tummy was warm and weightless, and she could barely catch her breath.

Figuring if they didn't want to get carried away then and there, they had better call a halt, Poppy reluctantly broke off the kiss. She stepped back slightly and caught the teasing glimmer in his eyes. "Are you going to behave yourself, Lieutenant?"

Another classmate couple beeped their horn lightly as they passed. Poppy and Trace turned to wave.

"Well?" Poppy commanded archly, brows raised.

"I don't know." He trailed a hand down her side. "Will you stop kissing me if I get serious?"

"How about I resume kissing you—at home sans clothes—if you stop clowning around and just let us get there?"

"Deal."

They got in the SUV. Able to see he was already thinking about the many ways he was going to make love to her, Poppy said, "Do you think I should legally change the name of my business, too, before the adoption? I mean, everything has been happening so fast, I hadn't really thought about that. But if I'm already doing the paperwork for one, maybe I should do the paperwork for the other at the same time."

He slid her a look. "Your business has always been in your maiden name."

"That's true. It's always been McCabe Interiors."

"So maybe you should just keep it the way it is. At least for now, to avoid confusion. I mean, it doesn't really matter if you go by one name professionally and the other personally, does it?"

"No," Poppy said. Either way, they were still married.

But, she thought wistfully, there would have been something nice—and traditional—about having the same last name in all respects, anyway.

And even nicer, if her husband had wanted it that way, too.

After a blissful evening of lovemaking, followed by a night of sleeping wrapped in Trace's arms, Poppy awakened rested and relaxed. Her only problem was—once again—a slightly nervous tummy, which she hoped to quell with a proper meal.

"So, how many are coming to the party?" she asked while making toast.

Trace plated the scrambled eggs and bacon. "Thirty-five so far." He turned off the stove and carried the repast to the table. "In the end, I expect it will be more like fifty. I just haven't heard back from everyone yet."

Poppy tried not to feel overwhelmed. Up until now she and Trace had mainly lived in their own little bubble. She hadn't spent a lot of time with his military buddies;

he hadn't put in a whole lot of time with her family, either. Yes, they had gone to formal occasions—such as her sisters' weddings—but most of the time they were alone. Talking, making love; just hanging out.

At their wedding, there had been little opportunity to do more than cursorily greet the guys who had helped him out, last minute.

"By the way, I told everyone it's potluck," Trace said.

Poppy's worry over fitting in with his work buddies vanished under the more pressing problem. She poured him a cup of coffee but, worried about a return of her acid indigestion during their upcoming meeting with Mitzy Martin, stuck to a soothing glass of milk for herself. "You're kidding, right?"

"It's the way we always do it. That way, no one has to bear the full expense of hosting a big gathering."

Made sense. Passing on the butter, Poppy took a small bite of dry toast. "What is everyone bringing?"

"I don't know. Stuff."

Realizing belatedly Trace might want something on his toast, she went to the fridge and brought back peach and raspberry jams. "You didn't organize some kind of sign-up sheet or something?"

He helped himself to the raspberry. "No need."

He was such a man sometimes! "We could end up with all desserts or all meats."

His mouth quirked slightly. "That won't happen. We're supplying the nonalcoholic beverages, meat and dessert. I told everyone I'd barbecue steaks for the adults and hot dogs for the kids."

"Which means the only things left for people to bring are side dishes."

He nodded.

She bit her lower lip, what little appetite she'd had, fading.

"There's no need to stress over this, Poppy. No one is going to walk away hungry."

She met his wry gaze. "Are you sure you don't want me to try to coordinate with everyone?" So they didn't end up with all potato dishes or all baked beans.

"No. You have enough on your agenda."

"Still…" This was for him and his friends. So, even if it was sort of impromptu, she wanted it to be as nice as it could be.

Trace covered her hand with his. "Listen, these guys are just happy they're not eating MREs. Their wives and kids are happy to be with them."

Abruptly aware she hadn't even seen a guest list, Poppy said, "They're all married?"

Trace helped himself to seconds. "Or divorced. But almost all of them have kids." He smiled. "And soon we will, too."

If it all worked out, Poppy thought. They were still waiting on the final approval.

Doing her best to ignore the mounting butterflies in her tummy, Poppy checked her watch and asked, "Ready to go?"

Trace gulped the last of his coffee. "Hopefully, the third time will be the charm."

As it turned out Poppy's anxiety was all for naught. The Laramie social worker had only a few more questions for them.

Once they were answered, Mitzy sat back in her chair. "When the two of you got married, I admit I had my doubts about the validity of the union." She smiled. "Everything that's happened the past week—the seriousness with which you took these interviews, the quick way you put the nursery together, attended a Lamaze class at the hospital, and Trace's desire to return home from overseas—has made me feel otherwise."

"Actually getting transferred back to the US may take a while," Trace warned.

"I know. But just the fact you took formal action and put in a hardship request with your CO speaks volumes." Mitzy paused. "And then there's Anne Marie's opinion. After meeting with you two last weekend, she is more convinced than ever that not only are the two of you the right people to love and care for the twins, but that you are madly in love with each other and will provide a great home for them."

Except, Poppy thought uncomfortably, she and Trace had never claimed, even to each other, to harbor anything but friendship and passion.

Mitzy smiled. "So I plan to let the Stork Agency know this morning that you passed the amended home study with flying colors and you're approved."

"Great news!" Trace declared, enthused.

Poppy nodded, outwardly pleased, while inside, her private discomfort grew. She'd always prided herself on her directness. To the point that, having to parse her words felt wrong. Even to achieve a lifelong goal.

Not wanting to spoil the moment, however, or to do anything that would throw a wrench into their plans at this late date, she gave the social worker a faint smile. "So what next?"

Mitzy made a note on the pad in front of her. "We wait for Anne Marie to go into labor. Which could be anytime now."

Poppy was buffeted by yet another wave of anxiety. She reached over and took Trace's hand in hers. "What do you mean?" She relaxed only slightly even as Trace squeezed her palm reassuringly. "She isn't actually due for several more weeks!"

Mitzy closed the file. "Twins typically arrive a few weeks early. If not, doctors will induce labor to prevent complications that occur if it gets too crowded in the womb. But not to worry. Anne Marie had a doctor's appointment this morning. They did an ultrasound and everything looks fine."

"That was all good news," Trace said as he and Poppy left the building. "It means I'll definitely be Stateside when the twins are born. So how come you're not smiling?"

Because you won't be here for very long after that, Poppy thought, studying the clouds looming on the horizon. Although the day had started out sunny, it was shaping up to be a gray and gloomy afternoon.

Instructing herself to get it together, she pivoted to face her husband. "I was just thinking that, even with them coming early, you won't have much time with the babies before you have to leave." Disappointment roiled through her, mixing with the residual acid in her tummy. *And that makes my heart ache for all of us.*

He paused on the entranceway sidewalk, briefly looking caught up in the anguish of the moment, too. Broad shoulders flexing, he shrugged. "Good thing we know how to make the most of every moment then, isn't it?"

It was. For all military families. And yet, somehow this was different...

He cupped her face in his hand. "You're really sad about this, aren't you?"

Stepping back, she dragged a hand through her hair. "I'm being selfish, I know. The important thing is the kids are healthy and are going to have a good home and we're finally getting the children we have both longed for, and we've had this time, to be together, and prepare for their arrival. I do know that, Trace."

Intimacy simmered between them as they stared into each other's eyes.

"You just don't want to go it alone after they're born," Trace guessed.

You're right, Poppy thought fiercely. *I don't want to do it without you. Not anymore.* Where had that thought come from? she wondered. Especially given that this had pretty much been the plan from the beginning, at least until he had put in for the hoped-for transfer back to the continental United States.

Aware he was still waiting for her answer, she said, "I don't want you to be deprived of bonding with the twins those first few months. I know from my own sisters' kids there are so many changes, so fast." Her breath stalled halfway up her windpipe. She blinked back tears. "I don't want you to miss anything wonderful."

Trace moved in close as pedestrians passed to their left. He caught her elbow in a light, protective grasp. "It'll work out, Poppy, even if the stars don't all align and I'm not here as much as I want to be in those first few months. I'll still experience every moment through you. I'll still be their dad. Still love them right along with you," he vowed huskily.

But he might not ever love her, not in the deeply romantic way that she wished. And while she knew she could handle them going along with the status quo, she still wished she could have it all. With him.

Chapter 13

"You're still frowning," Trace said as they walked toward the parking lot.

And she shouldn't be, given the news they had just received. Unable to say why, without going back on their deal, and putting Trace in an untenable position, Poppy said the first thing that came into her head. "I was thinking about the nursery." *Not about whether or not you'll ever love me the way I'm beginning to realize I've always loved you.* She swallowed. "Had I known we had this much time…" Her brow furrowed thoughtfully. "I would have painted it before we set it up."

Trace, who had reached into his jacket pocket as if to take something out, removed his hand. "What's wrong with the color in there now?"

"It's ecru. That was fine, for an office-slash-guest

room. Very neutral and relaxing. But the walls in a nursery should be more cheerful."

He shortened his strides to match hers. "So we'll paint it."

"We're having a big party this weekend, remember?"

He shrugged his broad shoulders affably. "We still have Sunday afternoon and evening free, if you want to do it together."

She raised a cautioning hand. "Actually, we don't. Callie gave us tickets to a matinee performance of the 'Messiah' in San Antonio on Sunday. It's so spectacular I try to go every year. But if you don't want—"

He caught her hand before she could finish. "Of course I'll go with you." He tugged her closer. "Maybe we could even do a little shopping before or after."

Poppy inhaled his brisk, masculine scent. "Which is another thing…" she confessed, savoring the reassuring warmth of his touch. "I haven't even started buying gifts for my family."

He put his arm around her shoulders and winked. "Then it's a good thing we're going to the city for a concert, isn't it? Where all the stores are open extended hours. We could even stay in a hotel Sunday evening, if you want." He waggled his brows suggestively.

Despite herself, Poppy laughed.

He went in for a kiss just as his phone buzzed. Their lips touched but it went off again. And again. With a sigh, he looked at the screen, frowned and lifted it to his ear. "Hey, Mom," he said. "What's up?" A short silence. "I'm with Poppy. We just came from a meeting." Another pause. "What do you mean, what are we wearing? She has on a dress and a cardigan and looks ravishing, if I do say so myself."

He grinned as Poppy playfully punched his arm. Holding the phone out of reach, he continued in exasperation, "A sport coat and slacks... Yes. I have a tie on... Because it was an important meeting." Trace blinked. "You want us to come now?... Well, sure, I'll ask her... Thirty minutes... Fine. See you then."

He ended the call.

"What's going on?"

Trace exhaled roughly. "My mom is looking at space for a florist shop in San Angelo. She wants my opinion."

This was weird. "What do you know about commercial space?"

He smiled knowingly, sharing her bemusement. "Absolutely nothing."

"Speaking of which...isn't your mom's current beau a commercial Realtor?"

Trace put his phone away slowly. "He's going to be there, too. And, as you might have gathered, she wants you there, as well, to give *your* opinion. She'd like us all to go to lunch after."

Poppy studied the taut planes of his face. The joy she'd evidenced only a moment earlier was all but gone. "Obviously you don't approve."

He grimaced. "I think something is up that she was reluctant to tell me on the phone."

As it turned out, Poppy soon discovered, Trace was right. Bitsy was not only glowing with excitement when she greeted them, she was also wearing a sleek white-satin suit, with a white lily corsage pinned to the lapel, and sporting a rock on her left hand that could support a family of six for a year. Her beau, Donald Olson, was not only beaming, too, but he was also dressed in a very elegant wool suit.

"So what do you think?" Bitsy asked as they toured the newly refurbished space.

Trace shrugged. "It seems fine. A lot smaller than your current store in San Antonio."

Bitsy tucked her arm in Donald's. She cuddled up to him, her dreamy countenance a counterpoint to her crisp, business-like tone. "Oh, honey, I'm selling that."

Trace turned. His tone hardened suspiciously as he asked, "Why? I thought it was doing great."

Bitsy smiled and continued gazing adoringly at her beau. "It is doing great. That is why I've had a very nice offer on it. Enough to fund a trust that will in turn fund my eventual retirement."

At least that was smart, Poppy thought, given Trace's mom was nearing sixty.

Trace checked out the stockroom. "I still don't get why you'd want to come back to San Angelo. When you were living here, you were always chafing to get out and move to the city."

"I was. *Then.*"

"So what's changed?"

"This is where Donald has his business, darling. And if we're going to be married today…"

Trace braced his hands on his waist, pushing the edges of his sport coat back. "You have got to be kidding me."

She wasn't, Poppy noted as the tension level rose, right along with the acid in her too-empty stomach. Too late, she realized she should have eaten breakfast. Or at least grabbed some crackers to munch on the way here. Would have, if only she had realized how stressful this meeting would be.

Bitsy continued, in that instant looking every bit as

mulish as her only son. "We have an appointment with the justice of the peace at one-thirty this afternoon. And we'd like you and Poppy to stand up for us."

Trace narrowed his eyes at Donald. "You know my mom has been married—and divorced—eight times."

The wealthy silver-haired Realtor remained unperturbed. "This will be my fourth marriage."

Trace dragged a hand over his face. Finally he looked over at the two elders. "Which is all the more reason why the two of you should take a little time to consider this."

Bitsy continued to glow from the inside out. "I don't need to consider it, Trace. I'm in love with Donald."

"And I love Bitsy, with all my heart and soul," her beau said in return.

Trace groaned again. Emotionally, he implored, "Mom, please, don't do this."

His words fell on deaf ears. "I want to be married before Christmas. And I want you and your new wife to witness," Bitsy insisted.

"At least take the time to get a prenup," Trace said.

"We already have," she answered. "Liz Cartwright-Anderson drew mine up."

That meant, Poppy realized, his mother was well protected since Liz was the best family-law attorney around.

"And Donald's attorney drew up his."

"For the record," the older gentleman said with the shrewdness of someone who had not only earned his personal fortune, but protected it, "both are iron-clad."

Against Trace's better judgment, they witnessed the ceremony. They did not, however, join the newlyweds for lunch.

"You should not have been so hard on your mother," Poppy said as they walked back to the SUV.

"I wouldn't have been if I thought there was a chance in the world this union would last. But it won't."

Poppy thought about the way the two lovebirds had looked at each other. It had been sweet. And seemingly sincere. To the point she'd gotten tears in her eyes when the smitten couple said their vows.

However, noting the tense set of his shoulders as he slid into the driver's seat, she tried to keep her tone neutral. "How do you know?"

Trace backed out of the parking space then gave her a sideways look. "Because my mom might like this guy—a lot—and be totally infatuated with him," he said, easing into traffic, "but she doesn't really love him, at least not in any lasting way. She just doesn't like being unattached during the holidays and, as a consequence, is always buffeted by the emotional winds."

Poppy could understand that. She'd been feeling unusually sentimental this Christmas season, too. For all sorts of reasons, she thought as her stomach gurgled.

"Yes, that was me," Poppy said dryly at Trace's stunned reaction, embarrassed she still couldn't get a handle on her acid-generating-anxiety.

He asked in concern, "You didn't eat much breakfast, did you?"

Try one bite of toast. One sip of milk. "I'm fine." Although, she was starting to feel a little nauseated.

"Look, we can stop for something on the way out of town."

It seemed wrong, to refuse to sit with Bitsy and Donald and then go straight to another restaurant in town.

What if they ran into each other? "Let's just wait until we get back to Laramie. It's only half an hour."

He braked at the stoplight, letting her know with a glance it wasn't too late. "Sure?"

No. Not really. "Yes," she said.

Big mistake. No sooner had they left the town limits than her stomach began to roil. She rummaged through her purse and came up with a peppermint candy. Maybe it would help.

"We need to get them a wedding gift."

His jaw clenched. "No way."

"Trace…"

"I mean it, Poppy. I'm not supporting this."

She understood this brought up all the issues and uncertainty of his childhood. Still… "Given that you couldn't dissuade her, you could at least wish her well."

He waited until the way was clear, turned on his signal and passed a slow-moving tractor on the two-lane highway. "I know you think that I should have let my mother do whatever she was going to do without weighing in." He accelerated until he had passed it.

"I do."

"And while it may well be her decision, it always becomes my problem when it all falls apart."

Poppy caught the apprehension in his tone. "What do you mean?" As her nausea rose, she did her best to concentrate on the peppermint taste in her mouth.

Trace's hands tightened on the steering wheel. "She calls me and writes me and emails me. Constantly. Wanting to know my opinion. Is she being unreasonable? Is he? Was the marriage a mistake? Should she divorce him or let him divorce her? Do I think he could be cheating, or if he's not cheating, does it count if he is having an emotional affair with another woman or has just lost all interest in…? Well—" Trace exhaled roughly "—you get the drift."

Poppy sent him a commiserating look. "Sounds pretty awful."

"It is. Mostly because I know, even before I get one word out, that whatever I say is going to be wrong."

Poppy rummaged in her bag for another peppermint. "So just refuse to weigh in next time." She unwrapped it with trembling fingers.

Luckily, Trace's attention was focused on the road. "It's not that simple."

"And maybe," she said, sliding the mint into her mouth, "it is."

Trace had no response. Either that or he just chose not to respond. An awkward silence fell between them. Feeling more carsick with every passing moment, Poppy looked out the window and studied the decorations on the homes and ranches they passed. Trace turned on the radio. Beautiful Christmas music filled the passenger compartment. Yet the tension between them remained.

Unable to bear it, because the last thing she wanted to do was to argue with Trace—now or ever—Poppy tried one last time to help him see the situation for what it was. "Look, my parents made their fair share of mistakes. The truth is, Trace, we all do. But the one thing they taught all six of us is that you have to let go when you love someone. Let 'em make their own decisions and suffer the consequences."

"You're saying I should support her fully and let her do whatever foolish thing she wants, no matter what?"

Ignoring the pressure rising in her esophagus, Poppy nodded. "And then let your mom *own* the aftermath, as well. Without you weighing in either before, during or after." She reached over and squeezed his forearm. "It's the only way either of you will ever be happy."

"Independence…" He guessed where this was going.

Poppy gulped in air. *Please don't let me be sick.* "Has always been…always will be…key, Trace," Poppy finished determinedly. "Especially for you and me."

It wasn't just the unusual quavering of Poppy's soft voice that had him worried. Or the way she kept gulping in air. It was the color of her complexion, too. Trace pulled over to the side of the road, put the SUV in Park. And was quickly glad he had. "Are you okay? You're looking a little green."

"Actually…" One hand pressed to her mouth, Poppy unlatched her seat belt and opened the passenger door. "I could use a little air."

She stepped out into the grassy field in the middle of nowhere. Took slow, measured breaths.

Alarmed, Trace moved up beside her. He wrapped his arm around her shoulders. "Are you going to be sick?"

Poppy shut her eyes. For once she let herself lean on him. "Not…if I can help it," she gasped.

And as a few moments passed, then a few more, and her color slowly began to normalize, Trace began to breathe easier.

"Do you think you're coming down with something again?" he asked when she finally straightened.

Poppy shook off the idea. "It's just stress."

He had a hard time buying that. "I've never known

you to suffer this way before—unless something else was wrong." Like the time she'd come down with mononucleosis her first year in college. Or the day she'd lost their baby.

"I had motion sickness as a kid, all the time. It didn't matter what the mode of transportation—car, boat or plane, I usually needed Dramamine beforehand if I didn't want to upchuck on one of my sisters."

He chuckled at her wry tone. The fact she was attempting a joke must mean she was doing better. "That must have made you popular."

She moaned comically. "You have no idea."

He could tell that the crisp, cold air was helping her feel better.

"Plus," she continued on a beleaguered sigh, "I was so nervous about our meeting with Mitzy this morning I didn't want to eat much before we left, and then because my stomach was so empty, I had a touch of heartburn this morning during the actual meeting. Couple that with the lack of lunch and the occasional bumps and curves in the road..."

He knew that had all been a factor, but he still felt she was keeping something from him. Perhaps the same something that had upset her during his mother's wedding.

And Poppy obviously knew it, too, which was why she turned away from him and headed a little farther away, until she was standing next to a strand of cottonwoods. She took a few more deep, calming breaths. "Well, what do you know!" She pointed to a branch. "Mistletoe. The real deal." She fingered the glossy green leaves with the white berries admiringly. "If this isn't a sign Christmas is coming, I don't know what is."

Trace reached into his pocket. Removed his artificial sprig. "And here I thought you were becoming rather attached to mine." He waved it over her head then slowly lowered it at the same time as he dipped his head, not stopping until their mouths were oh, so close.

She held up a hand before he could kiss her. "I may be better," she murmured ruefully, "but I'm not that good. Yet."

"Then we'll save it for later." He pocketed the fake strand that had enabled him to steal a kiss wherever, whenever. "And get this—" he extricated the real sprig from the tree "—for the house and the party tomorrow."

"Your military friends are a romantic bunch, I take it?"

He noted a faint wistfulness in her low tone.

Was he disappointing her on that level? Given how often and passionately they'd made love the past few weeks, it was hard to see how.

He shrugged. "Their wives and girlfriends seem to think so."

The question was what did Poppy really think of him—as a husband? He knew she had turned out to be a spectacular wife.

Suddenly looking younger and more innocent than he could ever remember, she remarked, "A lot of pent-up masculinity beneath those uniforms."

He ran a caressing hand down her spine. "And a lot of breathtaking femininity right here." He gave her waist a squeeze.

She returned his playful smile, but the usual enthusiasm seemed to be missing from her pretty brown eyes.

Hoping it was just the physical malaise dampening her usual good spirits, he walked back to the SUV, set the mistletoe inside and returned with a bottle of water.

"Thanks." Poppy took one sip, then another.

"So why are you so anxious about the party?" he asked eventually, as she continued to study the barren Texas landscape as if it held all the answers.

Her slender shoulders stiffened. "I don't know."

Now she really was fibbing. "Yes. You do."

Another pause.

Not sure if this was the time or not—but hoping it would help her mood, which admittedly had been all over the place ever since he'd returned to the States—Trace reached into his pocket. He withdrew the small velvet box he'd been carrying around "just in case" all day.

"What's this?" she asked in surprise.

Trace put it in her hand. "Open it and see."

Poppy flipped the lid.

She stared at the golden locket nestled in the satin folds. "It's a push present," Trace explained. "With room for photos of both kids. I think you normally give it to the new mom after she delivers the baby, but I figured that might not be appropriate, given Anne Marie's feelings and all, so... I was waiting until we got the word our adoption had final approval."

Poppy continued to stare at the gift, her lower lip trembling.

She had never reacted with this much ambivalence to anything he had ever given her before. "Is this not the right thing?" he asked gruffly, remembering Mrs. Brantley at the jewelry store—who'd been urging him to go with diamonds—hadn't been all that impressed with his choice, either.

Poppy shook her head, letting him know he was on the wrong track once again. And then promptly burst into tears. And from the looks of it, they weren't happy ones.

Chapter 14

Poppy prided herself on the fact that she almost never cried. Never mind "ugly" cried. But she was certainly doing it now. The sobs coming out of her sounded as if she'd just lost her best friend. And in a weird way, she had.

This hasty marriage of theirs had upset the dynamics of practically everything.

"Would you have preferred something else?" Trace persisted.

Poppy blotted her face with the back of her free hand. "The necklace is fine. It's b-b-beautiful, in fact." And so thoughtful, which was just like him, damn it.

"Then why are you crying?" Trace asked gently.

Poppy shrugged.

"There has to be a reason."

There was, but it was nothing she could say without

heightening the tension between them and making them both feel worse.

"There isn't," she lied, her lower lip still quivering with telltale emotion.

He stroked his hand over her back, rubbing in deep, soothing circles "Then how about you hazard a guess?"

How could she tell him watching his mother marry someone for all the wrong reasons had triggered an inner unease in her about their own situation that she had yet to shake? And that this gift he had just given her, out of duty and obligation, only made their situation seem even more disingenuous. Because the popular axiom was right: marriage changes everything.

But even if that's how she really and truly felt, how could she bring herself to admit it—when she had promised him from the get-go that getting hitched would change absolutely nothing between them? When she knew he still felt the same way he always had? It was only she who was changing. Wanting, needing, hoping, for more.

Aware he deserved some explanation, however, Poppy struggled to staunch the flow of tears. "It's everything," she choked out. The fact she *almost* had everything she had ever wanted. The knowledge that she *never would* have everything she had dreamed about, too.

"And it's nothing…" She gestured inanely.

He tucked his thumb beneath her chin and lifted her face to his. "Come on, Poppy. Level with me."

Still holding the jewelry box in one hand, Poppy rubbed a hand over her face with the other. She pushed away from him, away from the scrutiny.

"Okay, then, if you must know. I've never been newly married, never been about to adopt a child—never mind twins—before!" *Never spent so much time with you at one clip, loving every minute of it, while knowing at the same time that soon it will all be gone, because I'll have to say goodbye to you again for at least six months. Maybe more...*

He steadied her with a hand beneath her elbow then stepped back slightly. Compassion and concern glimmering in his eyes, he asked, "Are you that freaked out about caring for the twins by yourself?"

Yes. And that scared her, too. For years now she had been certain she could do it all on her own. Without even her family for backup. The same way she had accomplished everything else of merit and value in her life.

Now, only to find...maybe she wasn't so strong and so independent, after all. And that sucked.

As Trace continued to study her, an intimate silence fell between them.

With effort, Poppy pulled herself together. She pivoted, so he could help her put on the locket. "I'm sure my mood swings will stabilize once the babies are actually born."

They would have to, she thought, swallowing around the parched feeling in her throat as he fastened the necklace.

"I mean, with twenty to twenty-four diaper changes a day, and at least twelve feedings, I won't have time for all this self-defeating anxiety. I'll just be in emergency mode."

An inscrutable expression crossed his handsome face and he gave her a look that had her pulse jumping. "Which is likely the problem."

Now he was seeing her the way she had never wanted him to see her. Weak. And needy.

She exhaled in frustration. She needed to get a grip. "Like I told you before, I will have help," she said slowly, reminding them both there was no need to panic, even if she had already done so, at least a little.

She touched the locket as though it were a talisman.

"But what if it's not enough?" he asked, his brows pulling together in concern.

"It will be, Trace. I'm already getting emails from the in-home baby nurse agency my mom and dad recommended. And since I'll be living at their home temporarily once you head back overseas, I'll have a ton of family support. So it really will be all right."

These were, after all, solvable problems.

And if she had to accept that while she might be falling in love with Trace, he would only ever see her as his life and family partner, lover and best friend, well, then, so be it. The deep affection they felt for each other, and their mutual devotion to building a family together, would be enough to make her and the kids happy.

It would have to be.

There was no other choice.

Trace had heard from other airmen how their wives sometimes fell apart when they were about to be deployed overseas. It usually sprang from the fact they had kids and being the sole parent on duty could feel like too much over time. But sometimes it was just the fact that the wives got lonely. And felt abandoned. Or needed more.

But that wasn't Poppy. It never had been.

She had always weathered his subsequent sign-ups and absences just fine.

Always resisted putting unreasonable demands on

him. Hell, really any demands at all. That was what he had liked about their relationship. They were both free to pursue their dreams, and just as free to come together whenever they could.

Poppy's problems had always been hers to fix. Just as his had been his to rectify.

And that had worked for them just fine.

So maybe they should go back to more of a separation of lives that had worked so well in the past? And not keep trying to merge the two.

"Look, we can cancel tomorrow's party, if you like," Trace said quietly, taking her hand and leading her back to the SUV.

Poppy seemed clearly affronted by even the suggestion. "No way. I'm looking forward to meeting more of your friends and their families."

He slid open the passenger-side door and helped her inside. "If you're not up to it—"

She settled into the seat. "I had some air. I'm fine."

But she reclined her seat slightly, turned down the temp on her side of the vehicle and closed her eyes the moment the SUV started moving.

Fortunately they only had another fifteen minutes to go.

When they reached her bungalow, she evidenced a determined cheerfulness that was almost as scary as her sudden burst of tears had been.

But, knowing women who were about to give birth—and in a way that was exactly what was about to happen for Poppy via adoption—she was entitled to her moodiness.

As the "dad" in the situation, it was his job to make

sure she was physically comfortable and to allay those emotions.

He headed straight for the kitchen. Got out the chicken soup he'd purchased the day before and slid it into a saucepan to heat.

"Monte Carlo or plain grilled cheese?"

"Plain grilled cheese."

He got out the ingredients and assembled two sandwiches while she lingered nearby. He was glad to see the healthy color coming back into her face.

She released an exasperated sigh when she noticed him staring at her. "You know, you don't have to wait on me."

So she'd said before. Could he help it if he felt compelled to do so? Enjoyed doing so, more than either of them ever could have imagined?

He watched her take off the cardigan she'd thrown over her dress and loop it over the back of a chair. Her dress was sleeveless, which was good—it gave him a nice view of her incredibly sexy shoulders and toned arms. The locket looked nice on her, too, very momish and right.

Figuring he owed it to her to take some of the pressure off, however, he pointed out calmly, "And *you* don't have to throw me a party tomorrow."

"Touché." A slow smile tilted the corners of her luscious lips. She seemed to know instinctively this was one battle she wouldn't win. He was going to take care of her right now, and that was that. Best of all, she was going to let him.

"But seriously…back to the party," Poppy continued with a smile. "We are having it. So. What can I do to facilitate it?"

He gestured at the table. "Sit down and make a final list since I am guessing you're better at organizing social gatherings than me."

She rolled her eyes, grabbed a pen and paper. "No argument there."

He laughed, as he was meant to, and slid the sandwiches into the skillet. The buttered bread sizzled as it hit the pan. "Paper plates, cups, even disposable silverware are all fine. We don't need tablecloths…"

She made a disgruntled face. "We're having tablecloths."

"We can have the disposable paper kind, then."

He was overruled yet again. "We're having cloth," she said firmly. "In fact I'll use my Christmas ones. But disposable everything else will be fine."

He turned the sandwiches. "You sound like a wife."

"And you sound like a husband."

They exchanged smiles.

"Do you have any coolers or anything to put drinks in?" he asked, liking the way it felt, simply hanging out with her. Better yet, enacting a life with her.

Poppy propped her chin on her fist. "I've got three large stainless-steel washtubs we can fill with ice and drinks."

Trace poured the soup into bowls. "Great." He plated the sandwiches and brought their very late lunch to the table.

Even as they ate, she began to fade. To the point that by the time she had finished, she could barely keep her eyes open. He studied the faint shadows beneath her eyes. Reaching over, he brushed his knuckles along her cheek. "You need a nap."

She flushed the way she always did when he fussed

over her. "Is there mistletoe involved in there any-where?"

He appreciated the invitation to dally. "Maybe later." He growled playfully. "For now, all you get is sleep."

For a moment he thought she was going to argue. Stay there and say they had to do dishes, something. Instead she put her napkin aside and rose, hand extended, her slender shoulders slumping with exhaustion. "I'll go," she relented. "But only if you sleep, too."

He went with her up the stairs. Moments later, their shoes were off and they were on the bed. She turned onto her side, he snuggled up behind her. Within seconds, she was fast asleep.

He waited a few more minutes then carefully extricated himself. Covering her with a blanket, he pressed a gentle kiss to her forehead, stood looking down at her.

He hadn't seen her this vulnerable since she'd lost their baby, and a good portion of her fertility as a result.

Tenderness wafted through him, along with a fresh flood of guilt. Even though she'd put on a brave front earlier, he knew she was struggling with emotions she couldn't—wouldn't—detail.

He wasn't really sure what to do.

Yet he knew he was responsible for all of this some-how.

And that in turn made the idea of leaving her again all the harder.

Poppy woke to total darkness.

She was alone, on her bed. Necklace on. Still in the dress she'd worn earlier in the day.

Trace was nowhere to be found.

Feeling disoriented, she turned on the bedside lamp,

sat up and swung her legs over the side of the bed. A glance at the clock said it was nearly 9:00 p.m., which meant she had been asleep for approximately five hours.

And she was hungry again.

Go figure.

Still feeling a little unsettled, she walked downstairs. Trace was sitting at the dining room table, his laptop in front of him. Seeing him sitting there in her dining room, in jeans and a loose-fitting shirt, his sandy-blond hair all rumpled, it was as if Christmas had come early.

And often.

Grateful to have him there, in a way she had been too foolish to be earlier, she smiled.

She'd love to go to him and distract him with a hot and steamy kiss. But she could see from the logo on the screen that he was doing something related to the air force. Looked like paperwork of some kind. Official business.

That meant he was entitled to his privacy.

He turned, shifting so she could no longer see the screen. "Hey, sleepyhead."

Deciding her initial instinct was right—he really didn't want her to see what he was viewing—she moved out of eyesight and into the kitchen. "Sorry I disappeared on you like that." She opened the fridge and took out the milk, thinking a glass of the icy-cold liquid might ease the gnawing feeling in her stomach. "I didn't mean to nap so long."

"I'm glad you did," Trace called over his shoulder. He typed in a few more words. "Give me one second and I'll be done."

Poppy nodded and reopened the fridge. There was plenty of food inside, but it all required cooking. And this late, she really wasn't up for it. Maybe a bowl of cereal?

She went to the pantry, perused the shelves. They had a few wheat flakes left—but not enough for even one serving. She had to remember the next time she went to the market: Trace liked cold cereal every bit as much as she did. "Have you had dinner?" she called over her shoulder.

"No."

"Hungry?"

He was still typing. "Starving."

As was she. "Any ideas?"

He shut the lid on his laptop. Flashing a sexy grin, he strolled over to join her. "Pizza. With everything. Ice-cold beer. Maybe a slice of New York style cheesecake?"

Happy things were normalizing between them yet again, she retorted, "Sounds good. And we're in luck because Mack's Pizza is open until midnight on weekends."

He took her by the hand and led her to the spacious laundry room on the other side of the kitchen. She blinked at what she saw. "Wow. You've been busy."

Trace moved behind her to allow her an unobstructed view. Wrapping his arms around her waist, he tugged her against him. "You know there is practically nothing in this town you can't get delivered or ordered in advance?"

The warmth of his body was like the sweetest cocoon. She relaxed against the hardness of his chest. "That's because no one has very far to go." She studied the neatly stacked items. "I see you got all the beverages and party supplies."

"I also ordered an assortment of Christmas goodies from the Sugar Love bakery. The grocery is holding all the meats, condiments and rolls. I'll pick both orders up tomorrow, when I get ice."

Smart. Poppy turned to face him. Winked. "I think you may have a future as a personal assistant. To me."

With a wicked gleam in his eye, he stroked a hand through her hair, lowered his head to just above hers. "Oh, I could certainly do that…"

Poppy shook her head in amusement. "Yeah, right," she murmured, going up on tiptoe to kiss him.

He kissed her back, just as fervently.

Finally they broke apart. "I'm sorry I was such a basket case earlier."

He nuzzled the sensitive skin of her neck. "Ah, but you're *my* basket case."

Contentment swept through her.

He grinned. "Too corny?"

She shook her head. "Cute. Like you."

His gaze drifted over her. "Now that's corny."

She laughed. "Then we're even."

He kissed her again, briefly this time. Then pulled back.

"I was serious about the pizza."

"That's good." Poppy went to find her phone and the takeout menu she kept in a kitchen drawer. "Because I'm starving, too."

"Eat in or go out?"

Maybe it was selfish, but she wanted Trace all to herself, at least for tonight. And if they went to Mack's, everyone they knew who walked in would be stopping by to chat with them. "In. If that's okay with you?"

He nodded, abruptly looking no more eager to leave their little bubble of happiness than she was. "Perfect."

* * *

"Your home is just gorgeous, Poppy," Hallie Benton said once the party had gotten under way.

All the other military wives gathered in her kitchen, agreed.

"Thanks." She smiled. From her vantage point, she could see the men in the backyard, grilling, swapping stories and watching the kids, some of whom were playing freeze tag, others a bean-bag-toss game that had been set up.

"It's such a shame you're going to have to give it up," Fran Jones remarked.

Cara Cesaro arranged the beautiful array of homemade side dishes and salads on the buffet. "Not necessarily."

Everyone turned to the oldest member of the group.

"You and Trace could rent it. But you'd have to find a tenant who would love it and cherish it as much as you obviously do. Otherwise…" She shook her head.

A murmur of worry went through the group.

Linda Mayes stacked napkins. "At least Trace has put in a hardship request to be stationed in the continental United States."

Hallie shrugged. "They all do after a while or…get divorced."

Fran waved at one of her children in the yard. "Luckily, Trace is getting wise fast." She swung back around. "Now that he's finally married and ready to settle down."

"What are you going to do with your business?" Dawn Huff asked Poppy, cutting a large tray of cornbread into squares.

"Duh," Linda said. "She'll have to sell. Or move operations, I guess."

Cara sliced lemons for the iced tea. "Won't that be hard? Given how much pilots move around? You'd barely get set up one place, when you'd have to pick up and go somewhere else?"

Everyone looked at her.

Poppy knew there was only one way to shut this down. The truth. "Actually..." She paused. "The twins and I aren't planning to follow Trace around. He's going to continue to come to us instead."

A shocked silence fell. "Do you really think that's smart?" Hallie finally asked.

Fran was skeptical of their plan, too. "You're a military wife now. Military wives—good ones, anyway—are all about the careers and needs of their military husbands."

Poppy could see that that was true of the women gathered around her. Their devotion to their husbands and families was iron-clad. It had to be. But she and Trace didn't have just any marriage.

Linda said gently, "Our husbands love the fact that we support them one hundred and ten percent. Our willingness to put them and their service to our country first is what makes our relationships so successful."

"And if you and Trace are serious about starting off on the right foot," Dawn added firmly, "you should at least consider doing this for Trace, too."

Two weeks ago Poppy would have thought these words were heresy. There was no way she would have even considered it. But now that they had actually lived together as man and wife, she was beginning to feel differently.

The question was, did he? And how could she even ask without putting him on the spot?

Luckily, she had no more time to worry over it, as Trace and his buddies flowed into the kitchen, en masse. Poppy could tell instantly by the mischievous looks on all their faces that something was up.

Something fun.

"What have you-all been up to?"

Grins, all around.

"Trace has been telling us the secret to having a happy marriage," Paul Huff said, taking his wife, Dawn, in his arms.

Linda Mayes laughed as her husband, Jack, stepped behind her and cradled her close. "Oh, he has, has he?" she said skeptically.

Randy Cesaro tucked Cara against his side.

"Appears he's become quite the expert in just a few short weeks."

Tucker Jones took his wife in one arm, and shoved his other in the pocket of his jeans. Grinning boyishly, he looked at Trace. "So, Lieutenant," he drawled, using Poppy's pet name for her new husband. "Do you want to demonstrate the secret of your success? Or shall we all do it together?"

Poppy's heart pounded as Trace advanced on her, a predatory glint in his hazel eyes. "Oh, I think, in this case, it's one for all and all for one. This being the season to be merry and all that."

The women exchanged perplexed looks. Everyone turned to Poppy. "I have no clue," she declared.

Until Trace pulled a very familiar cluster of leaves and berries from his pocket, that was. He dangled the mistletoe over her head. "Perhaps this will bring it all back," he said.

Poppy gasped. "You're not... really..."

"Oh, yeah," he said, lowering his mouth to hers, where he bestowed a tender lingering kiss, at the same time all the other guys did the same with their wives. "I am. Because if there's one thing every serviceman or woman knows, it's how to appreciate the ones we love."

Poppy could see that was true.

What she didn't know was if Trace loved her like these guys all obviously romantically cared about their wives, or if he loved her in more of a familial, lifelong best friend kind of way. And if it was only the last, did it really matter, when he made her—and everyone else around them— feel so damn good all the time?

"What were you and the other wives talking about so intently this evening?" Trace asked after everyone had left.

Poppy would have liked to have something—anything—to occupy herself with, but the truth was there wasn't much to do since everyone had pitched in to help with the cleanup before they had left.

She moved out into the backyard. The day had been unusually warm. The evening was just as mild. Although in the distance she could see clouds moving in, obscuring the stars. As the breeze wafted over her, Poppy pulled her sweater closer around her. "Everyone was giving me advice on how to be a good military wife."

Looking as relaxed and content as he'd been with his friends, Trace checked the temperature of the coals and put the cover on the grill. "Well, not to worry. You are one."

She'd like to think so.

Poppy hovered near enough she could see the expression on his face. The lights from inside the house bathed them in a soft yellow glow, at odds with the darkness of the night. She wasn't sure why, but she felt like she needed to test him on this. "They all said I should pack up and move whenever you do."

A muscle flexed in his jaw. "I would never ask you to do that, Poppy," he returned gruffly. "You know that."

But what if I would? she wondered.

He came even closer, inundating her with his brisk masculine scent. Masculine satisfaction radiated from his eyes. "I like you just the way you are." He took her all the way in his arms. Determination tautening the rugged planes of his face, he said in that gruff-tender voice she loved, "Don't let anyone else tell you otherwise."

He lowered his head and captured her mouth in a kiss that had her senses spinning and her heart soaring. And then he deepened the kiss even more, reminding her that he knew what she wanted and needed better than anyone, even when she would have preferred he didn't.

She moaned; the possessive feel of his arms around her robbing her of the will to resist. And then she was kissing him back, just as passionately, even as he guided her into the house. Through the downstairs. Up to their bed.

Her pulse jumped as he lifted the veil of her hair and pressed light, searing kisses along the nape of her neck to the V of her sweater. Already feeling the dampness between her legs, and the desire pounding through her, she brought his lips back to hers. Their tongues mated until her whole body was alive, quivering with urgent sensations. She pressed her body erotically against his. Whenever they were together this way, she felt so many things. Wonder. Passion. Need. Yearning. He made her feel completely and truly alive in a way only he could.

Hands moving along the buttons of his shirt, she

opened the edges. Revealing the hard ridges and taut, broad planes of his shoulders and chest. His skin was satiny smooth, over it a mat of golden-brown hair that covered his pecs and arrowed downward to the goody trail. She smiled, exploring the warm hardness with both hands.

He stepped back, amusement flickering in his eyes. "You just can't resist me, can you?"

Slanting his lips over hers, his hands roved beneath the hem of her sweater, over her ribs, to her breasts.

She yielded to the way his hands swept over her curves, molding and exploring, defining and weighing the jutting nipples and gentle slopes. Desire trembled inside her, making her belly feel weightless, soft.

"I don't want to resist you," she whispered back, letting her hands fall to his fly. "Never have." She eased the zipper down and slid her hands inside. "Never will…" She found his erection, hot and urgent. Her heart pounded. They were practically combusting and they'd barely started.

He gave her a look that promised this evening would be every bit as memorable as she wanted it to be.

"When you say things like that it drives me wild," he growled, easing off her sweater and bra, even as she pushed his pants down.

His shirt came off next.

Then her jeans and panties.

He kissed her again as they lay on the bed. She surrendered to his every kiss and caress, burying her hands in his hair as he slid down her body and sent her into a frenzy of wanting. And then he was nudging her thighs apart with his knee, settling between her legs, sliding even lower. She cried out as he claimed her, touching her and kissing, taking her to new heights and depths, exploring every nuance of desire, until there was no more holding back, no more waiting, only the hot, wonderful, quivering sensation as he completely rocked her world.

He waited until her pulsing stopped then moved upward yet again, taking her legs and wrapping them around his waist.

"That's it," he whispered as their bodies melded. "Open for me."

She was suffused with sweet, boneless pleasure.

He surged deeper still. "Take all of me…"

For a moment Poppy didn't think it was going to be possible, not when he was this aroused, but then he slid home yet again, moving one arm beneath her and lifting her hips. With a soft, giving moan, she arched into him, letting her body do for him, with the most sensual part of her, what he had already done for her.

The connection left her feeling deliciously distraught.

She surged again, and again, and again.

Restless now. Needing. Wanting. Holding him tightly, she kissed him more and more rapturously as the two of them rocked together, offering each other refuge, until they were locked in an explosion of lust and feeling unlike either of them had ever known.

And it was only when they slowly came back to earth that Poppy remembered the question she'd asked.

Should she follow him? Just pick up and move wherever the military sent him?

He'd said no.

His lovemaking just now said yes.

But what was the real answer? And how would she ever find the nerve to pursue the matter further without wrecking what they already had?

Chapter 15

"I thought you were going to go into the office for a while when we got back, to catch up on email and return client calls," Trace told Poppy on Monday afternoon when they pulled into the driveway of her bungalow.

Relaxed from their day-and-a-half trip to San Antonio, Poppy got out of the SUV and headed for the cargo area. "That was the original plan." She lifted out the shopping bags containing Christmas presents for all her nieces and nephews, as well as a few things for their own soon-to-be-delivered little ones. "But then I got to thinking on the drive back that the babies really could be born any day..."

His arms full, Trace accompanied her up the steps. "Mitzy said when you called her it was likely to be another week before doctors induced labor."

Poppy unlocked the door. "Assuming she doesn't go

into labor naturally in the meantime. Which Mitzy told us was also a very real possibility."

They went back for one final trip, Poppy carrying more presents, Trace their overnight bags. They set everything down in the foyer. He helped her off with her coat then dispensed with his. Taking her by the hand, he led her into the living room and settled beside her on the sofa.

"Does it still bother you that we were never able to get you pregnant?" Draping his arm along the sofa back, he pulled her into the curve of his body. "At least without resorting to artificial means?"

Poppy basked in his warmth and strength. "Things happen the way they are meant to happen, Trace." She lifted his hand and kissed his knuckles. "I really believe that."

He turned her hand and kissed the inside of her wrist. "So do I. And it doesn't answer my question," he said in that low, easy tone of his.

Poppy wanted to tell him the truth, but what was the point when he couldn't do anything to fix it? They had made love so many times over the years, all the while hoping she would conceive the child she hoped for. And she hadn't.

Yet she knew she owed him at least part of the truth; the part that wouldn't hurt him. "If wishes were reality, I would have loved to have your baby inside me." She met his gaze without hesitation or resignation. "But it didn't happen. And instead…" She smiled, genuinely happy about this. "Here we are, about to adopt twins." The smile spread from her heart outward. "And when they finally get here, they are going to fill our lives with so much joy that the fact they weren't in my tummy for nine months is going to be completely inconsequential.

"Which is why," Poppy took a deep, enervating breath, "we really need to redo the nursery before the babies get here."

Trace frowned. "I thought we were just going to paint the walls."

As she snuggled closer to him, she breathed in his scent, realizing all over again how amazing he smelled. She would miss this when he was gone. "Well, I was thinking we might want to redo the linens, too. Once we get the wall color looking exactly right."

He raked a hand through his sandy-blond hair. "You're serious."

She wrinkled her nose playfully. "I *am* an interior designer."

"Don't remind me!" he moaned good-naturedly.

She sobered. "I just want this to be perfect."

Briefly, he looked worried, which was definitely not her intent. "Or as perfect as it can be," she amended quickly.

He flashed her an easy grin. "It's okay. The guys warned me on Saturday you'd be nesting."

Pulling away, Poppy propped her hands on her hips. "Really."

He lifted his shoulders in an affable shrug. "While you were getting your advice, I was getting a few tips on how to be a good husband. And one of the things I was told—repeatedly, I might add—was that we would be a whole lot happier if I would just cede control. Let you make all the decisions on the domestic front."

She took the news with the amusement with which

it was delivered. "And here I thought chauvinism was dead."

"Was that an insult or a compliment?" he asked, dead-pan. "I can't tell."

Poppy laughed despite herself. Reluctantly she stood. Their bedroom antics the night before had left her in serious need of a nap.

A fact Trace noticed, despite the fact she somehow managed to stifle the yawn rising in her throat.

"Just give me the paint swatch and I'll go down to the hardware store," he offered, rising.

Poppy hedged. "I can't."

He gave her an odd look. "Why not?"

"Because I need to actually put paint on a piece of whiteboard and look at it under different lights to even know which shades I want to try."

"Which shades?" he echoed, aghast. "How many are you planning to look at?"

"Ah. Eight. Maybe nine. I'll narrow it down from there." She raised a hand before he could protest. "That is why I need to get the paint samples right now. So I'll have plenty of time to study them before we paint on Thursday."

He walked with her to the door, all lazy, confident male. "So what can I do?"

"Disassemble the cribs."

Another long, thoughtful pause. "You do remember how long those took to put together, right?"

Unfortunately, yes, she did. But… "There's no room in there to paint with the cribs in there, so…" She gave him a sweet, cajoling look that promised she would make it up to him later. "If you wouldn't mind?"

Reading her mind, he returned her sexy smile. "You go get the paint swatches. I'll follow orders here."

If only their domestic bliss could continue more than a few weeks. Wistfully, she warned, "I could get used to this."

He gave her a playful swat on the derriere. "Better go now, woman, while the going is good!" He pulled her to him and planted one on her. "Otherwise, we might find ourselves beneath the mistletoe. Again."

Poppy was tempted to stay and let him put the moves on her, but knowing the hardware store had the best paint in town, and they closed at six, had her hurrying out to her minivan.

It took longer than she expected.

When she returned, her cousin Will's truck, with the McCabe Charter Air Service logo on the side, was parked in her driveway.

Hoping he wasn't stealing her husband for another out-of-town mission—she knew it was selfish but she really wanted Trace mostly to herself during the remaining fourteen days they had left—Poppy grabbed the bag with the paint samples and brushes then hurried up the walk.

As she let herself in, she could hear the sounds of furniture being moved around, and deep male voices wafting down the stairs. "That sounds great," Will said amiably. "In the meantime, I had the sense the last time I saw you, that you were restless."

Was he?

Guilt tightened around Poppy's heart. The last thing she had ever wanted to be was a ball and chain...

"It's true, I've never liked taking extensive leave," she heard Trace admit.

Poppy battled her disappointment, not really surprised.

Since Trace was military through and through.

"—wondering if you might fill in for us and take a few more flights on an as-needed basis. Seems the stomach flu that was going around, has a wicked boomerang effect that goes with it. Just when you think you're over it," Will observed lightly, as their steps grew closer overhead, "you're not."

No kidding, Poppy thought, thinking about all the acid indigestion she had been having since she'd been hit with her brief foray of stomach virus.

"Yeah." Trace said as he appeared at the top of the stairs, carrying several parts of one crib. His back to her, he continued. "Poppy had that same experience last week."

"Anyway, thus far we've been able to handle being short-staffed. But I was hoping that if we do need you, that— Poppy! Hey. I didn't know you were here." Will gave her an easy grin. Both men came down the stairs, carrying dissembled sections of the cribs.

That's because I was busy eavesdropping. Again, Poppy thought guiltily. What was wrong with her? She usually didn't have to resort to listening in on other people's conversations. She just asked people what she wanted to know outright. So why was she suddenly so insecure?

Aware both men were looking at her, Poppy forced herself to smile as if nothing was out of the ordinary. "I just walked in." Well, almost.

Will turned to Trace, still waiting for an answer.

As usual, her husband was a good guy. "If you need me before the twins are born, of course I'll be happy to help out." Trace stacked the crib parts neatly in a corner of the living room. "But after that, I can't do it. I'll be needed here until I have to head back to base."

A father himself, Will understood. "Thanks. Appreciate it." He shook hands with Trace. "Poppy." Her cousin gave her a familial hug then headed out.

Silence fell between Poppy and Trace.

Suddenly she wondered what else had been said between the two men. Had they been talking about Trace's recent request to be reassigned Stateside? An ex-navy pilot, Will knew how difficult it was to leave the service. But he had done so to be closer to family. Had he been counseling Trace to do the same? Or was that even more wishful thinking on her part?

Poppy wondered, aware all over again how much of a concession Trace had already made. When she'd made... exactly none.

So what did that say about her?

Trace moved closer. "You okay? You look a little pale."

She felt odd all of a sudden. Kind of woozy and nauseous. And just plain weary to the bone. Nerves again? Or the wicked boomerang from the stomach flu?

Feeling as though she had appeared weak in front of her new husband all too often the past few weeks, Poppy squared her shoulders and picked up the bag. She reminded herself she was a strong, independent woman. Always had been, always would be. She did not need Trace to take care of her. "I'm fine." She headed quickly up the stairs.

Once in the nursery, seeing there was still a second crib to be dissembled, she set down the bag from the paint store. Determined to do her fair share, and not put this all on Trace, she grabbed a screwdriver.

"You don't have to do that," he said from behind her.

Unable to locate the screws along the bottom rail, Poppy hunkered down so her head was almost even with her knees, and attempted to look upward. Finding what she wanted, she reached beneath the crib and, still squatting, pushed the end of the Phillips screwdriver into the head of the screw. "I really want to get the swatches up while we still have some daylight left." She grimaced, as the tightened screw refused to budge. She shifted positions awkwardly, tried again, failed.

"Here." Trace took her by the shoulders and, when she still didn't obey, guided her masterfully upright. A little too quickly, given the way her head abruptly began to spin.

"Poppy?" he said sharply.

Oh, Lord, she was going to faint.

Or puke.

Or something.

"Here. Sit down." He shoved the ottoman aside and pushed her into the glider rocker. "Put your head between your knees."

Poppy moaned as the seat of the chair moved like the deck of a pitching ship.

"Stay that way."

She did.

Trace hunkered down in front of her, his handsome face taut with concern. "Better now?" he asked.

Marginally. "Yes."

He tucked her hair behind her ear, ran a gentle hand over the nape of her neck. "You still look awful."

"Thanks. So much." And she still felt as though she

was going to either faint or puke, she wasn't sure which. Maybe both.

Another moment passed.

To her mortification, nothing got any better.

Grimacing, Trace stood. Hand beneath her elbow, he steered her to her feet. "We're going to the emergency room."

As if she wasn't humiliated enough. "No. We're not," Poppy declared even as her knees wobbled treacherously.

Noticing, Trace wrapped his arm around her waist and tucked her close to his side. "Listen to me, Poppy. You can't afford to be sick—with anything—with those twins on the way." His manner every bit as firm and authoritative as his voice, he slipped his arm beneath her knees and shifted her into his arms. Resolutely, he headed for the stairs. "So we're taking you to the hospital and having you seen by a doctor. And that's that."

As much as Poppy wanted to argue, she knew Trace was right. If she were harboring any germs she needed to get rid of them, lest she unwittingly infect the newborn babies soon to be in their care.

That didn't mean she didn't still feel a little foolish when she was taken to a patient exam room and asked to put on a gown. "The crazy thing is, I feel completely fine now,' she told the nurse taking her medical history.

So fine, she hoped that her parents—who were likely busy with scheduled patients of their own—didn't get wind of the fact she was here and decide to come down to see her.

"Well, it could be that stomach bug," the nurse said. "People are having a lot of trouble shaking it entirely. But we'll have the doctor come in to examine you."

She took Poppy's vitals. "In the meantime, we'll run a blood test to see what that turns up."

A quick minute later she exited, vial in hand. Leaving Trace and Poppy alone.

He stood next to the gurney she'd laid on, his big hand clasping hers. Poppy tried not to think what it would be like if he were around all the time, taking care of her, and vice versa. Aware she really could start relying on him, in a way that wasn't healthy given his chosen profession, she joked ruefully, "We have to quit meeting like this. With me ill and you the big, strong, military man rushing in to save the day."

He chuckled, looking as relieved as she felt to see her wooziness had passed. He rubbed the pad of his thumb across her lower lip. "Is that how you see me?" he asked her tenderly, his gaze roving her face. "A military man?"

And a husband and a lover and a friend, and now the father of the children they were about to adopt, too. "Isn't it how you see yourself?" she asked curiously.

The door opened before he could answer.

A young female resident doctor Poppy had never met before entered. The tall, thin blonde introduced herself as Dr. Keller. She looked through the notes on the computerized medical records on her iPad. "First of all, do you want your husband to be in here for the exam? Because if you would be more comfortable, he doesn't have to have access to either the exam or the results."

Poppy was familiar with health privacy laws.

They were how she had kept her previous miscarriage and emergency surgery from her family. Although she was beginning to think it was time she rectified that, too. Just in case another health crisis came up and Trace wasn't here.

"He can be with me. And you have permission to share any medical information with my husband."

How weird it felt to say that.

Dr. Keller handed Poppy a paper to sign, stating just that. When she had done so, the physician went back to the information gathered by the nurse. "I see you had an ovary and a fallopian tube removed years ago as a result of an ectopic pregnancy. There were complications and the tube burst…"

"Yes, that's correct."

Dr. Keller asked a few more questions about Poppy's efforts to get pregnant since. That, Poppy admitted, had been without any artificial fertility treatments, and unfruitful. She also asked about her periods—which had always been unpredictable and irregular. Extremely heavy one time, barely there the next.

"When was your last cycle?"

"Somewhere between Halloween and Thanksgiving."

"Any cramping or unusual spotting since?"

Poppy shook her head.

Dr. Keller asked Poppy to slide down to the end of the table and put her feet in the stirrups.

"What did the blood results show?" Poppy asked.

"We're still waiting on them." While Trace stood at the head of the table, holding her hand, the doctor examined Poppy's pelvic area. "Let me know if anything hurts," she said.

Nothing did.

"Well…hmm." Dr. Keller frowned. "Let's do an ultrasound to see if that tells us anything."

Poppy flushed.

"It's nothing to be nervous about," the doctor told her soothingly.

"I know. I've had one before." She was just beginning to feel like a hypochondriac, with her dizziness and the nausea gone and nothing at all apparently turning up in the physical exam. What if this was all some sort of psychosomatic episode, she thought miserably as the nurse came in to assist with the next test.

Sensing how nervous she was, Trace continued to hold her hand as the sheet covering her lower half was pushed to just above her pubic bone, her hospital gown lifted to just beneath her breasts. Cool gel was spread across her abdomen in advance of the wand.

Abruptly, on the viewing screen, they could see the fluid wavy image of the ultrasound.

Dr. Keller began to smile as she moved the wand with precision over Poppy's abdomen. "Aha! See this…" She pointed.

Poppy blinked. And blinked again.

Her throat went dry. "Is that—?"

"A baby." Dr. Keller laughed out loud. "It sure is! Looks to be about three and a half…almost four months along."

That meant when she and Trace were together in September…

"And look here," Dr. Keller announced with even more enthusiasm. "Right beside her is *another* little girl!"

Another? Poppy could barely wrap her mind around the first bit of news.

Trace looked equally gob-smacked.

"I'm pregnant?" she breathed.

Beside her, Trace began to grin from ear to ear.

"With twin girls."

* * *

The next few minutes were filled with joy. Shock. Disbelief. More joy. And every other emotion under the sun. Trace and Poppy hugged each other and cried and hugged each other again.

But by the time they got back to her house, still trying to absorb the news, another even more unsettling reality had settled in. Poppy shrugged off her coat.

"Trace. What are we going to do about Anne Marie's twins?"

He tensed; his eyes wary.

She rushed on, twisting her hands in front of her. "We're planning to adopt them!"

Trace nodded, maddeningly poker-faced.

"But if I'm going to have twins of my own—*our* own—in another six months…" She shook her head miserably, doing the math. "That would be *four* newborns in six months…and with you gone…" Her heart lurched, the pain of his leaving like a physical blow. "Is it fair to the first set of twins?"

Again, he gave her nothing.

Just stood there, watching, waiting.

Cautious. Way too cautious.

Poppy edged closer, searching his eyes for some flicker of emotion, some sign that he was feeling just as overwhelmed as she was.

She shook her head, tried again. "I remember how chaotic it got when my own twin sisters were born, and I was three. And then when the triplets came along two years after that, it was even more crazy. And I don't want to be in a situation where I don't have enough of me to go around."

That could well happen, she knew. No matter how well-intentioned she was.

"Not to mention the commitment we made to Anne Marie. We promised her we would adopt her twins. To back out at the last minute like this…"

"Seems really dishonorable, too," Trace guessed where she was going with this.

Relieved he understood, Poppy nodded. "But on the other hand, we promised Anne Marie we would give her babies a really good life, with tons of love, and how is that going to be possible with four infants, coming almost all at once, and you gone for at least the first six months, if not more…" She paced away, anxiety twisting inside her. In that light, even considering adopting the twins seemed incredibly selfish.

And then there was her secret fear.

Poppy pivoted back to Trace. "What if something does go wrong with this pregnancy and I am forced to go on bed rest, and can't care for them the way a mother should." Her voice trembled. "Or worse, I lose these babies, too?" At the memory of the child they had lost, her heart broke.

Tears misted her eyes. "If we do what's best for the babies and give up Anne Marie's twins, so they can have all the time and individual attention and love they deserve, and then I— If something happens. We might not get another chance to be parents, at least not for years if we have to go back on the waiting list." Which would surely be the case!

He wrapped a reassuring arm around her. Determination lit his eyes. "Whoa now. Dr. Keller said everything looked fine."

Yes, she had. But what if she was wrong?

Poppy folded her arms in front of her. "The doctor didn't think anything was amiss when I was pregnant the last time, either."

He tightened his grip on her protectively, before releasing her. "But they didn't do an ultrasound when you were first diagnosed, either, did they?"

"No," Poppy admitted, emotions getting the better of her once again. "There was no reason to, but..." She dragged in a breath and pulled herself together with effort.

Panicking would not help either of them.

Trace looked at her closely "So what do you want to do? Proceed with the adoption? Or reconsider our options?"

There was no clue in his maddeningly inscrutable expression as to what *he* wanted.

Wishing he would tell her what was on his mind and in his heart, Poppy fell silent.

She had thought—hoped—they were getting closer than ever, now that they were married, preparing to start a family.

But it had all been an illusion, albeit a heartrending one.

Trace was as unwilling to show her what was deep in his heart and soul, as he always had been. She swallowed a lump in her throat, aware this was their chance to really get close to one another. If only he would let his guard down, too. "I want you to tell me what to do," she said quietly.

He shook his head. "I can't do that, Poppy."

Her body felt locked up tight. "Then I want you to *help* me make this decision."

He grimaced. "I can't do that, either."

"Why not?" Her heart cried. "Don't you want children?" Where had that come from?

His body tensed in resignation. "Yes, I want to have children with you, either via adoption or the old-fashioned way, or if you think you can handle it—"

You. Not we. Not us.

"—then do both," he continued with a careful stoicism that seemed to come straight from his soul.

"Then why can't you tell me what we should do?" There! She'd said it! *We!*

He rubbed a hand across the scruff on his jaw. "Because you are the one with the family history of multiples. You're the one who lived it." His eyes held hers for a long beat. "I mean, I know how close you and your sisters are now, but to hear you talk about it, there were times when you were growing up when it wasn't all bliss."

Poppy ignored the growing ache in her heart. "That's true of all families, isn't it?"

He scoffed. "You're asking me about a *normal* family?" Taking a step back, he scowled. "I really wouldn't know. Which is why you have to make the decision."

"I can't," she said brokenly. "Not without you." This was too big, too important, for only half of a couple to decide.

His jaw tautened. "I'll support whatever you decide."

He just wouldn't be there in the trenches with her. And if he couldn't do that, what else would he be unable and or unwilling to do? "That's not an answer," she said, her own anger mounting.

He shrugged. "It's the only one I'm prepared to give."

She stared at him and knew trying to budge him was

like trying to move a brick wall. "You mean that, don't you?"

He opened his mouth and shut it. "Yes."

"And it's always going to be this way," she said, feeling raw to the bone. "You doing your thing, me doing mine?"

"It's what we agreed," he pointed out harshly. "It's what made us work so well all this time."

He was right, of course. She had said that, numerous times. She'd even believed it, for a time. But now, having lived with him—as his wife—for the past two weeks, she knew better. They were on the cusp of something really and truly wonderful, if only they would allow themselves to become true real-life partners in every conceivable way.

But he didn't want to do that.

And she couldn't pretend to be okay with it when she knew there was so much more to be had. If only he'd open his heart.

"Then I'm sorry, Trace," she said, her voice trembling with emotion. "I'm sorry for both of us. And most of all I'm sorry for our twins." Refusing to cry, she stepped past him.

He just looked at her. "What are you saying?"

Her heart hurting in a way she'd never imagined it could, she went upstairs and grabbed the duffel he'd never bothered to fully unpack. "I'm saying what I should have known all along."

Ignoring the hurt, disbelieving look on his face as he stood behind her, mutely watching, she grabbed the few things that had made it to hangers, and stuffed them inside. She went into the bathroom and added his toiletries, too.

"That it's not enough for us to be lovers and friends, and husband and wife in name only, not heart. Our children deserve more than that, and so do we."

He stared at her as she shoved his duffel into his hands. "You're kicking me out?"

Poppy inhaled a tremulous breath. "Yes, Trace," she confirmed sadly, going downstairs to get his coat and anything else he might have had. "I am."

Chapter 16

Wracked with guilt that she couldn't live up to their original agreement, Poppy agonized over her decision for several days. But in the end, she knew it didn't matter that she had already taken the twins into her heart and made a place for them in her life. She and Trace had promised Anne Marie that the twins would have a mom and a military dad to love them. They'd even gotten married to facilitate that! They just hadn't been able to make it work. And now she was alone again. Minus the husband, lover and best friend she had been counting on to see her through her first foray into parenthood.

So, still feeling torn up about what she knew in her heart she had to do, Poppy went to see Anne Marie. In one of the most difficult moments of her life, she explained sadly, "As much as I wish I could go through with the adoption, it wouldn't be fair to your babies. Not when there are other better options for them."

Her hand on her swollen belly, Anne Marie listened intently, looking as disappointed—but ultimately accepting—as Poppy felt. "I get it. I'm glad you're doing the sensible thing. Because you're right… There is no way you could manage two sets of twins in six months. Well," she amended wryly, "you probably could. You're so together."

Poppy didn't feel together at the moment. Since she and Trace had called it quits, the reality was she was an emotional mess. Although for the pregnant teen's sake, she was doing her best to appear both practical and encouraging.

"But I'm cool with the other couple that wanted to adopt them, too." Her gaze narrowed. "What I don't understand is why Trace didn't come to talk to me, too. Did he already go back to the Middle East?"

Poppy felt another pang in her heart. There had been a lot of them the past few days. "No. He's still in Texas."

"Then?"

This was even harder. Poppy swallowed. "We're calling it quits."

Anne Marie stared. "How come?"

Poppy shook her head; not sure she could explain it even if she wanted to, which she didn't. "It's complicated."

"Did he want you to keep all four babies?"

That was the hell of it, she didn't know. And now, probably never would. Poppy twisted her hands in her lap. "He didn't weigh in, either way."

Anne Marie nodded sagely. "Which made you feel like he didn't care."

And maybe never would. At least not as much as she needed him to, if they were going to be married the way she wanted to be married.

She blinked away the moisture gathering in her eyes. There she went, getting ridiculously emotional again. "How did you get so smart?" she asked hoarsely.

"Group." Hand to her lower back, Anne Marie got up and walked around the back of the chair. Resting one hand on the top of the upholstered chair, she admitted honestly, "We have to go every day and talk about our feelings and stuff. It's helped me understand a lot and see things I never would have seen before." She paused meaningfully. "Like how much you and Trace love each other."

The crazy thing was Poppy knew they still did care about each other—deeply. "Sometimes love isn't enough."

Anne Marie circled the chair and sat again. She leaned toward Poppy urgently. "That's what I told my dad the last time we saw each other, before he left. See, I was tired of him being deployed, time after time after time. And worse, volunteering for hazardous duty." She shook her head, in that instant, looking much older than her years. "And I just couldn't understand that. I always wanted him with me and Mom. But my dad said there were some things that had to be done, and he was the one to do it. His fellow soldiers needed him to be there."

That sounded achingly familiar. "I'm sorry," Poppy said quietly. She reached over and squeezed Anne Marie's hand. "I know how that feels, to have to keep saying goodbye time after time."

Anne Marie nodded. "The point is, the last time I saw my dad before he was killed in that firefight, we had harsh words. I said he didn't love me, when deep down I knew that he did. And I could tell I really hurt him." Anne Marie teared up.

It was all Poppy could do to choke back a sob.

"My biggest regret is that we ended it that way. I never got to tell him I was sorry, or that I did love him with all my heart. Don't make the same mistake with Trace, Poppy. Talk to him before he goes back overseas. Try to work things out. 'Cause he's a good guy."

"I heard you were bunking out here," Mitzy Martin told Trace when she caught up with him at the Laramie Air Field. At loose ends since he and Poppy had called it quits, Trace had volunteered to help decorate for the annual McCabe Charter Air Service's Holiday Open House.

He fastened the garland onto the steel beam overhead then came down from the ladder to get another. "Is everything okay?" With Poppy, her pregnancy, the adoption...

"Poppy went to see Anne Marie this morning, to tell her in person that she was not going to be able to adopt the twins."

Trace picked up the ladder and settled it to the left. He picked up another garland. "So she decided what she wanted to do."

Mitzy followed. "Have you?"

"I told her I was leaving the decision up to her," he said.

"I heard that, too."

He used a piece of dark green twine to secure the garland, then came back down and moved the ladder yet again. "So then you also know that you can stop giving me a hard time," he snapped, looking Mitzy in the eye.

Her eyes smiled but not her mouth. "I'm not so sure my work here is done."

He winced. "I can't imagine what would be left for you to do."

"Perhaps nudge you into telling your wife the plans you made *before* she realized she was pregnant."

Ah, yes, those, he thought, aware it was all he could do not to groan.

Mitzy stepped closer. "Those are still your plans, aren't they?"

His gut twisted in disappointment. "Yes. Not that it matters."

The social worker looked at him with perceptive eyes. "I think it might matter enormously—if Poppy knew what you were planning."

"That's never been our deal. Our relationship has worked—or at least it *did* work—because we always let each other go off and do our own thing. No pressure, no judgment, no—"

She gave him a baleful stare. "Commitment?"

"We were committed, to our own lives."

"Then why keep coming back to each other? For sixteen years, Trace!"

Because, for the life of me, I can't stay away. And up to the point where Poppy told me to take a hike, I had thought—hoped—that Poppy couldn't stay away from me, either.

Which just went to show, Trace thought sourly, how much he knew.

Not a whole hell of a lot, as it happened.

Mitzy continued to stare at him then finally put her

bag down and sat on one of the leather-and-steel hanger chairs. Realizing she was settling in for the long haul, this time Trace did groan.

"Did you ever think about why I worked so hard to put you and Poppy through the wringer, the way I did, during the amended home study?"

Figuring if this was going to take a while he may as well get comfortable, too, Trace settled across from her. "Because you're a Type-A social worker?"

Mitzy heaved an exasperated sigh. "I did that because I, and everyone else who knows the two of you, have gotten tired of watching both of you go through life so *blindly*—"

Trace lifted a warning brow. "Don't mince words now."

"—and refuse to admit to yourselves or each other, what we all know to be true."

"Which is what?" he demanded impatiently, wishing everyone would stop talking in riddles.

"That we only get one chance at life. And that it's Christmas. The time of giving. Of hope. And renewal. And the rest, Lieutenant, you are smart enough to figure out for yourself."

Poppy took one last look in the mirror then slipped on her red wool winter coat and scarf. Keys in one hand, she picked up her bag and the small gift-wrapped present, in the other. The doorbell rang just as she reached the front door.

Frowning, because she didn't want anyone or anything to waylay her from her mission now that she had finally made her up mind, she put on her most unwelcoming expression and opened the door.

Trace stood on the other side of the threshold.

In jeans, starched, blue, button-up shirt, tweed jacket and tie, he was a sight for sore eyes. Or he would have been had things not been so tense between them. His expression, already gut-wrenchingly solemn, turned even more purposeful. The wild hope that he had come to reconcile with her fled; replaced by a tight knot in her throat. And an ache in her heart.

Realizing maybe now wasn't the right moment, after all, she slipped the present into her pocket, out of sight.

"I can see I caught you at a bad time," he said gruffly.

"I was just headed out to the party at the airstrip," she told him. Where she had heard he would be. "Will invited me."

"Me, too."

Another thrill. A smidgen of hope. "Then...?"

His eyes were dark and so very intent. "I wanted to talk to you first, rather than meet up there."

Aware he had a point about that—it would have been awkward, especially with everyone they knew, watching—Poppy nodded and ushered him inside.

The lump in her throat was back, along with a throbbing ache in her heart. Was there any love left between them? Or was she going to have to start from scratch? Though it hardly mattered. She knew her goal. Even as she knew there were certain things they had to get caught up on, too. "I saw Anne Marie today."

Concern lit his hazel eyes. "How is she?"

"Good. Very pregnant and very understanding." Briefly, she elaborated.

He nodded, admitting he'd already been apprised of her decision. He then nodded at her midriff. "How have you been feeling?" His gaze caressed her tenderly.

"Fine." Physically, anyway. Emotionally she was a wreck. Inanely, she continued. "I have my first appointment with the obstetrician on Monday."

"That's good."

"Listen, Trace. I wanted to talk to you, too." Pretending to feel a lot more self-assured than she was, she took off her coat and folded it over the newel post. Still holding his steady gaze, she swallowed the growing knot of emotion in her throat. "I'm sorry about what I said the other day."

His expression inscrutable, he closed the distance between them.

She searched his face, still not knowing what lay ahead, almost afraid to wish...

He took her hand. "I'm sorry, too." He paused again, looking deep into her eyes, his expression raw and filled with the longing she harbored deep inside. "For not being there for you in the way that you needed me to be," he admitted hoarsely. "Because the truth is, I did have strong feelings on what we should do. Like you, I thought two sets of twins in six months' time was too much."

Relief filtered through her. She moved all the way into his arms. "Then why didn't you tell me?"

He threaded one hand through her hair, wrapped the other reverently around her waist. "Because we made a deal a long time ago to always be supportive, and never undermine each other's life decisions." He hauled in another rough breath. Admitted, "And because I didn't want to have the kinds of marriages my parents have had—with us always fighting to have things our own way, the end result being that one of us would feel like we got the raw end of the deal. I was afraid if I weighed in on something that important, and my opinion didn't match yours, that you'd resent me."

Poppy knew what it took for him to admit that. She splayed her hands across his chest, the rapid beat of his heart matching hers. "Whereas I needed to feel like I wasn't in this alone, that we were a team. And I should have told you that directly, Trace, instead of expecting you to know intuitively what I was thinking and feeling." She swallowed. "And I certainly shouldn't have pressured you to make a decision on the spot, when I couldn't do so, either."

"Why weren't you this honest and open with me the other day?" he challenged softly.

This, Poppy thought, was even harder. "Part of it was sheer hormones." She flashed a wry smile. "It's true what they say about pregnancy, the surges do make you feel a little overwrought and emotional. As you might have noticed…"

He grinned back. "I think I have."

Poppy sobered. "The rest was more complex and goes back to the time when we first met. I know how much you loathed being trapped in a domestic situation not of your own making, the way you constantly were when you were a kid, with families that never should have been formed in the first place. I promised myself that I would never hurt you that way."

"Which is why you didn't tell me you were pregnant the first time around," he surmised.

Poppy's voice broke. "I think I knew even then that I wanted to spend the rest of my life with you, but I didn't want to admit it to myself."

"Because you didn't think I felt the same way."

She nodded, the ache in her heart receding even as

the lump in her throat grew. "I convinced myself it didn't matter. That we didn't need to have everything everyone else had to be happy. When just being with you made me feel so good."

Emotion glimmered in his eyes. "For me, too," he said thickly.

Incredibly aware of the heat and strength emanating from his tall, powerful body, she teased lightly, "And if it ain't broke…"

"Why fix it?" he finished, smiling.

She nodded and he sobered once again.

"I haven't been honest with you, either, Poppy," he told her hoarsely, smoothing a hand gently down her spine. "Because I don't just want you to be my lover and my friend and the mother of my kids. I want you to be my wife, in the traditional time-honored sense. I want to love you—and I do love you with all my heart. And to protect you—"

"Whoa there, fella." Poppy stopped him, a fingertip pressed against his lips. "Back up." She stared dazedly into his eyes. "Did you say you *love* me?"

He nodded, all the affection she had ever hoped to see on his face. "And I have for a very, very long time. Probably since the first time I laid eyes on you when I first came to Laramie."

Joy bubbled up inside her until she was bursting with happiness. Poppy rose on tiptoe and kissed his lips. "I love you, too," she whispered tenderly. "So very much."

They kissed again, even more passionately. "So we'll stay married?" she reiterated.

Trace nodded seriously. "But under different conditions than we last agreed."

* * *

An awkward silence fell. Okay, so maybe he hadn't handled that announcement exactly right, Trace thought, studying Poppy's stricken expression.

She gave a slight nod of her head. "I understand if you want to go back to the Middle East and finish your deployment. Or even sign up for another." Her slender shoulders squared. "I want you to know I'm prepared to make whatever sacrifices I need to make to be a good, supportive military wife."

Her unwavering support helped, as always.

But there were things she had to know.

Things, as Mitzy had pointed out, that Poppy needed to be told. "That's good to know, darlin'," he told her. "Because I did withdraw my request to be transferred back to the States, and replaced it with another. Which, thanks to the help of my senior officers, was granted earlier today."

She blinked and he explained. "I didn't want someone else stepping in to be your Lamaze partner or to be there for the birth of our kids. And I couldn't wait six months or more to be with you, either. So I resigned my commission with the air force, effective immediately."

"Trace!" Poppy did a double-take. "You can't quit the military altogether, not even for me and our kids. It's in your blood!"

"I know." He nodded. "Fortunately there are other ways to serve our country, and I was able to arrange an inter-military-service transfer to the Texas National Guard. Starting in January, I'll be on active duty one weekend a month and two weeks every year, plus whenever I'm needed, in an emergency." He released a breath and went on. "The rest of the time, I'm going to work for your cousin Will. Turns out there is a growing need for air-ambulance pilots right here in West Texas. And that suits me very well, too."

Poppy stared up at him in wonder. "You'd really do that for me?"

He wrapped his arm around her and kissed the top of her head. "For you and for us." Their eyes locked. Encouraged, he continued. "For a long time, I thought the military was my home, but my real home is where my heart is. And that is with you and our babies. And to prove just how serious I am about that, I bought you a Christmas gift, which I am giving to you a little early." He removed a small velvet box from his jacket pocket and handed it to her.

Poppy opened it up. She gasped when she saw what was inside. A beautiful diamond solitaire.

"I should have asked you to marry me a long time ago. The right way. But I'm doing it now." Love rushing through him, Trace got down on one knee and took her hand. "Poppy McCabe, will you make our marriage a real and lasting one in every way, and be my wife and let me be your husband, for as long as we both shall live?"

Poppy laughed out loud with joy. Still grinning from ear to ear, tears glistening, she tugged on his hand and pulled him to his feet. "You bet I will!" Then, eyes gleaming impishly, she reached into the pocket of her coat and pulled out an equally small but very nicely wrapped present. "I have a little something for you, too."

He paused, reminding her, "You already gave me a gift—the party."

She wrinkled her nose then continued mysteriously, "This is symbolic. A token, if you will, of the many nights and days to come."

More curious than ever, he opened it. Inside the box was the sprig of plastic mistletoe that always brought a smile to both their faces. She kissed his cheek. "I figured it's our good-luck charm."

He chuckled. "That, it is."

"And a harbinger of our many holidays to come."

"I like that, too."

They paused for another kiss. And then another and another. Poppy hitched in a breath. "Want to skip the party for something much more important instead?" Their reunion.

He accepted the amorous invitation in the spirit with which it was given. Swinging her up into his arms, he mounted the stairs to their bedroom.

"Sweetheart, you read my mind."

Epilogue

One year later

"What do you think?" Trace asked. "Walk or drive?"

Poppy stepped out onto the porch to stand beside him.

The December night was beautiful. Starry and clear, with a slight breeze. She turned, admiring her husband's handsome profile. "It's only what—forty degrees?"

"I think so."

"If we bundle them up...?"

"They'd probably enjoy a stroller ride over to your folks' home."

Hand in hand, they went back inside.

The twins were lying on the blanket on the living room floor. Dressed in matching red-velvet dresses, white tights and satin ballet shoes, their wispy blond hair sporting matching bows, they looked adorable. As usual, they were facing each other, waving their stuffed toys at each other, and talking softly in a series of gurgles and coos only they could understand.

Trace paused to survey them, too, all the affection she had ever hoped to see in his hazel eyes. "I just want you to know," he stated huskily as he knelt with her, "they're not dating until they are thirty-five."

Poppy laughed as they each gathered an infant in their arms, and stood. "I think Ella and Emma might have something to say about that."

"Yeah, well," he continued to tease sternly, all doting dad, "I expect you to back me up."

Poppy patted the swell of his bicep. "I think they'll be okay. They're half McCabe and half Caulder, after all. Women don't come any stronger than that."

He grinned. "True."

He put on one coat and cap, she the other.

Together, they settled the girls into the double stroller, donned their own jackets, locked up and headed off down the street. All the decorations were up. Some of the houses even had Christmas music playing. As usual, the twins were enthralled with all there was to see and hear.

"I love this time of year," Poppy admitted as they paused to study a particularly delightful display of Santa Claus and his reindeer.

Trace put his arm across her shoulders.

When they'd looked their fill, he continued pushing the stroller down the sidewalk, in the direction of her parents' home, where the McCabe family Christmas party would soon be starting.

"I love it, too." He gave her shoulder a squeeze, kissed her temple. "Now that I finally have the happy family I've always wanted."

Poppy basked in his love, returning the affection full-force. "Is your mom still planning to visit after New Year's?" In the throes of yet another divorce, Bitsy had elected to take a Christmas cruise for singles to the Bahamas. His father was headed out west, to check out a new strain of cattle.

Trace nodded, having made peace with the fact that his parents were just not meant to be married to anyone for long. "Both are." He smiled good-naturedly. "At separate times."

"That's good," Poppy said. She wanted him to be close to both his parents, and thanks to their new grandkids, that finally seemed to be happening.

"The question is," he mused as they turned the corner and walked down another festively decorated street. "What are we going to get each other for Christmas this year?"

Poppy sighed wistfully, thinking about all the changes the past year had brought. "A full night's sleep, maybe?"

Trace nodded. "Twelve hours at a pop would be so great."

"Yeah." They reflected, laughing. "Not happening." The most they ever got at one time now was seven hours. And, given they had two infants who weren't always on identical schedules, that was still a rarity.

They chuckled some more.

"Maybe we should give each other a joint gift," she suggested.

He was all over that. "Like a king-size bed?" Delight sparkled in his eyes.

Poppy grinned, thinking how much fun they could have with that. And how much more comfortable her six-foot-four husband might be. "Sounds like a plan."

As they neared their destination, Trace halted the stroller. While the girls enjoyed yet another set of holiday decorations, he turned to take Poppy into his arms. "Have I told you today how much I love you, or that you and the girls have given me everything I ever wanted?" he asked thickly.

He had.

Unimaginable happiness swelled within her. "Or that you," Poppy whispered, rising up on tiptoes and wreathing both her arms around his neck, "have made all my dreams come true?" She kissed him again, with all the emotion she felt in her heart. Their gazes locked, held. "I love you so much, Lieutenant."

That was, as it turned out, the most lasting and wonderful gift of all.

* * * * *

Tina Leonard is a *New York Times* bestselling and award-winning author of more than fifty projects, including several popular miniseries for Harlequin. Known for bad-boy heroes and smart, adventurous heroines, her books have made the *USA TODAY*, Waldenbooks, Ingram and Nielsen BookScan bestseller lists. Born on a military base, Tina lived in many states before eventually marrying the boy who did her crayon printing for her in the first grade. You can visit her at tinaleonard.com, and follow her on Facebook and Twitter.

Books by Tina Leonard

Harlequin American Romance

Bridesmaids Creek

The Rebel Cowboy's Quadruplets
The SEAL's Holiday Babies
The Twins' Rodeo Rider

Callahan Cowboys

A Callahan Wedding
The Renegade Cowboy Returns
The Cowboy Soldier's Sons
Christmas in Texas
A Callahan Outlaw's Twins
His Callahan Bride's Baby
Branded by a Callahan
Callahan Cowboy Triplets

Visit the Author Profile page at Harlequin.com for more titles.

The SEAL's
Holiday Babies

TINA LEONARD

Many thanks to the wonderful readers
who embrace my work so loyally—
I can never thank you enough.

Chapter 1

"Hang on a sec," Ty Spurlock said to Sheriff Dennis McAdams, stunned as he watched a tall redhead wearing seriously tight blue jeans that complemented her seriously sexy figure walk into The Wedding Diner on the arm of Sam Barr, a bachelor recruit whom Ty had brought to town for the express purpose of matchmaking.

It appeared that a match might indeed be in the making. The problem was, the redhead wasn't one of Ty's intended bachelorettes.

Because he secretly had his eye on her for himself.

"What was that?" Ty demanded.

"What was what?"

"Jade Harper going into The Wedding Diner with Sam."

Dennis grinned at him. "Free country, isn't it?"

246 The SEAL's Holiday Babies

"Sure it is." Ty sank onto the hood of the sheriff's cruiser and pondered why the idea of Jade and Sam together bothered him, like a real bad toss from a bull. He'd had those, many of those. They were never any fun.

Neither was this. "Is there something going on there I don't know about?"

Dennis's eyes twinkled. "Do you *think* there's something you should you know about? Are you taking over from Madame Matchmaker, our resident maker of matches? That'll put Cosette's pink-frosted hair in a twist for sure, if she thinks you're butting in on her area of expertise."

Ty felt strongly that Sheriff Dennis might be keeping something from him, which only made Ty resolve to get to the bottom of the matter. Jade had no business going out with Sam Barr, as prime for matchmaking as Sam might be. "*Is* there something going on between Sam and Jade?"

Dennis shook his head. "You'll have to ask Jade. Or Sam."

The sheriff was being deliberately obtuse, prickling him because he could. Nobody understood him the way Dennis did. The man had been elected sheriff after Ty's adoptive father, Terence, had given up the sheriff's job— fifteen years of being a great sheriff undone by one rumor. A rumor that had never gone away. But Sheriff Dennis had always supported Terence Spurlock, and Ty appreciated that more than he could say. Maybe only another sheriff could understand how loose lips and bad information could strike down a career and a man. "Or I could just ask you, since nothing goes on in Bridesmaids Creek that gets past you."

Dennis chuckled. "True enough."

"So? Is there?" Ty asked impatiently.

Dennis crossed his arms and smiled. "Didn't you bring those four cowboys here to find them brides? Sam Barr, Squint Mathison, Justin Morant and Francisco Rodriguez Olivier Grant, otherwise known as Frog?"

"What does that have to do with Jade?"

Dennis laughed. "Ty, you can't blame her for dating someone. Jade thinks you don't know she's alive, except for her occasionally scooping you some ice cream in her mother's shop. You haven't exactly pursued her."

Ty grunted, glancing around the main square of the town he called home, even as an adopted son, and the town to which he owed so much. Owed them everything because they'd helped raise him, and because he'd had a great childhood because of them.

He owed them everything but his bachelorhood.

"Is there a problem?" Dennis asked.

"No." There was, but he knew Dennis wouldn't needle him about it further. Except he did.

"You could always try talking to her," he said, surprising Ty. Dennis prodded him in a gentle, fatherly way that made him miss his own dad.

"I'm good at talking," Ty said, "but I'm a couple weeks away from trying to make it into the SEALs. I have nothing to offer Jade." He'd be gone for six long months of training, and then a little longer, if he made it.

No. When *I make it.*

Mentally, he reviewed The Plan, which was so far working like a charm.

Bring home eligible, trustworthy, elementally studly bachelors with the intent of pressing some of the ladies— not Jade—into marriage. This would start a rollerball of reactions: namely, babies and families, new blood in Bridesmaids Creek.

Which was very important in a town that was one step away from dying off completely.

He wasn't about to let that happen. No, everything was working smoothly, with Mackenzie Hawthorne and her four darling little girls now married to rodeo rider Justin Morant. That was the beauty of goals and plans—they worked like charms because they were road signs pointing the way to the future. One needed merely to stick to a plan and not deviate; that was the key.

Victims number two, three and four—those being Sam, Frog and Squint—were certainly catnip to the many ladies in town. So there was no reason under the clear blue sky of Bridesmaids Creek, Texas, that Sam should settle on Jade Harper.

"Eat your heart out much?" Sheriff Dennis asked, jarring him back to the present.

"I'm fine."

"I think Jade would understand the whole BUD/S training thing, Ty. She's an independent girl. She works hard. Don't you think it might be better to speak than to hold your tongue to the point that you lose her forever?"

Lose her forever? Ty chewed on that a moment. He wasn't going to lose Jade, because he'd never had Jade. What he had was The Plan. Nothing could disrupt it, because you didn't get into the SEALs by being an indecisive doorknob. You accomplished that by having determination and focus, and by serving one master. And the only way to clear his father's name, to rebuild the Spurlock brand, was to return home a man of his word. The people of BC—Bridesmaids Creek—had ceased believing that Terence Spurlock was a man of his word when a stranger to BC had been allegedly murdered at the local haunted house, the Hanging H, Mackenzie Hawthorne's place. Folks said Terence had been bought off by the town's evil shyster in big boots, Robert Donovan, who owned significant chunks of town and was determined to own more, carving it up into retail parcels that enriched his considerable wealth. If he could get the Hawthornes to sell, along with the owners of the ranches surrounding Jade's place, Donovan would have the kingdom he desired. But because the people had mostly grouped together against him, refusing to sell, Donovan currently held smaller, disconnected and farther-flung chunks of land not suitable for his grand visions.

Ty's father would never have been bought off by anyone. It burned Ty's gut that some folks—not everyone, but enough—had put such a rumor out there. More than anything, he hated that Bridesmaids Creek was held hostage by Robert Donovan and his coterie of greedy swindlers.

"I understand the mission," Dennis said softly. "I'm just saying you don't have to pay for what happened to your father by losing something you love dearly."

Ty moved away from the voice of temptation, which was intended to be the voice of reason. Sheriff Dennis was a good man. He wanted to help. When Ty's father had died of a broken heart from losing the town's trust—and Ty was sure as the setting sun that that's what had driven his father to his grave—Dennis had been there to remind him of what a very good man his father had been.

Ty clapped Dennis on the back and walked in the opposite direction from The Wedding Diner—and Jade.

* * *

"It's a dumb idea," Ty said a half hour later, relenting on entering The Wedding Diner, because his curiosity was killing him. He inserted himself at the table in The Wedding Diner with his buddies Squint and Frog so he had an excellent visual on Jade and Sam, but whether he was torturing himself on purpose he couldn't say. "In fact, that idea is so dumb it makes me wonder if you've poured something strong in your coffee."

Squint shrugged. "You don't want a family. We do."

Frog nodded. "You brought us to BC to find women. We want what Justin got when he married Mackenzie. He got a family."

Ty swallowed, not about to admit that the idea was very appealing. "You wouldn't know what to do with Justin's four babies."

"I don't care how many babies are involved," Squint said, sipping his coffee thoughtfully. "I just care that babies are eventually involved."

"So let me get this straight. You're going to propose pregnancy to a couple of ladies. Not marriage, just pregnancy."

"That about sums it up." Frog eyed with pleasure the plate of steaming eggs, toast and bacon a waitress set down in front of him. "Women aren't looking for a ring anymore, Ty. They want to know that the man they choose can give them a family. And personally, I want to know that I have children in my future. So it's a win-win."

"We're not saying we couldn't love a woman who didn't want children," Squint said. "But we think Justin's got a pretty good setup, and it inspires us. Plus we're pretty good father candidates."

Ty grunted. "Have you chosen your victims?" This ought to be rich. He couldn't wait to hear more details from men whom he'd specifically brought here for the very purpose of finding brides and making families to grow BC.

Just not in the manner in which they were planning to go about it.

"Well, Sam's picked Jade," Squint said, nodding his head in the redhead's direction. "That's as far as we've gotten."

Ty winced. If Sam thought he could just propose pregnancy to an independent woman like Jade Harper, it might be worth hanging around to see him get handed his head. Ty almost laughed at Sam's plan.

Then again, maybe it wasn't that funny. What if Jade said yes? She was twenty-seven, and a beauty like her shouldn't still be on the market, except she claimed she wasn't ready to settle down.

That might be changing now that her best friend, Mackenzie, was happily married.

Ty shrugged off the vague sense of uneasiness the thought gave him. "Picking a lady and having her fall for you are two different things." He glanced Jade's way, commanded himself to quit staring.

"We thought you'd support our plan," Squint said, his tone surprised. "When you lured us to BC, you said there were plenty of ladies looking to settle down. When you've been in the military as long as we were, the thought of ladies looking to settle down is pretty inviting."

"Yeah, why are you beefing about this?" Frog glared at him. "Dude, if you have a better idea, speak up. If not, say nothing. You're leaving soon enough, and you won't be doing much communicating once you're trying to get through BUD/S. So our story won't be of much interest to you."

In other words, butt out. "Your plan is fine. Foolhardy, but fine. I wish you all the best." A horrible thought occurred to Ty. "What if Jade were to say yes to Sam's stupid pregnancy idea?"

His two friends/hires/tricksters stared at him.

"Well, they'd get married," Frog said. "As sure as my name is Francisco Rodriguez Olivier Grant, I'd probably be best man."

"That would be me," Squint said, "as sure as my name's John Squint Mathison."

It could be serious if his lunkheaded buddies were already scrabbling over who was going to get high honor at this imaginary wedding. *What possible difference does it make to me? Free country, like Dennis said.*

He sneaked another glance at Jade, all long and lean and capable and sexy, with a mop of burgundy-red hair that was a siren's call to Ty. She had a bright smile that teased, always laughing at him, and somehow with him. Captivating him. A laugh that never failed to bring a smile of response to his face, no matter what his mood was. No, when he'd thought up The Plan, the plan of bringing life back to BC, he'd put Jade on a pedestal out of sight, in a mental closet marked Private. Do Not Touch.

Mine.

Sam put his big, beefy hand over Jade's delicate one, and Ty could hear that musical laugh across the aisle, reaching his ears with a pang that lodged in his heart. Something blew in his brain, like a transformer struck by lightning, and the next thing he knew, he was sliding into the white booth occupied by Jade and Sam, tucking himself up against Jade in the most friendly, brotherly fashion, because she expected friendly and brotherly from him.

Only he knew it was more of an ambush.

Jade grinned at Ty when he bumped in next to her, jostling her arm away from Sam's. "Look at you," she said to Ty. "All buzz cut and ready to report for duty."

Ty palmed his newly shorn head. She'd loved his hair long and wild, but he looked just as hot with it short, too. That was the problem with a rascal like Ty—he *looked* irresistible shaved or wild and woolly.

Spiritually, he was way too woolly for her.

"I let one of the ladies buzz me down," Ty said, and Sam grinned.

"Your mother took the sheep shears to him," Sam said.

"Betty didn't have sheep shears," Ty said, "but believe me, she was determined the brass wouldn't be disappointed with me when I showed up for training."

"It's short." Jade smiled. "I can just imagine Mom giving you the treatment. In another world, she could have been a hairstylist. The ice-cream shop just happened to get to her first."

"A remarkable woman," Sam agreed, and Ty elbowed Jade so that she looked at him again.

"Did you just elbow me? In a brotherly, somewhat obnoxious way?"

He looked pained. "I'm not really your brother. As much as it felt like that growing up, I'm not exactly brotherly material, as has been well noted by just about everyone."

Including her, which was why she kept Ty very much on the outskirts of her radar. "Mom practically raised you, along with everyone else in this town. You even had a bunk at our place." Her gaze softened as she took in Ty's square, determined jaw and wide brown eyes. "You broke a lot of noses for my sake when we were growing up."

Sam laughed. "He tried to break everything when we were on the circuit. Now go away, *brother*. This is a private lunch."

"Private?" Ty glared at Sam. "Nothing's private in BC."

"This is," Jade said. "You have to take your overprotective, buttinsky self elsewhere."

She hated to send him off. But the thing about Ty was that the more he hung around her, the more her hopes rose. It was something she had almost no control over. He treated her like a little sister—and her heart mooned for him. Stupidly.

And this year, her resolution was to get on with her life and accept that Ty was simply too much bad boy for her. Her practical nature knew this, accepted that she wanted something completely different when she envisioned a husband.

But her heart—and her female side—wanted Ty. In fact, her mind and her body were practically enemies at this point, warring with each other, each convinced the other was right.

She'd done a darn good job of moving on, seeking new opportunities. And a new man. Okay, Sam Barr wasn't "the one," but he was the first man she'd gone out with in a long time, and he was nice, and she was looking for *nice* on her man list, wasn't she?

"Go," she told Ty, her voice a little urgent as she gave him a pointed push, practically edging him out of the booth.

He stood, put on his brown Stetson, looked at her a bit sadly with those big brown puppy-dog eyes and tipped his hat to her and Sam before returning to his own booth.

"Poor fellow," Sam said. "Doesn't know what he wants in life."

"Poor fellow?" Jade refused to glance Ty's way. "The man brought you here on a mission. He's not a poor fellow at all. Don't fall for the injured look he wears so well." She sipped water, glad for the coolness, but couldn't meet Sam's eyes.

"He's going to make it," Sam said, his tone admiring. "He's trained for a year to make it through BUD/S. Trained like a maniac. I predict he not only makes it, but he terrorizes all the other recruits."

"Of course he's going to make it!" Jade said, astonished. "All Ty's ever wanted to do was be a SEAL. A lean, mean, fighting machine, as I heard one of the men call him once. He's dedicated to his goal." She swallowed hard. "Ty will make it, and once he does, we'll hardly ever see him around here again." The thought was so painful it physically hurt her stomach.

"Yeah, that's what he told us."

Jade's gaze flew to Sam. "Told you what?"

He shrugged, a handsome lug of good intentions and impeccable character that she felt absolutely no zip, no zing for—not the way Ty kept her emotions all riled up.

"Ty's working on his Plan."

"Plan?"

Sam shrugged. "His life goal. Short list. One, settle

some good friends of his—bosom buddies—in BC to tempt the local population of females."

Jade felt her back stiffen. "Go on."

"Two, see his dear friends happily married, with babies, to stifle Robert Donovan's evil plan to turn BC into a concrete wasteland—a project already under way with Donovan in the process of bidding out parcels he owns to various government contractors."

"Let me guess. You and Frog and Squint are the bait for Ty's grand vision."

"And Justin." Sam grinned. "Justin was first, but he took so long to get down to business that Ty began to worry. So he brought the three of us along."

Alarm bells rang inside Jade. "Well, wasn't that thoughtful of Ty. And three?" she asked sweetly.

"Three is to clear his father's name. The murder that was never solved was pinned on his father's incompetence, and that's something Ty also lays at Donovan's door. He's convinced Donovan had a plan to oust his father as sheriff and bankroll the election of his handpicked pawn of Satan, as Ty puts it." Sam reached for her hand again, going back to the place where they'd been before Ty had butted into their booth.

But they couldn't go back, because once Ty had leaned up against her side, invading her space and her every sense, she'd felt herself slipping. And now that she was hearing of the perfidy of his Plan—who did he think he was, anyway, bringing in men to charm the ladies, as if the BC women were simply a herd of goats—she was really annoyed.

"Fourth, and finally," Sam continued, "the last part of The Plan is for Ty to make it into BUD/S, get his Trident and spend the rest of his days, as long as he can, in every far-flung locale of the world, chasing bad guys. Setting his brothers free." Sam looked thoughtful. "In another life, I do believe Ty would make the perfect assassin. He likes the loner lifestyle. Says he's most at peace when he's alone. Probably because he's adopted, is his theory."

Jade was stunned. She pulled her hand from Sam's, took another sip of her water to calm her racing thoughts. "That doesn't make sense. Ty was never alone. He was part of our family."

"But that's not how my brother feels. In his mind," Sam said, pointing to his own head. "Ty says he's alone. Got no family, got no one. Says it suits him fine. He was born alone, plans to die alone."

"Is that so." Jade hopped to her feet. "Well, I have something to say to Mr. Loner Spurlock about that. If you'll excuse me, Sam."

Ty Spurlock had another think coming if he thought his Plan was going to work on her. It wasn't—and he wasn't going to zip out of BC under cover of night and leave without her telling his majesty what a nonsensical dumb-ass he was.

This is one lady Ty's going to find it's impossible to bait.

Chapter 2

"Hello, Ty," Jade said, astonishing him because she'd arrived at his booth with something on her mind, judging by the compelling grip she had on his sleeve. "Could I speak to you privately for a moment? Outside?"

Ty glanced at Squint and Frog. "Fellows, I'm being called to duty."

They raised mugs of root beer to Jade. "When duty calls, a gentleman always answers," Frog said.

"If there was a gentleman around," Jade replied, and Ty thought he heard a bit of an edge in the darling little lady's voice. He followed her outside into the bright sunlight, having no choice, really, because she'd let go of him only once he'd left his booth.

Following her was no hardship, since he got to surreptitiously watch that sweet, heart-shaped fanny of hers move ahead of him in a determined locomotion of female-on-a-mission.

Sam must have dropped the ball somehow and upset his conquest. Ty couldn't remember seeing Jade so steamed before, the results of her temper obvious by the lack of a smile on her face and the light frown pulling her brows together. Poor Sam. Nice guy, but a bit too beta male—gentle, sweet, bearlike—for a heart-stopper like Jade.

It was known that women went for the alpha male, the bad boy in boots, which was something Justin Morant, Squint Mathison and sometimes Frog had in abundance. Okay, maybe not Frog; he was pretty beta as beta males went, somehow mellowing after life in the navy. Ty had worried about bringing Sam Barr along for The Plan, fearing he was too easygoing and nice and free-spirited—almost hippielike in his approach to life— then figured maybe BC had a librarian or a kindergarten teacher who might be looking for a plainspoken, existential bear of a man who wouldn't raise her blood pressure.

"Ty Spurlock," Jade said, stopping so fast in the middle of the pavement that he had to reach out and grab her to keep from knocking her down, "who do you think you are?"

He registered soft female and sweet perfume in his arms before he reluctantly released Jade. "What do you mean?"

"I know all about your stupid Plan. And it really is stupid!"

He grinned. "Sam has a big mouth."

"And you have a big head!"

Ty laughed. "Aw, Red. Don't worry." He tugged her back into his arms for a hug disguised as brotherly, but which was just an excuse for him to hold her again. "I didn't leave you out. There are plenty of men to go around." He hesitated, lost for a moment in the scent of peachy shampoo, and the feel of soft curves wriggling against him, before he started to give her a good, brotherly knuckle-rubbing on her scalp. Then his hand suddenly arrested as he realized the knuckle-rub wasn't as satisfying as he'd thought it would be.

Holy crap, she felt good. And sexy as hell.

Jade kicked his ankle, a smart blow he felt even through his jeans and boots. He released her, surprised. "What was that for?"

"You think you're *so* smart."

"Look, Jade. There aren't enough men in this town, you know that. The ladies outnumber us four to one or something. Or ten to one. I'm just trying to do the right thing."

She gazed at him, and he could see disgust heavy in her eyes. "I don't want you doing the right thing for me. Your right thing. Leave me out of The Plan."

He shrugged. "Sweetcake, if you don't like the goods, don't buy them. But it looked like you might like Sam a little bit, from where I was sitting. Pretty cozy lunch the two of you were having."

"So I should fall in with your plan and marry Sam? Is that how this is supposed to work?"

A streak of pain lanced Ty's heart, but just for a moment, and he ignored it for the greater good. "If you fall in love with one of the fine gentlemen I've brought to BC, I would call that a happy ending."

"You're an ass, Ty Spurlock."

He was honestly mystified. "It's no different than a

blind date, if you think about it. You've been on a blind date before, haven't you?"

"Yes, but—"

"You'd participate in a bachelorette auction for charity, right? We do those events here every year. The Best Man's Fork run, the Bridesmaids Creek swim—"

"Am I going to the highest bidder?" she asked, and Ty recognized a warning tone in her voice, which he actually didn't want to hear. He moved quickly to soothe her and ameliorate any damage.

"Now, Jade, as one of Bridesmaids Creek's most generous supporters, you deserve nothing but the best. And I've brought my very best to BC. That being said, if you don't like the fellows, don't go out with them. Sam, Squint and Frog will find other ladies to chat with." Ty tipped his hat, hoped he'd moved off the hot seat, and headed toward his truck with a sigh of relief.

Jade got in the passenger side before he'd even situated himself in the driver's seat. "And what about you? I noticed you left your name off the bachelor offerings."

"I'm not eligible." He started his truck, backing up. "If you're riding with me, buckle up. If not, advise me where I may drop you off. You wouldn't want to keep Sam waiting, I would presume."

She gave him a decidedly annoyed eyeing. "You really are a jackass, aren't you?"

"So they say. You coming?"

Jade leaned back, buckled her seat belt. "I'm not done telling you off."

"Fine by me. We ride together, but you may not like the destination." He glanced at her, ridiculously happy to have Jade in his truck—and happy as hell that she wasn't back at The Wedding Diner being romanced by Sam.

Which was kind of bad, because Sam had only been doing what he'd come to BC to do: find a wife. Or at least that's what Ty had told Sam and the guys they wanted: a wife, and a chance to have a family, become dads. Ty had promised them that BC was ripe, full-to-bursting ripe, with ladies who would leap at the chance to run to the altar.

He sighed. "So what's the topic?"

"Topic?"

He looked at her long, slim legs in Wranglers, the dangerous look in her eyes. Curves in all the right places. Was pretty certain his libido was starting to smoke. "The topic you're in my truck to discuss."

"Let's start with your Plan."

"Everybody has to have one, little lady. Otherwise nothing ever gets done." He rolled down his window, happy to smell fresh country air, be driving a truck in the greatest little town on earth, and have the most dynamite sexy redhead he knew glaring at him from the safety of her seat belt. "You have a problem with plans?"

"*The* Plan. The Plan that seems to start with you bringing bachelors to town, getting them married, and then you skittering off like a cockroach."

"I see no problem with that plan. Sounds like all the holes are filled." He frowned. "Maybe a slight quibble with the cockroach part. Don't think I ever saw myself in that role." Ty brightened. "You could rephrase it as Ty rides off into the sunset, leaving behind a grateful town. A veritable hero, and the townspeople cheered their thanks."

"Ass," she murmured under her breath.

"*Hero.*"

"Okay, but say someone decides you're the catch of the day before you go—"

"Riding off like a *hero*."

"Skittering off like—"

"It is understood by all," he interrupted quickly, before she could bring up the roach bit again, because in the mood she apparently was in, she was going to get around to saying something about how roaches got squished under female boots, "that I've never been a marrying man. This has never even been questioned."

"Ah, the happy, footloose, untamed cowboy."

"Exactly," he said, pleased now that they understood each other perfectly.

"Which is why you interrupted my lunch with Sam."

"Why?"

"Because you don't think Sam's the man for me. Obviously."

"Well," Ty said, uncomfortably acknowledging that what she'd said held the ring of truth, "there are better options."

"And who would those better options be? Because quite frankly, Sam suits me."

"How?"

"He's nice. He's gentle. He says what he means. Unlike some people, who are full of baloney."

Ty supposed she meant him. She certainly had that you're-the-guy-full-of-baloney tone in her voice. "I take it you're not happy I interrupted your lunch."

"Face it, Ty, you've always been something of a showboat."

"You mean I live life large." He sneaked another glance at her shapely body, red-hot from the flaming topknot of hair to her boots. "I remember when you and I used to play with our friends all day in the fields. Ball, chase, Red Rover—if it was a game, we knew it." He sighed. "I miss those days sometimes." He didn't understand how his best friend had grown up to be such a siren. Jade had him tied in knots he wasn't sure could be undone, except maybe by some kind of spell. Or his absence. "I'll be leaving soon," he said, reaching for the easiest knot to untie.

"Good," she said pleasantly.

His lips twisted of their own accord. "Guess that means no going-away party." Or kiss, for that matter.

"I wish you the best of luck. I hope you make it through BUD/S. You've worked hard enough to get there."

He turned his head at the soft, earnest note to her voice, surprised. "I believe you mean that."

"With all my heart." She opened the door when he stopped at the last crosshatch of road at the town's edge. "See you around, Ty."

"You can't get out here." They were a good two miles from the main drag. He didn't want her to leave, anyway. He'd been enjoying having her in his truck, even though he sensed she had something urgent on her mind.

"I'll be fine. Sam followed us."

She waved, closed the door, and as she headed to the truck behind his, which was indeed Sam Barr's vehicle, Ty's last glimpse of Jade was her sweet fanny as she got on the running board and scooted up into the passenger seat. He blinked, stunned by how fast he'd lost her. Damn Sam for being such a resourceful fellow, Ty thought, recognizing at the same time that Sam had many fine qualities, resourcefulness notwithstanding, or

Ty would never have brought him here as an outstanding, trustworthy candidate to be won by the ladies of BC.

But he didn't have to be *so* darn resourceful.

"It was like taking candy from a baby," Sam observed to his two friends as they perched in the bunkhouse at the Hanging H ranch. Their friend—and project—Justin Morant had married Mackenzie Hawthorne here not so many months ago, making himself the proud father of four little girls. Justin had kept the three amigos—as he called Squint, Sam and Frog—on at the Hanging H, saying he had big plans to expand the spread and operations. They would also need a lot of help when they put the Haunted H into full swing, the renaissance of Bridesmaids Creek's beloved "haunted" house and amusement place for kiddies and families. This October, they'd be putting the haunted back in the Hanging H, and BC was buzzing with the return of one of their most profitable and renowned projects.

"Candy from a baby?" Squint said. "Even a baby has better sense than Ty."

Frog grinned. "I figure putting you up to following Ty around was a stroke of genius. There you were, the proverbial white knight, when Jade decided she needed a ride away from temptation."

Sam sank into the leather sectional sofa in the comfortable bunkhouse, sighing with pleasure. "They say a man doesn't know what he's lost until it's gone. And the only way to capture Ty in his own snare is to make him think the bait is about to be stolen."

They all crowed about that, lifting beer bottles to each other in victory.

"What we need is a real challenge," Frog said.

The room went silent.

"I don't believe there's anything more challenging than getting Ty Spurlock to pull his head out of his butt," Sam offered. "What do you have in mind?"

"Well, let's see." Frog gazed at the ceiling. "The haunted house will start by the end of this month, for nine glorious months of family fun. Then BC kicks off Christmas Wonderland all over town, and Santa Claus takes over right after Thanksgiving. What do you say," Frog said, warming to his idea, "if we give ourselves a two-week deadline to get Ty and Jade engaged?"

Squint looked at him doubtfully. "What you're really aiming for is to get Ty off the dime before he leaves for BUD/S. That's just not going to happen. You know as well as anyone, since you were by my side in Afghanistan, that a BUD/S candidate is encouraged to take care of any detail that might be a distraction before he gets to training. Along that topic, a candidate is also discouraged from taking on new decisions, such as a wife. I say hold your horses, there, son. BUD/S is serious stuff."

"Then why are we doing this? Why are we trying to pull the rug out from under Ty?" Sam shook his head. "It'd be unfair to Jade if we're all going to wave goodbye to Ty in a couple of weeks, and her heart is broken."

"That's why an engagement is even more important." Frog nodded wisely. "No questions left unanswered."

"There are too many questions," Squint said direly. "You forget there was a murder here years ago that was never solved. Ty hasn't forgotten that the lack of an arrest was put down to his father's bungling of the investigation. He's not going to pop any questions until his dad's name is cleared. And the only way to clear it is to reopen the Haunted H, and let everyone see that the past is the past. Whatever happened then no longer matters."

They considered that.

"I guess so," Sam said. "We're not being fair to Jade, then. She doesn't want a man who's all hung up in his head."

"No," Frog agreed. "She'd be better off with you."

"Yeah, but I don't want to settle down," Sam declared. "I want to see Ty caught in his own trap!"

"Then we'll have to work around the murder angle," Squint said, "Frog and I'll focus on Daisy Donovan, since it was her old man who was determined to destroy the Haunted Hanging H and brought this whole house of cards down on Ty. And you try to wrangle Ty to the altar, preferably before he ships out."

"Great," Sam said. "You took the easy assignment, and left me to corral the man who brought us here to find brides for ourselves."

"Thought you just said you don't want a bride," Squint pointed out.

"It's true," Sam said, downcast. "I just came along for the ride, and to see the two of you suffer. Then you decided to make Ty suffer, and that seemed like even more fun. But it's not so much fun anymore," he groused.

"It'll be worth it when we see Ty heading up the altar path," Frog said, exhorting his friends to action. "Shake on it, fellows. We've got a lot of work to do."

Ty was so annoyed with his friends and a certain sexy redhead that when Daisy Donovan slid up under his arm in the parking lot of the sheriff's office, all he could do was muster up an unenthusiastic, "Hi, Daze."

She gave him a friendly enough squeeze, but where

Donovans were concerned, it was like being in a boa constrictor's grip—you knew it wasn't going to end well unless you could get away fast.

The tempestuous brunette bombshell had no inclination to remove herself from his side. "So much man, Ty Spurlock, and somehow, all I ever feel for you is sisterly emotions."

"That's what they tell me. What's on your mind?"

She laughed, hot allure practically snapping sparks his way—which meant Daisy wanted something.

"You."

"I'm not available." His gaze lit on Jade heading into Madame Matchmaker's comfortable, cheery, pink-fronted shop, and his stomach bottomed out. What could Jade possibly want with Madame Lafleur?

No doubt it was just a simple visit. Madame Matchmaker and Mssr. Unmatchmaker—Cosette and Phillipe Lafleur—had offices right next to each other, connected internally by an arched door that could be locked for privacy when they had clients. Phillipe and Cosette had been married for fifty years, bickered constantly, loved each other like mad and had recently decided they were going to unmake their own marriage. This decision had BC residents in a twist, not certain whether the matchmaking/unmatchmaking services still had good karma. Cosette kept a book of all the matches she'd put together—and of the "mismatches," only one was recorded in her book: that of Mackenzie Hawthorne's marriage to Tommy Fields. Tommy had left Mackenzie for a twenty-year-old, and since Ty had been responsible for bringing Tommy to Cosette's attention to make the match, he'd felt compelled to bring a replacement to BC for Mackenzie: Justin Morant.

It was a match made in heaven. But since Ty knew that Cosette's matches didn't always go off as planned, he worried about Jade slipping into the pink shop with the scrolled lettering on the window that read Madame Matchmaker Premiere Matchmaking Service. Where Love Comes True.

He didn't want love coming true for Jade, at least not with anyone but himself.

"I really am a rat bastard," he murmured, and Daisy said, "What?"

"Nothing." He looked down at the brunette attached to his arm. "Did you say you needed something, Daisy? I have to be somewhere."

"I want you. Remember?" She smiled at him, a veritable temptress with something on her mind.

Stepped right into that, and now he was almost afraid to ask. "You just said you have sisterly emotions for me. Can you be more specific about this 'want'?"

She glanced at the jail, which was buried deep inside the courthouse, just the way Sheriff Dennis liked it. "Going to see the sheriff about something?"

He'd forgotten all about seeing Sheriff Dennis once he'd spotted Jade. It almost didn't bear thinking about what pink-haired Cosette and his sassy redheaded darling might be dreaming up between them.

It certainly didn't bear thinking that Jade might be chatting with Cosette concerning Sam. *Sam, my friend, who I brought here,* Ty reminded himself. "Nothing set in stone."

"Good. Because I have a problem. And I need your big, strong muscles and wise mind to help me."

She beamed up at him, daddy's little girl, who'd never heard the word *no* in her life. Ty cleared his throat.

"What, Daisy?" He couldn't wait to get away and make an unscheduled visit to Phillipe, see if he could figure out what was going on behind the arched doorway of the two shops. Maybe the door would be open, and he could listen to what Cosette and Jade had up their dainty sleeves.

"I need a man," Daisy said. "And you'll do just fine."

Chapter 3

"What are they doing?" Jade asked, peering through the white slats at the window of Cosette's private sanctum. She couldn't see Daisy and Ty; Cosette had a much better vantage point. "If I know Daisy, she'll be kissing Ty before he even knows it's happening."

"I don't have a great view." Cosette strained her femininely plump body a little harder to peer out. "But it looks like Daisy's plastered all over him. She wants something."

Jade backed away from the window, telling herself it didn't matter. She shouldn't care. She plopped into a pink velvet antique chair and waited for Cosette to give her a further bulletin.

"Ah, there goes the kiss," Cosette said. "I knew Daisy would hit her mark."

Jade shot out of her chair, mashing the slats flat in her

hurry to see what she really didn't want to see. But all she saw was Ty striding away from Daisy, who watched him from in front of the small courthouse as he crossed the street. Jade snapped the blinds shut before he could catch her spying.

"Gotcha!" Cosette laughed delightedly, taking the pink chair opposite as Jade returned to hers.

Jade stared at her friend. "You mean Ty and Daisy weren't kissing?"

Cosette looked coy. "Of course not. That would never happen. But what do you care?"

"I don't." She did. Terribly.

"My girl, it's no use protesting. That's no way to catch a man. It's very American to be hard to get, and with some men that works. However, Ty's leaving soon. You don't have time to set traps."

Jade wrinkled her nose. "Let's talk about why I've come to see you." It would be best to get Cosette off the topic of trapping Ty. She had no idea how badly the man annoyed Jade.

It annoyed her even more that Cosette could tell that she did care if Ty kissed Daisy, or anyone.

"You can talk about whatever you like," Cosette said pleasantly. "In your mind, you'll still be thinking about Ty."

Jade drew a deep breath, telling herself to be patient with her older friend. "I assure you, I'm not thinking of Ty."

"Did I hear my name?" Ty appeared in the arched doorway, broad-shouldered and fine, and Jade's breath caught in spite of her wishing it wouldn't.

"Why would we be talking about you?" she asked, giving Cosette the don't-say-a-word eyeball.

"Why wouldn't you be?" He walked in and lounged on the prim white sofa across from their pink tufted chairs, eyed the delicate teacups on the table, ready for tea, and the pink-and-white petits fours invitingly arranged on a silver tray. "I saw you two spies. You're leading Jade down a bad path, Madame." He laughed, pleased with himself, a big moose with way too much confidence.

Jade scowled. "Everybody spies on Daisy."

"Of course we were spying on you!" Cosette said. "Jade had just told me how very handsome you looked today." She smiled hugely. "You don't mind if we ladies checked you out, do you, Ty?" Cosette rose with a distinctly coquettish air. "If you will both excuse me for a moment, I think I hear Phillipe calling my name. No doubt he's sniffed the aroma of petits fours and tea all the way from his dusty office. The man adores my petits fours." She swept out of the room, a vision in pink, white and silver, a lady on a mission.

Jade turned back to find Ty's gaze on her, his eyes squinting with internal smirk-itude. "Oh, don't go getting a big head over Cosette's comments."

"Where there's smoke, there's fire. Do please pour." He nodded toward the teacups.

"There was no smoke, no fire. We weren't looking at you." Jade leaned over to pour out the tea, then handed him a cup. "You can get your own petit four if you want it."

He laughed. "I do, in fact, want to try Phillipe's favorite treat. What is it about these tiny things you ladies find so irresistible?"

She hoped to get him off the topic of his handsomeness—which she had said nothing about to Cosette, though she had, in fact, been thinking that he was extraordinarily hunky—and the topic of tiny frosted cakes was as safe as any. "It's the art involved in a petit four."

"So in other words, you really don't want me to bring up that Cosette gave you away?" He winked, bit into a cake. "Whatever you want, doll."

Jade sent him a sour look. "What did Daisy want?"

"This is good," Ty said, his tone surprised. "Sugary, sweet, delicate. Couldn't eat a lot, far too rich for that, but tasty all the same. If you eat too many of these, you'll have to watch that sexy figure of yours."

"Back to Daisy. Quit avoiding the fact that you were conversing with the enemy."

"Oh, that." He put his plate down, picked up his tea and sipped. It looked quite ridiculous, she thought, a big man holding a fragile cup and saucer—and yet, somehow, she wanted so badly to kiss him she didn't know what to do.

Which was such a bad thought to have she wished it right out of her brain. "Yes, that. I'm going to bug you until you tell, so get on with it."

"Nothing important. And on that note, I should depart—"

"I'll ask Daisy myself, and whatever she wanted, she'll embellish," Jade warned.

"She wants me to escort her to the grand opening of the Haunted H," Ty said, his tone reluctant, his expression even more so.

Jade blinked. "But why? She and her father got up a petition to keep the Haunted H from starting again. They were violently opposed, and part of the reason we waited was to make sure folks in Bridesmaids Creek supported it."

"Daisy says it'll show everyone that bygones are bygones. She doesn't want to go by herself, and being escorted by—"

"By the man who brought the bachelors to Bridesmaids Creek will make her look like the belle of the ball," Jade interrupted.

Ty seemed confused. "I don't think that was what she's after. Granted, Daisy's no innocent flower, but she really sounded sincere."

Jade raised a brow. "Really, really sincere. Daisy, sincere." Surely that wasn't jealousy in her tone. But then she realized by the reappearance of his smirk that he was thinking the same thing.

"You know you're a special girl, Jade," he began.

She hopped to her feet. "Ty, you bigheaded oaf, don't you take that tone with me. I don't care if you go with Daisy. I just think you're a traitor. It's not fair to Mackenzie and Justin, because Daisy's done everything she can to destroy the Hanging H getting its haunting back. You *know* that."

"Yeah." Ty sounded momentarily confused again. "You have a point."

"And you know what Daisy's father said about your own father," Jade stated, warming to her subject, wanting badly for Ty to see for himself that he'd fallen prey to Daisy's charms, as every man in BC seemed to do eventually. "Robert Donovan said your father bungled the investigation of the murder out at the Hanging H—"

"Daisy said us going to the opening together would let everyone know that those days were past," Ty said. "I really thought it was in the Haunted H's—and Bridesmaids Creek's—best interests that I escort her. I'm leaving in less than two weeks. What I want more than anything is to leave behind a town with a secure future, with everyone on the same page."

He looked distressed. Jade felt sorry for him, so sorry her heart hurt. Maybe she was beating him up because she was jealous. *I am jealous,* she admitted to herself. But nothing good ever came of associating with Daisy Donovan and her land-grabbing father. "I've got to go."

"Hang on a sec—" Ty said, but Jade couldn't stay any longer. She hated all of it—hated that Ty was leaving most of all. What if she never saw him again?

She hurried out the door and jumped into her truck, vaguely aware that Daisy stood on the pavement outside Madame Matchmaker's shop, smiling her infamous bad-girl smile.

Ty was thunderstruck, and could not have been more shell-shocked, when Jade left in a hurry. He'd been this close to her—in the same room, and kindly left alone by Madame Matchmaker—and he'd blown it. Big mouth, big feet into big mouth, bad combo.

"Crap," he said, when Cosette hurried back into the room, her eyes distressed and her pink-tinted hair slightly mussed from her rush. "I think I just blew that."

"Oh, dear." She handed him a small plate of homemade lasagna, steam rising from the cheesy top. "Eat for strength. Eat for intuition."

He looked at the lasagna, a four-by-four piece he would have devoured under any other circumstances, say, had Jade not ditched him, leaving him with a guilty conscience and a terrible case of buyer's remorse where Daisy was concerned. "Will it help?"

"Oh, lasagna always helps," Cosette assured him.

"A big man like yourself doesn't do well on an empty stomach."

He thought that sounded like the first sane advice he'd had all day, and dug in with the silver fork she'd put on his plate.

He actually felt a little stronger, and perhaps a bit of clarity come over him—it was too soon for intuition—as the warm food hit his stomach. "I'm in the doghouse with Jade."

"Yes." Cosette nodded. "Probably so."

"Trying to do the right thing isn't always easy."

"Indeed it's not. But doing a dumb thing is very easy."

He gazed at her. "Were you just subtly trying to prod me into self-discovery mode?"

"Not so wordy, dear. Just trying to help you pull your head out of your keister, as you young folks put it."

"Ah." He ate some more lasagna. "Does Jade like me?"

"A little," Cosette said. "You did spend a lot of time being raised by her mother, if you recall. She got used to you."

"Yeah. Jade was an awesome little sister." Only he hadn't felt sisterly toward her in a long, long time.

"Things change," Cosette observed.

"Daisy might have changed."

"And some things don't ever change."

Ty nodded. "You think there's no way to leave the past behind and move on with our lives? The Donovans can't mean it when they say they want to be part of BC?"

"Some things are just habit." Cosette shrugged. "No, I don't think the Donovans are being any more forthright than they've ever been."

Why was he training to be a SEAL if he didn't believe in the greater good? "Eventually this town has to move on."

"I'm impressed that you want to forgive the Donovans, given how your father was treated by them when he was sheriff."

Ty's blood hit low boil, began to simmer at the old, painful memories. He put his plate on the marble-topped coffee table. "I'm just trying to leave town on a good note. I want there to be healing, Cosette. No divisions in the town on my behalf."

"Are you not planning on coming back, then? Because this town wrote the book on divisions. We feel pretty safe with black and white, good and evil. We're not trying to be a storybook town, Ty. We sell our charms and our legends, always with a hefty dose of fairy tale evil villains."

He looked at her. "You and Phillipe aren't really getting a divorce, are you?"

She stared at him. "Young man, how is that any of your business? I suspect you have plenty of your own love life to attend to."

He got up from the chair. "You never did say whether you believe Jade feels more than sisterly to me."

"But we've already established your head is firmly lodged in your hindquarters, dear, so what good would it do for me to try to help you with the answer?" Cosette walked him to the door. "I have no words of wisdom for you."

"No words of guidance from the local matchmaker?" He was teasing, but only slightly. He really wanted to know how Jade felt, because he was definitely getting some kind of strange vibe from her.

"A little bit of guidance, just a smidge, if you're in

the mood to hear it," the matchmaker said. "Jade needs to be able to trust a man. Completely."

Cosette closed the door behind him.

Great. Jade didn't seem to trust him much.

Right now, Ty really didn't trust himself.

Suz Hawthorne, Mackenzie's little sister and part-owner of the Hanging H ranch, launched herself at Ty the moment he returned to the bunkhouse. "Are you an idiot?" she demanded. "A certifiable idiot?"

Ty slumped into the leather recliner, noting that Sam, Squint and Frog were all there to witness his takedown. "Probably. On which topic are we speaking?"

The thing about Suz was that she instantly commanded respect—if a fellow wanted to keep his hat attached to his head. Twenty-three and spunky, recently retired from the Peace Corps, she had come home to help her sister save the Hanging H, preserving it for herself and Mackenzie, but mostly for Mackenzie's four newborns. You only had to look at Suz to realize she probably could make your life miserable if she cared to, Ty realized. He eyed her short spiky hair, streaked blue over blond, and the cheek stud that complemented her dark eyes—eyes that glared at him even as he stared back at her.

"Kissing Daisy?" Suz demanded. "You're not a certifiable idiot. You're a certifiable dumb-ass!"

"I did not kiss Daisy."

Suz's glare went DEFCON on him. "The grapevine says differently. You of all people know Daisy Donovan is poison to us!"

His brothers-in-mischief looked at him with great sympathy.

"She has a point, bro," Frog said.

"Poison or not, Daisy's *hot*," Squint said, earning himself astonished stares from everyone.

Sam grinned. "Doesn't mean she'd be good for you."

"You can talk, Sam," Ty said. "You're just going to ride away one day. This is my town. I have to stay on everyone's good side because eventually I'll be pushing up daisies here with the rest of my fellow residents, and I don't expect to get any more peace in the afterlife than I've gotten in BC in the present life. Staying on everybody's good side is an art form." And right now, he wasn't on Suz's good side. "Look, little sister—"

"Don't 'little sister' me." Even with the wild hair, the piercings and the discreet tats, Suz was beautiful in her own way—and her expressive eyes right now stabbed him with guilt. "Daisy and her father tried to kill off the haunted house before it ever got started. If you're so interested in saving Bridesmaids Creek, you'll know that you can't show up with the enemy. Or be sucking face with her, either."

Suz shot the men a last look of disgust and departed. Ty's friends checked him for his reaction.

"She has a point," Squint said. "I'll save you. I'll suck face with Daisy."

"She's a fireball. Won't ever glance your way unless there's something she wants from you." Ty looked at his boots, which he'd propped on the coffee table, in direct violation of the house rules he had engraved on his mind from years of living under Jade and Betty's roof. "In fact, I think I got snookered."

"What were you thinking?" Frog peered out the window after Suz. "That is some fine little lady, by the way."

"And that's not going to happen, either." Ty got to his

feet. "Not at the pace you three are moving." He felt distinctly glum about his dilemma. "Do you knuckleheads understand I'm leaving town soon? I won't be here to guide the reins of romance for you."

Sam laughed. "There's no such thing, bro. Romance isn't guided. It's a whirlwind of passion, joy, misunderstanding and longing."

They all gazed at Sam, who shrugged.

"I'm just saying," he told them. "If you really want romance, you have to let the whirlwind suck you into its vortex."

"I've had enough of sucking faces and whirlwind vortexes. One of you is going to have to escort Daisy to the opening. You must go in my stead, as my representative. It'll be a poor substitute," Ty said grandly, "but a man doesn't go back on his promise." He pulled a quarter from his pocket. "Here's how we'll decide which of you will—"

"Lash himself to the mast of misfortune," Frog butted in. "None of us wants to be saddled with the mistress of mayhem."

"You're all so poetic today. This is how this works." Ty put the quarter on the top of his fist. "Each of you will call heads or tails. The one who calls wrong wins the prize."

"Some prize," Sam said. "I don't see why we should have to clean up your mess, dude."

"Because I brought you here."

"In other words, no gain without pain. I call heads," Sam said.

"Is it a two-headed coin?" Squint asked. "It'd be like you to have a two-headed coin."

Ty gawked at his friend's lack of trust in him. "Would a SEAL candidate scam his best buddies?"

"I'll call heads, too," Frog sighed.

"I'll take tails," Squint said, "just to liven things up."

Ty tossed the coin, let it land on the Southwestern-style loomed rug. The quarter stared at them.

"That's it, then," Squint said, "I'm your fall guy."

Frog and Sam leaned back on the leather sofas, oozing relief. Ty picked up his quarter.

"I thought you said you wanted to kiss Daisy," Ty said to Squint.

"I thought I did. I think I just got really cold feet." He looked suddenly apprehensive. "It was one thing to have the fantasy. It's another to have the fantasy sprung on you in all its—"

"Soft, delicate flesh." Sam hopped up, clapped Ty on the shoulder. "Thanks for the good flip. I'm off to hunt up trouble at the big house."

"Big house?" Ty watched Frog shoot to his feet, following Sam to the door. "You mean the Hanging H? Are you going to see Suz?"

"I am," Sam said. "Frog's not." He glared at his buddy. "You stay here with them. I don't need any deadweight."

Frog hurried out the door in front of Sam, in a rush to get to Suz first. Sam glanced back at Squint and Ty with a grin. "He's so easy to work. A little spark of jealousy and watch those boots fly."

He closed the door. Ty sighed. "Thanks for taking Daisy on for me. I just can't afford any drama right now. Not when I'm leaving." He sank into the sofa. Of course, his relief had nothing to do with his departure; it was all about Jade. Once he'd realized he had stepped in a huge pile of cosmic poo, he knew he had to back out on Daisy no matter what it took. There was no way he wanted Jade upset with him.

"You're crazy about that little lady, aren't you?"

Of course he wasn't crazy about Jade. What a dumb thing to say. "Don't try to make romance bloom in a desert, Squint."

Jade blew in on a flurry of cold wind and a gust of snow that slithered from the bunkhouse roof. Ty straightened, stunned that she was here, glad as heck to see her.

"I think I'll join the fellows and see what trouble we can conjure up," Squint said, disappearing.

Some friend, taking off when it was clear there was going to be a sonic boom leveled at him. Ty looked at Jade, appreciating the tall redhead's sass as she put her hands on her slender hips and gazed at him with disgust.

"Daisy Donovan," she said.

"I felt sorry for her."

"You did not." Jade glared at him. "Daisy tried to ruin my business. She's trying to ruin the Hawthornes' haunted house, which, may I remind you, is something that could bring Bridesmaids Creek back to life. As I recall, that was your stated purpose in returning with three bachelors, wasn't it? New blood to breathe new life into the moribund shell that is Bridesmaids Creek?"

He loved looking at this woman. He loved hearing her talk, even when she was railing at him. When she said words like *moribund,* her lips pursed so cutely it was all he could do not to jump up and take those lips with his mouth, hungrily diving into the sweet sex appeal that was Jade.

Hell, he wasn't 100 percent certain what *moribund* meant—although it sounded distinctly dire—but maybe if he let her talk long enough, she'd say something else that started with *m-o-r*. He decided not to confess that he'd already dumped Daisy off on Squint, and to let the little lady fuss at him.

"Don't you have anything to say for yourself?" Jade demanded.

"I'm content to let you do all the talking." He settled himself comfortably, watching her face. "You have something on your mind, and I'm happy to let you clear the deck."

She sat next to him, so she could look closely at him to press her case, he supposed. But the shock of having her so near to him—almost in his space—was enough to brain-wipe what little sense he had. Damn, she smelled good, like spring flowers breaking through a long, cold winter. He shook his head to clear the sudden madness diluting his gray matter. "You're beautiful," he said, the words popping out before he could put on the Dumb-ass Brake.

The Dumb-ass Brake had saved him many a time, but today, it seemed to have gotten stuck.

"What?" Jade said. Her mesmerizing green eyes stared at him, stunned.

He was half drowning, might as well go for full immersion. "You're beautiful," he repeated.

She looked at him for a long moment, then scoffed. "Ty Spurlock, don't you dare try to sweet-talk me. If there's one thing I know about you, it's that sugar flows out of your mouth like a river of honey when you're making a mess. The bigger the jam, the sweeter and deeper the talk." She got up, putting several feet of safety between them, and Ty cursed the disappearance of the brake that had deserted him just when he'd needed it most.

"Okay, so if sweet talk won't save me," he said, reverting to cavalier, since that's what she seemed to be expecting, "all I can say is that Daisy asked me to take her to the grand opening, and you didn't."

"I didn't want to ask you!"

"Then why are we having this conversation? Good old-fashioned green-eyed monster, maybe?" He got up, took her in his arms. "I'll talk sweet to you if you want me to, beautiful."

She stomped on his toe and moved out of his arms. He bent over, his toe impressed by the sudden squelching it had cruelly received.

"What I want you to do is tell Daisy Donovan you wouldn't be caught dead escorting her to the haunted house. No smart remarks about puns." Jade glared at him. "And from now on, I suggest you remember who your real friends are."

He fell onto the sofa, wondering if she'd broken his toe. Definitely he was going to donate a toenail to the cause. Not a good thing to have happen right before he left for BUD/S. "I know who my friends are. They're the ones who don't try to damage me right before I leave for SEAL training."

"I don't care about that," Jade said sweetly. "I care that you don't fall into one of Daisy's many traps, and leave drama back here in BC for me to clean up. You're just lucky I got to you before Suz did."

"She's already been here. Only she didn't wound me." Ty glanced at his secret sweetie's boots with respect. Square-toed and sturdy, they could have been registered weapons.

"She didn't? Maybe she's going soft. But I'm not. I know who my friends are." Jade walked over, tugged his boot off. "I also know how commerce works in this town, and I understand Daisy's tricky little mind. Oh, you big baby," she said, staring at the toe she'd rescued from his boot and sock. "It's just going to be a little black-and-blue. You'd better toughen up if you're going to make it through training."

He smelled that sweet perfume again, was riveted by the soft red sweater covering her delicate breasts. Wondered if playing the pitiful card would get him attached to her lips—and decided he probably didn't want to do anything to upset the grudging sympathy he finally saw in her eyes. "My toe is fine. My life is fine. Everything is fine."

"It's not fine yet." She smiled, leaned over and gave him a long, sweet, not-sisterly-at-all smooch on the lips. Shocked, he sat as still as a concrete gargoyle, frozen and immobilized, too scared to move and frighten her off.

She pulled away far too soon. "*Now* it's fine."

Indeed it was. He couldn't stop staring at her mouth, which had worked such magic on him, stolen his breath, stolen his heart. He gazed into her eyes, completely lost in the script.

"What was that for?"

Jade got up, went to the door, opening it. Cold air rushed in and a supersized sheet of snow fell from the overhang, but he couldn't take his eyes off her.

"Because I felt like it," Jade said, then left.

Damn. His toe still throbbed, but his lips were practically sizzling from her kiss, far outweighing the complaining from his phalange bone. Ty had no idea what the hell had just happened here—but it dawned on him through his shell-shocked, sex-driven, Jade-desiring brain that if he were a smart man, he'd better decline

Daisy's invitation on the double, let her know he was sending a stand-in.

If he ever wanted to be kissed like that again.

Chapter 4

The night of the grand opening of the refurbished, re-born Haunted H was glorious, by anyone's standards. Ty felt a real sense of satisfaction as he looked at the new lights his buddies had put up in an elegant arch over the long drive-up to the ranch. Lights were everywhere, twinkling and beautiful, highlighting the butt-freezing weather and somehow making it romantic.

Maybe his three bachelor candidates weren't totally useless, after all. They could at least decorate, apparently, if not appropriately seduce the women he'd brought them here to romance.

Ty hurried after Jade when he saw her moving with long strides toward the jump house, which was teeming with kiddies. Parents with strollers watched, smiling, as their kids bounced inside the huge, inflatable pink-and-purple castle.

"Hi, Raggedy Ann," he said, and Jade turned to look at him. He thought she was amazing with her red curls springing out everywhere, completely negating the need for a Raggedy Ann wig. The red-and-white stockings were killer, clinging to dynamite legs Raggedy Ann never dreamed of having in her cloth-stuffed world. He nearly had a coronary over the cute painted freckles speckled across Jade's nose and cheeks, never mind the white apron over the blue dress, which for some reason made him very horny. He supposed the truth was that everything about Jade caught him between a coronary and an erection, a delicious in-between hell of longing and teeth-grinding lust.

She gave him a once-over. "What are you dressed up as?"

He was pretty proud of his efforts, and drew himself up to showcase the black cape, boots and swashbuckling ebony hat he thought he wore so stylishly. "Zorro. You couldn't tell?"

"You look silly." She offered him the tray she held. "Cupcake?"

"What do you mean, I look silly?" Ty demanded. "Ladies love Zorro. They think he's a dashing hero. And sexy."

"Guy Williams was sexy. Antonio Banderas was a sexy Zorro." She gave Ty another once-over. "Please take a cupcake so I'll feel better about deflating your monstrous ego."

Ty ignored the cupcake, wishing he could have a kiss instead. "Where did I go wrong?"

"I don't have time to tell you all the ways that costume is wrong." She laughed and started to move away. "Where's your date?"

Ah. The little lady was prickly because she was expecting Daisy to land on his arm any moment. He felt better now that he knew her lack of charmed respect for his costume was thanks to jealousy. "Squint's escorting her."

Jade moved away. "By now you have to wonder where you're going wrong, Ty. When Daisy Donovan throws you over, and you only put on half your mustache, something's not working for you."

She disappeared into the crowd. He felt his upper lip. Frog and Sam banged him on the back. Ty coughed, thinking he could easily survive BUD/S, since he could survive the camaraderie of his so-called friends in BC. "Easy on the lungs and rib cage, fellows."

"Where's your 'stache?" Frog demanded.

Ty looked at Frog, dressed as a fairly convincing Robin Hood, and Sam, who was masquerading as a pirate. Both of them had their mustaches firmly in place. Ty felt around in his pocket for the left side of his. "Thought I had it on."

They smirked. "Smart-asses," he said, realizing his friends had let him walk out of the bunkhouse missing half his facial prop. "Friends don't let friends go out missing the most important part of their costume. The mustache is the sex-magnet angle for Zorro."

They seemed to think that was hilarious. "Look," Frog said, "Sam snapped a photo when you weren't looking. It's pretty much gone viral on the internet."

The photo showed Ty trying to get his hat just right in the mirror, really working hard for Zorro-mysterious, completely missing the fact that one side of his upper lip was traumatically bare. "You guys are such a riot."

"Yeah." Frog wiped tears of laughter from his eyes and put his phone away. "That we are."

"So, was Jade bowled over by your sex appeal?" Sam asked, loudly enough that half the county could hear the question, even over the whirring of air keeping the bounce house inflated, and the squeals from delighted kids.

"Not really," Ty admitted. "She seemed to be under the impression that I was here with Daisy. Every piece of gossip transmits itself at warp speed in BC, but for some reason not the one bit of info that really mattered reached her ears." He glared at his buddies. "You two are useless."

"You gotta talk your own book, brother," Frog said. "We can't do all your heavy lifting for you."

"Yeah, don't expect us to sell the steak if it ain't sizzling on its own," Sam said, and they drifted off, vastly amused with themselves.

Ty sighed and went to man the dunk booth as he'd promised Jade's mother, Betty, that he would.

"Don't you look hot," Daisy said at his elbow. She was dressed like a princess, of course. What else would anyone have expected? "Hot as a pistol!"

Ty perked up at the rather corny appreciation of his efforts. "Thanks."

"No problem." She traced his upper lip where there should have been a sweet Zorro-inspired clump of faux bristles. "I have my face paints with me, since I'm in charge of face painting. I can fix that in a jiff."

He was pretty relieved to hear it, even though he was surprised Daisy had been given any assignment at all, up until the point she began slowly, sensually painting on his upper lip with a brush. A crowd gathered around the princess and Zorro, and he wondered desperately where Squint was.

Ty could have predicted with the accuracy of seven oracles that Jade would catch him with his chin firmly clutched in Daisy's, well, clutches, her face inches from his.

"Well, at least it's a mustache now," Jade said, "instead of half a confused black caterpillar."

"I think he looks sexy as hell," Daisy said, and planted one right on his cheek. Ty's eyes went wide. His body recognized hot sex appeal and his inner guide reacted urgently, screaming *Fire! Fire! Danger!*

He leaped away from Daisy, just in time to see Jade heading off toward the ice cream booth her mother ran, a very popular spot surrounded by anxious kids wanting sprinkles on their ice cream and parents wanting hot chocolate.

"I heard a rumor," Daisy said, "that Jade Harper made you dump me tonight."

"Ah…" Ty tried to glimpse Raggedy Ann's hot red curls in the crowd near the ice-cream stand. "She didn't approve," he said, his brain belatedly registering that he probably should have censored that remark.

"I see," Daisy said. She leaned up against his chest. "You don't know what you're missing."

He stared down at the determined, dynamite bundle of feminine firepower his buddy Squint seemed to think he could handle. *Hell, no, Squint can't handle this. I can't handle this.* It would take the real Zorro to tame this tiger.

"You tell Jade Harper that nobody dumps Daisy Donovan. Nobody that doesn't end up regretting it. And it goes double for her. She and Suz and Mackenzie Hawthorne aren't the queen bees of BC, even if they think they are. And for some odd reason, I get distinctly brotherly vibes whenever I'm near you. It's really tragic. All kinds of man, and something about you makes me want to pat your head like a puppy. I just don't get it."

She sauntered off, sexy in a white Cinderella ball gown that bordered on safe-for-kiddies-and-somehow-unsafe-for-bachelors. Ty wiped his brow under the gallant black Zorro hat.

"You're smearing the 'stache," Squint told him, suddenly appearing through the crowd.

"Crap!" Ty quit trying to wipe off Daisy's kiss and the sweat on his brow. "Where the hell have you been? And why haven't you got a hold on the princess of peril?" He stared at his pal. "And what is that you're wearing?"

Squint laughed. "*Where* the hell I've been is helping Justin Morant put up another six tables and accompanying chairs. The Haunted H has a much bigger turnout than expected. They also needed about another six dozen wienies for the wienie roast."

"That's nice. Glad you're making yourself useful," Ty growled.

"Why I'm not holding my hot princess is the simplest part of your question. I believe in keeping the lasso loose, brother. But not too loose. I'll be catching up with the Cinderella in question momentarily. Believe me, I'll teach her all about magic pumpkins and wands that do a different kind of magic."

"That's nice," Ty said, still staring at Squint's outrageous getup. "Anyway, what the hell are you?"

"Can't you tell? I'm you." He pointed to the camo bandanna, boots, camo pants, black Kevlar vest and helmet equipped with night-vision goggles. "I'm you going into BUD/S."

"That's so funny I forgot to laugh," Ty said sourly. "It's all fine for you to mock my efforts, since you and Frog are already SEALs. I sense a little rivalry, or perhaps the essence floating through that you don't think I can make it, so mock away. But you're scaring the kiddies and, I might add, their parents. People are looking at you like sharpshooters, assassins and military-grade security were hired for this shindig," he said, keeping his voice low. "At least take off the goggles and hide the artillery, okay?"

"It's a toy," Squint said, shifting the long gun on his back, letting the strap hang over his shoulder. "It's a water cannon, doofus."

"It doesn't matter. Don't you remember what happened? We don't want anyone recalling that someone died here at the last haunted house."

"He wasn't shot," Squint said.

"We don't want any dangerous vibes. Go put it in your truck! And find Daisy before she starts any more trouble!"

"All right, dude. *Cálmate.* Keep your 'stache on. Damn." Squint went off, obviously a bit insulted.

"Hey, mister," a little boy said. "Are you running the dunking booth?"

"Yes. No." Ty grabbed Sam as he meandered by, and shoved him into his place. "The pirate is tending to the water exhibit. Have fun."

Ty trotted off to locate Raggedy Ann, finding her spinning cotton candy onto paper cones. "Can we talk?"

"Talk away. Want some?"

"Uh, no. Thanks." He handed the fluffy stick of

puffed pink sugar she gave him to the first kid in line. "From Zorro to you, kid."

"Thanks, mister!"

The boy hurried off.

"That's not how we make profits here. Weren't you the one who believed that the haunted house and bachelors were all BC needed to get back in the black?" Jade said.

He slapped a hundred dollar bill on the wooden ledge of the ice-cream-and-sweets stand. "Can we talk?"

"We're talking now," Jade said, oozing darling and too-sweet-for-tea.

"I want to talk to you alone."

She gazed at him, her green eyes wide. "Will Daisy allow you to? She just came by here with a—"

"That's it." Ty went into the crowd, grabbed Frog, propelled him to the stand. "Robin Hood's robbing the gremlins and warlocks and giving to the kiddies right here. I mean, the ninjas and pint-size ghosts. Make yourself useful and give these tiny customers a good show," he told Frog, tugging Jade out from the booth. He pulled her into the bunkhouse a little unceremoniously, but he was running out of days to break through the ice with this little gal. "There are way too many urchins around here. It's enough to make a single guy nervous as hell."

He dropped onto a sofa, pulled off the Zorro hat and the mask and the one side of the mustache that wasn't painted on. There was just no help for it; he had to do something before he went mad. So he swept Jade into his lap. "Now you listen to me and you listen good. I want nothing to do with Daisy Donovan, and you know it. You're just having a helluva good time teeing me up about it."

"Yes, I am. You deserve every moment of it."

He stared into Jade's dangerously green eyes, which reminded him of a hidden forest, and wished he knew of a forest somewhere to drag her off to. The closest one was near Bridesmaids Creek's creek, and it was far too cold to drag her there. She didn't fight—or even move—to get out of his lap, so he decided she liked being with him more than she was saying.

"You smell good. Like cotton candy."

"And peach ice cream and sprinkles and hot cocoa and popcorn. Sexy stuff." Jade looked at him. "I wasn't being honest. You're a really hunky Zorro."

He looked at her, suspicious. "Now you tell me."

"Couldn't tell you with Daisy hanging on to your face."

That sounded like an opening he couldn't pass up. "Okay, you hang on to my lips, and I'll probably get the message."

To his astonishment, Jade kissed him, long and slow and sweet, taking a tantalizingly hot tour of his mouth. Ty's brain blew a short circuit that fried The Plan and all his good sense and intentions in one fiery explosion.

"Get the message?" she asked, pulling back to study him.

He certainly had gotten something. "I'm not quite sure. If you do that again, I can probably—"

She put a finger against his lips. "You're leaving in, what, eight days? Nine?"

"Yeah. Wanna give me a private going-away party?" He wrapped his arms around her, mashing her closer to him, sighing against her neck. Wondered if he dared unzip the Raggedy Ann dress. "God, you taste better than cotton candy. Do it again."

"My point was, you're leaving. And according to The Plan I've heard so much about, the last thing you need are entanglements and issues back home when you go. That's straight from the BUD/S training bible, or the code you live by, or something, isn't it?"

The heat she was causing by sitting on him was just about unbearable. Even his eyeballs were heating and his brain was smoking, fogging his heretofore perfect reserve around Jade. "I can handle any issue you throw at me, doll face."

"How punny of you."

"No. You are a doll face, even when you're not Raggedy Ann. I don't care what you're wearing, you make my brain go bye-bye just by looking at you."

She stared at him. "What has gotten into you?"

"You," he said, thick desire terminating his normal inhibition. "You're in my blood, and I don't know why the hell I never realized it before."

Those dark green eyes stayed on him. "You know this is a very bad idea," Jade stated.

"It may be," Ty said, "but that's exactly what makes me so convinced I need to take this walk on the wild side."

"So you want to make love to me?"

He hadn't gotten that far in his thinking, but as soon as she mentioned it, he went straight up like the pirate sword his buddy had been carting around. "The question is, do you want me to make love to you?"

She straddled him, kissing him, and the bits of his poor Jade-addled brain hot-wired right into another dimension. All he could think of was that he better kiss the daylights out of her before she changed her mind, before she convinced herself that this really was the bad idea of all bad ideas.

But she rocked against him instead, and he slipped his hands under the blue dress and white apron, nearly dying at the sweet feel of her butt cheeks in his palms after he'd been surreptitiously lusting after them all this time. Jade moved against his crotch, getting as close as she could, her kisses matching his for urgency and passion. He held her tight, crushing her fanny against him, his tongue sweeping inside her mouth, tasting peppermint and even a little sweet cotton candy. He wanted her more than he wanted his next breath, but no way was he going to do anything to scare her away. Talking about making love and actually doing it—well, a man couldn't take anything for granted, no matter how much he wanted inside the soft, welcoming heaven he knew Jade would be.

"Well?" she asked softly.

"Well what?" He stared, mesmerized and still, into her big eyes, hardly daring to believe that this moment was actually coming true for him. Holding Jade was so much more amazing than his dreams had ever been.

"Are you going to make love to me or not?"

He gulped. "What about all that business about me leaving, and The Plan?"

She began unbuttoning his shirt. "I'm a big girl."

Dear God, she was, a big, beautiful girl. Nothing like the playmate with whom he'd roughhoused. "I don't want to—"

"Leave me holding the bag?" Jade kissed his mouth, tracing his lips with her tongue. "Will you quit being a gentleman and act a little more like your costume?"

He blinked. "Just to clarify—"

She got up, dragged him to his bedroom. Closed and locked the door. "Listen up, cowboy. You brought your buddies here to settle the ladies. You need to do your part."

"That part of The Plan was about bringing eligible, marriage-seeking bachelors to BC." She had his shirt off now and was working on the bottom half of his costume, and Ty wondered if he could survive for the next six months without this woman.

"I'm not looking for marriage. I'm not looking for anything but a little dangerous costume sex and maybe some playacting. Can you handle that?"

"I can sure man up to the occasion." He caught her hands in his. "And then what?"

"And then you go off and do your thing, and I do mine." Jade smiled. "You'll tell your buddies you nailed Raggedy Ann, and they'll be totally impressed. I'm just hoping my Zorro fantasy lives up to the real thing."

Well, there was a challenge a man just had to accept. Ty slowly unzipped the blue dress, pushed it down over her arms, dropped that and the white apron to the floor, nearly asphyxiated from the desire clogging his throat. She was perfect. Long and lean and tall, just like he'd imagined. Peach-sized breasts, freckles in some spectacularly sexy places and a navel he planned to get very familiar with.

After he licked every centimeter of that deliciously heart-shaped ass. "Come here, doll face. Zorro's going to show you exactly why his blade made him a legend."

Chapter 5

Jade was horrified when she awakened in the bunk-house, realizing that Zorro was gone, and maybe so was her reputation as a Haunted H volunteer. She slipped her costume back on, annoyed that she'd dozed off—but then again, those moments in Ty's arms had been wonderful. She'd finally managed to seduce Ty Spurlock. How long had she waited for the right moment to kiss that footloose cowboy? Forever. When the opportunity had finally presented itself, no way would she have passed it up, even if she felt silly wearing painted-on freckles. A pass by the mirror showed that the freckles were a thing of the past—Ty had kissed her senseless, every centimeter of her body. A few dot-on lip liner freckles were no match for that man's roving, heated kisses.

He was dynamite in bed, and she'd fibbed like mad, telling him he wasn't sexy in his costume. Protecting herself, putting up barriers that, thankfully, she'd let down just in time. Her body sang with delirious joy at the amazing things he'd done to her.

The thought of Ty leaving for BUD/S was terrifying in a way—but she'd sold him the notion that they would go their separate ways, no strings attached.

"And I'm sticking to that story, because it's the only one I've got." Jade slipped out the back so no one would notice where she'd been for the hour she'd been gone. The haunting was still in full swing, though the kiddies were looking a trifle spent. Parents began strolling with their tired children toward the massive parking lot manned by BC volunteers. She returned to the ice-cream stand, picking up her duties smoothly from Frog, who'd been doing a creditable job of twirling cotton candy. "Thanks for working my shift. Head off and have some fun, Frog."

He grinned at her. "I saw Ty go by a while ago, and he's missing half his mustache again. It's about time someone gave that cocky dude something to do with his mouth besides run it."

"I can't imagine what you mean." Jade handed a couple of mugs of hot cocoa to a young couple who looked exhausted by their small fry's evening out. But they smiled at her as they left, mentioning how much fun they'd had at the haunted house, and a funny arrow of longing hit Jade as she watched them walk away, pushing their stroller, enjoying their cocoa and the togetherness with their family.

She was never going to have that. To have a family she would need a man, and the only man she'd ever loved was Zorro, er, Ty Spurlock. All that business about them going their separate ways was just big talk to get him loosened up enough to say yes to her seduction of him.

"Well, I suppose I'll go see if I can hunt up a pair of lips to snack on. All this sweet stuff has made me hungry," Frog said, winking. "Your smile is a little crooked, Raggedy Ann, but I guess that won't come as a surprise, since you disappeared into the bunkhouse with Ty."

"Mind your own business, Frog." She tried to scowl at him, but he was so pleased that he thought he'd guessed her secret. She was too happy to frown, anyway; her heart was singing one minute, diving into uncertainty the next.

Frog ambled off, and her mother leaned over and whispered, "Daisy knows you and Ty disappeared together somewhere. She hung out here for a good half hour to see when you'd return."

"For all she knows, I was on parking-lot duty." Jade didn't care what the woman thought—Ty was never going to be Daisy's. Jade had caught him first, and she was going to keep him for the few days he had left in BC. Daisy could go jump in the creek.

"I tried to tell her you were helping with other stands," Betty said, "but she seems to have radar where Ty is concerned."

"Tough." Smiling, Jade helped her mother close down the stand, packing away the food and the condiments and serving utensils to take back to the ice-cream shop in town.

All was going well until an ostentatiously large Hummer limo pulled into the Haunted H grounds. Robert Donovan got out, and the limo slipped off, leaving him surveying the running tots and happy visitors with a frown. Standing about six-four, Robert was a man who struck fear into the hearts of many. He had black hair threaded with gray, massive shoulders, and boots that seemed too large to be real.

"Don't look now, but the destroyer of light and happiness has arrived," Jade told her mother.

There were still about two hundred guests at the park, lingering because of the romantic stars and pretty strung lights, and probably because they were having a grand time at a fun family event that had been closed for years.

"He's only here to make trouble," Betty said. "You can count on that."

"I suppose I'll take him a cup of hot cocoa, since we haven't emptied the pot out yet. Maybe the sweetness will keep him from his mission of mischief." It was the only possibly reason he could be here. The man had done everything he could to block the Haunted H from reopening, and so had his daughter. Which was kind of strange, since Daisy had been working the carnival tonight. Jade frowned as she walked toward Robert with the cocoa.

She was beaten to him by Suz Hawthorne. "Come to spoil our success, Robert?" Suz demanded. Her petite frame was a good foot and some shorter than the man she'd accosted. But Suz was fearless. Jade hurried to her friend's side.

"What success?" Robert looked at both women, his eyes eagle-stern, his hawklike nose somehow expressing his disdain. "This isn't a success. There are so many code violations here the Haunted Heap won't be open long." He smirked. "Be a good girl and go get your big sister. I have something I want to tell Mackenzie."

Suz drew herself up. "My sister and I are partners and co-owners. You can say whatever needs to be said to me, or not say it at all."

"My words can come just as easily in the form of a legal complaint."

Suz shrugged. "It's your money. I'm not interrupting Mackenzie's big night just so you can spout off. You can see we're a huge success and you're just ticked as ticked can be."

Ty's hand suddenly braced Jade at her back, his other hand supporting Suz at her shoulders. "You bugging my best girls, Donovan?"

Robert frowned. "What the hell business is it of yours?"

"Just as much as it is yours. As far as I can see, unless you've bought a ticket, you're trespassing." Ty jerked his head toward the Hummer limo idling a discreet distance away in the outbound lane. "Overcompensate much?"

Robert's eyes flamed. A slight gasp escaped Jade, and Ty's hand moved from her back to her shoulder, supporting her as he was Suz.

"You tell your sister," Robert said to Suz, "that this dump is closed. There'll be no more of this once I file a cease-and-desist motion. According to the petition drive, a great many BC residents don't want this grubby little flea market bringing crime and vagrants to our quiet town, and I believe the law will be on my side." He looked triumphant.

"The only people who signed that petition against us were people you threatened with some kind of financial wipeout. Like Mssr. Unmatchmaker," Jade said. "Anyway, most all of BC is here. Including your daughter."

Robert frowned, his massive forehead looking as if divots had suddenly been furrowed in the granite. He opened his mouth to speak, but a sudden scream from someone in the crowd cut him off.

"Call an ambulance!" a voice cried.

"Is there a doctor here?" someone else yelled.

Suz, Jade and Ty ran toward the people surrounding Betty's ice-cream stand. The older woman looked terrified.

"He was fine a minute ago!" Betty exclaimed, pointing to a man lying on the ground. "He bought cocoa!"

Jade looked at the cocoa in her hands, which she'd never given Robert, and glanced down at the prone figure. People were bent over him, trying to give him assistance and checking his pulse.

"He's dead," Sheriff Dennis said, kneeling at the man's side.

"It was the cocoa!" someone in the crowd whispered. They all gazed at the ice-cream-and-sweets stand, and at Betty, who appeared confused and frightened.

"It was *not* the cocoa," Jade called loudly, raising the cup. "This is cocoa I poured myself from right here, at our family's stand. Our own home recipe, I might add. I was taking Mr. Donovan a cup," she said, glancing at Robert. "There's nothing wrong with the cocoa."

People gazed at her, suspicious and nervous that they might have consumed something poisonous from the little stand. Jade raised the cup again, and with about a hundred pairs of eyes on her, drank every bit of it.

Silence fell, eerie compared to the laughter and joy that had marked the evening all night long. Even the children were still and silent, confused by what was happening.

"It's clear to see," Robert Donovan began, "that this repeat performance, just like so many years ago—"

"Oh, for crying out loud, Donovan." Sheriff Dennis rose from his abandoned attempts at CPR. He placed his jacket over the victim's face out of respect. "Don't start that crap, with this poor soul not gone from this life a full five minutes." He barked at his deputy to get the coroner on the double.

People still eyed Jade, convinced that any second she'd fall to the ground dead.

Then, to her everlasting thankfulness, Ty's voice split the tension. "Betty, pour me a big-ass mug of that cocoa, would you?"

Gratitude hit Jade square in her heart. She watched her mother's hands shake as she poured and handed a cup to Ty. He raised it to Robert. "Bottoms up," he said, and finished it off, smacking his lips. "Best cocoa I ever had, just the way it's always been, Mrs. Harper. Ever since I was a boy, I looked forward to coming home on cold days to your house. I always knew there'd be a pot of hot cocoa and chocolate-chip cookies waiting in your kitchen. Did I ever thank you for that?"

Betty finally smiled, timidly but thankfully. Jade felt something bloom inside her, something that had been there a long time as just a tiny seed, but now blossomed into feelings much more deep. She smiled at Ty, who winked at her.

He turned to the sheriff. "Why don't you get Donovan to donate his vehicle for a couple of hours to haul this unfortunate soul over to the medical examiner's place?"

"I'll do no such thing!" Robert looked as if he might strip a gear, relaxing only a little when he saw his daughter, Daisy, standing at the edge of the crowd. "Honey, you need to come away from this place. It's dangerous."

"Nobody's going anywhere," Sheriff Dennis said. "My deputies will see to that. Until the M.E. arrives and gives us a preliminary guess as to how this individual died, everybody's staying right here. My deputies will see that you're comfortable as can be. Bridesmaids Creek is known for its hospitality. I'd say the appropriate medical personnel will be here any second, so relax, folks."

Betty began unpacking her stand, setting everything back up so that people could have something to eat and to feed their kids.

"I'd better help Mom." Jade looked up at Ty. "Thanks for everything."

He smiled at her. "I wouldn't miss tweaking Robert Donovan for the world. You know that."

"I heard that." Daisy frowned, suddenly appearing at his side. "You're just under Jade's spell, Ty Spurlock. My dad's trying to help BC, while the Harpers and the Hawthornes are trying to destroy it."

"You didn't look like anybody was hurting you tonight, Daisy," Jade said. "Who gave you the assignment of painting faces, anyway?"

"No one." Daisy sniffed. "I just wanted to participate."

"Why? You're too much like your father to want us to succeed. Was the goal to frighten off our customers?" Jade was too mad to be polite.

"We don't have to frighten off your customers. You do such a good job of *killing* them off." Daisy huffed, then went to stand beside her father.

"Pay no attention to her." Ty put his arm around Jade. "Let's figure out a way to keep these folks occupied with happy thoughts."

Jade went with Ty as he rounded up the guys, determined to put the best face possible on the Haunted H. But even she knew that after what had just happened, it would be almost impossible to dispel the rumor that something was very, very wrong in Bridesmaids Creek.

Chapter 6

Ty walked across to the bunkhouse, dead tired and ready to tuck in for the night. After the events of the evening, he couldn't help worrying that he was leaving his little town when it needed him most. The Donovans were definitely up to no good, and they had a pretty firm grip on BC. Jade and Suz and Mackenzie were tough, ready to face up to the Donovans, and they had a lot of community support. But there were still people who would fall in with the Donovans simply because money bought power—and silence.

Jade walked inside the bunkhouse behind him, following him to his room. "Thanks for sticking up for Mom. And our business."

He hadn't done much. Ty looked at Jade, tossed his hat on the dresser, tugged off his belt. "I didn't do anything anybody else wouldn't have done."

"You kept the Donovans from completely decimating our business."

"Maybe. For tonight." He shook his head. "I've got a bad feeling the haunted house may be damaged for good. All that hard work the Hawthornes, you and your family, the town and my guys put in trying to build BC into something better." Fury boiled inside him. "The Donovans just don't give up."

She walked over to him, caressed his cheek. "Ty, there's only so much you can do. We'll be fine here in BC."

He wished he knew that was true. Jade stood too close, clouding his senses. Ty relaxed into her palm, allowing himself to take the comfort she offered. He was angry for her sake, too. He'd seen the distress on Betty's face—and there was Jade, immediately stepping up to defend her mother. These two women gave constantly of themselves to BC—but they were like tiny acorns standing up to a giant, mighty oak for space. Robert Donovan was too ruthless, and the Harpers very fragile and defenseless.

Ty stepped away from Jade. "The sheriff said it appears the visitor died of a plain old garden-variety heart attack. So this time we have a conclusive cause of death, unlike the first time." The first death would never be solved, and people had long memories. He supposed that was why he felt so strongly about doing what he could to raise BC from the ground, because he knew what Donovan had done to his adopted father with rumors and scandalmongering.

And now it might be happening again. "I'm running out of ideas to stop Donovan."

Jade plopped down on his bed. "Look. You've got to

think about packing that locker over there," she said, pointing to where he'd been gathering up everything he needed for training. "You need to think only of your future, and getting into the SEALs. We're going to be fine here, Ty. I promise. We're a pretty resilient group. You know that."

"Yeah." He took a long look at Jade, tried not stare at her face, drink her in. She was so optimistic, so spunky. He'd hate to see all that ironed out of her by Donovan. It had happened to his father. Gradually, even resilience could be worn down by continued pounding, like rock worn away by the relentless sea.

Then again, Ty had his own team in place. The thought wasn't exactly heartening, but it was something. "Where are the three musketeers?"

Jade smiled at him, melting his heart. "They're about to rumble with Daisy's gang. I think Frog said they were going to duel—"

"What?" Ty stared at Jade. "Why didn't you tell me sooner?" He crammed his hat back on, grabbed his belt, thrusting it though his belt loops as he hurried to the front door.

She followed him. "I didn't tell you because I knew you'd do this."

"Do what?" He peered out the window, seeing that the last people had packed up their stands and deserted the Haunted H for the night. Hardly anybody was left on the ranch, and a full moon shone overhead—a perfect night for a full-on squabble between rival factions. "What am I doing?"

"Rushing off to play peacemaker." Jade dragged him from the window. "They're big boys. They can handle themselves. That's why you brought them here, right? To handle things?"

"I'm not sure why I brought them here anymore." Ty realized Jade was bent on keeping him away from the fight. "What's really going on?"

"What do you mean?"

She gave him such an innocent look that Ty belatedly realized she'd been sent to waylay him with a little faux seduction. He grinned. She was so charming and darling, thinking she had him right where she wanted him.

Well, if she was going to go to the trouble to seduce him, he might as well show up for her efforts. He pulled her into his arms. "It doesn't matter what the *tres* knuckleheads are up to. I'd rather find out what you're up to." He kissed her, taking his time with her mouth, enjoying sinking into her soft lips over and over.

The best part was how hungrily Jade kissed him back. Ty's head swam, and momentarily he lost his place in his own plan. "Hey," he said, pulling back to gaze into her eyes.

"Yes?" Those eyes had nothing but sweet shyness in them, and Ty wanted to surrender completely to her.

"You're supposed to be keeping me busy."

"I'm doing my best, cowboy."

That she was. All kinds of attraction was steamrolling him. It was killing him not to let his desire for Jade completely entice him into her scheme.

Her hands roamed across his back, and Ty's heart rate kicked into high gear. Whatever she was hiding, it was something she wanted to keep hidden for sure. She kissed along his jaw, made her way back to his mouth. Ty closed his eyes, hoped he wouldn't black out from denying himself the pleasure of Jade's temptress act.

"Okay, little lady." He set her away from him. "I'm giving you an A for effort. I'm not the kind of schmo who falls for a few kisses." He pushed his shirt back into his jeans, since it had worked loose thanks to Jade's clever little hands.

"Yes, you are. You're exactly the kind who falls for a few kisses."

This was dangerous ground. "Yeah, well, not anymore. Take me to this rumble you're trying to keep me from."

"No."

"I'll find it myself."

She blocked the door with her curvaceous body, flattened like a protective shield to keep him from leaving. "You won't."

Ty wanted to press Jade up against that door and kiss the daylights out of her, but she was trying so hard to waylay him that he had to see how far she'd take this newfound protectiveness. "I'll want more than a kiss or two if I'm not going to join the fun, cupcake."

She wrinkled her nose. "Thickheaded, much?"

Ty grinned. "If you can't stand the heat, don't wander into the kitchen. Now lead me to trouble."

"You're leaving for BUD/S soon. You need to be in good shape, not all busted up from a fight."

Ty stared at the most kissable mouth in town. "I've played this totally wrong."

"What do you mean?"

"I brought the three doorknobs here to settle the ladies. What I didn't realize was that it was the men in this town who needed settling." He couldn't get over how sweet she'd felt in his arms. Every man needed that kind of sweetness in his life—then there'd be no rumbling.

"Daisy's gang of five creepos. They need women. Then there'll be no fighting, just five happy family men tied down by diapers and wedding rings."

Jade locked the door, turned the bolt. Stayed right on her marker, not moving an inch.

"You can't stay there forever, sweetheart," Ty said. "This standoff between you and me is going to end one way or the other. Either I go join the fun, or I pick you up in my big, strong arms and lock you in my room so no one can interrupt what I'm going to do to you." He couldn't imagine what the ruckus was about, but he could hear shouts and smack talking. Jade looked more worried by the moment, glancing behind her at one particularly loud yell.

For a moment he thought she might relent and allow him to leave. She settled a meaningful gaze on him instead.

"I want a baby."

Ty stepped back a pace, stunned. "What does that have to do with me?"

"I want you to give me a child."

He blinked, took in her very serious expression. "That's a pretty good tactic, beautiful. You nearly gave me heart failure. But I'm not falling for it, so move your sweet little buns away from that door. My brothers need me."

She shook her head. "I want a baby, and you're the man who can help me."

He smiled, staggered by her charming ploy to keep him in the bunkhouse. "Well, of course I can help you. But as we both know, I'm leaving. I don't have time for romance and nonsense, and I'm not getting married, so—"

"I didn't say I wanted to marry you," Jade said, annoyed. "You're never coming back to BC, so you're the perfect man for what I need."

He went to the playbook to save himself. "SEALs are advised to get all their affairs wrapped up and put their private lives at rest—"

"That's fine. You go be a SEAL, and I'll be a mother." Jade's eyes softened. "Ty, you weren't here for years. You only came home to save BC. You were going to ride in, disperse some Prince Charmings, leave behind some happy newlyweds to blossom into families, thus seeding the town with more BC-friendly citizens, then ride off into the Technicolor sunset."

He could hear a full-blown rumble erupting around the bunkhouse. "I wish I could help you, but I can't."

"You can't get me pregnant?"

"Well, sure I could." Ty was pretty confident he had the right stuff for that, if she was inclined to give him a shot. "I could probably do it in one try," he boasted.

Jade shook her head. "Please wait a moment while I remind myself that your cockiness is one of the reasons I chose you to be the father of my child."

He cupped her face with his palm. "You chose me because your ovaries clearly recognize good genes." He stroked her soft skin, thinking there was nothing he'd rather do than toss her into his bed and make long, slow love to her again. "However, what would Betty think if I knocked up her only daughter and left town?"

"My mother will be delighted to finally have a grandchild." Jade moved his hand away. "And it's ovary."

A siren shrieked outside and Ty gazed into Jade's eyes, wondering what was going on that she was so willing to keep him out of it with the intriguing notion of sex and fatherhood. He studied her. "Ovary?"

"That's right. I only have one."

He pondered this. "So you're looking for a mighty big gun to hit the target."

She laughed out loud. "To go with your big mouth. Really? You're that cocky?"

He shrugged. "One man's cocky is another man's confidence. Move away from the door, angel face."

"You're turning me down?"

He scoffed. "Of course I'm turning you down. You're just trying to keep me away from a good old-fashioned brawl. The whole premise of you getting knocked up and me leaving my child here with no father is absurd. Which I think you know." He leaned in for a kiss, then scooted her away from the door after he'd lingered over her lips. "Nice try, though."

Jade moved. "You brought your friends here to populate the town. I'll pitch my plan to Sam."

Ty stopped cold, his hand on the knob, at the word *plan*. Even Jade had a plan—everybody in BC did—and he should have factored that in. Instead, he'd seen her as a sweet, sexy woman he was leaving behind because he had no other choice—nothing could interfere with *his* Plan. "Sam?"

Jade nodded. "He's a wonderful man. You wouldn't have brought him to BC if you didn't know that beyond a shadow of a doubt."

Ty couldn't deny it, so he didn't bother.

"Besides which, he's not a bad kisser," Jade teased. "Or so I hear."

Something hard hit Ty in the gut, the same punch

that had hit him the day he'd seen her walking into The Wedding Diner on Sam's arm. "Sam is a great guy."

"Obviously."

Ty didn't consider himself a jealous man—he just wasn't. And he wasn't going to be today. "Well, whatever you have to do, sugar," he said, and headed out the door to find his friends and the trouble they'd cooked up.

He was certain he'd left bigger trouble behind, redheaded trouble looking to give him a surefire coronary. Yet despite Jade's plan, and her sassy little mouth and hot body, there definitely wasn't going to be a baby, at least not from his gene pool.

The little lady was going to have go swimming elsewhere.

Chapter 7

Jade followed Ty, having stalled him as long as she could. She didn't want him joining the fight, or getting involved with the ongoing trouble brewing in BC. The conflict could go on forever, thanks to the Donovans and their wealth.

Ty needed to leave town. His desire to get into the SEALs was part of who he was; he'd talked about it, prepared his body and spirit for it for years. Part of the reason he'd brought Frog, Sam and Squint here was because he'd gotten to know them on the rodeo circuit, where they'd drifted after their time in the SEALs, still wanting action and to be part of a community, a brotherhood. To be fair, Ty had never wanted to settle in Bridesmaids Creek. Life could be slow here, not the adventure he longed for. Jade understood that—everybody in BC did. They were all rooting for him to go off and achieve his dreams.

In Bridesmaids Creek, achieving your dreams made you a hero, a legend. It wasn't just the men, either— women dreamed as big as the sky, too. Even Daisy had dreams—although they were counterpoint to what was best for BC, at least in Jade's opinion.

Maybe the scuffle was over. Daisy and her gang of five hangers-on faced off against Squint, Frog and Sam just as Justin Morant came over, holding one of his four babies. Mackenzie Hawthorne Morant stood by her husband, pushing a stroller with the other three tucked inside under soft, warm blankets. Jade's mother hovered protectively nearby, doing her best grandmother-in-training routine.

Sheriff Dennis looked crossly at the men eyeing each other, facing off in the light from the barn's kid-friendly haunted-house decorations, pumpkin-shaped globes and a few strings of smiling ghosts mixed among the white, twinkling lights.

"What's going on?" Ty demanded, and Jade hurried up behind him, fully intending to drag him away if any punches were thrown. Under no circumstances was he going to SEAL training messed up from fighting.

"Your band of merry men," Daisy said, "jumped my guys."

"We didn't jump them," Frog said. "We just played a friendly prank."

"Friendly? How friendly?" Ty demanded.

Daisy's friends glowered at Ty's buddies. Jade could feel hostility oozing from every pore of all the men. *Testosterone,* she thought, disgusted. *There's far too much of it in BC.* And the smell of horse manure was really strong, so strong Jade raised a hand over her nose for a moment.

"Nothing to cause a ruckus over," Sam said. "Donovan's doing his best to ruin a good thing here. We just want these fellows to know we're keeping an eye on them."

"How much of an eye?" Ty asked. "What did you do?"

His friends smiled, pleased with themselves.

"We just gave them a small roll in the dirt," Squint said.

Jade's eyes widened as she realized the smell of manure was coming from Daisy's gang. "Oh, no. You didn't!"

Frog laughed. "We did. And it was awesome!"

That was too much for Daisy's friends. The five men leaped onto Frog, Squint and Sam. Justin handed the baby to Betty and jumped into the fray, and before Jade could get a hand on Ty, he'd thrown himself into the fight. Fists and curses flew.

"Aren't you going to do something?" Jade asked Sheriff Dennis.

"Nope. In fact, I'm heading into the kitchen. Betty had a couple of cinnamon cakes put by for the workers, and that means me." He went off, whistling.

Jade looked at Mackenzie and Betty. "We have to stop them."

"They brought it on themselves," Betty said.

"Mom!" Jade stared at her mother. "You don't condone fighting!"

Betty sighed. "Let's let the fellows sort it out. I'm taking the babies inside before they get cold."

Jade's mouth fell open. "Mackenzie, Ty's supposed to leave in a few days to try to make it into the SEALs.

He came home to save your Hanging H ranch, and your Haunted H business. Tell them to stop fighting!"

Mackenzie, her dearest and best friend going back years and years, shook her head. "Ty isn't going to thank you if you go rushing in there all mother hen."

That was true. Jade scoffed in resignation. "Why are men so stupid? What is this solving?" It looked as if the men were having the time of their lives, acting like children. "Women should rule the world," she muttered.

"We do. Quietly." Betty made sure all the babies were comfortable, and pushed the pram toward the big, lovely old Hawthorne house. "These men have brought BC back from the dead. We're just getting life breathed back into them. If they want to fight, I say let's go warm up some cocoa and cider. And find bandages."

Jade glanced at Ty, worried. No one seemed to understand the importance of him not getting his clock cleaned right before he left town. What if he broke something, was seriously injured?

This was too stupid—and she hadn't exactly succeeded in her mission of keeping Ty out of this fight once she knew it was going down. He hadn't bought the let's-get-pregnant bombshell she'd tried to waylay him with. She couldn't take the testosterone overload a second longer.

"That's enough!" Jade strode over to Daisy, who was watching and encouraging her guys, clapping when one of them landed a good blow. Jade grabbed her by that fabulous chocolate hair, dragged her to the ground and sat on her. "Make them stop, Daisy. Call them off."

"No way!"

"Now. Or I cut off your hair. I mean it."

"You wouldn't!"

"I *would.*" Jade looked up as she realized Mackenzie stood next to her. "Got any scissors?"

"Sure." Her friend handed her a large pair of shears.

"Why do you have these?" Jade asked, ignoring Daisy as she suddenly squalled something that wasn't very ladylike.

"It wasn't hard to tell where this was going." Mackenzie laughed. "You had blood in your eye for Daisy. I figured it was either douse her in the creek, dunk her in a horse trough or take scissors to that pretty hair. I came prepared. Besides which, I was working the balloons at one point tonight and I needed scissors to cut the ribbons."

"Excellent. Call them off, Daisy." Jade bounced on her to emphasize the words.

"No. The Hawthornes are not the princesses of Bridesmaids Creek. Suz and Mackenzie aren't royalty around here! We're going to buy this dump, and—"

"You never learn." Jade picked up a good-size handful of chocolate locks and snipped them right next to Daisy's scalp.

The scream her victim let out was bloodcurdling—and so were some of the words she leveled at Jade.

"Call them off!" Jade commanded.

Daisy tried to buck her off, but Jade was too strong, and Mackenzie helped hold her still. "I shouldn't get involved in this. I have four daughters to set an example for," Mackenzie said. "Cut fast."

Jade picked up an indiscriminate handful from the back and clipped it off. Daisy was going to look like she'd fallen under a lawn mower.

The scream Daisy unleashed this time was probably

heard in the next county. Jade winced, but the men quit fighting, turning to stare at the three women.

"What are you doing, Jade?" Ty demanded.

"Just playing a friendly prank," she said sweetly. "Nothing to cause a ruckus over."

"Help me!" Daisy yelled at her friends.

"No," Jade said, brandishing the pointy scissors. "Not unless you want me to take another, oh, six inches out of Daisy's pride and joy."

When she was satisfied that no one was going to try to save Daisy, she nodded. "No more fighting tonight. You look ridiculous, every one of you." She glared at Ty, so he'd know she was including him, even though he looked hot as the dickens all roughed up and tough from battle. But it was the wrong battle. "And you stink to high heaven."

All the men seemed to finally realize that manure and testosterone was a bad combination. Not women-friendly in the least.

"This isn't going to be settled tonight, but Daisy, you and your father are on the wrong side. One of these days you're going to figure that out." Jade flexed the scissors in the air with a snicking sound to keep Daisy quiet, and it worked like a charm. "I want you and your gang off this property right now, or I won't be responsible for the buzz cut I'm going to give you. All of you." She snicked the scissors in the air again. "Got it?"

"Fine," Daisy said, "but just know I live to fight another day. Probably tomorrow."

"Fine. Tomorrow I'll have had some sleep, and I'll be ready with something better than scissors. Maybe green hair dye. You'd look good as a lettuce-head, matching that money you're always bragging about. Or maybe a bleached blonde."

"Witch," Daisy spit, leaping to her feet when Jade let her up. "You won't win. You're the one on the wrong side. You have no man, Jade Harper, and no hope of one. You'll live and die in this town a spinster, or marry nothing more than a farmer."

Jade smiled. "Frankly, I'd be proud to marry a farmer. That might not be big enough for you, but the farming, small-town life suits me fine, Daisy. It's the reason you've never really fitted in here after all these years—you and your father are trying to change us into something we're not. The grand Donovan vision."

She handed the scissors back to Mackenzie. Satisfied that the brawl was over and no one was going to be seriously injured for the night—and annoyed as heck with Ty for getting involved when he knew very well he shouldn't—she walked toward her truck. She'd seen blood on his face and his lip was split open—that mouth that had kissed her not too long ago, kissed her senseless—and her temper simmered at the stupidity of it all.

It was time to go home—before she let fly all over that rugged cowboy.

"Hang on," Ty said, looking as if he was about to hop into the passenger side before she could even turn the key in the ignition. "I want to talk to you about this having-a-baby and marrying-a-farmer business."

Jade shook her head. "I'm done talking. Don't you even dream of getting into my truck after you've been rolling in horse crap. I tried to save you, but no. You had to go all Rambo."

"Oh, no, little lady. You're going to patch me up."

She was too steamed to pay attention to his plea for attention. "You're fine, barely scratched. Go home."

He grinned. "You tried to save me from myself, and I'm ready to express my gratitude."

Ty wasn't letting Jade leave without him. He wasn't about to let his fiery little friend get away, so he talked her into hanging around while he took first a hose-off in the barn, then a shower in the bunkhouse, and finally hauled ass into her truck before she could change her mind. When he'd seen her straddling Daisy like a too-tight saddle, snipping off chunks of her hair, he'd nearly had heart failure. No man ever envisioned a full-on catfight without getting a little chuckle out of it, but Jade hadn't been messing around and he hadn't laughed.

No—he'd realized he was totally, irretrievably falling for her. She'd been trying to defend him, and Bridesmaids Creek, and why he'd never realized she was such a devoted heroine, he didn't know. What he did know was that everything had changed tonight. Just sitting in the truck with her as she drove toward her house had his heart hammering and his jeans way too tight in a certain area.

Jade Harper was the woman of his heart.

"So I've been considering your offer—" he began.

"Rescinded," she interrupted.

"Not so fast," he said, his tone soothing. "We need to get back to the single-ovary issue. I believe I'm your man."

She shook her head, visibly aggravated with him. "You are not my man."

"Well, you certainly don't want a farmer."

"I would want a farmer, if he understood hearth and home, and that fighting never solves anything."

"Says the woman who just gave Daisy Donovan the haircut from hell."

"She needed that," Jade said. "She's had that coming for years."

He wanted to laugh, but held back to keep himself out of trouble. "Let's talk about that baby you want. Or was that just a ploy to keep me from the fight?"

She turned into the drive of the small farmhouse where she and Betty lived. "It was a ploy, and I do want a baby."

"So the offer's still open."

"No. It's not." She got out of the truck. "You know what? This is so not a good idea. You can walk back, since I didn't invite you into my truck in the first place."

He swooped her up, deposited her in the porch swing and sat down beside her. "Not until we finish the discussion you started earlier."

"It's late." Jade scowled at him, her expression clearly visible in the soft lights that decorated the wraparound porch.

"There's an important rule about never going to bed mad," Ty said, reaching out to twine a strand of her hair around his finger. It was so soft, and she was so soft. He was dying to hold her again.

"I'm fine with going to bed mad. I just want to go to bed." Jade removed his hand from her hair. "Go away."

"I'll be completely out of your hair in just a few days," Ty said. "Let's stay friends."

"Ty, you don't understand. We're sort of friends, the way we always were because we're both from here. But you need to go, and I need to stay." She looked sad.

"Wherever you go, you'll find trouble, I have no doubt of that."

She went inside, abandoning him. Ty thought he'd utterly struck out until the door opened again and she came out with a damp cloth.

"Wipe your mouth," she said, "I don't want you bleeding all over the porch. It's been freshly painted."

It had been; he could smell the paint, and the whiteness gleamed in the moonlight and lamplight. Garlands of pine twined around every banister, decorated with red ribbons. A big wreath hung on the door, very festive in the chilly weather. He dabbed at his mouth where it felt as if he'd split it again from grinning at Jade, and she sighed, reaching out to take the cloth from him, pressing it against the spot where he'd taken a slight punch earlier. Strangely, it didn't seem to hurt as much now that Jade was ministering to him.

"You scared me tonight," she said. "I didn't want you fighting, and getting yourself all busted up before you go to training. What would you have done if you've broken a hand or some fingers?"

"It would've sucked," he admitted. "But I had to back up my brothers."

"Those aren't your brothers. Those are your bachelors." Jade shook her head. "The problem with you is that you're always working your plan."

He brightened, caught her hand in his, tossed aside the damp rag she'd been soothing him with and pulled her into his lap. "I'm trying to add you to my plan. Let's get back to your problem. It's more interesting."

"No." She snuggled into him. "Go home, Ty."

"This is my home," he said, looking around the small

farmhouse. "I practically grew up here. Betty is like my mother."

"That would make us some kind of siblings, and that would be so weird."

He laughed. "Just because I love your mom doesn't mean I feel brotherly toward you. Let me romance you, Jade. I'll put such a glow on that ovary of yours it'll be spitting out little Tys in no time."

She wrinkled her nose. "Nothing about that convinces me to let you anywhere near my ovary. And can we please stop talking about it?"

"I don't see how you expect me to stop talking about the most interesting proposition I've had in years. Make a baby with a sexy redhead? Hell, yeah!"

She got out of his lap. "Begone."

"I know you want me, Jade Harper. You shouldn't deny yourself the pleasure just because I had to defend the Hanging H from some hardheaded rascals. And may I just remind you one more time that you're the one who did the most damage tonight? Daisy's going to have it in for you like she's never had it in for anyone before. You cut off the thing she loves the most." He laughed, still amused by the spectacle of Jade at work on Daisy's tresses. "You're quite a fighter."

"Men are always so amused by women fighting." Jade shook her head. "I wasn't about to let Daisy get away with hurting Mackenzie and Suz. They're my best friends."

"Besides me."

She looked at him. "Not even close, cowboy."

"So no goodbye party of the sexual variety?"

"As I said, I changed my mind the minute I saw you throw the first punch. What were you thinking?" She put her hands on her hips, and Ty could tell she really was angry with him. "Don't you realize how important your dream is to Bridesmaids Creek? You don't have the right to throw it away on a stupid brawl."

"My dream?"

"We've heard about your SEAL dream for years. We've watched you swim laps in Bridesmaids Creek for hours, watched you run for miles, half the time dragging a tire or something on your back for conditioning. When you came back to BC, we all thought you'd come just to say goodbye. None of us suspected you'd bring eligible bachelors to populate the town, and somehow, that made us think all the more of you." Jade's eyes softened. "You love Bridesmaids Creek almost more than anyone, and the last thing we want is to weigh you down."

He leaned back in the porch swing, astonished. "Weigh me down? This place is my touchstone. It's not a weight."

"Then go achieve your dream. Most of us here will never leave, so we're looking for a hero to live vicariously through."

"You could leave," Ty said.

"I don't want to. I want—" Jade pulled him up from the swing and guided him off the porch "—you to go become a kick-ass SEAL. It's going to be hard, and you need to be in the best shape possible, not all busted up from fighting. Trust me, if you come back in ten years, we'll still be fighting here. It'll be like you're Rip van Winkle and just woke up and nothing changed."

"Jade—"

"And you need to be in great emotional shape, not dragged down by our silly problems. We lived without your guiding hand while you were on the circuit, and we'll be fine without you now. We're tough here, Ty. We don't need you to solve anything for us. So just go."

He stared at her, knowing beyond a shadow of a doubt that the last thing he wanted was to leave this woman behind forever. "Were you serious about having a child?"

"Yes. Absolutely. Betty needs to be a grandmother, and I want to be a mother." For the first time tonight, Jade smiled. "I want exactly what Mackenzie has. And I'll get it, too. Don't worry."

"I'm not exactly worried." He was practically staggered by the thought that she might find a farmer—or Sam—as soon as he was gone to training, and Ty would come home one day to find a mini-Jade following her mother around. "Damn, Jade, I'm pretty sure you need to let me tickle that ovary of yours."

She pointed to the road. "Go. Be the SEAL this town has always known you could be. We live to brag on our own."

She went inside, closed the door. Ty looked around in the darkness, his heart feeling as if it was bleeding. For a guy who considered himself smooth when it came to the ladies, he hadn't put a dent in Jade's armor against him. Sudden armor, he reminded himself. She sure had seemed eager back at the bunkhouse.

A woman didn't turn off her feelings just because a man got involved in a tiny scuffle, did she? He sank into the porch swing, pondering what the hell had just happened to him. "First she says she wants to have a baby, and I'm the father she's chosen. Then she cuts off Daisy's hair." A moment that had strangely afflicted him with a mixture of horniness, pride and admiration. He went back to his dilemma. "So the hair went poof, and so did Jade's desire to give me a chance to rock that ovary she was so worried about not thirty minutes before." He was so perplexed he felt as if the secure ground he'd been standing on had crumbled.

She *had* tried to keep him from the fight, and she had used sex as a lure. And yet he'd sensed she was very serious underneath the obvious wish to keep him from fighting. Jade wasn't being honest when she blamed her lack of desire to be alone with him on the fact that he'd jumped into the fight; he was going to be a SEAL, and anybody knew SEALs weren't opposed to a little action.

It didn't make sense. But the redhead that gave his heart severe palpitations of the good kind had definitely closed up on him tighter than a clam, both emotionally and physically.

If he hadn't gone to help his brothers, would Jade really have made love with him? Did she really want his child?

There was only one way to find out.

He got up, banged on her front door.

Chapter 8

Jade opened the door, which sort of surprised Ty because he wasn't sure that she would.

"Go away," she said.

See, that was exactly why she needed him—she didn't know how sexy she was, and how much she fired him up, sassing him like that. Ty grinned. "Can Jade come out to play?"

"Very funny. That worked when we were kids, but those days are long over."

"And to think I never even tried to play doctor with you, or Spin the Bottle, or any of the other kid games."

"I would have slapped you into next year."

He smiled bigger, couldn't help it. That spunk had his name written all over it. "I need a shotgun rider. Drive out to the old place with me."

Jade's eyes widened. "You're really going to your family home?"

He shrugged. "I'm leaving for a long time, won't be back. I need to rattle the ghosts before I go."

"And you want a fellow rattler."

Ty smiled again. "If anybody is up to the job, beautiful, it's you. Those ghosts don't stand a chance against you."

"So you want me for protection."

He laughed. "Sure. Come on, cowgirl."

She came out onto the porch, closed the door. "You're sure you want to do this?"

"I don't want to at all," he admitted. He hated going out there. It wasn't just the ghosts that got stirred up; it was the memories and the painful knowledge that he hadn't been here for his father when he'd wasted away from grief. "It's best if we face our ghosts. It's the only way to kill them."

"I don't know," Jade said, but she went with him. "There's something wrong with the idea of killing a ghost. I don't think they ever die. Hence, ghost."

These ghosts could die, if time would let them. At least he hoped so. The freight train of sexual attraction he felt for Jade should send them scattering—and he could leave BC with a clear conscience.

At least for a while.

"When's the last time you were there?"

He shrugged as he started the truck. "Whenever I was in town last."

He felt Jade's eyes on him. "You're never curious?"

"Nope. I know it's in good shape because Madame Matchmaker goes out there with a cleaning crew a couple times a month. I get a list as long as your arm whenever there's anything she deems needs to be fixed up." He glanced across at the gorgeous woman in his passenger seat. "Cosette says the place is in museum-quality shape."

A testament to his father's memory. Ty didn't want a single possession of his dad's moved or given away. He wanted to know, every time he returned home, that it was as if he was just coming home again, the way he had when he was a boy, to a father who'd loved him enough to adopt him. Honestly Ty didn't want the ghosts disturbed; he wanted them staying just where they were. The good ghosts, at least.

"You were a good son, Ty," Jade said. "Mom says she felt like you were even a good son to her."

"I tried." He really had tried to be helpful. When his dad had been at work, Betty's house, close to the Hanging H, had been a welcoming place. He'd had the run of it, too. For a kid who might have ended up in an orphanage, he'd been aware of the need to stay in everyone's good graces. He'd wanted so badly to belong.

Then he'd found rodeo, and that family had welcomed him, as well. Suddenly, he didn't have to be the extra addition in everyone's homes; he had a home of his own—the road. His duffel was his portable chest of drawers, his truck his way to a livelihood.

And always, his father told him he was proud of him.

Ty shuddered past the guilt that his father had needed him, and that he'd let him down. "Hey, so about this baby thing. Were you trying to have sex with me because you want a baby, or because you were trying to keep me out of the fight? Tell me the truth and you win the prize."

He stopped the truck in front of his house, gazing at

the porch lights, which were on though no one had lived there in years.

"No one just wants a baby," Jade said. "And it was both."

"It's a lot to hang on a guy who's leaving."

"Don't be a wienie." She jumped out of the truck.

"A wienie?" he grumbled to himself. He got out and waited for her to get to his side of the truck.

"I want a baby," Jade said when she got close enough that he could smell her perfume and the scent of sweet cotton candy clinging to her. "But it doesn't have to be you, so don't get yourself in a twist."

He caught her to him. "I am in a twist, and if you say one more word about Sam and your ovary, I'll probably have to spank you."

"No worries. Come on," Jade said, pushing him away from her. "Go inside and quit stalling."

"I like stalling." He pulled her back. "Let's get in my truck and make a baby."

She gazed up at him. "No strings attached?"

He kissed her. "Of course there'll be strings attached. Don't be weird."

She pulled back to gaze up at him. "Excuse me? I'm the weird one? And you're what?"

"Not weird." He allowed himself to taste the sweet heaven of her lips again. It was really the only way to keep her quiet. Anyway, kissing her had the knock-on effect of getting that freight train roaring inside his head again, which was awesome, because it really did run off the ghosts and the past he didn't want to examine closely. Or at all.

"Listen," Jade said, jerking away from him, taking a few deep breaths. "I'm just in this for a baby."

He laughed. "You're such a fibber. You have a seriously hot thing going for me, Jade Harper."

She sniffed. "Wouldn't you like to think that?"

"I do think that." He glanced at the star-speckled sky, delighted to have gotten under her skin. She simply didn't want to admit that she was crazy about him. But she was here with him now, wasn't she?

"Whenever I kiss you," Ty said, "my mind goes totally blank. All I can think about is you, and your mouth, and that body of yours."

She stared at him. "You're a little hot yourself. A little."

He laughed out loud, picked her up, tossed her over his shoulder. Carried her up the porch steps over her protests, slapped her rump once just to let her know he was the boss and that everything was going his way tonight, stuck his key in the lock and pushed the door open.

The warm fragrance of his father's pipe hit him, even though the man had been gone a few years. A combination of cherrywood and tobacco, the aroma brought the feeling of home rushing over Ty. He set Jade gently on her feet as he took in the single lamp that burned in the kitchen. The wood floors gleamed with polish, and not a speck of dust marred any of the furniture. If he listened hard, he could hear the sound of his father's big boots coming down the stairs. Ty's heart hammered; he held his breath, waiting for something that wasn't going to happen.

Those big arms weren't waiting anymore to scoop up the little boy when he came rushing in the door from school, anxious to see his father. "Damn," Ty muttered.

Jade stood very still beside him, not intruding on his memories. After a moment, she very gently inserted her hand into his, and he tightened his grip, grateful for the contact.

He took a deep breath, walked into the kitchen. Cosette had had a new refrigerator put in, a big silver affair that could hold an army's worth of food. He smiled, liking the way it looked in the big kitchen. Many a meal had been consumed here, the three of them at the round table with four wooden chairs, in the nook window overlooking the garden, and past that, the fields. "Damn," he said again, and Jade pressed up against his side, supporting him.

He went out of the kitchen, walked up the stairs, Jade at his side. Three bedrooms at the top led from the central hall. Ty pushed open the door to his room, his heart thudding.

The bedroom took up the entire east side of the upstairs. His toys and childhood memorabilia were in their right places, his trophies stacked on the shelves. Nothing had been moved.

"It's like a time capsule," Jade said. "As if you never left."

But he had. And he wouldn't have come back except that he wanted to say goodbye to the small town that had been his home. He'd had this grand dream that he could save the community, or weight the scales more in the favor of good.

Tonight's fight had shown how difficult that was going to be.

"Listen, we probably ought to go." Ty took a deep breath. "Thanks for coming out with me."

She put her hand in his. "Your parents loved you a lot, Ty. You know that. Terence never thought of you as his adopted son. You were the son of his heart."

"I know." He'd been a father in every way. Which made the fact that Ty hadn't been around for him much a pretty rotten guilt trip. "Hey, Jade."

"Yeah?" She looked at him with those big green eyes, and he felt himself falling in.

"About your situation." He gestured with a hand, feeling frustrated, not sure how to bring up such a delicate topic. "I know we were kidding around earlier about your, um, ovary—"

"It's okay," she said quickly, trying to ward him off. "It was a while ago."

He scraped a hand through his short hair, a military-ready cut that reminded him he had a future he was heading to in a few brief days. "I missed a lot of things, not being around. But I want you to know that—" he took a deep breath "—I'm sorry for whatever you went through. I know it wasn't easy."

"I had a cyst that burst." She looked sad. "It wasn't much fun, I'll admit. Pretty horrible, actually."

"I'm so sorry." He felt pain in his chest, physical pain, that she'd suffered in a way he could never imagine, not only physically but psychologically. He knew the emotional trauma was there, or she wouldn't have brought up her wild plan of trying to get pregnant. Which was feeling less wild all the time, and somehow strangely like a really good idea.

A clear sign it was time to leave. "Hey," he said, pulling her close, "let's blow this joint."

She relaxed against him just for a moment. "Good idea."

There was too much heat searing him. He was glad she wanted to leave as much as he did. Being alone with her wasn't his best idea—there weren't any barriers here.

Nothing to keep him from making the huge mistake of getting entangled where he definitely wanted most to be tangled up.

They went down the stairs together, side by side, not speaking. Suddenly Jade slipped, and he reached to grab her, and they fell the last few steps into the foyer.

"Are you all right?" He got up, went to inspect her. She gazed up at him with those incredible eyes, looking stunned.

"I'm fine. I think."

"Let me help you to the sofa."

"Not yet. Let me lie here a second and gather my wits."

He wasn't sure his wits could ever be gathered if she'd gotten injured because of him. "Are you hurt?"

"I'm trying to figure that out. Don't look, but I'm going to do an indelicate kind of roll to my side, get up kind of thing."

"Whatever works for you. Let me know how I can help."

His heart was racing way too hard. He was pretty certain she was blinking back tears as she got to her knees, thankfully making it to the large, soft rug that graced the living area.

"I'm just going to lie here on this comfy rug for a few moments," Jade told him. "Please stop looking like that. You're scaring me."

"Do you want me to call someone? A doctor?"

"I'm fine. I think I knocked the breath clean out of me and stunned myself. I see a few spots when I try to get up. I'll be fine in a second."

He glanced back at the stairwell. "Luckily, it was only two or three steps. I'm sorry I didn't catch you."

"My foot slipped right out from under me. I can't imagine why."

She was wearing boots; maybe she'd caught a slick spot on the uncarpeted stairs. "Let me help you move to a sofa."

"Okay. Thanks."

He helped her to a sitting position. "How's that?"

"Fine so far," Jade said.

"Great. Put your arm around my neck, and—" Dear God, he could smell perfume and see just a bit of cleavage beneath her red sweater. Thankfully, she'd been wearing a puffy coat or she might have really hurt herself. Ty tried not to think about how warm and soft she was, and he was almost succeeding when he realized that holding Jade this close, her arm wrapped around him so trustingly, had given him an erection of epic proportions.

This was not good.

He was crazy about this woman. And she wasn't exactly pushing him away. In fact, if he didn't know better, he'd think she might have just snuggled a little closer against his chest, in the opening his sheepskin jacket provided. Close enough to feel his heart beating, which was thumping as hard as a drum in a parade.

The front door opened, and Cosette peered in at them, her mouth opening a little in surprise.

"Ty!" she exclaimed.

"Hi, Cosette." He noticed Jade trying to wriggle away from him, realized a strand of the red hair he adored was caught on one of his jacket buttons, making escape impossible.

"I saw the lights on," Cosette said, sounding breathless and worried. "I was on my way home. I wasn't expecting you to be here, and I only ever leave the kitchen lamp on. The door was open—"

"Cosette, it's fine. I'm glad you're here." He really was—he desperately needed separation from Jade in more ways than one. "Can you help me with Jade?"

"Of course! What's wrong?"

"I tumbled down the stairs," Jade said, "although I don't know if you can call three steps a tumble. And now I'm caught in Ty's jacket."

"I can see." Cosette nodded and closed the door, but didn't do anything to help release her from the proximity of Ty's chest. If anything, she seemed completely happy for Jade to remain in his arms, and Ty reminded himself that she was named Madame Matchmaker for the exact reason that she had a matchmaking business, and she was, in fact, damn fine at it.

Too good, in fact, as testified by the matchmaking ledger she kept in her office.

"Cosette, Jade's hair is caught in my coat," he reminded her. "Can you help her? Because I can't see it, obviously." Not with the way Jade was crushed up against his chest. He was afraid to move her lest he pull her hair and hurt her.

"I feel like we need a photo of this moment," Cosette said, pulling out her phone and snapping a quick picture. "There," she said, pleased. "We'll have something for the memory books. We do love our memory books in Bridesmaids Creek."

His jaw dropped, and yet he shouldn't be the least bit surprised by anything the inhabitants of BC did. "Cosette, a little help, please? Jade is hurt and I want to get her to the sofa."

"Yes, please," Jade said, sounding very tired suddenly.

It scared the hell out of him. She was always so perky. He began to worry about a concussion, which was stupid, because he was pretty certain she hadn't hit her head. But maybe he hadn't noticed. His heart started that uncertain hammering again, reminding him that this woman meant so much to him he couldn't bear for anything to happen to her. He should have protected her. How could a man feel like a competent protector when he let her fall down a staircase?

"Have you had the stairs polished recently?" he asked Cosette, as she peered at the hank of Jade's hair snagged on his button.

"No," she murmured. "They're in fine condition. Your father made those stairs with his own hands, remember. We're going to have to cut this, I'm afraid, Jade. Your hair got caught in the buckle."

"I guess it's my just deserts for cutting Daisy's hair," Jade said.

"No. It's not any dessert." Ty wished he could shrug out of his jacket so he could see how to help, but if anybody could figure out how to disentangle them, it was Cosette.

"Where are your scissors?" she asked. "Never mind. They're in a kitchen drawer."

He was happy to hear it, because he hadn't lived here in so many years that he didn't even know if a pair of scissors remained. Cosette beetled off, and Ty wrapped his arms tight around Jade.

"Let me get you over to the sofa."

"I'm fine. I just tried to knock myself silly, is all."

"That would be a very hard thing to do, since you're

one of the smartest women I've ever met." He helped her to the sofa, and they sat down together.

"This is so awkward," Jade whispered. "Cosette is going to tell everyone about this."

"Hell, yes, she is. She has the photo to show. Luckily for us, it's pretty tame stuff." If she'd opened the door and found him kissing the daylights out of Jade, as he wanted to be doing—now that would have been awkward.

He wished he had been kissing Jade. Ty felt that a golden opportunity had slipped away from him.

Cosette returned, peering at him, her big eyes illuminated by her pink-cast hair. "Don't look."

"Why not?"

"Because I don't want you being a big baby about it," she said. "It's just hair. It'll grow back. By the time you make it back to BC the next time, you'll never be able to tell the difference."

"Very funny," he said, noting her dig about his frequent absences. "Just do it, already." If she didn't get Jade away from him, get the sweet scent of her shampoo and body away from him immediately, he wasn't going to be able to think straight for a month. He was already pretty much lost in the fantasy of kissing her—and that wasn't going anywhere very fast.

"There!" Cosette exclaimed, examining her handiwork as Jade pulled away, rubbing her head. "Free as a bird!"

"Thank you, Cosette," Jade said.

"Ah, well, curly red hair has its dangers. And now I must be off!" The older woman wound her scarf tighter around her neck, beamed at the two of them. "Lock up tight, Ty."

"I will."

She went to the front door, hesitating as she watched him settle Jade on the sofa.

"It's good to see you back here in the old place, Ty," Cosette said. "Good night, you two."

She went out, locking the door behind her.

Jade looked up at him. "Sorry about that."

"Sorry for what?" He couldn't imagine what she had to be sorry about.

"For—I don't know. Making an ass of myself."

He couldn't imagine any woman ever being less of an ass than Jade. "You'll be happy to know that you won't miss this little bit of hair."

"Right. Because it's right in the front." Jade sighed. "It's karma for what I did to Daisy."

"Nonsense. And you look totally hot with short hair. That angled look is really wickedly hot." He wanted desperately to kiss her, so desperately that he decided to busy himself inspecting the staircase—anything to stay away from her until she felt steady enough to leave.

The stairs had been barely used in all the years he'd been gone. Cosette hadn't had them polished. Possibly Jade had simply had a clumsy moment, but she wasn't a clumsy woman. He peered at the spot where she'd slipped, realizing there was a crack in the stairs. A slight crack only an eighth of an inch wide, separating the stair board from the box underneath.

That would have to be repaired. Clearly, she'd somehow caught her heel on the uneven step and slipped. He moved his fingers along the edges to see if he could push them back together until it could be properly repaired. It wouldn't do to have Cosette taking a tumble.

The stair glided back into place as easy as a jigsaw

puzzle piece locking into its correct match. He tugged at it to test the stability, and the wood moved toward him again. "This is definitely not secure," he told Jade.

She came to stand beside him. "Maybe the house has shifted, loosening the boards."

"Maybe." Anything could happen, but his father had been a fine carpenter. He'd even built the balustrade and carved the stair rail, a beautiful, polished mahogany work of art that had stood the test of time. Ty tugged at the board once more, determined now to pull it apart so that Cosette wouldn't step on it until it could be fixed.

The wood piece completely separated from the stair, and though he expected to find nothing at all underneath, a metal box came into view.

"Yikes," Jade said. "This place *is* like a time capsule."

A strange sensation came over Ty, a sense that something wasn't right. Nobody hid gray metal boxes in stairwells unless they didn't want them found.

No one could have put this here but his father.

"Are you going to open it?" Jade asked.

"I don't think so," Ty said softly. "I think I'm going to close up this house and get the hell out of Dodge." While he still could. Before the tendrils of BC could pull him any deeper.

She put a hand on his shoulder. "Maybe that's a good idea."

"You think so?" Nothing good came of opening hidden boxes and releasing another person's ghosts.

"Yeah. Navy SEAL advice, remember? Get your affairs in order, and leave everything—"

"Yeah. You're right." He pushed the wood piece back over the box, shoving it into place again. The hole disappeared like magic.

Before he left town, he was going to buy some serious, ass-binding wood glue to seal this off. Whatever it took, that box wasn't going to see the light of day again.

"I guess it could always be gold," Jade said. "Buried treasure."

"I'm not much for believing in fairy tales." Besides which, his father had been an assiduous businessman. Everything had been noted down to the penny; the records and accounts had been easy to find and settle after his death. If he'd left gold, money or valuables in a safe somewhere, he would have marked that in his business records. There'd only been one safe deposit box, and then an old iron safe in the basement that would take a crane to move. Ty had known about those. But his father had built the stairs, and whatever he'd secured away there he hadn't wanted to ever be found.

Which meant nothing good was in this box. "Let's get out of here."

Jade kissed Ty when he stood up.

"What was that for?"

"Because I think you're brave."

He wasn't brave. Not at all.

But he wasn't about to admit it. He pulled her into his arms instead, reigniting the passion they'd shared earlier, taking the gentle kiss she'd just given him into the inferno he wanted—needed—right now.

The one thing he had in his life that was secure and sane was this crazy redhead who drove him out of his mind. He'd taken too long to admit it to himself, but he was going to miss the hell out of her.

His affairs were not in order, not by a long shot.

"Either we leave now or I'm going to lose the battle between my conscience and my—"

She stopped his words with a kiss. "Lose it, already. I've waited way too long for you to get over that schoolboy conscience of yours."

Well, hellfire. There it was, the invitation a man could not pass up. He couldn't, not when kissing Jade was the best thing that had happened to him in a long time. He wanted to spend hours losing himself in her, thinking about nothing but her beautiful body and her sassy mouth and the way she made him grin.

He carried her up the stairs to his old room, laid her gently on the bed, turned on a lamp.

She stared up at him, her eyes huge in her pale face, the slight freckles standing out. He had never seen anything more beautiful, never desired anyone the way he did her. She pulled off the red sweater, revealing a white lacy bra with a tiny pink bow in the center, and something about that trusting, inviting gesture was so sexy that Ty knew in that moment that Jade Harper had completely, irrevocably stolen his heart, in spite of his best efforts to keep his heart selfishly to himself.

"You know what we're doing here," Jade said, and Ty halted in the act of diving in and ripping her clothes six ways from Sunday.

"Making love?"

"Avoiding the buried box."

He nodded, his full-on erection urging him to get on with the diving in he so desperately wanted to do. Still, if Jade was having a change of heart, he'd tell his poor, tortured body and soul that there'd be no diving of any kind today, unless it wanted to go for a really long, cold swim in Bridesmaids Creek. "Probably. Are you okay with that?"

"I'm *so* okay with that." Jade undid his belt buckle

and looked up at him. "Whatever excuse works is fine by me."

There was sweet satin and lace waiting for him, and a redhead who wanted him. There might never be this much willing paradise in his life again.

He dived in.

Chapter 9

The hours of holding Jade in his arms could never be replaced by anything better—never. Ty felt as if he'd died and gone to heaven, on rocket propulsion and faster than angels flew. As she lay on his chest, he stroked her skin, trying to figure out what he was going to do now.

He had to do something.

"I'd better go," Jade said. "It's almost morning."

He didn't want her to go. They'd spent hours making mind-blowing love, hardly speaking, letting their bodies do the talking. "I can't let you."

She laughed softly. "I never thought I'd hear those words from the mouth of such a rolling stone."

"I'm not kidding." He wasn't. His life had changed in ways he couldn't have imagined. You just didn't make love to a woman and then go off as if it hadn't mattered—at least not if you'd finally caught the woman of your dreams and something very, very close to love had smacked you right upside the head, bringing you to a very clear realization of how wonderful your future could be if you could keep that woman of your wild and crazy dreams.

She rolled up on his chest to gaze down at him. "It's not like I haven't always been here in BC. You know where to find me."

"Yeah. So does Sam."

She smiled sexily at Ty. "You brought those fine hunks to town."

He hadn't meant for one of them to make Jade fall in love with him. And as Jade appeared to be on something of a baby-making mission, it was a concern that weighed on Ty. "Hunks, huh?"

She raised a brow, kissed him. "Just a little."

He could tell she was teasing him and enjoying it, but the thing was, he had this really strong urge to put a name on whatever it was they had between them. "I don't like Sam," he said with a growl.

Jade laughed. "You think the world of Sam. Anyway," she said, kissing him again, making him think about the fact that he should be kissing her, and in the most strategic places possible. "Sam isn't a stayer."

"A stayer?"

"Mmm-hmm. Haven't you noticed? Sam isn't going to be your success story. You're far more likely to settle down than Sam. And Frog and Toad are guaranteed."

Frog and Toad? Ty might have laughed if he wasn't so worried. "Frog and Squint are good guys. Sam is, too," he admitted grudgingly. "How do you know he isn't going to settle?"

"He's just along for the ride."

"You spent enough time with him to figure that out?" Ty asked, unable to help himself from sounding like a jealous schmuck.

"He just doesn't have any desire to stay in one place, Ty. Sort of like you."

She pressed gentle kisses on his chest, tantalizing him.

"So what if we made a baby?" he asked.

The kisses stopped. "You're good, handsome, but I really don't think you're so good that a couple of nights—"

"I'm trying really hard. And I have a confession to make."

"Do confess." She cocked her head, waiting.

"I'd like to spend the rest of time before I leave dedicating myself to that goal."

She looked at him for a long time. "I have a confession to make myself."

His heart hitched. He hoped like hell she wasn't going to tell him that this was a one-shot deal. "Your turn."

"I'm on the same drug that Mackenzie was on when she got pregnant. It's to help women conceive when it's been difficult for them to do so."

"Why were you already on it?" He refused to think she might have been playing up to Sam for the very purpose of getting that baby she wanted.

"The day you came home, I went and talked to the doctor."

His jaw literally sagged. "You never once let on that you wanted to date me. Or even be more than friends."

She wrinkled her nose. "It's not the kind of thing a woman just blurts out to a man. Although I did mention to you tonight that—"

He sat up. "Yeah, you mentioned it tonight, a handful of days before I'm leaving, and simply to keep me from jumping into a fight!"

She shrugged, which made her very tempting breasts jiggle a little. He was utterly fascinated—but forced himself back to the conversation. "It took me a while to get my courage up. The fight sort of pushed me to the moment."

"I'm glad something did," he groused. He hated to think he might have gone off and never known that this woman had sexy plans for him. "Holy crap."

"Yeah."

"So there's really a chance we could make a baby, since you're on this turbo-ovary-booster stuff."

She smiled. "It worked for Mackenzie."

He could be a dad. Holy, holy crap.

"But I'm pretty sure it's not the right time of the month," Jade said.

His world crashed. "How do you know? Doesn't the medicine override all that?"

She laughed. "I'm afraid not."

"Hell."

"It's okay."

No, it really wasn't. He didn't have enough time to give this his best shot. And something inside him really, really wanted to do just that. "So you wanna get married?"

"No." She laughed again and got out of the bed. "You're going to do your SEAL thing. Don't try to use me to get out of it."

Use her, hellfire. He wanted to have her for the rest of his time here. He wanted everything she wanted to give him and then some. "But if I did hit the target, you'd marry me, right?"

She reached for her panties, clearly getting ready to bolt. "You're going into the navy. That's all you ever talked about. Let's focus on that goal."

"I just don't want to come home to find you married," he grumbled, knowing he was being totally unreasonable. He didn't like the way she'd skirted the issue of marriage, either. It hadn't been much of a proposal, as proposals went—more something that had flown unbidden out of his mouth. But she hadn't so much as blinked or smiled when he'd said it, and from that alone he discerned a decided lack of enthusiasm on her part.

He supposed she didn't have much to get excited about, since he really had nothing to offer her. She was right. He was leaving, and there was absolutely no knowing when he'd be back.

"I'm not done with you." He grabbed her, tugging her back into bed with him, encircling her with his arms and holding her against his chest. Anything to keep her with him just a little while longer.

"I have to leave."

She didn't sound all that convinced. Ty figured he knew what a woman sounded like when she was ready to hit the door, and Jade made no move to leave his arms, either. He nuzzled her neck, sighed against the soft skin. Felt himself get hard, and stroked a hand across her nipples, which perked up instantly. She was fitted against him in such a nice, comfortable spoon fashion, and he moved into place easily behind her, finding the soft sweetness he craved, sliding inside her as if they'd never been apart. Didn't belong apart. She moaned with pleasure, tucking herself closer against him, and Ty's every muscle tightened with desire he couldn't control. Something about her drove him completely out of his mind. Jade was the only woman who made him this insanely hungry. He teased her nipples, and when she gasped, rocking against him urgently, he slid a hand between her legs, stroking her, letting his fingers glide against her softness, taking his time bringing her to pleasure until she was gasping his name, begging him for release.

Still he gently kissed her neck, taking his time before sweeping her over the edge, enjoying her heat and her desire for him.

"Ty," she said, her voice an urgent plea.

He knew what she wanted. He could give it to her—he would. But he wanted her hovering with him at the edge of pleasure as long as possible, wanted her in his arms feeling this magic as long as he could keep her.

She tightened up on him, and he steeled himself, but between her soft words asking him to release her, and the wild tension of her rocking against him, Ty knew he couldn't last much longer. Taking a gentle bite of her shoulder, keeping her as close to him as he possibly could, he thrust into her as he teased her with his fingers until he could feel the soft, slick folds all around him tense, waiting. He tweaked her gently, burying himself deep inside her, and was rewarded by his name on her lips again as she gasped and cried out.

Then he allowed himself his own release into her welcoming body, his every muscle shuddering, his arms holding her for all he was worth.

This was what he wanted.

This was his new plan.

He didn't know how it could work out. It seemed impossible.

But if there was any way on God's green earth he could keep Jade for his own, he intended to do it.

Jade had Ty take her home just before the sun came up. After the excitement last night with the fighting, and then somehow them ending up in bed together, everything had changed. Jade barely knew what to think. She slipped quickly from his truck before the moment could get awkward between them. If it never happened again, she wanted to remember last night just the way it had been—spontaneous and somehow magical.

She went inside her house, headed upstairs for a hot shower and a change of clothes before she went to find Betty.

Her mother looked up, smiling brightly, as she made it into the kitchen. "Good morning! There's coffee and I have a cake fresh out of the oven."

"It smells fabulous." Jade realized she was ravenous as she got a cup of coffee and slid onto a bar stool. "Thanks, Mom."

"Busy day ahead." Betty pulled out some eggs. "Thanks for all the help last night."

"Mom, I don't want you to do everything yourself. You can't run the ice-cream shop and do the treat stand at the Haunted H." Jade sighed with appreciation as her mother put a fresh-baked slice of cinnamon cake in front of her. "I can run the stand at night myself."

"I look at this two ways," Betty said, whipping the eggs in a bowl with some milk and other ingredients. "One, we're lucky to have the extra income the Haunted H is bringing in, and with the Donovans being totally against it, we have to make hay while the sun shines, because who knows how long it'll last. Two, I have help at the ice-cream shop. It's not that much work to run the stand, too."

Jade barely realized she'd wolfed down the entire piece of cake. "I was starving."

"You were out late," Betty observed mildly. "Probably didn't have dinner."

Jade sipped her coffee. "I don't know what I'm doing, Mom."

Betty didn't stop stirring, didn't glance up. "Does it matter?"

And that was her mother's subtle way of saying that she shouldn't overthink the situation with Ty, which had just taken a major complication turn. "You're right."

"Anyway," Betty said, "Cosette called me last night."

Jade looked at her mother. "I'm fine. I just fell down a couple of stairs."

Betty glanced up. "You fell down stairs?"

"Cosette didn't tell you?"

"My word, no. She called to tell me that Robert Donovan is continuing to put the squeeze on Phillipe. I don't think Mssr. Unmatchmaker's going to be able to hold out. And I think the divorce is going ahead, unfortunately. Too many financial issues, with Donovan pulling the strings." She looked puzzled. "How would Cosette have known you fell down some stairs?"

"Never mind. Long story." Maybe Cosette hadn't gone into full gossip mode as soon as she'd left Ty's place. Anyway, it didn't matter. Jade supposed she didn't care if people knew she'd gone out to Ty's place—even if folks would be a little surprised that he'd finally darkened that door after so many years. She certainly had been.

Strangely, it had felt so much like he'd come home. She'd felt him relaxing, unbending.

Until they'd unearthed the metal box. He hadn't said another word about that during the night, and she didn't figure he would. "I don't understand why Phillipe and Cosette's little matchmaking business is the immediate target of Mr. Donovan's evil plans."

"They're in the center of the block in town. If he can take that, he'll have more leverage with the other businesses." Betty put steaming eggs on a pretty blue plate in front of her. "Cosette is just devastated."

Jade's phone buzzed in the back pocket of her jeans. "This is delicious, Mom. I should be making you breakfast, though."

"Nonsense."

Jade pulled out her phone, smiling when she saw the message from Ty: Come back tonight—I have plans for you.

She texted back Plans?

Just dinner, beautiful. Don't be greedy.

She laughed. He did have high opinions of himself.

"Ah, young love," Betty said with a happy sigh.

Jade blinked. "I'm not in love, Mom. We're not in love."

"Ty and you, you mean."

Jade realized she had no secrets from her mother. "Yes." She texted back I'll bring dessert. Going to the Haunted H tonight?

Wouldn't miss it.

She put her phone away, her body already glowing with the secret knowledge of what she knew would happen tonight. "What do you think it would take to get Robert Donovan off our necks forever?"

"If I knew that," Betty said, sitting down with her own piece of cake and a cup of hot coffee, "I'd be blabbing it all over town."

"I feel sorry for Cosette and Phillipe." Jade lost her appetite. Cosette was just about the nicest person in Bridesmaids Creek. In fact, there was no better place to have grown up than BC. Everybody helped look out for each other. Jade had never been tempted to leave—not like Ty had wanted so badly to do.

She completely understood his reasons. "I think I'm going to spend some time with Ty until he has to go."

"That's nice, dear." Betty had her head buried in the Bridesmaids Creek newspaper now, looking for gossip items. "Try to keep him out of any more fighting until he leaves, is my advice. He needs all his strength for BUD/S."

Everybody supported Ty in his dream. Any time a BC son or daughter made something of themselves, the town celebrated, feeling a part of that success. Town pride was built in from birth. "I know. Thanks, Mom." Jade got up, took her dishes to the sink. "I'm going to clean the kitchen, then I'll run the stand tonight. Will you promise me to stay home and relax?"

Betty glanced up from the paper. "Why wouldn't I want to be where all the action is?" She laughed, shook her head. "Jade Harper, just because you're spending time with a hot man does not mean I'm ready to suddenly put on my slippers and sit in front of the TV. You couldn't keep me from the fun!"

Jade smiled fondly and shook her head, then began putting a few things away so Betty wouldn't have to. She'd gotten a lot accomplished when she heard the back door open.

"Hello!" a man's voice yelled into the house, like he'd done a thousand times before.

"In here, Ty!" Jade called, irrationally pleased that he'd shown up so soon.

He walked into the kitchen and Jade smiled. "Just like old times. You must have smelled the cinnamon cake a mile away."

He was so big and handsome—so sexy she could hardly stand it. All she could think of was the magic his hands worked on her, and his mouth, and his body against hers.

A flush of desire stole over her.

"No cake today, thanks." He kissed her mom on the cheek. "Do you mind if I steal your daughter for a moment?"

"Steal away." Betty waved her hand. "Do you want the kitchen?"

His gaze hitched to Jade's. "Can we chat outside, Jade?"

This was odd. He never passed up Betty's cake or pie. She looked him over, hearing an urgent tone in his voice. He wore jeans, a freshly pressed long-sleeved shirt, his sheepskin jacket—and a really serious expression. A shiver of concern ran over her, and maybe even a splash of premonition that she wasn't going to like whatever he'd come to say.

Chapter 10

Jade walked outside with Ty, catching his serious mood like a virus. Lighthearted, daredevil-with-a-grin Ty—when was he ever this dark and quiet?

"What's going on?" she asked, anxious to get whatever it was out in the open.

He took a deep breath as they reached his truck, and leaned against the door. As if he meant to drive off at any second. Jade's heart rate kicked up.

"I have to leave today."

She hesitated. "Didn't we just text about getting together tonight?"

He nodded, his gaze dark and focused. "Those were the plans. The weather forecast is ugly, and flights are already being canceled around the U.S."

"I saw that on the news," she murmured, her heart sinking.

"I can't risk not showing up to BUD/S on time."

"No. Not at all." There would be no second chance, and being late wasn't an option. "You're absolutely right to go." Her heart felt as if it was shattering. She'd caught the weather report on the edge of her subconscious, barely paying attention to it, wrapped in the happy glow of the wonder of spending time in Ty's arms. "It's a wise decision to get ahead of flight cancelations. This winter has been busy with storms."

She took a deep breath, unable to say any more. The last thing she wanted was to make him feel guilty that he had to leave, when he was doing the exact thing she knew he needed to do, and which she wanted him to do.

"I want you to do something for me. It's a lot to ask." He took a deep breath, pulled her up against him.

"What do you need me to do?"

"I'll understand if you can't make the commitment. It's a huge favor."

She looked up into his eyes. "Okay."

"I want you to take over Cosette's job of watching the house. I don't know when I'll be back, and she's done it for me for years, but I'd feel better knowing you were in charge."

Jade nodded, understanding. He was trying to get his affairs in order, which underlined the finality of his imminent departure. She swallowed hard, not about to dim his leaving with news that Cosette and Phillipe's marriage appeared to be pretty much on the rocks. "It's fine. I can do it. It's probably for the best. Cosette's so busy these days."

His arms wrapped around her more tightly. "No one's busier than you are, lady. But you're special to me, you know that. And I keep thinking about that loose step, and Cosette stepping on it—"

"It's no problem. Take that off your plate of worries."

He kissed her forehead. "Here's the thing. I have a bigger favor to ask."

"Go on." At this point, she was going to say yes to whatever he mentioned. The best way to have him leave with no worries in his rearview mirror was to do whatever she could to help.

"About the box…"

She watched him carefully. "Did you open it?"

"Hell, no. As I said, I knew all of Dad's business affairs. There's no hidden gold or something fantastic in that box. Whatever it is, he meant to keep it hidden. I have no desire to open Pandora's box. Not now."

"It can wait until you get back." She had a suspicion he was right about leaving whatever it was buried.

"I've had a will drawn up," Ty said. "You're the sole executor and beneficiary of my estate, should anything happen to me."

Her mouth dropped open. "Why?"

"Who else is there?" He kissed her gently on the lips. "And I would have no peace of mind whatsoever if that supercharged ovary of yours decided it had bingoed."

She was stunned. Couldn't say anything. "Ty, you're going to be fine. Nothing's going to happen."

"All affairs have to be in order."

She knew that. On one level it made total sense. On the other hand, it forced her to realize that what he was doing was very dangerous—and more so in the future, if he was accepted into the SEALs.

Of course he would be. He'd worked his ass off to realize his dream.

"All right," she murmured, not happily.

"You'll write me if you're pregnant? I'd be the world's worst dad not to be here—"

"I'm not pregnant," she said. "I told you, I don't even think I'm in the right time of my cycle."

"Damn." He looked a bit crestfallen, though he smiled. "I really worked hard at that."

She laughed. "I noticed. It was wonderful."

He kissed her long and sweetly, drawing a sigh from her when he finally pulled away to look at her.

"Which brings us back to the box," he said.

She waited.

"I want you to open it after I'm gone."

A gasp flew from her before she could stop it. "I don't—"

"Hear me out." He cut off her words, holding her protectively in his arms. "You're the only person I trust with whatever's in there. Take care of what needs taking care of, in regards to the contents. I just don't want to know whatever secret Dad might have been keeping. I hope you understand."

"I do," she murmured. "I really do. I'm not comfortable with it, but I do."

"It's a huge favor, like I said. But I really want to leave with a clear head, and no BC drama hanging on to me."

"It's the least I can do." Jade took a deep breath. "You realize it's probably nothing other than… I don't know, maybe some important papers."

"Those were all in the vault. Anyway, here's the thing," Ty continued, obviously not caring to linger on whatever secrets his father might have left behind. "After you go through the contents, I want you to seal the step back up. I've left the materials to do that. I figure you know how to work with wood, since you help your mother set up the stand at the haunted house."

"It's no problem." She was actually pretty handy at repairing lots of things. Small-business owners learned how to do things for themselves. "I can take care of it."

He kissed her one last time, his lips lingering over hers. "This isn't how I wanted to say goodbye. I had planned for something more romantic, not dumping all my final requests on you."

"It's fine." She was still stunned that he was leaving so quickly. It felt as if part of her was being ripped away.

"I've told Cosette she's off the case. Here are the keys." Ty handed Jade financial documents and a key ring. "Believe me, I'd rather be giving you a different kind of ring, Jade."

Her gaze flew to his. "I think we both know that's not realistic."

After a long moment, he nodded. "I guess not."

"Go," she said, feeling on the verge of tears she didn't want to cry in front of him. "Be the best damn SEAL the navy ever trained."

He smiled, his mouth a little crooked. "You always believed in my dream."

"Of course I do. If Frog and Squint and Sam can be SEALs, you ought to really make BC proud."

He grinned. "Your faith is inspiring."

"I just know you. You've never set a goal you didn't achieve, Ty."

He looked at her. "I never really thought of myself that way, but I guess you're right."

"Of course I'm right." She kissed him one last time. "Please hit the road." The papers and key ring felt heavy in her hands. She wanted to drop them and throw her arms around his neck, beg him not to leave, at least not so quickly.

But he had to.

"You mean a lot to me, Jade Harper."

She smiled bravely. "And you mean a lot to me. You'll mean even more with a Trident."

"I don't know when I'll be back."

"You don't know if you'll ever be back," she said. "And that's exactly the way it should be. You haven't dreamed this dream for so long to be pulled back to Bridesmaids Creek, Ty. The only reason you came home was to save us. In lieu of a going-away party from BC, I freely tell you to get your ass in that truck and don't look in the rearview mirror. Nothing ever changes here. We're a mirage in time."

"A town of carnies," he said. "Everybody selling their shtick and the BC legend."

"That's right. Now go sell yours."

Ty looked at her for a long time. "I would have swum the creek for you. Even done the Best Man's Fork run. And that's something I've never said to anyone."

"Our BC legends are pretty entangling. Be careful what you say." She smiled, but he didn't return it, his gaze serious. Her heart ached, but he had to go. He'd always feel he'd fallen short of his goal and his dreams if he didn't. A few hours of wonderful lovemaking shouldn't change everything he'd planned for. "Now go, cowboy."

He nodded, got in the truck. "But if there should be a baby—"

"There isn't. Goodbye." She kissed him on the mouth through the window opening, smiled as big as she could, selling shtick as hard as she could. "Good luck."

"Thanks."

He looked at her for a long moment, his eyes serious and dark, then started the engine. He drove away, his truck headed down the road toward the Hanging H, where he'd say his goodbyes to his buddies. She imagined shouts and laughter, and assumed Sam would drive him to the airport. She wished Ty would have asked her to take him, knew that would have been a really bad idea. Airports were no place for goodbyes, not goodbyes that were forever.

She carried the papers and the house keys inside.

Her heart rode off with Ty.

Chapter 11

Eleven months later

"These little ladies don't look like their father," Sam observed, looking down into the bassinet where little Marie and Eve blinked their eyes like tiny dolls.

Jade shook her head. "Considering most of the town thinks they're yours, you better not say that too loudly."

He grinned. "Aw, I wouldn't mind if they were."

She raised a brow.

"I just mean I wouldn't mind having some kids," he said hurriedly. "But I'm sure not hitting on you, Jade."

She laughed. "I know."

Sam hung around a lot now that she'd had the girls, as did Frog and Squint. She'd never admitted that Ty was the father, not to a soul except Betty—and her mother would never give up her secret. Sam was just fishing, doing his usual trickster thing.

"I just want that to be clear," he continued, "because one day Ty is going to ride back into town, and I don't want him beating my head in if someone tells him I was flirting with his girl."

"I'm not Ty's girl." Jade swallowed hard. "Don't be silly."

"It's not a matter of silly. You're taking care of his house. Ty wouldn't let anyone take care of his homestead unless he trusted them and felt strongly about them."

"Sorry to blow up your theory," Jade said breezily, reaching into the bassinet to pick up Eve, "but you're aware that Cosette used to do this same job I'm doing? Keeping an eye on the Spurlock place?"

Sam shook his head. "I'm not buying the story you're selling, sister, but whatever." He scooped up Marie. "I do love babies. And these girls are sweet."

A little uneasy that he'd guess her secret, Jade wanted to get Sam's attention on a different topic. "Maybe you should consider running in the Best Man's Fork race."

"Maybe I shouldn't." Sam nuzzled the baby. "I think you may have done something unattractive in your diaper, little one, and yet somehow I can't find it entirely unattractive."

Jade laughed. "That's bad, Sam."

"I can change diapers faster than Houdini can disappear. I've had lots of experience." He did just that at the change table with impressive speed and efficiency.

"Are you sure you won't at least consider the Bridesmaids Creek swim? It's very, very lucky," Jade said. "Guaranteed to bring you a bride, if you win."

"Oh, I could win," Sam bragged, "but I don't want

a bride. My goal is to be free and easy for the rest of my life."

"We have lots of pretty ladies around here." She looked up as she tested a bottle. "Anyway, Ty brought you here to find a wife. Aren't you stating that you have conflicting goals?"

"Look, it's easy. Squint and Frog want women. Justin didn't think he wanted one, but he got five. I think that's hilarious." Sam grinned. "Frog's trying to romance the socks off of Suz, much good may it do my brother in arms. And Squint's determined to tame the tornado known as Daisy. I figure everybody's settled and accounted for, and if I slip through Ty's net, that's fine. He'll just have to be happy with his success rate, and then get his own house in order." Sam glanced at Jade. "You still haven't told him, have you?"

"I'm not going to, and neither are you." She took a deep breath. "The time will be right one day, but it's not now. And you know it as well as I do."

"He was pretty proud when he wrote that he was now truly one of us," Sam said.

"And he took off for Afghanistan as fast as he could get sent. Or wherever he really went." There hadn't been a lot of news from Ty, and Jade felt a twinge about that. She'd stayed awake many nights during her pregnancy, wanting so badly to tell him, but not about to rock his world. "Anyway, what should I have done? Told him before he was even finished with BUD/S that he was going to be a father? You and I both know he would have come rushing back home." She swallowed hard, knowing it was true. Ty felt strongly about family, and the fact that he was adopted poured determination into his soul. He would have returned—and they would have had no future. You didn't take someone's long-held dream and dash it on the rocks, then expect that he wouldn't look back with some regret. Oh, Ty was too good of a man to be bitter or resentful—but it wouldn't be the same as it had been during that blissful time they'd shared in his house.

"I have to go do something." Jade had put this particular errand off long enough. "I'm going to call Mom over to watch the babies."

"I can do it," Sam said.

"You should be working." She went to find Betty, who'd staked out her place in the kitchen. "I need to run over to the…the Spurlock place real quick, Mom. Can you watch the girls?"

"Of course I can!" Flour flew as Betty put the lid on a canister. "Let me wash up."

She glanced over her shoulder at her daughter as she stood at the French sink. "I thought you were on the once-a-month schedule of going over there."

"I am." Jade covered the cookies her mother had baked with a paper towel, knowing they wouldn't be around long enough to bother putting them in a canister. "There's something I need to take care of."

"Suits me. I needed a baby break!" Betty sailed out of the kitchen, and Jade could hear her admonishing Sam to go find the cookies because he was looking too thin.

Sam wasn't too thin—but if he and the fellows didn't quit hanging around here so much, they were going to gain very un-SEAL-like pounds. Jade put on a scarf and coat to protect her against the cool wind—December was bringing much colder weather—and hurried to her truck.

Fifteen minutes later she was at Ty's, cautiously unlocking the door. As always, the house seemed welcoming and secure to her—but she never opened the door that her gaze didn't go straight to the stair step she had yet to repair.

She'd put off pulling out the metal box as long as she could. Today was the day, she vowed. The babies were two months old; Ty wasn't coming back. No one went into the house except her and Betty. Jade dropped in from time to time, checking over the place, turning on every tap to make sure everything was running properly, running a light rag over every surface to pick up dust. When she'd been ordered to bed for three months during her pregnancy—the doctor had been worried about her carrying the babies to term—Betty had come over in her place. Jade had told her mother that the third stair was loose, and not to step on it. Ty planned to repair his father's handiwork when he came home one day.

Betty had thought that sounded reasonable, and the subject never came up again. Jade had mostly put Ty's wishes concerning the box out of her mind. Part of her had hesitated because there was the tiniest chance he might come home—but that would mean he hadn't made it through BUD/S, and she definitely didn't want that.

It was really hard to think about opening a box Ty's father had left behind, but she understood why Ty didn't want to do it, why he was happier closing up the past for good. She'd promised herself that by the twins' two-month birthday, she was going to quit putting off the special mission Ty had entrusted her with.

She briefly considered repairing the step and not examining the contents of the box, but it was a small favor he'd asked, considering all he'd done for her. Anyway, it would take only a moment.

Jade tugged the step apart, finding the box undisturbed, though it still surprised her in some way to see it. The box's placement was so odd, nestled into the dark shelter of the stairs. Whatever was inside was something Sheriff Spurlock couldn't toss away, and yet didn't want Ty finding, a perfect hiding place from an active boy who might randomly see something his father didn't want him to see.

Yet maybe it was something good. Love letters, or a tiny statuette blessed for the house the sheriff had built.

Encouraged, Jade pulled the box out, and sat on the bottom step. Slowly she opened it, staring down at the pile of papers inside. On top of the stack lay an envelope with no writing on it. She picked it up, took a deep breath and pulled out the letter inside.

Dear Ty,
If you're reading this letter, I've probably gone to the big ranch in the sky. I left instructions with Phillipe LaFleur—Mssr. Unmatchmaker—that if you ever decided to sell the house— -or if Robert Donovan managed to take over Bridesmaids Creek for good—that he was to give you a sealed letter I'd left in his possession. The letter gave you instructions on how to find this box, and I ask you in advance to forgive me for not telling you the truth in person. I never wanted to, could never see the reason to honor a man by ruining your life, which I think would have happened if you'd learned my secret during your formative years. If I had my way, this secret wouldn't ever make it to the light of day—certainly not until after Donovan's death.

But skeletons don't always stay buried, and the

fact is, you are Robert Donovan's true son. Donovan's wife, Honoria, who was born and raised in BC, came home here and confided to my wife, Emily, during her pregnancy that Robert didn't know she was expecting, and that she planned to leave the state to have you, and give you up for adoption. Emily talked her into allowing us to adopt you, as long as we never, ever told Robert the truth.

As Emily couldn't have children, we jumped on the opportunity to have a child of our own, and Honoria was happy to know that her child was going to be living with us. We didn't know Robert that well then—he wasn't from here, and we figured our secret was safe. They were living at the time in Houston. It wasn't that she didn't want you, son. Honoria had realized she didn't love Robert, and she wanted no part of having a child with him. By then he'd already begun to show the seeds of the evil he'd later develop, and Honoria had quickly realized she didn't want to stay with him, wanted no ties with him. He would have never left her alone, anyway, if he'd known she was having his child.

Of course, you know this means that you're Daisy's older brother. You'll wonder how the Donovans ended up staying together, and even having a child together.

Honoria told Emily years later in confidence that upon her return from having you in Pennsylvania (we met her there and picked you up as soon as you came into the world), Robert professed his undying love for her and swore to change his ways. He'd missed her during her extended absence, fearing she had no intention of returning. Honoria decided to give her marriage one last chance, and Daisy was born a couple of years later. They moved here to BC for good when Daisy was about three years old. Secretly, I think Honoria was thrilled with the chance to keep an eye on you as you grew up. I think she also didn't realize that by then Robert had chosen BC as the perfect place to launch his empire, or she might never have returned here. I know their marriage wasn't a happy one after Daisy's birth, as Robert became hungrier and hungrier in his ambitions. Something about having a child of his own seemed to spur those ambitions. He was determined to create a kingdom for his name and his only child.

Jade stopped reading, stunned beyond words at the secrets spilling from the pages. It was almost too horrible to contemplate. She was fiercely glad Ty had never opened the box. She felt certain he would have never left BC, would have made it his mission to stay here and thwart his birth father at every turn of his evil steps.

A shudder ran over her that had nothing to do with the cool temperature at which she kept the house, or the gathering dark clouds outside, warning of a massive snow dump before the night was out.

She returned to the letter, her hands trembling a little.

Son, inside the box you'll find your birth certificate, as well as a gift from Honoria. The end of the story isn't a pleasant one. As you know, Daisy is straight from the DNA of her father, which

you somehow escaped, thankfully. You brought
your mother and me a lot of joy over the years, Ty.
After Emily died I could sit in this house and think
about the happy memories we had as a family. I
can still hear your little footsteps thumping down
the stairs. I can see your happy smile every night
when I came home. I can see you running footballs
into the end zone, and escorting the Homecoming
queen. More than that, you were good to us, son.
You were the miracle we would have never had in
our lives. Forgive us, please, for keeping you to
ourselves. You were the hope and the dream we
never expected to have, and you were the son we'd
always prayed for. You grew into a good man, and
you made us proud. As far as Emily and I were
concerned, you were ours, and the thing we loved
the most.

I love you, son.

Dad

Tears jumped into Jade's eyes, streaming down as
she put the letter back inside the envelope. She flipped
through the other paperwork, but there was nothing else
other than what Terence had mentioned, and a tiny box
she assumed was the gift from his mother. Jade opened
that quickly, wiping at her tears.

It was a small sterling Saint Michael medal, almost
identical to the one Frog wore. Ty's full name was engraved on the back. Jade returned the medal to the velvet
pouch, thinking that Ty would have liked such a gift. She
closed the box, hesitated only a moment as she realized
with dawning horror that Robert Donovan was the blood
grandfather to her children, and Daisy the girls' aunt.

It was too much to contemplate right now. Jade crammed the box back into its secret nest and went to get the repair items Ty had left for her. She sealed the step back into place with wood glue, making sure it was tight and secure.

No one would ever know Sheriff Spurlock's secret. It would certainly never fall from her lips.

Satisfied with her handiwork, she put the toolbox away, then slipped on her coat, anxious to be away from the house. A promise was a promise, and she'd kept her promise to Ty. She felt immensely better now that she'd discharged her final duty—but her heart was heavy.

The door blew open on a gust of wind and icy puffs of cold. She gasped, staring into Ty's eyes as he filled the doorway, dark and forbidding and somehow not the Ty she remembered. A dark stranger gazed back at her, his face lean with hard planes, his body taut and muscle-packed.

"Ty!" Jade exclaimed. "You're home!"

He nodded, closed the door. "Yeah. I guess you could say that." He jerked his head toward the door. "I saw your truck. Hope I didn't scare you."

"No." She backed up a step. "Of course not."

She wasn't frightened, but her heart raced in spite of her words. The man she'd made love to no longer seemed to reside in his dark eyes. He didn't smile, didn't seem glad to see her.

If anything, he seemed remote.

"The roads are getting bad. You shouldn't be driving in the dark."

"No." She tightened her jacket, gulped a little nervously. "I should go."

He sniffed the air. "Do I smell glue? Paint?"

She shook her head. "I just cleaned the kitchen sink. You're probably smelling that."

He nodded, sighed tiredly. "Probably. Thanks for watching the house for me."

"It wasn't a problem at all," she said nervously, doing a little skitter around him to get to the door.

His hand shot out, grabbing her arm as she edged past. Her eyes caught on his gaze, her heart banging wildly inside her.

"I'm wiped," Ty said. "I've been on flights and in airports for the past three days, and I'm probably only close to being human. I don't mean to be rude."

"It's all right," she said quickly. She went to the door, opening it. "I understand."

He put a palm on the door to detain her. "I really do appreciate you taking care of everything while I was gone. Though I noticed you didn't take any of the cash I put in the account to pay you."

"I didn't need it. There was really nothing to do. Good night." She hurried out the door, sleet stinging her face. Oh, God, that had been so awkward. It was as if their idyllic time together had never happened.

And yet it had. She was going to have to tell Ty the truth eventually, now that he'd come home. She got in her truck, gazing at the house with rapidly blinking eyes, trying hard to fight back tears.

She missed the Ty who had left BC.

Strangely, irrationally, the Ty who had returned to BC was really hot, dangerous looking. She swallowed, recognizing that her whole body had come alive when he'd walked in the door. So alive she'd forgotten to tell him everything she'd wanted to tell him—even congratulate him on becoming a full-fledged SEAL.

No, in the heat of the moment, caught off guard and worried that her own secrets would somehow be revealed, she'd babbled, saying nothing meaningful.

She hoped he didn't discover that the step had just been repaired. He'd definitely ask questions.

She took a deep, worried breath, astonished that her children were related to Robert Donovan. The thought was shattering. And she'd cut their aunt's hair off, giving Daisy a hairdo that had taken a long time to return to any semblance of attractive.

One thing was crystal clear: Jade wasn't going to make the decision that Honoria had had to make. She would tell him the truth, so that he could know his children.

And hopefully, he wouldn't bring up the marriage promise he'd demanded before he ever even kissed her. She had no desire to be married to a stranger.

And that's what Ty had become.

Ty stared at the closed door, a little startled by how quickly Jade had disappeared. It was almost unfair how much more beautiful she'd become in his absence. He swallowed, his gut hollowed out by the sudden rush of emotions hitting him since staring into those big green peepers of hers. Peering through the window at her truck, Ty thought about how many cold nights, how many muscle-tearing exercises her smile had gotten him through.

She hadn't smiled at him tonight, not once.

In fact, she'd looked like she'd seen a ghost.

"Hell, maybe I am a ghost," he muttered. He turned to glance through the house once he saw her taillights disappear into the darkness. "A ghost that definitely smells glue."

There was an obvious difference in chemical makeup between glue and dishwashing soap, or even whatever sink cleaner she might have used, and Ty frowned. He left his duffel on the rug and walked into the kitchen, switching on some lights. He'd almost gone to the Hanging H to bunk in with Frog, Squint and Sam, but decided he didn't want anyone to know he was in town just yet. He needed sleep desperately, so desperately he didn't bother to stop at The Wedding Diner to grab a meal, even though he knew there'd be nothing edible in the house, and he missed the hell out of Jane Chatham's home cooking.

He wasn't in the mood for company, needed a few days of sleep to get human again. Once he'd seen Jade's truck parked in his drive, he'd suddenly felt a burst of something he hadn't felt in a long time.

Happiness. He'd been happy as a kid in a candy store to know that little redhead was in his house. She was the only person on this planet he cared to see right now.

"Think I scared her off," he told the salt and pepper shakers on the kitchen island, before turning his gaze to the living room sofa, where he had once held Jade after she'd stumbled down the stairs.

It had been the happiest time of his life, holding that curvy body in his arms.

She'd barely written while he'd been gone, just a few breezy notes reciting the happenings in BC. He'd searched every line she'd penned for the announcement that she was pregnant, and as the months passed, he'd realized her one ovary had been immune to him, after all.

She was even more beautiful now, somehow almost

glowing. Something soft and gentle had rounded out her body, and his had responded instantly. If she ever gave him the chance to try to overcome that ovary again, he wouldn't be saying no.

He went to grab a glass of water from the tap, and hesitated, arrested by the dry, clean sink.

Whoa, the little lady had totally tossed off a humdinger of a fib. This sink was clean, but it had not just been cleaned; it was dry as a bone. Even the sponge was dry. He drank the glass of water and walked back to the front door.

Yep. Glue.

His gaze fell to the stair. He'd forgotten all about that, had put the whole thing out of his mind. Bending, he touched the seam, his finger coming away with a trace of wetness. Definitely glue.

She'd waited this long to go through the box and repair the stair? He wiped the glue on his jeans, and thought about why that might be.

They were three weeks from Christmas. Maybe she hadn't had time to do it before—and not sure whether he'd be able to return for the holidays, maybe she'd decided to get on with it.

Which would mean that for nearly a year, she'd just stepped over the broken step.

Shrugging, he decided it didn't matter. She'd done what he wanted done, and he didn't give a damn what was hidden away there. He went back to the kitchen, grabbed a warm beer from a case that was stored in the pantry, cracked it open. Guzzled it, wrinkled his nose, searched out a bottle of whiskey he had in the bar.

"That's more like it," he said, after a satisfying,

straight-up gulp. Maybe one more would relax him enough to fall asleep.

He thought about Jade's cloud of soft red hair cascading over her white parka. Maybe she and Sam had gotten together, after all, or maybe someone else had caught her fancy. There was no reason she wouldn't be dating.

Jealousy hit Ty so fast and hard it was stunning. Which was stupid as hell. Why would she wait for him? They'd made no promises to each other, outside of that silly promise he'd extracted from her that if he'd gotten her pregnant, she'd marry him.

Jade would never have married him. She'd been completely focused on his goal.

He'd succeeded in that goal beyond his wildest dreams. Had no regrets.

Except for losing her.

He sat at the kitchen table where he'd eaten meals with his parents. Stared out the window into the back garden, not seeing much thanks to the darkness. Beyond their yard lay Robert Donovan's land, the beginning of his fiefdom. Land that his father had sold Donovan, believing the man when he'd said he wanted to run cattle on it.

Cattle had not been the kingdom Donovan had planned to build. Steel and concrete and a consortium of government-owned buildings was Donovan's plan, turning BC into some kind of outlying big-city-in-the-country—if he could figure out how to push out the hardy, intractable citizens with their thick, stubborn roots buried deep in BC soil.

Ty put the glass to his mouth, hesitating when the doorbell rang and the door swung open.

"Ty?"

He set the glass down at hearing Jade's voice. Sounded like an angel calling to him. Hunger rushed over him, a burning desire he'd never fully extinguished. "In here."

The front door closed, and he waited with his heart hammering. She walked into the kitchen with a huge sack, her red hair windblown and wild, looking like all his dreams come true. Her gaze fell on his nearly empty glass and the whiskey bottle beside it.

"I figured you were hungry."

He was. God, he was hungry. And Little Red Riding Hood had just walked in with her bag of goodies. "I am."

"I stopped at The Wedding Diner and picked you up some food. It won't last you long, but I figured you'd need something." She started unpacking the contents onto the counter. "Pot roast, lasagna or pork roast?"

She glanced at him. His throat dried out.

You. Just you.

"Whichever's easiest. Thanks," he blurted out instead.

"I can't stay," Jade said, pulling out the lasagna. She set it in front of him, retrieved some utensils and put those out, too. "Now, the other two entrées are hot as well, so you're going to have to let them cool before you stick them in the fridge. But you'll have food for the next couple of days if the roads are icy, or you just feel like sleeping." She smiled at him, a smile that electrified him. "I'm putting some of Mom's blackberry cobbler and apple pie in the fridge, too." Jade moved away, a busy whirlwind, intent on her mission. He glanced at the steaming lasagna, but then his gaze ricocheted back to her. That was where his temptation lay, in those round hips, long legs, the sweet smile he remembered so well. "Mom's going to wonder where I am, so I'm off."

He got up, wanting to detain her. But he couldn't.

There was a barrier between them that hadn't been there before. So he walked her to the door, following the motion of her sexy butt under the parka with a tight throat. "Appreciate the food."

"Not a problem." She opened the door.

He closed it. "I do have a small question."

She gazed up at him. "Okay."

"I actually have lots of questions." He took a deep breath. "Any chance you'd want to have dinner with me tomorrow night, catch me up on the hometown news?"

The smile slid away, and the shadows he'd seen earlier returned to her eyes. "I can't, Ty."

He nodded. "Okay." His heart plummeted into his stomach.

"Listen," she said suddenly, "eventually we'll talk."

"Eventually?"

"When you've had a chance to sleep. When you've—"

A sudden gust rattled the front windows. Ty opened the door, staring outside. "Snow's really coming down now."

"I have to go." She slipped around him, zipped up her parka on the porch.

"The roads are going to be bad," he warned. "Maybe you should stay here for a while." *Until morning. Sofa, guest room, wherever, just stay.*

"I can't," she said. "Goodbye, Ty."

She went to her truck, got in, switched it on and drove down his drive without looking back.

A lot had changed in eleven months.

He wished it hadn't changed so much.

Chapter 12

Jade was still so stunned by Ty's sudden appearance that the next day she kept herself extra busy. The babies, at two months, were starting to become more interested in their surroundings. She set them on the kitchen island counter in their carriers, where they could watch her bake cookies for the Christmas village tonight. Baking would keep her mind off Ty, and it would help out her mother. Jade glanced at her darling girls, cooing at them, still shocked that their grandfather was the horrible, merciless Robert Donovan.

Ugh. The thought made her hands tremble slightly. Jade took a deep breath. "Chocolate-chip cookies it is, girls."

Suz came into the kitchen, her smile huge. "I was hoping these little ladies would be awake! Mwah!" She kissed both babies on their foreheads. "Guess what?" she said to Jade.

"Anything I might guess right now would be wrong," Jade replied. She couldn't have guessed anything that had happened yesterday, from what the box had revealed to Ty suddenly showing up, sending her heart into overdrive.

She was no more over him than she'd ever been.

"We've got the loans on the business paid off!" Suz radiated joy, twirling around the kitchen with an elflike jig. "Robert Donovan can't call them in, can't bulldoze our business, can't hurt us anymore!"

Jade smiled. "That's awesome!"

"It is." Suz finally parked herself on a bar stool so she could play with the babies' toys. "And the guys have promised to stay on another year."

"Frog, Squint and Sam."

Suz nodded, took a few chocolate-chip kisses out of the bag Jade was about to use for the cookies. "This means ol' Mr. Donovan can get *stuffed.*"

Jade couldn't help a laugh. "Yes, he can." Probably it was bad of her to speak unkindly of her daughters' grandfather—but then again, he didn't know about them, and what he didn't know didn't hurt him.

Maybe he never had to know.

It's not like he would care, she thought, remembering Sheriff Spurlock's letter to his son.

"Blast," Jade said. "I'm a butterfingers today." She looked at the egg she'd just splattered all over the countertop, the yolk missing the bowl by at least an inch.

Suz grinned. "Guess who's about to come in for a fridge raid?"

Jade stiffened. Surely not Ty.

Oh, she hoped it was Ty. "Who?"

"Who else raids refrigerators like they were personal picnic baskets?" Suz turned to face Sam Barr as he walked in, hands in his jeans pockets, a grin on his handsome face.

Jade was so disappointed it was all she could do to smile.

"Hi, womenfolk," he said cheerfully.

"Womenfolk?" Suz scowled. "Are you a manfolk?"

"I'm not sure. I'll ponder that sometime, princess." He kissed Suz on the cheek, drawing a squeal from her, then dropped a kiss on each baby cheek, as well. Then he looked at Jade, who brandished a wooden spoon at him.

"No, thank you," she said.

He laughed. "You don't know what you're missing."

"I can do without."

"I'd be hurt, except I know you gals who protest the most usually have a secret you're keeping." He went to peer inside the fridge. "Betty said she put some pumpkin pie back just for me. Has my name on it and everything." He foraged around for his treat.

"Well, what about it, Jade?" Suz grinned at her. "Do you have a secret?"

"Not about Sam." Jade shook her head. "I'm sure I have a secret or two, but—"

Sam backed up from the fridge with the pie in his hand, smooching Jade on the cheek before she could pull away.

"You do that again, Sam Barr, and that pie is going in your kisser by a different route than you planned," she promised.

"Phew. Tough case." He sat across the island from

her and proceeded to enjoy his pie. "What would you do without me around here?"

"Yes, Jade," Suz said, egging them on. "Did you never figure out that Sam has a huge crush on you?"

Jade looked up from measuring sugar into the bowl, startled. Sam raised a brow, waved a fork dismissively.

"I have a crush on two women in this room, but I'm afraid neither of them is over the age of three months." He ran a gentle hand over the babies' slightly fuzzy heads. "Sorry, ladies, my heart is taken by these angels."

"Hmm," Suz said, "you're the kind of man who'd set your sights on a woman with a mother who bakes the world's best pumpkin pie." Suz got up to cut a piece of her own.

"I might be that kind of man," he said, winking at Jade, "but I get the pie for free. No need to confuse the process with a wedding ring."

"I'm so disappointed," Jade said wryly. She packed brown sugar into a cup, eyed it carefully. Since neither of them had mentioned Ty's presence in town, she figured he hadn't left the house yet. He was probably sleeping like a fallen log.

"Then again," Sam said, putting his dish in the sink, "that pie is so good I might have to rethink my position." He planted a quick, friendly kiss on Jade's cheek, in the spirit of the teasing.

Suz gasped, then leaped up from the stool, throwing her arms around Ty's neck as he walked into the kitchen, startling Jade so much she nearly dropped the sugar.

"You're back!" Suz exclaimed. "This is going to be a very merry Christmas! Jade, look who it is!"

She was looking—and trying hard not to drink him

in as if he were some kind of sexy, exotic cocktail— her eyes caught on Ty's, her heart thundering madly.

Sam went over, slapped him on the back, doing the guy version of greeting. "You old dog! When did you get in?"

Ty grinned at his friend. "Last night."

"Look at you," Suz said. "A real SEAL."

"Hey," Sam said, "*I'm* a real SEAL!"

"You're retired," Suz reminded him. "This one's live and in the flesh."

"Whatever," Sam said, scooping Eve from her carrier. "Look at this, Ty!" He grinned proudly, holding the baby up for Ty's inspection. "Have you ever seen anything so beautiful as these two little ladies?"

Jade froze, wondering how Ty would react. He looked at each baby in turn, his gaze returning to hers. "Congratulations," he said. "They're beautiful."

"That's right," Sam said proudly. "Gonna be rodeo queens one day." He nuzzled Eve's nose. "'Cause I'm planning on rigging the vote if I have to."

Suz laughed. "Cheaters never win."

Ty hadn't broken eye contact with Jade, and she had the feeling something was terribly wrong. She couldn't move—except to pick up Marie, who'd let out a squawk of protest at being left in her carrier.

Then she returned her gaze to Ty's, not sure how to broach the sudden elephant in the room. Suz looked at her strangely, no doubt wondering why she wasn't proudly showing Ty her newborns—only Suz didn't know what Sam had figured out on his own: Ty was a father.

Sam, of course, was no doubt enjoying her discomfort in a friendly, devilish-like-a-brother way.

"Congratulations," Ty said again. "I'm going to head over and see the guys. I just wanted to stop in and thank Betty for all the cookies and candy she sent to me overseas."

He left the kitchen. Suz's jaw dropped. "Wow, what was that all about?"

Jade shook her head, cuddling Marie to her. "Maybe he doesn't like children," she said.

Sam laughed. "Well, he would if they were his."

Jade gave him a warning look. Sam winked again, determined to torture her a little. "The problem is," he said, "Ty left because he thinks these babies are mine."

Suz's gaze flew to Jade. "Are they?"

"No! Oh, for heaven's sake!" She glared at Sam. "Why can't you keep your mouth shut?"

Suz appeared dumbfounded. "Oh, I get it. You mean these babies are…" She stared at Jade. "Ty's the father?" She counted quickly on her fingers. "Oh, my God! Ty is the father!"

Jade shook her head. "I didn't say that." She hadn't wanted anyone to know, hadn't even hinted at it. Betty had backed her on that, saying it was nobody's business.

"Oh, wow," Suz said. "Ty would never have left the country if he'd known you were expecting. And twins!" She gazed at Marie and Eve. "I'm not sure he would have left BC!"

"Exactly." Jade leveled the wooden spoon at Suz and then Sam. "And neither of you is going to tell him."

"You have to tell him," Suz said. "You don't want him thinking that these angels are this knucklehead's." She pointed at Sam. "Ty could be talking about the fact that he was over here, and got to meet Jade and Sam's babies just now. And that would be horrible!"

"Hey!" Sam exclaimed. "I'm a catch! I know I am!"

"You'd be the catch that got tossed back," Suz said.

Jade pulled off her apron, flung it at her friend. "Suz, you mix these cookies for Betty. Just follow the recipe. And Sam, you're on babysitting duty."

"I'd like to complain," he said, "but since I get to graze in Betty's fridge all I like, I'll just sit here with these little pumpernickels and pretend like I'm not the overlooked Prince Charming of BC."

Jade flew out the door, not waiting to hear any more nonsense. It wasn't fair to Ty not to tell him about Eve and Marie. Their old agreement wouldn't be in force any longer—too much had changed. Too much time separated them now.

But he deserved to know the truth—because history shouldn't repeat itself.

Suz stared at Sam as he settled himself with another slice of pie and a big cup of frothy organic milk. "I hope you're pleased with yourself."

"Indeed I am." He grinned at her, thinking that for a short stack, she really had a lot of personality. Not his type, of course, but in due time, he could help Frog Francisco Rodriguez Olivier Grant see what he was missing out on. Sam knew when a woman was crushing on a guy, and Suz wore her crush like a beacon, even if she did think she was keeping it on the down-low. "Ah, young love."

Suz narrowed her eyes. "You're going to look like a dunce if you've messed up everything between them. Jade obviously didn't want Ty to know. She didn't want him being tied to BC. She doesn't want him getting himself killed because his mind is on the family he didn't know he had, and the shenanigans back here."

"Tell me about it, cutie pie." Sam munched with contentment, undisturbed by the pot of steam that had become Suz's head.

"You don't have a thing for Jade, do you?" Suz looked at him, mystified, one slim brow raised.

He winked. "I have a thing for you."

"Oh, bull-oney. Bull-*oney*." She shook her head, whacked him on the hand with the wooden spatula, then turned her attention to the recipe she was supposed to be mixing up.

Sam went back to enjoying the pie, his heart completely in love with the luscious blend of creamy pumpkin and cinnamon spreading across his tongue. He had never met the woman who could steal his heart, and knew he never would. Which was why it was so much fun to play matchmaker for his buddies, and watch them fall like babies trying to take their first steps.

"One day, girls," he told Eve and Marie, "one day you're going to get to eat a bite of your granny's pie, instead of sucking on those unsatisfying bottles. And then you'll know why a man will do anything for a woman who cooks like Betty Crocker and Betty Harper. My two favorite ladies."

"Oh, brother," Suz said with disgust. "You have to help me put the holiday decorations up at the Hanging H later. And I don't want any of this nauseating wheezing about how the way to a man's heart is through his stomach."

Sam laughed. "Just don't burn those cookies, cookie, and you and I will get along just fine."

* * *

Ty headed into the bunkhouse at the Hanging H, hoping to find Frog and Squint for some answers. His head whirled, his breath coming too short for comfort. He'd never felt this wound up, not even in Afghanistan.

Jade was a *mother*. And those babies were *tiny*. Two doll-like babies, clearly not that old. He did the math as fast as his poor, stunned brain could manage: They couldn't be more than a few months old, or they'd be bigger.

So those babies weren't his. He'd left in January, so any offspring of his would have been born in October.

Those babies were almost brand-spanking-new.

Damn.

There was no one in the bunkhouse, so he headed over to the main house. He had to have answers. Who was the father?

Of course he knew the answer. Sam had been hanging around, holding a baby, acting very comfortable in Jade's kitchen.

Ty felt as if a huge hole had been blown in his heart. His stomach seemed to be compacted into a cramp he couldn't relax. His dream of coming home to Jade, and the minimal chance that she might have waited for him, faded away.

He opened the back door, as he always had, and five pairs of eyes turned to stare at him, as if he were some kind of specter.

Ty felt like a specter.

Frog, Squint, Mackenzie, Justin and even Daisy hovered around the island, sticking M&M's onto an enormous gingerbread house that covered the entire kitchen island.

"Ty!" Daisy exclaimed. "Welcome home!"

Mackenzie came to hug him, and his buddies slapped him on the back, gave him a punch in the arm and a high five. Daisy gave him a fast hug, then got him a glass of milk and a brownie with peppermint sprinkles on top, pointing him to a bar stool.

"Sit," Mackenzie said, "and tell us everything. We thought you were never coming back to BC!"

God, it was good to be home, among faces that smiled at him and people who loved him. He sat on the bar stool, enjoying the warmth of friends, and briefly wondered why Daisy was in the mix. He hoped like hell Squint hadn't finally decided to fall for her tricks, but Ty had enough problems of his own with a certain fiery red-head.

"Well," Mackenzie prodded, "gobble that brownie, drink that milk and then start with BUD/S. We want to hear about every second from our hometown hero!"

He swallowed hard. He wasn't sure he could push anything past his seriously tight throat. Jealousy seemed to be sitting in his airway like a rock. "Thanks, everybody, for the welcome. It's good to be back."

They grinned, pleased. "We have so much to tell you," Mackenzie said. "But you first!"

"Um, okay." He took a bite, sipped the milk so they wouldn't be disappointed. "Hey, I stopped by the Harper place to check in on Betty and—"

Mackenzie clapped her hands. "And you saw the babies!"

He forced a smile onto his face. "I did, actually."

His friends all looked pleased as could be, as if they were related to the babies or were proud godparents or something. Ty cleared his throat. "Um, Jade didn't mention who the father is, and I didn't really want to pry. What's the story there? She wasn't wearing a wedding ring."

"Well, it's interesting," Frog said. "No one knows who the father is, and we don't have a good guess."

Squint nodded. "We have guesses, but none of them are good."

"Guesses?" Ty swallowed again. "Was Jade dating somebody?"

"No. No one, as far as we know." Squint shrugged. "It's all very mysterious. We have no clue."

"For a while we suspected Sam," Mackenzie said. "But Sam says hell, no. He likes those babies, adores them. Hangs around there all the time."

"Yeah, like a bad smell," Frog said. "But Sam says he hasn't even kissed a girl in BC, and doesn't plan to. Idiot," he added cheerfully. "We were brought here to find brides, weren't we? So why not spread our kisses around?"

They all laughed, relaxed. Ty had a horrible headache, all the jovial banter not easing his shock over finding Jade had somehow figured out a way to get that ovary working just fine. *Damn, damn, damn.*

"They're so small," he said. "I never saw such delicate little things."

Mackenzie grinned. "You should have seen my four when they were born! No bigger than small baking potatoes. Want another brownie?"

She put one in front of him, and Ty couldn't say no. It felt so good to be home among his friends—except for the problem with Jade.

"So, buddy," Frog said, "tell us everything."

"When were the babies born?" He had to know.

"October first," Suz said.

His mind went into major mental-math mode. "October?" He'd left in January. *My God,* it was possible. Holy hell, it was more than possible that those babies were his. He perked up, feeling a little light suddenly shining into his life—then crashed. Jade had been at his house last night, hadn't breathed a word about babies, a pregnancy, nada. They weren't his. The damning realization crushed his heart. "Jade's never given a hint about who the—"

The back door blew open. Jade came in, stomped the snow off her feet on the mat.

"Hello-o-o, little mama," Frog said. "Join us to welcome home this brave SEAL. And have a fortifying brownie on me!" He gave Jade a big, sloppy smooch on the cheek, which had Ty bristling in spite of himself.

"Hi, everybody. Uh, and Daisy," Jade said awkwardly. "Ty, do you have a second? I need to talk to you."

Everybody looked very interested in her announcement.

"Aha!" Squint exclaimed. "I told you, guys! Ty's the baby daddy!"

They all whooped and carried on something ridiculous around the kitchen island, high-fiving each other and laughing. Ty thought he even might have seen money change hands between Squint and Frog.

"I was sure it was Sam," Frog said. "Until I wasn't sure it was Sam. Then I put my money on a dark horse."

Jade looked embarrassed. Her cheeks got a bit pink and her gaze skittered away from Ty's. "Guys, if you could just go back to building this fine gingerbread house, that'd be awesome."

Well, she hadn't denied that he was the father—that

was something. Ty's world spun like mad. Could he be a father? To twins?

That would be the welcome home gift to end all welcome home gifts.

He strode to Jade's side. "Let's go into the fireplace room. If you don't mind, Mackenzie? Justin?"

"Of course not!" They smiled at him demurely—too demurely. Which tipped him off to the fact that there was a baby monitor on the kitchen island, and it was on.

He reached over and switched it off.

"Aw!" Frog looked chagrined. "We would have turned it off, dude."

"I doubt it. Come on, Jade." Ty led her into the comfortable living room.

"You know they'll turn it right back on."

"Either that or they'll have their ears stuck out to pick up any sound we make. It's like a family of drones." He didn't much care; he was with Jade. It was Christmas, and he couldn't think of any place he'd rather be than here with her, in BC.

"Nice tree," he said to break the tension, tossing a glance over at the beautiful Christmas tree in a corner of the lovely blue-and-white-decorated living room. But that didn't interest him as much as the red-hot mama who took a seat near the fireplace.

"I have to talk to you," she said, and he said, "Yeah, I got that. I'm listening."

His heart thundering, he sat on a sofa, keeping a careful distance between them. He didn't want to get too close, accidentally smell her hair, touch her, have to fight to keep from taking those sweet, cupcake-soft lips.

"First, let me tell you how proud I am that you got your Trident. All of BC celebrated, Ty. It's a huge ac-

complishment. And everything else you've done, too."
She smiled at him and he felt a small glow start inside
him—except that she sounded like they were in a job interview and she was about to give him the you're-really-
awesome-but-you're-not-quite-right-for-the-job speech.

"Thanks," he said, numbness stealing over him.

"Ty," Jade said, "I became a mother while you were
gone."

"I did notice."

"As you know, I wasn't expecting to be able to get
pregnant, so it was quite a surprise."

"I'm pretty surprised myself."

He was going to kill Sam. Damn Sam. It had to be
him. No one hung around someone's babies, holding
them and acting all goo-goo-eyed and mushy, unless
they were his own progeny.

Yes, Ty was going to kill Sam, even if he had no rational reason to.

"Congratulations. That's great," he said, realizing
something more than what he'd said so far was required.
He had to play nice, act pleased for her, cover the fact
that he was dying inside.

"I was hoping you'd feel that way."

He nodded, completely destroyed. "I know how much
you wanted a baby, Jade. I'm really happy for you."

She took a deep breath. "I just want you to know that
our previous agreement obviously isn't necessary. After
all, so much has changed. You've been gone nearly a
year, and—"

"Agreement?" He was lost, needed a map terribly.
Maybe if he wasn't so immersed in her beautiful green
eyes he could pay attention better, but he had to hang on

to something, and drinking her in was something he'd longed to do for a long time.

"Our marriage agreement." She laughed, sounding somewhat nervous. "We were both in a different place then, and it was a rash agreement."

"Our marriage agreement?"

Her face took on a pink cast, and he realized she was embarrassed.

"I shouldn't have brought it up. Never mind Forget I said anything."

"Hang on a minute." He held up a hand. "What are you talking about, Jade?"

She looked at him, obviously torn about saying more.

"Don't leave me in the dark." He glanced at the Christmas tree twinkling in its corner and scratched his head. "I remember saying that if you happened to get pregnant, I wanted to marry you."

"Yes." She looked relieved. "But you don't have to anymore."

Finally they were getting someplace. "Won't the father marry you? I mean, if Sam's being an asshole, I can sure beat his head in for you."

Her eyes went wide. "Sam's not the father of my children. Sam doesn't want any part of marrying anyone, and he certainly wouldn't get a woman pregnant. He avoids what he calls women traps like the plague. For that matter, so do Squint and Frog—even if they claim to be here looking for brides. I just don't think they're all that serious. Playing the field, is my guess."

"Back to the father issue." Ty couldn't get the whole story straight in his head. "We'll worry about the home team and their field-playing later."

"The babies are yours, Ty," Jade said softly, and it felt as if wings rushed into his heart, lifting it skyward.

"Mine?"

She frowned. "Well, of course! Who else's would they be?"

He swallowed hard, stunned. "I don't see how."

She raised a brow. "You don't see how?"

"We don't, either," Frog called down the hall. "Can we have a few more details? There's a big hole in this story!"

Jade grabbed Ty's hand, led him down the hall to a guest room, closed the bedroom door. "Of course you're the father. You don't remember working really hard to help me get pregnant?"

She looked seriously disappointed in him, so Ty reached out, pulled her to him. "Slow down a minute, beautiful, and let me catch my breath. I'm still processing the fact that I don't have to tie Sam to a cactus and leave him for an unpleasant, prickly end."

"I can't believe you think Sam and I... I mean, I would never—" Jade looked at him, disgusted. "No. Never Sam. He's just really good with the babies, and he loves them. And I think they're comforted by his deep voice. Actually, the girls love Frog and Squint, too, but they don't come around daily, even hourly, like Sam does."

Ty grunted. "I'll try to thank him. Won't be easy, because I'm a bit jealous." If those tiny little pink-wrapped babies were his, he was totally jealous of all the hours Sam had spent holding them that he had missed out on. "So, mine, huh?"

"Of course they are. I just didn't tell you because I was...afraid."

Ty gazed into her eyes, seeing her apology in her honesty. "Because of my training."

"I really felt like it was best if I waited until later to tell you. I'm sorry if I did the wrong thing." Jade took a deep breath. "Believe me, it wasn't the easiest decision I ever made."

He pulled her into his arms. "I'm a father. That's just about the best welcome-home gift I could have ever gotten. I don't know if it's totally hit me yet."

She smiled. "Sometimes the fact that I'm the mother of twins hasn't totally hit me yet, either."

"Twins." His brain struggled to take that information in. Then he laughed out loud. "I told you your ovary would like me."

She tried not to laugh, moved out of his arms. "Yes, you did. Crow all you like. You deserve it."

"I certainly plan to. So now, about getting married—"

"No, no. That's exactly what I came here to tell you." Jade's face turned serious. "Marriage is out of the question."

Chapter 13

Ty hurried after Jade as she exited the bedroom. "What do you mean, out of the question? Of course we're getting married! Those babies are going to have a father, and it's not going to be Stand-in Sam!"

Jade stopped in the hallway and put a hand against Ty's chest, sending his pulse skyrocketing. He wanted to kiss her desperately, celebrate his good fortune of becoming a father—sensed that would be a mistake. Jade was far too defensive, her demeanor closed off from him.

Nope. No kissing.

But as soon as he could manage it, he was going for those sweet lips. He'd gone far too long without kissing Jade.

"I don't want anything to change, Ty."

He caught her hand in his. "Sorry, darling, it's changing."

"It can't." Jade shook her head, adamant. "Ty, look. I spent the last several months eaten up with guilt because I wasn't telling you that you were a father. I didn't know if that was the right decision or not. What if you'd died? Gotten killed by a roadside bomb or something?" Her eyes filled with tears, astonishing him. "You have no idea how hard it is to watch the news every night with your heart in your throat, wondering if your babies are ever going to get to know their father."

Their friends trooped out of the kitchen.

"Ty's really the father?" Squint asked. "I did not see that coming."

"I thought about it once," Frog said, "but I dismissed it as being too impossible."

"Oh, wow," Mackenzie said. "What a great home-coming gift for you, Ty!"

"Congratulations, Ty," Daisy said, and he wondered again why his friends had suddenly let trouble into their tight-knit circle.

"That's awesome!" Mackenzie flew down the hall to throw her arms around his neck. "Now Justin will have a fellow father to talk baby with!" She glanced with delight at her husband, and he saluted Ty with a grin.

"Uh, yeah. I hadn't exactly thought of it that way, but yeah. Me and Justin. Fathers. Who would have ever thought it?" Ty said, feeling a little panic come over him. But he wasn't going to be a husband, not like Justin. The sparky redhead who'd drifted into the kitchen with the rest of the group seemed pretty clear on that.

"Excuse me, gang," he said, following Jade as she tried to sneak out the back door. "Just a minute, mother of my children."

Jade kept walking toward her house. "I have to get back. It's almost time to nurse the babies."

"I can help you." He was damned if Sam would be Drop-In Daddy any longer, not while he was around.

"Not with nursing, you can't." Jade walked faster. "Ty, I get that all of this is a shock to you, and you're welcome to come around anytime you like to see the babies, but I don't want anything to change between us. I mean it."

He caught her hand, stopping her. "As I said, everything has changed. So get ready for that." It felt so good to hold her hand, hold any part of her, that he forgot his earlier vow about keeping his distance, and pulled her against his chest. "Now *this* feels like home."

She remained against his chest, surprising him, because he'd expected a bit of a tussle. She was plenty strong-willed, and he'd been gone long enough to give her time to get really set in her ways. "I know you have some bug in your head about me, and the babies, but we're getting married, beautiful."

She pulled away. "I can't marry you. I'm sorry."

"Because?" He stopped her when she prepared to dart off again. "Because you don't want to be married to a guy who's not going to be around much?"

"Of course not!" She thumped his chest with a stern finger. "No one has supported your dreams more than me, so don't even go there."

"Then why? Marrying me is the smartest thing you could do. We have babies who need the Spurlock name."

She seemed to go a little pale, though it was hard to tell in the very frigid weather, which was already pinkening her cheeks. "Oh, God, Ty."

"What?" He looked at her. "What is it?"

"I can't marry you. I'm sorry, I can't. I appreciate

that you want to do the right thing by the children, but I promise you, Eve and Marie will be just fine."

He stopped, his brain scrambling. "Eve and Marie?"

"Yes." She looked at him curiously. "Didn't I tell you?"

"I might have missed it, but—" He tried on his daughters' names, turning them over in his mind. "Those are beautiful names. Eve and Marie Spurlock. Perfect."

"No," Jade said, "they're Eve and Marie Harper. It's just the way it has to be."

She headed off, her boots crunching in the crusty snow.

"Why?" He stopped her again. "A promise is a promise, doll face, and you did promise me that marriage was my reward for overcoming your timid ovary."

She shook her head. "Neither of us knew what we were promising then, Ty. Forget it."

"I'm not forgetting a damn thing. My daughters are going to have my name."

Jade sighed. "Ty, how much more bad news do you want in one day?"

"Bad news?" He considered that. "I haven't had any bad news today. All I've gotten is good news, so go ahead and hit with me with whatever you're keeping under that sexy red hair of yours. Be prepared, you're talking to a navy SEAL. I don't hear a whole lot of bad news. Everything filters into best possible outcomes."

"All right." Jade took a deep breath. "I didn't want to tell you this. I know you said you didn't want to hear, and God knows, I'm still pretty floored by the whole thing. But I finally opened that stupid box."

"So? Nothing that was buried in a box is going to keep me from being a father to my children, Jade." He tucked her against his chest once more, wanting to chase away the sudden shadows in her eyes. "I promise you, everything is going to be fine. I suggest you start thinking of what kind of wedding gown you'll be wearing."

"Ty, I don't really know how to say this," she said, pulling herself from his arms, "but Robert Donovan is the girls' grandfather."

Ty stared at her, caught and wary. "No, he's not. Not if I'm the father."

"You're the father," Jade said slowly, softly. It came to him that she was trying very gently to point him toward information she thought he needed. "And Robert Donovan is your father."

The earth shifted beneath his feet, then Ty realized it was his legs going rubbery. His brain felt rubbery, too, unable to process what the mother of his children had just said. "What?"

She took another deep breath. "Ty, I'm so very sorry. Sheriff Spurlock and your mother adopted you from Robert Donovan's wife. Robert doesn't even know you're his son. That's why the box was buried. Your father never intended anyone to know." Jade's eyes filled with sympathetic tears. "I so didn't want to tell you, Ty. I know you said you never wanted to know what was in it, and I tried to keep to the letter of our agreement. But as you can see, that's a promise I just can't keep."

He shook his head, refusing to acknowledge what he was hearing. Felt himself grow dark inside. It explained so much. God, how he despised Donovan. Almost hated him.

This was insanely bad news. "So Daisy is my sister."

Jade nodded. "I invited her to come to a few more of our functions and projects, Ty. It's not easy for me. But there's a part of me that feels that family should be... family."

"I don't see how. She's as evil as her father." He straightened. "So I'm evil, too."

"Not hardly. Of course you're not!" She rushed into his arms to comfort him. "Don't say that! You're one of the most admired men in this town."

He shook his head. "Jade, you don't understand. I'm more Donovan than I am Spurlock."

"You're pure Spurlock. Nurture versus nature. You know that."

"I don't know that." He had a dark side, he knew. Now he understood where that darkness came from.

"Look, that's a silly theory. If I gave my babies to Cosette Lafleur to raise, they'd grow up very artsy, thinking pink hair was normal, and chatting in French. Of course you're your father's son! Sheriff Spurlock was a fine man, and so are you."

Ty's whole world had changed, sliding into some kind of strange abyss he hated. He couldn't take it in. "You're positive that's what was in the box?"

"I'm afraid so." Jade backed away, feeling horrible for him, not sure how to comfort him. "I really didn't want to tell you, but I'd already kept one thing from you, which I felt horribly guilty about, and still do. I couldn't keep two secrets that would change your life."

"I know." He shook his head. "I'm not angry with you. I'm just cursed."

"You're not cursed! That's ridiculous!"

"I'm going," Ty said suddenly, making up his mind. "I'm going to see the babies."

She looked worried. "And then what?"

He walked away, no longer sure.

But one thing he did know—he was going to be a father that his daughters knew loved them.

Ty couldn't say he was relieved to know that the reason Jade didn't want to marry him had to do with his newfound family lineage, and her own feelings of remorse over keeping things from him. Part of those guilty feelings he could have honestly told her to forget about—he'd insisted he didn't want to know what his father had hidden away in the staircase, and he wasn't sorry about that decision at all.

In fact, a big part of him wished he still didn't know. He was surprised by the amount of anger that had rushed into him at her revelation—anger and questions and fury. But not with her. All his fury was directed at Robert Donovan, who apparently had been an ass for so many years that even his own wife hadn't trusted him.

The anger Ty would deal with later.

As for Jade, just worrying about why she'd been keeping him at arm's length had been plenty to have on his mind. But now that he knew, he agreed with her; there could be no marriage between them. The last thing he was going to do was sully his daughters' lives and reputations by announcing their relationship to Robert Donovan.

God, what a hellish curse that would be to live under.

And it wasn't a secret that could be kept. Right now, their dearest friends knew that Ty was the father of Jade's babies. Daisy had been in the room with the others, so by now, all of BC had heard the news. That was how secrets worked in their community—they just didn't stay buried forever.

It sucked, really sucked, to know that Donovan was

his birth father. And yet Ty could be a better man than Donovan; the curse didn't have to perpetuate itself.

"Listen," he said suddenly, as Jade returned to the kitchen, where he'd sat himself at the table. He'd tried to nibble on one of Betty's oatmeal-raisin cookies, but frankly, his appetite was gone like the wind. "Has Sam left?"

She nodded, sat across from him. "One look at your face seemed to convince him that his presence wasn't needed. He shot out of here and didn't even give me a report on the babies." Jade smiled at Ty and selected a cookie for herself. "Sam usually likes to give me the rundown of every single thing the girls have done while he was babysitting, from first poop to possible smile."

"Yeah, well." Jealousy sparked inside Ty again. "While I'm here, I don't want Sam babysitting. I'll babysit." He pondered that for a second. "I guess it's not babysitting if I'm the father. Then it's probably dad-sitting or something."

"Fine by me."

"So anyway." He took a deep breath. "You and I are going to keep this deep, dark secret, okay? For as long as we can, anyway. I don't want the girls growing up with a shadow hanging over their heads. You have to admit it's a big, nasty shadow. I don't know how long something like this can stay hidden. Part of me wonders if there's another shoe that might drop." Or someone else who knew.

"I leave that decision up to you, although part of me wonders if Robert has the right to know."

"He has the right to nothing." Ty got up, paced the room. "He'd figure out a way to use them to get something he wants. Trust me, I know the man. He's an open book. When it comes to his ambition, everyone is a sacrifice."

"Except Daisy."

"I'm not so sure." Ty sat down at the table again, reached for Jade's hand, held it between his. "For now, let's agree that particular skeleton stays buried in the closet."

"Staircase," she murmured. "Fine by me. I sealed that box up tight. Very tight."

"Why'd you wait so long to look in the box?"

Jade shrugged. "It was your personal business."

Ty stared at her. "You realize you may be the only woman on the planet who doesn't have killer curiosity. I'm betting any other one would have looked that first night."

"I waited in case you didn't make it through BUD/S. If you'd decided to come home, then I could have made you do it—"

"Ha! You were the one who told me to stay in training no matter what!" Ty squeezed her fingers lightly.

"I know. But being a SEAL isn't for everyone."

"You think I can't do what Squint, Sam and Frog did? I don't know that I appreciate your lack of faith," he teased.

"I just thought I'd wait to see what happened." Jade pulled her fingers from his, got up to get coffee. "And then I was pregnant. The last thing on my mind was the box, and I kind of forgot about it. I went over to your house once a week, but I'd put the stair back together, and taped it off so Betty would know which one to avoid."

"Your mother's been going to my house, too? And you didn't tell her about the box?"

"Nope." Jade poured them each a cup, set one in front of him. "I told her you had mentioned the stair came loose, and that we were supposed to be careful. I don't think Mom paid any attention. When I was put on bed rest in the sixth month, she went over there all the time in my place."

"I'll thank her later," he said gruffly. "I didn't mean to cause trouble for your whole family. I was trying to take care of you in case something happened to me." He scowled. "You didn't touch a dime of the money in the account, but you had my daughters! You should have taken some of the money to help raise my children. Why else does a man bother to draw up a will except to take care of his responsibilities?"

Ty wasn't satisfied with her clear-eyed gaze, which stubbornly reminded him that she could take care of herself. "Anyway, you should have written to tell me," he grumbled, knowing very well why she hadn't. "Were you going to tell me when they were walking down the aisle with their husbands?"

"I was going to tell you when I knew it was safe to do so," Jade said. "Now drink your tea and get warmed up before I kick you out. It's almost time for me to nurse. The girls will be awake any second."

"I want to meet them. I barely glanced at them earlier. I think I was in shock." He shook his head, remembering the punch in his gut at seeing the babies. "I know I was in shock."

"You'll meet them. Soon."

"I will today," he said stubbornly, walking around the table to take the seat next to her. He held her close against him, putting his face against her neck, sighing with happiness. "I thought constantly about the way you smell. I dreamed of your red, springy hair and your sweet lips that kiss me like I'm the only guy in the world."

She tried to wriggle away, but he was having none of it. "You just sit still, beautiful. I came a long way to hold you, and I plan to do it often. Now that the whole town knows you've had my children, I figure there's no need to hide my feelings for you."

Jade turned to gaze into his eyes. "You're not angry?"

He kissed her neck, taking his time. "Oh, I'm a little peeved. I underestimated your desire and ability to keep secrets. I wish you'd told me about the babies. It would have given me something to occupy my mind with."

"I didn't want you occupying your mind with anything but staying alive." Jade got up, moved to the counter to refill her cup, but he knew she was just creating distance. A little squeak came over the monitor, and a serenely happy look settled over Jade's face, hitting Ty like an arrow shot into his heart.

He'd never seen anyone appear so joyful, so peaceful.

She was thrilled to be a mother.

"You get to meet your daughters now, although I'm going to warn you, it's not a romantic thing. It's dirty diapers and spit-up—"

"Lots of things in the navy make me think I can handle a little baby hurl. Lead on," he said drily.

She went down the hall and he followed her into a nursery where a night-light glowed softly and the scent of baby powder hung in the air. He could see two small heads barely moving, and a tiny hand flailing.

"Girls, this is your daddy," Jade said, picking a baby up from the crib where *Eve* was scrolled in delicate letters. "Eve, meet SEAL Ty Spurlock, your father and one of the finest men I've ever known."

He took the baby, memorizing everything in that first touch. Eve was warm from sleeping, her tiny body a little taut from the wail she wanted to let fly, until he held her to his chest. Then she went still, surprised by the new arms cuddling her.

"And this is Marie." Jade held the other baby and unbuttoned her blouse as she sat in a rocker. "If you walk around with Eve, she'll stay calm until I've got Marie fed."

"Second fiddle, are you?" he murmured to the baby, and Jade laughed.

"No, she just has my patience. Marie has your impatience."

"I don't think I'm impatient." Of course he was. Nothing ever moved fast enough or smoothly enough to suit him. "Okay, I'm impatient."

Jade smiled. "I'm glad you came home."

He cleared his throat, still kind of lost in the soft, sweet scent of his daughter and the warmth of her tiny body against his chest. He was lost in the beauty of Jade nursing his other daughter, and the love sweeping over him as he realized that this was the most amazing moment of his life.

He was a father. A real father. He had two daughters, and the three females in this room had just become his entire world.

"We're going about this all wrong. You're going to have to marry me," Ty said, his tone tight with emotion. "I know you've got a thousand bugs in your brain because of the way that everything happened, and the secrets that you had to keep for so long, but babe, if you don't marry me, these little girls are going to grow up thinking their father is a lightweight in the dad department." He kissed Eve, loving the tiny, downy hairs that sparsely adorned her head. Then he stared his stubborn lady down. "I did my part, angel face. Now it's time for you to do yours."

Chapter 14

The wedding was a fast, beautiful affair that took place right before Christmas. Jade couldn't believe how quickly everything was happening. After lots of soul searching, she and Ty had agreed that marriage was the right thing for the children.

They'd never talked about love. But she did love Ty, with all her heart and soul. She understood why he hadn't mentioned it, though it pained her a little. Until Ty came to terms with who he was—the new him he'd just discovered—she didn't figure he could love anyone.

Except the babies. Oh, how he loved Eve and Marie. Jade smiled as she took off the cream-colored gown she'd worn to the courthouse. Ty had insisted the girls be at the wedding. He'd held Eve and she'd held Marie, and thankfully, the ceremony had been swift, because

Jade had been nervous the girls would get cranky and her breasts would start leaking.

Funny thing to worry about on one's wedding day. But she had bigger things on her mind now, the biggest of which was the fact that she knew good and well that Ty hadn't completely forgiven her for not telling him he was a father.

He hadn't said much about it, but she sensed it was in the back of his mind. Trust was a huge factor in a relationship, and when he'd just learned he was related to people with whom the word *trust* was never associated, he needed to be able to count on someone, absolutely.

She'd have to build that up in their marriage.

"Hurry up!" Betty called from the bottom of the stairs. "It's time to cut the cake. The natives are restless!"

Jade sent one last appraising glance over the red velvet dress she'd bought months ago at the maternity store, glad it covered the full curves she was working on diminishing just a bit, and hurried down the stairs.

"My goodness, is all of BC here?" she asked Ty, who looked quite pleased with himself as he held his daughters in his arms.

"Wedding cake at Christmastime. Nobody in town is ever going to pass that up."

"As the best man, I'll pass the cake," Frog said. "That way I make sure I get the biggest piece."

Everyone booed him playfully, and Betty gave her a slight nudge toward the cake. Jade picked up the knife and glanced at her husband. "I think the way this works is that I'm supposed to cram some of this into your mouth."

He grinned. "Do your worst, Mrs. Spurlock."

She jumped at hearing her new name on his lips,

and everyone gathered in the dining room crowed with delight.

"I'll pass the plates around," Suz said, coming forward. "Here, you take a baby," she told Mackenzie, handing her Eve. "And you take the other munchkin, Daisy. It might just stir something warm in your heart."

Jade froze, and beside her, she felt Ty do the same. They watched as Daisy took little Marie, cooing to her. It was astonishing to watch Daisy act as if she actually didn't mind holding an infant, even was happy to be included. Jade looked at Ty uncomfortably, and after a moment, he shrugged.

There was no point in being ugly in front of everyone in BC. People were standing six deep in the dining room and were spilled out on the lawn. Jade put a smile on her face. "I'm going to cut as fast as I can, and you guys make an assembly line of sorts. Grab your cake and then head into the den area, where the Christmas tree is, so everyone can make it in out of the cold."

That seemed to be a plan the crowd liked—as long as they got cake—and Jade cut the first slice. "Here goes," she told Ty, and carefully put a piece into her husband's mouth.

"Excellent cake, Betty and Jane," he said, "but I know one thing that's sweeter." He gave Jade a big smooch on the lips that had everyone laughing.

"Help me with this," she said, wiping a little frosting from his face.

She and Ty sliced the cake swiftly, and Mackenzie and Betty passed it along to grateful wedding guests, all of whom had congratulatory words to say to their hometown son and daughter. Jade couldn't stop smiling. Why had she worried? This was turning out to be one of the most magical days of her life. It was so hard to believe that this big, strong, handsome man was now her husband. How many years had she dreamed of this very moment?

"You got off easy, you know, old son," Squint said as he passed by. "The folks are grousing that you got set up with a bride and didn't even have to swim the creek."

Ty grinned. "That's right. No Bridesmaids Creek swim for me to find a bride. I got mine without magic."

"Yeah," Sam said, "you didn't have to navigate Best Man's Fork, either. The folks feel a bit cheated."

"That's just fine." Ty laughed, and Jade loved the sound of it. Just hearing him so relaxed and happy gave her hope for their marriage, as strange as it had started out. "I've run the fork and swum that creek so many times training for BUD/S that the magic already did its thing." He gave Jade another smooch, and people laughed. She had just turned to finish cutting the last several slices of the lovely three-tiered confection trimmed with gold roses and latticework when the room went totally silent.

So silent it felt as if everyone quit breathing.

Robert Donovan walked in, a plate of cake in his hand, a big grin on his face. Jade froze. Beside her, she felt Ty go totally tense, protective in his stance near her.

"Donovan," Ty said. "You didn't have an invite."

"Don't need one." He glanced at the guests, his gaze falling on each person's face, which somehow felt threatening. Jade was glad the babies had been taken into the den by Cosette and Phillipe.

Daisy came into the room. "Dad, what are you doing here? Weddings aren't your thing."

"Everyone likes a wedding." He grinned hugely, sort

of nastily, and Jade wondered if that was just Robert Donovan's normal expression. Looking at him, knowing his history, made her sick to her stomach.

"That's it," Betty said, bustling into the kitchen. "Out you go, Donovan. This is my house, and you aren't invited. And there are still laws we follow in this town about trespassers."

"That's interesting, Betty. You're just the person I came here to see." He glanced around. "Now that your only chick's going to move out, you won't need a place this big. Ten acres is far too much for you to handle."

"Don't see that's any of your business," Jade's mother snapped.

"It's connected to the Hanging H. Only divided by a fence," Robert said. "Makes it very valuable, Betty. I could make you a nice offer. In fact, I'm making you a very nice offer. A property like this could easily go for a million dollars."

The guests who had filed back into the dining room to see what was going on gasped. Betty put her hands on her hips, frowning. "Donovan, if that's all you came to say on the day of my daughter's wedding, then get the hell out."

He looked at her like a cat about to pounce on a bird. "Betty, you don't want to be out here all by yourself."

"*Your* chick hasn't flown the coop," Betty snapped. "Anyway, even when mine does, I'll be just fine."

"A lot can happen to an elderly woman in a place this big," Robert said, and everyone gasped again.

"That's enough," Ty said. "You've had your say. Betty's asked you to leave, so I suggest you do so before we help you."

Sam, Squint, Justin and Frog came to stand at Ty's

side for backup, a scrum of dangerous-looking men. Jade breathed an internal sigh of relief.

Robert glanced around the room. "A fall, a broken hip. You'd be much better off in a smaller place, Betty. Now where are those tiny newcomers to Bridesmaids Creek I've heard so much about? No bigger than Christmas stockings, apparently, since they were born a few weeks early. Not too healthy, are they? A million dollars could make a lot of difference in their lives."

Jade caught Ty's arm to keep him from jumping across the table and punching Donovan. Her husband was not going to jail on their wedding day.

"Robert Donovan, let me ask you something," Betty said, getting right up close to him so she could poke his chest with her finger. "What's all the empire building about, anyway? You can't take any of this with you when you go."

"I don't have to. I have my daughter." He glanced at Daisy, but strangely, she didn't smile back at him. In fact, Jade thought she looked mortified by her father's behavior. "She'll inherit everything."

"Really," Betty said. "Well, maybe she won't. Maybe all your empire building is for nothing."

The whole room went silent.

"What do you mean, Betty Harper?" Donovan growled.

"I just mean that you might find your empire being split up one day." She poked him again. "So if was you, I'd mind myself."

"I don't have any other heirs," Donovan said.

"I'm tired of you, Robert," Betty said. "I'm tired of you scaring folks half to death in this town because they're afraid you're going to buy up the debt on their ranches and their homes, and call the loans on them. I'm tired of you running roughshod over everyone, and hurting people, and ruining every damn thing this town's tried to build. So here's a little news flash for you. You do have other heirs, and they happen to be my granddaughters. How does it feel to know that kingdom you're building isn't exactly the one you thought it was?"

Jade stiffened. "Mother!"

"He deserved it," Betty said. "I'm sorry, I—"

Ty leaped on Robert Donovan, throwing a right hard enough to knock the older man down. The entire room had gone deathly silent as Daisy stared at Jade and asked the question everyone wanted answered.

"Is it true?" Daisy demanded.

The guests had left in a hurry after Donovan was helped to his feet. He'd been carted off to the hospital, and Jade didn't care even if he did need to have his jaw reattached to his face. He deserved it for the many miseries he'd caused everyone in BC for so many years.

But her mother—oh, God, what was she going to do about her mother? Ty hadn't spoken a word to Jade since Betty's big reveal—in fact, he'd been the one to take Donovan to the hospital.

Ty had barely looked at Jade or Betty when he'd left, with Squint, Frog and Justin following him for backup. Probably to keep him from murdering Donovan on the way to the hospital.

"Mom!" Jade exclaimed when Betty bustled into the room. "Mom, what were you thinking?"

"I wasn't." Betty took off her apron. "The girls are asleep in the nursery, completely worn out from their big day." She looked at her daughter as Suz and Mackenzie came into the room to help carry dishes to the kitchen. "Well, yes, I was thinking. I was thinking just how badly I'd like to see Donovan get his just deserts."

"You had no right, Mom!" Ty was never going to speak to Jade again; she just knew it. He'd been adamant that the girls' true parentage remain a secret forever.

But even he had noted that secrets didn't stay buried in BC.

"How did you even find out about that, anyway?" Jade demanded.

"I heard you two talking over the baby monitor," Betty said, looking shamefaced. "You didn't know I'd come in the front door. I went down to check on the girls in the nursery, and I heard. I switched the monitor off as soon as I could, but it was too late. I am sorry for eavesdropping." Her shoulders drooped. "In fact, I'm sorry for spoiling your big day." She shook her head, collapsing onto a sofa with a sigh. "I guess I'm not as good as folks always try to paint me to be. But Lord, he got my nerves up, and I just wanted to pop that fat head off his fat neck!"

Jade sighed, sank onto the sofa next to her mother. "It was a beautiful cake and a lovely wedding day. I know you worked hard to pull all this together for me."

Betty put her head on her daughter's shoulder. "You know, I think it was all Robert's horrible talk about me getting old, and falling, and being helpless, and my daughter leaving my roost. And my grandbabies." She wiped at her eyes. "I think the old goat hit me on so many of my worst fears that I just wanted to give him a taste of his own medicine. Let him know he wasn't the big dog he thinks he is, and that this is one town he can't rule like some kind of king. We've got spirit here that he can't crush!" She gave a dramatic sigh. "I am so sorry, Jade. This town will be talking about your wedding day until the end of time."

"Yes, it will." Jade couldn't help smiling at her mother's statement, despite her forlorn tone. "Let's not worry about it anymore. What's done is done."

"Yes, but my son-in-law is going to think I'm a dragon. He tore out of here like a tornado was after him."

"Daisy went with him. They can have some bonding time."

"I doubt it very seriously. That's a brother-sister duo that isn't going to gel very quickly." Betty sat up. "Anyway, we have the girls. As far as I can see, you're sitting in the catbird seat, Jade Harper Spurlock."

"What do you mean?"

"It means," Betty said, "that Robert Donovan can't touch you. Can't threaten you, can't make your life miserable. You've got his granddaughters, and it could be years before Daisy gives him any bundles of joy!"

"Mom, Ty doesn't want our daughters anywhere near Donovan. I doubt very seriously Mr. Donovan would want any part of them, either. They're not going to be part of the Bridesmaids Creek power struggle."

"Doesn't matter. Everything changes for that smug old goat now." Betty giggled, sounding a whole lot less remorseful.

"Yes, and everything changes for me, too," Jade reminded her. "My husband's reeling from everything that's happened since he got home. This was supposed to be a simple holiday leave. Now he'll go back a different man than he was before he came home."

"Yes. But you're different, too." Betty shrugged. "When you read that letter, your life changed, too, Jade."

"Mom, you eavesdrop far too well." She sighed. It didn't matter now. All the cats were out of their flimsy bags. In her heart, she'd known that Ty was right: secrets didn't stay buried forever, not these kinds of secrets, anyway.

"You realize that your marriage stole a little bit of Madame Matchmaker's thunder." Betty got herself a piece of cake, plopped down next to her daughter, taking a bite with a sigh of pleasure. "Not bad cake, if I do say so myself."

"I think Cosette understands that things just happened."

"She likes to wave her magic wand, though. I feel like the Lafleurs might get back on a solid marital footing if they had some good luck, and that matchmaking business of theirs is key. I've been thinking this over, and I know how we can make things better for her and Phillipe." Betty grinned. "We're going to let her work her matchmaking magic on *Daisy*."

Jade got herself a piece of cake, too, figuring she might as well enjoy another slice, since she was the bride. "But Daisy and who? I don't even have a good idea for that."

"We'll let Cosette handle that little snare."

"To what end?" Jade wondered. "Daisy doesn't want to get married, and I haven't heard anyone but Squint mention he'd want to tangle with that whirlwind."

Betty straightened. "Not Squint. He's too nice. Too damaged. He needs something good in his life—not Daisy Donovan and her gang of wild men."

"And then there're those guys." Jade licked her fork. "Whoever marries her is going to have to put up with her gang. They're not exactly a barrel of monkeys, and

I'm pretty sure every one of them is on Robert's payroll over and beyond the work that they do for his kingdom, as you referred to it."

"I thought that was inspired." Betty beamed. "Maybe I'll go into the wedding-cake business."

"Mom, you don't have any time to do one more thing."

"You know what I wish? I wish you'd had time for a honeymoon." Betty shook her head. "You know, your father and I went to Oklahoma for ours. We camped out under the stars. It was nice."

Jade wasn't sure Ty had even thought about a honeymoon. There wasn't time before he went back to his military service, and besides, she was still nursing.

She just wanted her marriage to be a real one, and the look on Ty's face today when Betty had spilled the beans—okay, flung the whole pot of beans right at Robert's head—hadn't boded well. "I'm glad Dad and you had a lovely honeymoon. And I'm sure Ty and I will do something, one day."

Betty set her plate on the coffee table. "I'm going to start cleaning up. I want you to do nothing but be a bride today. Suz and Mackenzie can help. You just relax."

"I'm not going to relax," Jade said, getting up with her. "All the fun's in the kitchen."

Betty hugged her. "Be mad at me, but don't be mad at me forever. I couldn't bear it. Robert was right, I dread the thought of my darling chick leaving me. You might move to another state to be with that hunky SEAL husband of yours. I would if I was you."

"I don't think so." She relaxed into her mother's hug, enjoying the love. "I'm not sure what Ty's got in mind. And I'm not mad at you. I'm astounded by what you did, but then again, you're my mother. I suppose the apple didn't fall far from the tree."

The back door flew open and Daisy marched in, her long, chocolate hair flying.

"I hope you're both happy!" She glared at them.

"Sit down, Daisy," Jade said, recognizing that her new sister-in-law was in a twirl. "Let me get you a nice, hot cup of tea. It's really cold outside."

Daisy didn't sit, didn't move. The glare in her eyes could have frozen water. "I hope you're both happy with the way you behaved today. Very happy."

"Look, Daisy, it wasn't—" Jade began, but Betty put a hand on her arm.

"What's wrong, Daisy?" Betty asked.

Daisy's dark eyes blazed. "My father's had a heart attack, and it's all your fault! You just couldn't keep your big mouth shut. You had to tell all those horrible lies!" She looked completely wild and unsettled. "You've always been horrible and mean, Jade, you and Mackenzie and Suz. You're regular queen bees." Daisy burst into tears, something Jade had never seen her do.

"Now, girlie," Betty said, but Daisy rounded on her.

"Don't you say a word! This is all your fault! You just had to be horrible, and if my father dies, I'm going to, well, I don't know what!"

"You're upset, Daisy, and rightfully so. Sit down here and rest a minute." Jade steered her to a chair at the table. "Tell us what happened."

She quickly got a plate of wedding cake and some cookies, putting them in front of Daisy. Betty grabbed the teakettle and poured a cup of hot water for tea, setting a floral cup next to the sweets.

"You know what happened. Your horrible husband practically shattered my dad's jaw—"

"Shattered?" Jade asked.

"Well, no," Daisy said. "It's just badly bruised, the doctor says."

Jade let out a breath, glancing at her mother before she sat down across from Daisy. "And the heart attack?"

"Well, it's not actually a heart attack. It's a severe attack of angina. Brought on by stress!" She glared at Betty, then scarfed a cookie in record time. Started in on the wedding cake. "Mmm, this is good. Maybe I'll hire you to make my cake when I get married."

Jade raised a brow. "Are you getting married?"

"Do you think I'm going to let your daughters become my father's sole heirs after me?" Daisy asked.

"I don't expect that your father cares anything at all about my children," Jade shot back.

"He will. Dad's all about progeny and the future-generations thing." Daisy sighed. "I'm thinking about Francisco. Wouldn't Mr. and Mrs. Francisco Rodriguez Olivier Grant look nice on wedding invitations?"

Jade and Betty both gawked. "Frog?" Jade asked. "Why him?"

"He's ripe for the picking." Daisy shook her head. "Then again, Squint isn't hard on the eyes. It's just that Frog is so obviously on the hunt for a bride." She beamed. "I want a very stylish wedding gown from France. And a real wedding. None of this justice-of-the-peace stuff like you did."

Jade rolled her eyes. "I don't think you're going to get Frog. I think Suz has got her eyes—"

"Shh!" Betty said, her shushing startling both women.

"Here, Daisy," she added, too brightly, "let me get you another cup of tea."

"Did you say Suz has her eyes on Frog?" Daisy looked positively electrified by this news. She hopped up from the table. "Thanks for the chat, girls. I have somewhere to be. By the way, congratulations on your wedding, Jade, though I don't think your marriage will last too long." She took one last piece of cake for the road. "I heard Ty telling a nurse that he thinks he's leaving the navy. Can you imagine? After he worked so hard to become a SEAL?" She shook her head. "It's a shame. But he says he needs to be here with his daughters and wife. I think no marriage lasts when one party has to give up everything to please the other partner, but what do I know?"

"Yes, what do you know, Daisy?" Betty demanded. "I don't recall you having a degree in marriage counseling."

Daisy laughed and waved as she headed out the back door. Jade sank into a seat.

"Don't listen to her," Betty cautioned. "She came in here to stir up trouble, and she has."

She certainly had. But Jade knew Daisy was telling the truth. If Ty had said he was planning to leave the navy, then he was. He wasn't the same man who had left BC. No doubt he felt turned inside out.

Jade's heart sank. It was too soon for him to make that decision. There were a lot of emotions flying around from the holiday homecoming, the wedding, finding out he was a father, finding out who his father was.

But Daisy was right: he'd worked too hard to become a SEAL. And Jade was the reason his life had totally blown up, from a too-talkative mother to secrets Jade herself had kept from him.

When he came home tonight, she was going to do her best to convince her handsome SEAL that everything was going to be just fine. He had to go back, had to follow his dream.

She intended to fight for her marriage.

Chapter 15

A storm had turned loose inside Ty. Everything he'd once thought was the firm foundation of his life had been swept away.

He looked at his birth father lying on a bed in the hospital, giving commands to the nurses as if they had nothing better to do than be his personal servants. And of course, this was Robert Donovan, so who was going to tell him to pipe down?

"You need to pipe down," Ty said. "You don't need to always act like everywhere you go is part of your personal fiefdom. Your ticker is clearly telling you to chill out."

Robert stared at him, startled to hear a type of advice no one had dared give him before. "Why are you here?"

"Because." Ty sighed tiredly. "Because I hit you in your stupid mouth, because you had a small cardiac

event and because you're my daughters' grandfather."
He waved a hand dismissively. "Trust me, I don't want
to be here any more than you want me to be."

"So now that you know you're related to money, you
want to keep your eye on the golden goose?"

Ty looked at Robert with emotions bordering on disgust. "Really? That's your best shot? Always falling
back on your big, fat wallet?"

Robert didn't look thrilled by Ty's lack of respect for
his wallet. "You won't be in my will. And I expect some
blood work to be done to prove this spurious claim your
wife has come up with." He grunted, displeased by the
entire turn of events. "In fact, I may have the nurses
stick you while you're here."

"I think a simple swab will do," Ty said, "but knock
yourself out. Look, just because we share a bloodline
doesn't mean you're my father in any real sense of the
word. So don't try to act like one at this late date."

Robert's bushy brows rose. "What does that mean,
exactly? Are you turning your back on my money?"

"I couldn't care less if you have five dollars or five
million. By an unfortunate turn of circumstance, your
wife didn't like you enough to want a child with you." Ty
felt that was a travesty. Still, Jade hadn't told him about
his children, either. If he hadn't come home, he still
wouldn't know. Might never have known. He drummed
his fingers on the stiff metal-and-vinyl chair. This whole
business with Jade trying to keep everything quiet was
going to have to stop. Eve and Marie were his, and he
wanted to know everything and anything about them.
Maybe not with the attention to detail Sam apparently
liked—down to the pooping schedule—but all the stuff
that made a man a father, Ty planned to be in on.

"I'm staying in Bridesmaids Creek," he said. "Just to keep an eye on you, old man."

Robert's frowned at the disrespect he perceived from Ty's comment—and the adjective. "Old man! What son refers to his father that way?"

"I am not your son. Only in the blood sense. Please leave off all guilt trips. You're embarrassing yourself."

"Brave talk coming from a man on the government payroll." Robert sniffed. "See how much you have to live on and then I'll hear a different tune. You can't raise two babies and have a wife on a—"

"People do it all the time. Besides, I'm not exactly hurting financially."

"I'll buy your house, as I've offered to do many times. That should send your daughters to college."

Ty shook his head at Robert's endless calculations. "My dad sold you the land behind his house. You've had enough from the Spurlocks. You're not getting any more." He stood. "I have to go. Get on the mend, so I can give you hell."

"You know, Jade was awfully proud when you made it."

He felt a warm spot grow in his chest. "How do you know?"

"She went around town, telling everyone. She talked about you a lot."

This was news to him. Based on the amount of information he'd had from her while he was away, he'd have banked on the fact that she hadn't thought about him much. "Butt out, Robert. If I want a marriage counselor, I'll track one down. Just because we're unfortunately related doesn't mean I want any father-son chats, either."

"Yeah, well, I could use some assistance." Robert looked at him speculatively.

"With what?" Ty dreaded what he was about to hear. Donovan was as manipulative as the day was long. But he'd tried to coldcock the guy, so maybe he owed him a listen.

"Your sister—"

"Start over," Ty warned. "I'm serious. I want no discussion of us being a family. Do not try to tweak my heartstrings. As far as I'm concerned, I just learned that my family tree has a very undesirable root."

The older man shook his head. "I could use some help with my daughter."

"Can't help you."

"When I look at you," Robert said, drawing a deep breath, "I'm pretty proud."

"I don't care."

"What I'm saying is that I get why your mother… wasn't eager for me to raise a son. Raise you. Why she changed her mind about Daisy, I don't know." He sighed, sounding older than Ty had ever heard him sound. "Maybe she thought having a daughter would change me."

Ty remained silent, unmoved.

"Daisy is the apple of my eye. Having her just made me determined to conquer the world. You learn a little late in life that world-conquering is fine and dandy, but you really need to incorporate a few other elements into child rearing." He looked at Ty for a moment. "Your parents did a real fine job with you. Honestly, you're the kind of man any father would be proud to call his son."

Ty shook his head, not about to go there.

"So," Robert said heavily, "back to Daisy. She's already so much like me, and now that she knows she has a fractured family tree, she says she's on a mission to marry."

Ty snorted. "Sorry," he said, holding up a hand. "It's just that we're talking about Daisy."

"She says she's not going to let your daughters be the talk of the town. That they're not going to be my only legacy, as far as grandchildren go."

"That ol' family tree thing biting you in the ass, huh? Kind of wish you'd read *The Book of Virtues* to her when she was growing up?"

Robert shrugged, closed his eyes. "I don't know what I would have done differently. Everything, I suppose. All I know is that now I don't want my kingdom fought over."

"No fighting here. I don't want a dime of your dirty money." Ty was incensed. "You've made that money off the backs of folks in this town that you either flat-out robbed by manipulation, or tried to crowd out with fear." He stood. "Your entire kingdom, as you call it, is very safe from the Spurlock clan. You have my word on it."

"But you'll help me with Daisy."

Ty hesitated. "What exactly do you want me to do? Daisy's hell on wheels. She's going to do precisely what she wants."

"I don't want her running off and marrying some joker who's after my money."

"You've been lording your money over this town for years. Where do you think someone could be found who wouldn't want in on a chunk of change?" Ty hated the fact that he was even thinking through Robert's dilemma. "What you need is Madame Matchmaker's expertise. Only problem is you've about ruined her and

Phillipe's marriage by putting them under a load of financial pressure. You've wrecked his business in your pursuit of his little shop on the—". Ty stopped at the cagey look on Robert's face. "Oh, I get it. You've ticked off everyone in this town who has the resources to help you, and you want me to run interference. Hell, no. You made your bed, now lie in it."

Robert dolefully rubbed his chin where Ty had cold-cocked him, then pitifully massaged the area over his heart in a silent effort to stir up a little guilt.

"Oh, for crying out loud, Robert," Ty said, relenting slightly. "Who, exactly, do you have in mind for your wild-child daughter?"

"I was thinking," he replied enthusiastically, "maybe Sam or Frog, or Squint. You picked them, after all. You wouldn't have brought anyone to this town who wasn't honorable."

"You're asking me to hang one of my buddies out to dry."

Robert smiled. "There's gold at the end of the rainbow. Maybe one of your friends would think that's a plus."

"I thought you just said you didn't want anyone in the family who was after your dough."

"Those boys aren't from here. They know nothing about me, to speak of. And besides which, I'm not above trying to sweeten the pot. I just don't want anyone marrying my daughter who loves my money more than he loves her."

"You want the moon. What you're asking for is going to take matchmaking into a whole new gear." Ty edged to the door. "It would need skilled manipulation, with maybe even a little miracle or magic on the side."

"And you're the man who came up with the idea to bring a bunch of high-quality bachelors to town to marry off the local population of women, and improve the gene pool. All in an effort to save this town, namely from me." Robert grinned hugely. "I think I've come to the right place for what I need."

"This sucks," Ty said. "I'm not saying I'm helping you."

"If you quit the navy, it'll look like you're scared of me."

"Where did that come from?" Ty stared at the old man. "Does your mind never quit working?"

"Nope." He laughed, pleased. "I'm just saying, you need to remember that you're a hero for this town. Stay a hero. And find my daughter someone just like you. Maybe a little less stubborn, but otherwise the same."

"Stubborn comes with the brand. You don't get a SEAL without a heavy dose of stubborn, old man. Know what you're getting into."

Robert closed his eyes with a smile, and waved a hand majestically to dismiss him.

Ty rolled his eyes, still stunned that this ornery man could be his father, and departed, disgruntled beyond words.

All he wanted right now was Jade. It was his wedding day, for crying out loud, and he still hadn't had the kiss he'd been waiting for.

Jade gasped when the back door blew open and her husband walked in. "Ty! You scared me!"

"That is not what a man wants to hear when he returns to his bride's arms." He pulled her close, kissing her thoroughly, melting into her. "Oh, God, I missed this."

"I missed you, too."

She sounded breathless, and that was exactly how he wanted her. "Let's go have our honeymoon," Ty said.

"I think we should talk first, not that I want to talk on my wedding day." Jade sneaked her arms up his back, pressing him against her. "But in the spirit of the Christmas season, and in the spirit of being a totally honest, up-front bride, we probably should."

"And then we kiss. And other things."

She laughed. "Lots of other things. Betty's going to keep the babies, I've pumped some milk, and you and I are going away for the night."

"Where?" He didn't care, he just wanted to hold her.

"Your house for tonight. We'll stay close in case something comes up with the girls. Not that Mom isn't totally competent, but just in case. Then—" Jade kissed him more deeply, in a way that started his body sizzling "—Mom's wedding gift to us is a honeymoon in Paris."

"Paris?" He leaned back. "That's awesome. Expensive, but awesome."

Jade smiled, and he wanted to see that smile on her face always. "Apparently, Mom has saved up over the years for my wedding day. She wasn't counting on me having a home wedding in a post-maternity dress. She said the amount of money she'd put back for a wedding dress alone will cover the airfare."

"I love your mom." Ty was the luckiest man on the planet. "So what are we talking about?"

"Right now, we're taking our slices of wedding cake and going to your house. I'm all packed. Mom's fretting that I don't have a trousseau or a going-away outfit, and that no one threw birdseed or paper hearts at us, and I didn't toss a bouquet. Most of all, she's worried that I don't have a wedding negligee."

"It wouldn't be on you five seconds. Tell her it was good money saved."

"That's what I told her. But she's a mom. She's going to worry. Just like we're going to worry about our girls."

He actually had a lot of worries going on at the moment. "Let's get you on my white horse, then, and hit the honeymoon trail."

"But we talk first. We really, really have to talk, Ty."

He knew what this was all about. He would set her mind at ease, and then he was going to make love to her for the entire length of their honeymoon night. He picked up the honeymoon hamper Betty had thoughtfully packed.

"Let's go, bride. Talking isn't exactly my idea of foreplay."

She suddenly looked a little sad. "I know. But we really have to talk, because I promised you I wouldn't keep things from you anymore. And that's a promise I intend to keep."

It was that last bit that had Ty apprehensive. He didn't like his wife sounding so worried. He knew they needed to talk. But talking was something they should have done before, and she was right—she'd held things back from him. And he'd held things back from her.

He couldn't get a man-pass for that. He was just as guilty. So he took her to his house, opened the door and bent down to scoop her into his arms. "I'm a traditional guy," he said, and she kissed him.

"I like being in your arms. You can carry me over this or any other threshold."

That sounded better. More like she wasn't about to tell him to hit the road. He should be grateful if she wanted him to hit the road, because he was going to need a push to leave her behind.

"Wow," he said, and she got down from his arms, stunned by the transformation of his house.

"Yes, wow. Did you let the Christmas elves in?"

The Christmas tree alone was worthy of a Hollywood fairy tale. In fact, he couldn't remember how many years it had been since a tree had been in this house, and certainly never decked out like that. It was lovely, with silver and gold balls shining from every branch, reflecting the colors of the lights and the red velvet bows in every ornament. He didn't know much about decorating, but he could tell a lot of love had gone into the gift in their home.

"Changes our humble abode significantly, doesn't it?" Ty said.

"Humble? You call this house humble?" Jade laughed, and he put his arms around her, taking in the joy of sharing his first real Christmas tree with his brand-spanking-new wife.

"Oh, look!" Jade crossed to the fireplace mantel, admiring the handmade stockings. "We all have a stocking, including the girls."

He grinned hugely. "I probably have my old childhood stocking upstairs someplace, but I have no idea where to find it."

"I'll find it eventually. I'd like to see that." Jade smiled at him. "I remember when you were just a kid who got in lots of trouble. The sheriff had his hands full with you," she teased.

Ty felt slightly remorseful about the fact that he'd been a bit of a handful. "Yeah, I'd do a lot of things differently."

"I'm sorry, Ty. I shouldn't have said that." Jade hugged him. "Your father loved you so much."

"I know. He was a good man. If I'm half the dad he was—"

"You will be. Now come help me tear up this step."

"But we haven't finished the Christmas tour. And I'm not pulling up that stair. You did an awesome job repairing it." He had to remember he was the one who'd left his family secrets in her hands. Okay, he hadn't foreseen those secrets being spilled all over Bridesmaids Creek, but actually, it was better to get everything out in the open.

"Get your tool belt. We *are* tearing this stair apart. I'm not starting this marriage with any more skeletons waiting to jump out."

He did as she asked. "You're going to freak when you see the kitchen. By the holiday handiwork around here, I'm beginning to suspect your mother, Mackenzie, Suz, Cosette and Jane, at the minimum. They really went all out."

"That's what happens when you're the town's favorite son." Jade took the tool she wanted from his belt, then gazed at him thoughtfully. "You look really hot in that belt. Just so you know."

He grinned. "Just so you know, I'll be happy to put it on anytime for you. Let me do this. I'm the SEAL, remember? I'm supposed to be manly and tough."

"Go for it." Jade got down next to him, watching as he pried the stair apart. "I hope you're okay with this."

"I'm okay with it. I should have manned up in the first place." He pulled the board off the step, revealing the metal box, just where it had been before.

"It's not a matter of manning up. You were leaving for BUD/S. Wasn't your mind nice and clear when you left?"

"Not exactly." He stole a fast kiss from her. "I had a certain redhead on my mind all the time." Pulling the box free, he sat down with it. "You think this is necessary?"

"Absolutely." Jade nodded emphatically. "The more you know, the less Donovan can get to you."

"Yeah, about Donovan," Ty said. He looked at Jade. "He's decided he wants on Team Ty."

"Good. It's a step in the right direction. Of course, he's only doing it because of his granddaughters, but I'm okay with that. As long as you don't quit the SEALs, I'm good with learning to be a little nicer to Mr. Donovan. A *little*. And to not cut my sister-in-law's hair off anymore."

Ty looked at her, wondering if she knew exactly how much he loved her. Could it even be put into words? "I don't feel right about leaving you here holding the bag. It's not entirely fair if I leave you while I chase my dreams. You've got two new babies—"

"And that was *my* dream, if you recall." She touched his face. "Remember those days? Me worrying about my poor, underappreciated, untried ovary? You let me live my dream. I've got two darling babies to prove it."

"I told you that ovary was going to like my stuff."

She shook her head at his bragging, but he noted her lips were curved in a smile. "Read, Ty."

She sat next to him on the stair, putting her chin on

his shoulder. God, that felt good. She felt good. He'd waited a long time for this. Ty hesitated before opening the envelope, just so he could enjoy the feeling of Jade supporting him a little longer.

"I can read it to you if you want," she said softly.

"I'm okay. I was just sitting here admiring your legs."

She kissed his cheek. "And I was admiring your hands. We can get on with a whole lot more than admiring if you do your book report, student."

"Yes, teacher." He pulled out the letter, reading fast, his heart hanging like a wild bird on the wind as he read his father's words to him. It was as if Ty could hear his voice, speaking his thoughts aloud. "Jeez," he said finally, his throat tight with emotion.

"Yeah. You weren't such a bad kid, after all." She kissed his cheek again, and Ty shook his head.

"Oh, I had my moments. But Dad was my best friend. He really was. I never felt like I'd let him down."

Ty picked up the box Robert Donovan's wife had left—he couldn't think of Honoria as his mother—and opened it. The Saint Michael medal gleamed, and he turned it over, seeing that she'd had his name engraved.

"Saint Michael is a strong protector, an archangel," Jade murmured against his shoulder. "You could think of Honoria's gift as a blessing that manifested in your life. You are strong, you are a protector." She kissed him. "I think she loved you a lot, Ty. From afar. And maybe she did the thing she knew was best by keeping you from Robert. Not to be mean, but you're certainly a good man. And he's not."

"Robert said something along the same lines." Not that he was anywhere near forgiving Robert for being a cretin, but Ty certainly didn't regret that his real family, the couple he would always remember when he thought of family, were the Spurlocks.

"Thank you for allowing me to share this moment with you," Jade said. "I was worried you'd never forgive me for the way everything got sprung on you."

He put everything back in the box, put the box in its hiding place again. "It wouldn't be Bridesmaids Creek if everything wasn't sprung. Secrets don't come out gently and quietly around here. We do everything with dramatic intent. But what else would we expect from a town of carnies?"

She put her hand in his. "I think the box can go in our closet now, don't you?"

"You're right." He picked it up. "I'll fix the stair later. Right now, I have a wife to kiss."

"You'll note the mistletoe hanging from the arch," Jade said.

Ty shook his head, his whole world better with her in it. "It's sort of anticlimactic, don't you think? Kissing because of a pagan weed or whatever it is?"

"I think it's actually a fungus of sorts," Jade said.

"Which begs the question, what type of fungus would we hang to give us permission to make love?" He kissed her, then scooped her into his arms as she smiled at him. "I don't need a piece of mistletoe to kiss my Christmas bride."

"Good, because I plan on you kissing me every day," Jade said, "and frequently."

And those words were exactly what he wanted to hear. Ty Spurlock, U.S. Navy SEAL, husband, father and son, had finally come home for good. And nothing was going to ruin the best homecoming and Christmas ever, one he couldn't have dreamed up in his wildest delusional imaginings.

Wherever he was stationed, his heart would always be here. And there was nothing the Donovans or anyone else could do to ruin it.

He wasn't going to blow his second chance.

Chapter 16

Daisy ripped up the main drag of Bridesmaids Creek, her gang of stooges following behind on their motorcycles. Since she'd discovered she wasn't an only child, she'd had very little to say to Ty.

Today, it seemed, she'd changed her game plan.

She stopped in front of Ty and Jade, her motorcycle roaring. "If it isn't my happily married big brother."

Ty winced. "Let's go easy on the family connections thing."

Jade glanced down at their daughters in the large-wheeled pram, making sure the blankets were covering them securely as they walked through Bridesmaids Creek, taking in the lovely holiday decorations.

"Here's the thing, Daze," Ty said, "you should start thinking about toning down your gig."

"My gig?" Daisy stared at him, her eyes piercing despite her helmet. She pulled it off, the chocolate locks flowing free. "My future husband is fine with my gig, thanks."

Ty stilled. "Future husband?"

"Yeah. Didn't you hear? I've got my sights set on Frog."

Jade glanced at him, startled. "Why Frog?" she asked Daisy.

"Suz didn't really have a chance, although secretly I think she's been setting her cap for him. And I think he'd be open to marriage. He protests a lot, but you know men. They change their minds pretty quickly when a baby comes on the scene, don't they, Jade?"

Ty shifted, knowing full well what was on Jade's mind. Her best friend was Mackenzie, and Mackenzie's little sister was Suz, and Suz had long had her eye on Frog.

Things always had to be complicated in BC.

"We should set up a Bridesmaids Creek swim for you," Ty said, feeling a bolt of inspiration hit him. "Or a Best Man's Fork run. That way, let the best man win." And he'd make sure Frog was pretty well out of commission before participating. Daisy winning Frog away from Suz would set up bad blood for years in BC.

"I'm not doing any of those silly things. It's just a bunch of fairy tales." Daisy shrugged, looking wildly beautiful in her skintight and somehow body-baring black catsuit. "You didn't. Why should I, brother?"

He hesitated. "I already had my lady." He hugged Jade close to him. "There was no reason to do any of the normal activities."

Daisy smiled. "If you don't, I don't. You can't say that your hurry-up wedding is a precursor to forever happiness. Jade just wanted a baby. Everyone knew it. The man was totally secondary. And you don't need a swim in the creek to know that."

Jade gasped. "That's a terrible thing to say, Daisy Donovan! Why are you bent on making trouble?" She hurried to pull the babies' tiny red knit caps down more fully over their ears, as if to protect them from the vile things their aunt was saying.

Ty took a deep breath. "Look. Life just happened for us. Let me set up a run or a swim for my little sister, okay?" He smiled winningly, figuring either one she chose, he could think up a way to have Squint win. Squint, at least, had half an eye for this completely wild woman who was now Ty's sister. Half an eye, he thought, that's just great. *He'd be better off blindfolded if he winds up married to Daisy.*

"I don't believe in the superstitions of BC," she said, not falling for his con. "Why are superstitions the mother's milk around here?"

"I don't know, but it's worked for every single person in Bridesmaids Creek," Jade said. "Except for Mackenzie's first marriage. She didn't do a swim, either. Maybe it was bad luck. Let Ty set something up for you."

"As I recall, Ty fixed her up with that first deadbeat." Daisy smirked. "My brother doesn't have the first clue about what makes a successful match. Or marriage."

Ty could tell they were in dangerous territory. Beside him, Jade had stiffened up, tense and unmoving. Any moment now, things could get ugly. More ugly than they were already. "You want the BC ways, Daze, you know you do."

"I just want a baby, Ty. Preferably a son. I don't need a big day of glory for that." She looked at the pram with a huge dose of loathing. "They really are cute little things. And if Jade can do it, so can I."

She tore off on her motorcycle, then looped back around to stop in front of them again. "I tell you what, brother. I'm pretty sure I see through your plan. You don't want me with Frog because of dear Suz."

He didn't say anything. Just watched his new sister carefully.

"I don't believe the creek is magical. I don't believe Best Man's Fork is, either. Frankly, I think Dad was better off when he wanted to mow this town down to the ground and bring in government offices. Make this the Washington, D.C., of Texas." Daisy looked at him speculatively. "But if you have such strong faith in the powers of our superstitions here, I'll let you set up a swim for me, or a run. I don't care which."

He nodded. "Good. I'll get right on it. Maybe just before Christmas."

"Oh, absolutely, just before Christmas." She grinned at him. "But I'll only agree to a run if Jade does, too."

Jade shook her head. "What will that prove?"

"It will prove that my brother married the right woman," Daisy said, her voice silky. "I mean, after all, it was such a hurry-up wedding, who can possibly know? Poor guy is home on leave, finds out his nighttime love had his children—what's he supposed to do?"

"That's disgusting, Daisy, even for you." Jade pushed the pram forward, moving off.

"She's scared to know the truth. When you've been born and raised in BC, these fairy tales mean everything. Me, I'm a transplant, as everyone always likes to remind me. But even I know when a marriage has started off on the wrong foot," Daisy told Ty.

He had started to deny it when his darling, hotheaded wife whirled around.

"A swim," Jade said. "All the guys will swim. And you'll eat your words, Daisy Donovan. I married the only man for me. I just hope Ty can talk one man into showing up for you. It's twenty-five degrees outside. It would take a really strong man to want to prove that he's the right man for you."

Daisy smiled at Ty. "Do not try to keep Frog from the competition. He's going to want in."

"How do you know?"

"Because Daddy's putting up a hundred thousand dollars for the winner. Every bachelor in town will want to swim." She laughed, gunned her bike and roared away, and Ty realized he'd been caught in a neatly set snare.

Crap-a-monkey. He didn't believe in superstitions, either. But he did believe in BC.

He certainly believed in his marriage.

So he'd swim. Like a SEAL that wanted everything to be just as magical as possible for the only woman he'd ever loved.

Jade was nervous. She couldn't relax. Two days before Christmas, on Christmas Eve eve, the whole town was gathered on the banks of Bridesmaids Creek. She'd left the babies at home with Betty, because snow was falling and the forecast said it would snow all day.

"If you swim," she told Ty, "you're probably going to catch something besides me. Pneumonia."

"Not me. I've swum this creek many a time in the freezing cold." He zipped up a black wetsuit that fitted him quite nicely, Jade noticed.

Too nicely.

"I don't want any other women looking at you."

He laughed. "I'm going to be swimming so fast I'm going to be merely a shadow in the water. No worries."

She was worrying.

Ty came over to her, cradled her face between his palms. "I've got this. Everything's been taken care of."

"Meaning?" Jade wanted more reassurance than just confident words. Suz had been on the warpath for days, knowing exactly what Daisy was up to. Suz wasn't happy, either, that Frog had readily agreed to the swim.

She hadn't wanted to hear that any sane man would swim for a hundred thousand dollars. It had nothing to do with Frog having feelings for Daisy, because he didn't.

A knock at the front door caught their attention.

"Expecting someone?"

"No." Jade walked behind Ty to the front door of the house she was coming to love, where she felt very much at home with her husband.

Sheriff Dennis McAdams stood on the front porch.

"Hello, Sheriff. Come in," Ty said. "It's good to see you."

Dennis stepped inside. "You've really fixed the place up." He looked around, admiring the decorations.

"We didn't do this, actually. A team of elves decorated the place." Ty glanced at Jade, winking at her, which warmed her heart. "We think the ladies of the town sneaked in here, since Betty has access to Jade's key, but no one will admit to being our Secret Santas."

Dennis laughed. "Some secrets will stay secret, I guess."

"Let me get you a cup of tea, Sheriff." Jade turned

toward the kitchen. "It's cold outside, and these guys are determined to swim."

"Believe me, I know. Daisy's gang started a bonfire in town. They're pretty liquored up, standing around, trying to stay warm." Dennis shook his head. "Somebody's going to drown if they keep drinking like college kids. Anyway, I can't stay, Jade, so I'll have to skip the tea. Thanks, though."

"What's on your mind, Sheriff?" Ty asked.

"Well, as you know, Robert Donovan is doing his best to turn over a new leaf. Just happens to be that leaves aren't that easy to turn." The lawman sighed, glanced around the cheery room as Jade leaned against Ty for support. She had the strangest feeling Dennis's mission today wasn't good news for them.

"Just so long as he decides to stay a changed man, that's fine by me," Ty said.

"The two deaths at the Haunted H—the one when your father was still…sheriff," Dennis said, carefully not using the word *alive,* "and the one earlier this year— Robert claims were accidental. But he did bring those men here for mischief. Both of them were meant to cause trouble. He's confessed to that."

"Awfully coincidental, don't you think? That both of his henchmen would die?" Ty asked.

"Donovan claims he just wants to start over. Wants a clean slate with everyone. Hence his confession." The sheriff zipped up his sheepskin jacket. "He's real worried that Daisy's gone over the edge. She liked being an only child. Hard to give up her kingdom, or princessdom, I guess you'd say."

"Tough luck on that," Jade said, feeling a little guilt wash over her. Daisy still wouldn't know, and the town wouldn't be splitting apart, if she hadn't ever opened the Pandora's box under the stairs. And if she'd kept her mouth shut.

But it was too late for that.

"Confession's good for the soul, I guess. It wasn't Robert's fault that the men died," the sheriff continued. "There's nothing I can charge him with."

"Criminal mischief?" Ty asked. "There has to be something."

"One charge is beyond the statute of limitations, and the other—hell, what would we prove?" The sheriff gazed at him. "Look, this might be a case where we realize Robert's trying to change, and we support him. For the sake of BC. Because honestly, I think Daisy's got more potential for mercilessness than her old man ever had."

"How do two men just randomly die at our haunted house?" Jade asked. "Something doesn't make sense. I know he was trying to destroy our dreams, and BC, but he's not telling you everything."

"Well, the first man had a serious heart condition, which Robert knew about. He chose him deliberately because of it. The man also needed money and was open to causing trouble—but it was just too much good fortune that he died on your father's watch. My guess is that both of these men were ill, and stress may have triggered their deaths. Unfortunate? Yes. Coincidental? Maybe. Partly. Robert chose men who would do his dirty deeds, and who had nothing to lose. The thing is, we'll never know for certain. The only thing you can do is not let it rule your life going forward." Dennis looked at Ty sympathetically.

"So two men die, and he blames it on Betty's toxic

cocoa." Ty shook his head. "The man is a monster. He should be run out of town on a rail."

"He's admitted that he was behind the rumors that your father didn't look into the case seriously, and that his policies were flawed."

"Jackass," Ty said, and Jade could feel her husband breathing hard. "He destroyed my dad. His admission does my father little good now. Terence Spurlock died knowing this town had lost their trust in him."

"Yes." Dennis nodded. "I'm not saying you have to forgive Donovan for that. But forgiveness is just as meaningful for Bridesmaids Creek as it is for your life, Ty. You don't want to be imprisoned by the past forever." The sheriff sighed. "Donovan seems to be shedding his snakeskin and wants to make amends, ask forgiveness. He's started with his confession. He's also offered to set back half a million dollars for your girls, either for their education or their wedding, or—"

"We don't want a penny of Robert Donovan's money," Jade snapped. "In fact, I'm sick of hearing about it. And if you've come here on a mission of mercy from him, you're going back empty-handed."

Ty shrugged, proud of his wife's fire. "I'm afraid Jade's right."

"I totally understand. Think about it."

"So what did the second man really die of?" Jade demanded, unwilling to give much thought to the state of Robert Donovan's soul. "Since Robert's being so honest? Because I think he's lying through his teeth."

"According to him, and I've verified this through the autopsy results, that man had only a few months to live. Hence he was very open to the financial remuneration Robert offered him to come to the Hanging H that night. He, too, was supposed to cause a ruckus. Robert claims his goal was to set a small fire, maybe near the bunkhouse. To spook the customers and families, give the Haunted H a reputation for being an untrustworthy event."

Ty shook his head. "This is ridiculous. Donovan should be in jail, if for nothing else but being a creep and a son of a—"

"You tell Robert Donovan that he's footing the entire bill for the next ten years of haunted houses out at the Hanging H," Jade said, and Ty felt a surge of pride wash through him. "You tell him that he pays for ten years of Haunted H family gatherings, every single penny. And then maybe, just maybe, we'll think about whether we ever want to invite him to Christmas dinner!"

Ty glanced at her. Jade looked at him, feeling like a firecracker ready to explode.

"That's what this is all about, Ty. He's trying to clear the past so he can get forgiveness. So he can be with his granddaughters, and so he can be invited into our family."

"Is that likely?" Ty asked the sheriff. "Does Donovan actually think in terms of family?"

"My guess is yes. At least that's what it sounded like to me. He's an old man who's done a lot of wrong. It's time for him to come clean. And he's a smart man. He knows that eventually skeletons pop out of closets."

"Tell me about it," Ty said.

Jade grabbed her coat. "And he cancels every single sale and contract he may be negotiating, or may have negotiated, with any entity to come here, whether it be government or not. He stops trying to bulldoze people out of their homes and their businesses, and most especially, he leaves Phillipe and Cosette Lafleur alone." Jade buttoned her red coat and slipped on some white mittens, looking very Christmassy and darling to Ty. Sexy, and somehow like a Christmas angel, too.

"And all business decisions he makes concerning sales, any sales of any property, have to go through the town council, which consists of Ty or myself, and Cosette, Phillipe, Jane Chatham and her husband, Ralph, Betty, Mackenzie and Justin Morant, as well as yourself, Sheriff. Those are my conditions. He'll have to take it or leave it."

Jade glanced at the two men, who seemed disinclined to argue with her, or tell her that she was asking for the moon.

"If he wants to see his granddaughters, and hold them, and be part of their lives. If he wants to darken the door of this home at Christmas or any other time, that's my final and only offer. And now, if you gentlemen will excuse me, I'm off to man the hot-cocoa stand at the creek. My husband has a race to win for me today." She rose on her tiptoes to kiss her hunky husband goodbye. "I love you. Swim like Flipper."

He grinned. Time and two babies had not knocked one ounce of sass out of his lovely redhead. "See you at the finish line, gorgeous."

Jade went out, bundled to the max, her red-and-white scarf flying in the breeze.

"I guess you know that she's the only woman who could have tamed your heart," Dennis observed. "She's got a helluva lot of spunk."

Ty just smiled hugely.

Chapter 17

To say that Ty swam like seven devils were after him was no understatement. He felt awesome, as if he was back in BUD/S, pitting himself against himself, the weather and all the men who had the same goal he did—to be the very best.

He won, easily. Way ahead of the pack. Climbed out of the frigid water to be rewarded by his wife throwing herself into his arms.

"Superstition or not," he said, gasping for air, "I know I'm married to the only woman who is my better half. My significant other. The apple of my eye," he announced to the cheering crowd. "The milk in my cereal, the cherry on my pie. Long live Bridesmaids Creek!"

Jade laughed, kissing him. "You'd better sit down, husband, and drink some cocoa. You sound a little punchy. A little bit like you've been to Daisy's bonfire and gotten into the hooch."

"Yeah, but it was romantic," he said, collapsing on the bench where she led him. "Wasn't it?"

She smiled and put a warm blanket around him. "Very romantic. Silly, but romantic. When you catch your breath, there are warm, dry clothes waiting in your truck."

Clothes could wait. He got to his feet, lumbered to the side of the creek to see how the other fellows were doing. How fast could men swim for a hundred thousand dollars?

Daisy stood on the bank, wearing a drop-dead black cashmere pantsuit that clung to her every curve. She had on black boots, and her long hair whipped around as she cheered the swimmers on.

It looked as if Squint was going to win. Ty breathed a sigh of relief. The Plan was, as he'd instructed his brothers, that all three of them would swim faster than Daisy's gang—but then, at the last second, Squint was to touch the bank first. Frog and Sam were to cede the lead, though discreetly, thereby throwing the race to their friend.

The three would split the money, according to the terms Ty set forth for his brothers.

They'd readily agreed. They'd had to. It was his sister, he'd pointed out, his father-in-law's money, and Ty planned to beat their heads in if they didn't do exactly what he told them.

Squint was the fall guy, the sacrificial lamb, because he actually had, as Ty had pointed out with no thought to a pun, half an eye for Ty's dangerous sister. And Squint wasn't as easygoing as Frog. Frog wasn't capable of handling a woman like Daisy—she'd run all over him.

"Swim, Squint!" Ty yelled, unable to help himself. He'd known he'd be far in front of his brothers, but they seemed to be swimming slowly, by his calculations.

Even retired SEALs should be in reasonable shape.

To his shock, Daisy's gang began to pull in front. Something was terribly wrong. His brothers were slowing to a crawl.

"What's happening?" Jade asked. "Does something seem not right to you?"

He shook his head, his jaw dropping when all of a sudden, Frog touched first and jumped out of the water, dripping and gasping from the last-ditch effort he'd put forth.

Daisy's gang came in second, third, fourth, fifth and sixth.

Sam came in seventh. And Squint—he was dead last.

And everyone knew what coming in last meant.

It meant he didn't have a chance in hell of a happy marriage—or any marriage at all—in Bridesmaids Creek.

"It doesn't matter," Jade said as they went upstairs to their bedroom that night. Ty let his bride tuck him into bed, insisting he get under a pile of blankets. She was just certain he'd caught a chill.

Ty had never felt better. But he certainly wasn't opposed to letting his wife warm him up. She had that look on her face, as if she was in the mood for some Christmas fun, and he smiled. This was the real prize, the real win, being in bed with his beautiful wife, with the babies tucked into the nursery down the hall. The tree was twinkling downstairs, and so many presents billowed out from under it that it was clear Santa had arrived early.

Santa SEAL. "Come here, wife."

She snuggled up to him, warming him the way he'd known she would. "It's just a race in a pond, a fundraiser for our small town. Deep inside, you know that, Ty."

"You're trying to say it doesn't matter that somehow Squint didn't win. How does Squint suddenly get a leg cramp? He knows better than to let pain be his guide! What a wienie." Ty was outraged by his friend's sudden weakness. "I think he threw the race on purpose."

"We'll never know." She kissed Ty, trailing her fingers along his jaw. "Daisy gigged herself a Frog, and he claims he had to take one for the team because he could tell that Sam and Squint were struggling."

"I don't believe a word of it. I think Frog's competitive side kicked in."

"The money helped his time, no doubt." Jade laughed. "And although Suz is beside herself, it's for them to straighten out. But I have a question. Why did you do the swim? Truthfully? You didn't have to."

"For the traditional reasons, and then my own personal reason." He thought he felt a bit of breast underneath the frilly white gown Jade wore, and it was making it hard to concentrate on what was a very important conversation. "I wanted you to know that I wanted to win you. I knew those guys couldn't beat me. I'm in shape, and clearly, they're not."

"Frog, Squint and Sam donated their winnings to the BC hospital. What do you think about that?"

He kissed her fingertips, loving every minute he got to spend holding her. "That I picked them because I knew they were good men. So I expected nothing less from the three wild boys. They get a little crazy on occasion—"

"And that's why we love them. All of you."

Her hand drifted lower to his abdomen, her fingers moving over his muscles, which he wasn't too proud to admit were washboard tight, thanks to the SEALs. "You're going to be all right with being a navy wife?"

"You mean, with you being gone all the time?" Jade nipped his shoulder lightly. "I plan to give you plenty to remember while you're gone. So, about these reasons."

He smiled at his wife's curiosity. "I wanted you to know that I believe in us. That I trust you. All that bit about you ruining my trust because you didn't tell me about the babies, and other things, is something that belongs in the past. Buried." He kissed her, loving how she melted against him. "Some things *can* stay buried in BC."

Jade looked up at him. "You mean that, don't you?"

"Of course I do. Didn't I just prove it? I've still got the shivers that back up my words," he said, fibbing a bit. "You can get a lot closer. It'll help me warm up."

He put her on top of him, and she kissed his lips, bringing him a hot, sexy rush. "And the other reasons?"

He looked at Jade, the woman he'd dreamed of for so long. "Why else does a man rise to meet a challenge? I wanted you to have your own memory to brag about. And I believe that people will be talking about today's race for a long time to come."

He stroked the burgundy-red hair that stayed aflame even in his dreams. "I told you, I'm a traditional guy. I go by a plan, although I'm learning that sometimes the plan goes rogue, which, when it comes to you and my daughters, is okay. Redheaded-and-rogue suits me fine. And I love you. Like crazy."

"I love you, too." She smiled down at him. "Merry Christmas, my sexy SEAL."

He grinned and pulled Jade against his chest, holding her close to his heart. It *was* a very merry Christmas, and as Christmases usually went in Bridesmaids Creek, it was magical.

* * * * *

When Grace Williams topples from the balcony at the new Hotel Fortune, the last thing she expects is to find love with her new bosses' brother. Wiley Fortune has looks, money and charm to spare. But Grace's past makes her wary of investing her heart. This time, she is holding out for the real deal...

Read on for a sneak peek at
Her Texas New Year's Wish
by Michelle Major, the first book in
The Fortunes of Texas: The Hotel Fortune!

"I didn't fall," she announced with a wide smile as he returned the crutches.

"You did great." He looked at her with a huge smile.

"That was silly," she said as they started down the walk toward his car. "Maneuvering down a few steps isn't a big deal, but this is the farthest I've gone on my own since the accident. If my parents had their way, they'd encase me in Bubble Wrap for the rest of my life to make sure I stayed safe."

"It's an understandable sentiment from people who care about you."

"But not what I want."

He opened the car door for her, and she gave him the crutches to stow in the back seat. The whole process was slow and awkward. By the time Grace was buckled in next to Wiley, sweat dripped between her shoulder blades, and she felt like she'd run a marathon. How could less than a week of inactivity make her feel like such an invalid?

As if sensing her frustration, Wiley placed a gentle hand on her arm. "You've been through a lot, Grace. Your ankle and the cast are the biggest outward signs of the accident, but you fell from the second story."

She offered a wan smile. "I have the bruises to prove it."

"Give yourself a bit of…well, grace."

"I never thought of attorneys as naturally comforting people," she admitted. "But you're good at giving support."

"It's a hidden skill." He released her hand and pulled away from the curb. "We lawyers don't like to let anyone know about our human side. It ruins the reputation of being coldhearted, and then people aren't afraid of us."

"You're the opposite of scary."

"Where are we headed?" he asked when he got to the stop sign at the end of the block.

"The highway," she said without hesitation. "As much as I love Rambling Rose, I need a break. Let's get out of this town, Wiley."

Don't miss
Her Texas New Year's Wish *by Michelle Major,*
available January 2021 wherever
Harlequin Special Edition books and ebooks are sold.

Harlequin.com

ove Harlequin romance?

DISCOVER.

Be the first to find out about promotions, news and exclusive content!

 Facebook.com/HarlequinBooks

 Twitter.com/HarlequinBooks

 Instagram.com/HarlequinBooks

 Pinterest.com/HarlequinBooks

ReaderService.com

EXPLORE.

Sign up for the Harlequin e-newsletter and download a free book from any series at **TryHarlequin.com**

CONNECT.

Join our Harlequin community to share your thoughts and connect with other romance readers!
Facebook.com/groups/HarlequinConnection

HSOCIAL2020